"MEMORABLE. . . . There's no escaping the overall impact. . . . O'Brien is a fine writer with a distinct and distinctive vision of his time and place."
—*Houston Chronicle*

"FUNNY AND PROVOCATIVE AS WELL AS TERRIFYING. Those who enjoyed Tim O'Brien's firm grasp of the absurd in *Going After Cacciato* will be delighted with this excellent book."
—*Richmond Times-Dispatch*

"AN IMPRESSIVELY SUSTAINED EXAMPLE OF SHEER AMBITION AND RELENTLESSLY STRONG WRITING."
—*The Sun* (Baltimore)

"*The Nuclear Age* is set in 1995. Whether we live to turn the pages of that or any subsequent calendar depends in part on the quality of our collective imagination. This novel establishes Tim O'Brien as an eloquent shaper of that imagination. In the hands of writers as skilled and humane as he, the pen might yet prove mightier than the missile."
—*The Milwaukee Journal*

"*The Nuclear Age* is about the brink we're standing on. And no one wants to look over unless someone coaxes them along with an off-the-wall entertaining story, as Tim O'Brien does here. . . . Suspense and poignancy, too."
—*The National Catholic Reporter*

The NUCLEAR Age

THE NUCLEAR AGE
TIM O'BRIEN

A LAUREL TRADE PAPERBACK
Published by
Dell Publishing Co., Inc.
1 Dag Hammarskjold Plaza
New York, New York 10017

Portions of this novel appeared in different form in *The Atlantic, Esquire, Ploughshares, Granta,* and *The Pushcart Prize 1985.* The author wishes to thank the editors of those publications and to express gratitude for support received from the John Simon Guggenheim Foundation.

The principal characters and incidents in this book are wholly imagined. By and large, the author has tried to remain faithful to the flow of public events between the years 1945 and 1995, but on occasion it has seemed appropriate to amend history, most conspicuously by exaggeration. After all, this is a fable. And what is important, the author believes, is not what happened, but what could have happened, and, in some cases, should have happened.

"Those Were the Days": Words and music by Gene Raskin; TRO © Copyright 1962 and 1968 Essex Music Inc., New York, New York

For my mother and father,
for Kathy and Greg,
and for Ann

And the dead will be thrown out like dung,
and there will be no one to offer comfort.
For the earth will be left empty and its
cities will be torn down. None will be left
to till the ground and sow it. The trees
will bear fruit, but who will gather it?
The grapes will ripen, but who will tread them?
There will be vast desolation everywhere.
For one man will long to see another, or to
hear his voice. For ten will be left, out of
a city, and two, out of a field, who have
hidden in the thick woods or in holes in the rocks.

The Second Book of Esdras
16:23–29

FISSION

1

Quantum Jumps

AM I CRAZY?

It's after midnight, and I kiss my wife's cheek and quietly slide out of bed. No lights, no alarm. Blue jeans and work boots and a flannel shirt, then out to the backyard. I pick a spot near the tool shed. A crackpot? Maybe, maybe not, but listen. The sound of physics. The soft, breathless whir of Now.

Just listen.

Close your eyes, pay attention: Murder, wouldn't you say? A purring electron? Photons, protons? Yes, and the steady hum of a balanced equation.

I use a garden spade. High over the Sweetheart Mountains, a pale dwarf moon gives light to work by, and the air is chilly, and there is the feel of a dream that may last forever. "So do it," I murmur, and I begin digging.

Turn the first spadeful. Then bend down and squeeze the soil and let it sift through the fingers. Already there's a new sense of security. Crazy? Not likely, not yet.

If you're sane, anything goes, everything, there are no more particulars.

It won't be easy, but I'll persevere.

At the age of forty-nine, after a lifetime of insomnia and midnight peril, the hour has come for seizing control. It isn't madness. It isn't a lapse of common sense. Prudence, that's all it is.

Balance of power, balance of mind—a tightrope act, but where's the net? Infinity could split itself at any instant.

"Doom!" I yell.

Grab the spade and go to work.

Signs of sanity: muscle and resolve, arms and legs and spine and willpower. I won't quit. I'm a man of my age, and it's an age of extraordinary jeopardy. So who's crazy? Me? Or is it you? You poor, pitiful sheep. Listen—Kansas is on fire. What choice do I have? Just dig and dig. Find the rhythm. Think about those silos deep in fields of winter wheat. *Five, four, slam the door.* No metaphor, the bombs are real.

I keep at it for a solid hour. And later, when the moon goes under, I slip into the tool shed and find a string of outdoor Christmas lights—reds and blues and greens—rigging them up in trees and shrubs, hitting the switch, then returning to the job.

Silent night, for Christ sake. There's a failure of faith. When the back door opens, I'm whistling the age-old carol.

"Daddy!" Melinda calls.

Now it starts.

In pajamas and slippers, ponytailed, my daughter trots out to the excavation site. She shivers and hugs herself and whispers, "What's happening? What the heck's going *on?*"

"Nothing," I tell her.

"Oh, sure."

"Nothing, princess. Just digging."

"Digging," she says.

"Right."

"Digging what?"

I swallow and smile. It's a sensible question but the answer carries all kinds of complications. "A hole," I say. "What else?"

"Yeah, I guess."

"Just a hole. See? Simple, isn't it? Come on, baby, back to bed now—school tomorrow."

"Hole," Melinda mutters.

She folds her arms and looks at me with an expression that is at once stern and forgiving. A strange child. Twelve years old, but very wise and very tough: too wise, too tough. Like her mother, Melinda sometimes gives me the willies.

"Well, okay," she says, then pauses and nibbles her lower lip. "Okay, but what *kind* of hole?"

"A deep one."

"I know, but what—"

"Now listen," I say, "I'm serious. Back inside. Pronto."

Melinda squints, first at my spade, next at the Christmas lights, then at me. That mature gaze of hers, it makes me squirm.

"Tell the truth," she demands, "what's it *for?*"

"A long story."

She nods. "A dumb story, I'll bet."

"Not at all."

"Daddy!"

I drop the spade and kneel down and pat her tiny rump, an awkward gesture, almost beggarly, as if to ask for pardon. I make authoritative noises. I tell her it's not important. Just a hole, I say—for fun, nothing else. But she doesn't buy it. She's a skeptic; Santa Claus never meant a thing to her.

What can I do?

I look at the moon and tell her the facts. And the facts are these. The world is in danger. Bad things can happen. We need options, a safety valve. "It's a shelter," I say gently. "Like with rabbits or gophers, a place to hide."

Melinda smiles.

"You want to *live* there?" she says. "In a gopher hole?"

"No, angel, just insurance."

"God."

"Don't swear."

"Wow," she says.

Her nose wiggles. There's suspicion in that stiff posture, in the way she slowly cocks her head and backs away from me.

Kansas is on fire.

How do you explain that to a child?

"Well," she sighs, "it's goofy, all right. One thing for sure,

5

Mommy'll hit the ceiling, just wait. God, she'll probably *divorce* you."

"We'll work it out."

"Yeah, but I bet she'll say it's ridiculous, I bet she will. Who wants to be a gopher?"

Melinda sniffs and kicks at the hole.

"Poop," she says.

I try to lift her up, but she turns away, telling me I'm too sweaty, too dirty, so I lead her inside by the hand. The house smells of Windex and wax. My wife is meticulous about such things; she's a poet, the creative type; she believes in clean metaphors and clean language, tidiness of structure, things neatly in place. Holes aren't clean. Safety can be very messy.

Melinda's right—I'm in for some domestic difficulties—and if this project is to succeed, as it must, it will require the exercise of enormous tact and cunning.

Begin now.

I march my daughter to her bedroom. I tuck her between the all-cotton sheets. I brush a smudge of soil from her forehead, offer a kiss, tell her to sleep tight. All this is done tenderly, yet with authority.

"Daddy?" she says.

"Yes."

"Nothing."

"No," I say, "go ahead."

She shakes her head. "You'll get mad."

"I won't."

"Bet you *will*."

"Won't. Try me, kiddo."

"Nothing," she mumbles. "Except."

"Yes?"

"Except, God, you're pretty nutto, aren't you? Pretty buggo, too."

I don't say a word. I smile and close the door.

In the kitchen, however, I feel some pain coming on. Buggo? I pour myself a glass of grape Kool-Aid and then stand at the big window that looks out on the backyard. It's late, and my head hurts, but I make myself think things through rationally, step by step. Mid-April now—I can get it dug by June. Or July. Which leaves three months for finishing touches. A nice deep hole, then I'll line the walls with concrete, put on a roof of solid steel. No cutting corners. Install a water tank. And a generator. And wall-to-wall carpeting. A family room, a pine-paneled den, two bedrooms, lots of closet space, maybe a greenhouse bathed in artificial sunlight, maybe a Ping-Pong table and a piano, the latest appliances, track lighting and a microwave oven and all the little extras that make for comfort and domestic tranquillity. It'll be home. I'll put in a word processor for Bobbi, a game room for Melinda, a giant freezer stocked with shrimp and caviar. Nutto? I'm a father, a husband, I have solemn responsibilities. It isn't as if I enjoy any of this. I hate it and fear it. I would prefer the glory of God and peace everlasting, world without end, a normal household in an age of abiding normalcy.

It just isn't possible.

I finish the Kool-Aid and rinse the glass and return to the hole. I'm exhausted, yes, and a bit groggy, but I find the spade and resume digging.

I'm not crazy. Eccentric, maybe. These headaches and cramped bowels. How long since my last decent stool? A full night's sleep? Clogged up and frazzled, a little dizzy, a little scared. But not crazy. Fully sane, in fact.

Dig, the hole says.

Patience and tenacity. An inch here, an inch there, it's a game of inches. Beat the Clock. Dig and dream.

A rough life, that's my only excuse. I've been around. I've seen the global picture and it's no fantasy—it's real. Ask the microorganisms in Nevada. Ask the rattlesnakes and butterflies on that dusty plateau at Los Alamos. Ask the wall shadows at Hiroshima. Ask this question: Am I crazy? And then listen, listen hard, because you'll get one hell of an answer. If you hold your breath, if you have the courage, you'll hear the soft drip of a meltdown, the ping-ping-ping of submarine sonar, the half-life of your own heart.

What's to lose? Try it. Take a trip to Bikini. Bring your friends, eat a picnic lunch, a quick swim, a nature hike, and then, when night comes, build a bonfire and sit on the beach and just *listen*.

I've done it.

And I'll be candid, I blinked. I ran for it. Ten years on the lam, hideout to hideout, dodging bombs and drafts and feds and all the atrocities of our machine-tooled age. You bet I'm eccentric. I was a wanted man; I was hounded by Defense Intelligence and the FBI; I was almost shot to death at Sagua la Grande; I watched my friends die on national television; I was a mover in the deep underground; I could've been another Rubin or Hoffman; I could've been a superstar.

But it's finished now, no more crusades.

The year is 1995. We're late in the century, and the streets are full of tumbleweed, and it's every man for himself.

Times change—take a good hard look. Where's Mama Cass? What happened to Brezhnev and Lester Maddox? Where's that old gang of mine, Sarah and Ned and Tina and Ollie? Where's the passion? Where's Richard Daley? Where's Gene McCarthy in this hour of final trial? No heroes, no heavies. And who cares? That's the stunner: Who among us really cares? A nation of microchips. At dinner parties we eat mushroom salad and blow snow and talk computer lingo.

And me, I'm rich. I'm on a uranium roll. I'm well established and there's no going back. My assets include a blond wife and a blond daughter, and expensive Persian rugs, and a lovely redwood ranch house in the Sweetheart Mountains.

Call it what you want—copping out, dropping out, numbness, the loss of outrage, simple fatigue. I've retired. Time to retrench. Time to dig in. Safety first.

2
Civil Defense

WHEN I WAS A KID, about Melinda's age, I converted my Ping-Pong table into a fallout shelter. Funny? Poignant? A nifty comment on the modern age? Well, let me tell you something. The year was 1958, and I was scared. Who knows how it started? Maybe it was all that CONELRAD stuff on the radio, tests of the Emergency Broadcast System, pictures of H-bombs in *Life* magazine, strontium 90 in the milk, the times in school when we'd crawl under our desks and cover our heads in practice for the real thing. Or maybe it was rooted deep inside me. In my own inherited fears, in the genes, in a coded conviction that the world wasn't safe for human life.

Really, who knows?

Whatever the sources, I was a frightened child. At night I'd toss around in bed for hours, battling the snagged sheets, and then when sleep finally came, sometimes close to dawn, my dreams would be clotted with sirens and melting ice caps and radioactive gleamings and ICBMs whining in the dark.

I was a witness. I saw it happen. In dreams, in imagination, I watched the world end.

Granted, I was always extra sensitive—squeamish, even a little cowardly—but it wasn't paranoia or mental illness. I wasn't crazy. Fort Derry, Montana, was a typical small town, with the usual gas stations and parks and public schools, and I grew up in a family that pursued all the ordinary small-town values. My father sold real estate, my mother kept house.

I was a happy kid.

I played war games, tried to hit baseballs, started a rock collection, rode my bike to the A&W, fed the goldfish, messed around. Normal, normal. I even ran a lemonade stand out along the sixth fairway at the golf course, ten cents a glass, plenty of ice: a regular entrepreneur.

Just a regular childhood in a regular town. Each summer, for instance, Fort Derry staged a big weekend celebration called Custer Days, and even now, decades later, I can still see that long parade down Main Street, the trombones and clowns and horses, the merchants dressed up in frontier clothes. I remember the carnival rides. And the rodeo. And my father, I remember him, too. Every summer he played the role of George Armstrong Custer. Every summer he died. It happened at night, out at the fairgrounds—Custer's Last Stand—a dazzling historical pageant, blood and drama, the culmination of Custer Days. Up in the grandstand, among neighbors, my mother and I would eat ice cream and cotton candy while my father led the U.S. Seventh Cavalry to its annual reckoning at the Little Bighorn.

"There!" I'd cry.

Spotlights.

The National Anthem, the high call of a bugle, then my father would ride in on his big white stallion. He wore buckskins and a yellow wig. At his side was a silver sword; his face had the leathery gloss of a saddle.

I remember sabers and battle flags.

And then a drumroll.

And then a procession of mounted soldiers in blue uniforms and yellow neckerchiefs. I felt pride, but also panic. Jangling spurs and weaponry, canteens clanking, wagons, my father's posture in the saddle. Tall and straight, those bright blue eyes.

I worshipped that man.

I wanted to warn him, rescue him, but I also wanted slaughter. How do you explain it? Terror mixed with fascination: I craved bloodshed, yet I craved the miracle of a happy ending. When the battle began—tom-toms and howls and gunfire—I'd make tight fists and stare out at the wonders of it all. I was curious. I'd shiver and look away and then quickly look back again. It was the implacable scripting of history; my father didn't stand a chance. Yet he remained calm. Firing, reloading, firing—he actually smiled. He never ran, he never wept. He was always the last to die and he always died with dignity. Every summer he got scalped. Every summer Crazy Horse galloped away with my father's yellow wig. The spotlights dimmed, a bugler played Taps, then we'd head out to the A&W for late-night root beers.

A mountain town.

Elevation, just under six thousand feet.

Population, just over a thousand.

Ranch country. Scrub grass and pine and dust. An old hitching post in front of the Strouch Funeral Home. A courthouse, a cemetery, the Ben Franklin store. What else? The Thompson Hotel. The Sweethearts, of course. A stone-walled library. The air, I remember, had the year-round smell of winter, a brittle snapping smell, and at night, brushing my teeth, I could taste something like sulphur at the back of my tongue.

A pretty place, I suppose, but boring.

"Culture's that way," my dad would say, pointing east, "and if you want it, civilization's somewhere over that last ridgeline, more or less," then he'd hook a thumb westward, as if hitchhiking. Isolated. Fifty-eight miles from Yellowstone, eighty miles from Helena, twenty miles from the nearest major highway.

We were not high on the Russian hit list. But how could you be sure? Fort Derry, it *sounded* like a target.

And, besides, mistakes happen.

Even as a kid, maybe because I was a kid, I understood that there was nothing make-believe about doomsday. No hocus-pocus. No midnight fantasy. I knew better. It was real, like physics, like the laws of combustion and gravity. I could truly see it: a sleek nose cone, the wiring and dials and tangled circuitry. Real firepower, real danger. I was normal, yes, stable and levelheaded, but I was also willing to face the truth.

Anyway, I didn't have much choice. The nightmares had been squeezing my sleep for months, and finally, on a night in early May, a very quiet night, I woke up dizzy. My eyeballs ached. Things were so utterly silent I feared I'd gone deaf. Absolute silence. I sat up and wiped my face and waited for the world to rebalance itself. I'd been dreaming of war—whole continents on fire, oceans boiling, cities in ash—and now, with that dreadful silence, it seemed that the universe had died in its sleep.

I was a child. There were few options.

I scrambled out of bed, put on my slippers, and ran for the basement. No real decision, I just did it.

Basement, I thought.

I went straight for the Ping-Pong table.

Shivering, wide awake, I began piling scraps of lumber and bricks and old rugs onto the table, making a thick roof, shingling it with a layer of charcoal briquettes to soak up the deadly radiation. I fashioned walls out of cardboard boxes filled with newspapers and two-by-fours and whatever basement junk I could find. I built a ventilation shaft out of cardboard tubing. I stocked the shelter with rations from the kitchen pantry, laid in a supply of bottled water, set up a dispensary of Band-Aids and iodine, designed my own little fallout mask.

When all this was finished, near dawn, I crawled under the table and lay there faceup, safe, arms folded across my chest.

And, yes, I slept. No dreams.

My father found me down there. Still half asleep, I heard him calling out my name in a voice so distant, so muffled and hollow, that it might've come from another planet.

I didn't answer.

A door opened, lights clicked on. I watched my father's slippers glide across the concrete floor.

"William?" he said.

I sank deeper into my shelter.

"Hey, cowboy," my father said. "Out."

His voice had a stern, echoing sound. It made me coil up.

"Out," he repeated.

I could see the blue veins in his ankles. "Okay, in a minute," I told him, "I'm sort of busy right now."

My father stood still for a moment, then shuffled to the far end of the table. His slippers made a whish-whish noise. "Listen here," he said, "it's a swell little fort, a dandy, but you can't—"

"It's not a fort," I said.

"No?"

And so I explained it to him. How, in times like these, we needed certain safeguards. A line of defense against the man-made elements. A fallout shelter.

My father sneezed.

He cleared his throat and muttered something. Then, suddenly, in one deft motion, he bent down and grabbed me by the ankles and yanked me out from under the table.

Oddly, he was smiling.

"William," he murmured. "What's *this?*"

"What?"

"This. Right here."

Leaning forward, still smiling, he jabbed a finger at my nose. At first I didn't understand.

"Oh, yeah," I said. "It's a fallout mask."

Actually, of course, it was just a paper bag filled with sawdust and charcoal briquettes. The bag had ventilation holes in it, and the whole contraption was attached to my face by strings and elastic bands. I grinned and started to show him how it worked, but my father raised his arm in a quick jerky movement, like a traffic cop, as if to warn me about something, then he squeezed my shoulder.

"Upstairs," he said. "On the double. Right now."

He seemed upset.

He pulled the mask off and marched me up the stairs, coming on strong with all that fatherly stuff about how I could've caught pneumonia, how he had enough to worry about without finding his kid asleep under a Ping-Pong table. All the while he kept glancing at me with those sharp blue eyes, half apprehensive and half amused, measuring.

When we got up to the kitchen, he showed my mother the mask. "Go ahead," he said, "guess what it is." But he didn't give her a chance. "A fallout mask. See there? Regulation fallout mask."

My mother smiled.

"Lovely," she said.

Then my father told her about the Ping-Pong table. He didn't openly mock me; he was subtle about it—a certain change of tone, raising his eyebrows when he thought I wasn't looking. But I *was* looking. And it made me wince. "The Ping-Pong table," he said slowly, "it's now a fallout shelter. Get it? A fallout shelter." He stretched the words out like rubber bands, letting them snap back hard: "Fallout shelter. Ping-Pong."

"It's sweet," my mother said, and her eyes did a funny rolling trick, then she laughed.

"Fallout," my father kept saying.

Again, they didn't mean to be cruel. But even after they'd scooted me in for a hot bath, I could hear them hooting it up, making jokes, finally tiptoeing down to the basement for a peek at my handiwork. I didn't see the humor in it. Over breakfast, I tried to explain that radiation could actually kill you. Pure poison, I told them. Or it could turn you into a mutant or a dwarf or something. "I mean, cripes," I said, "don't you guys even think about it, don't you worry?" I was confused. I couldn't understand those sly smiles. Didn't they read the newspapers? Hadn't they seen pictures of people who'd been exposed to radioactivity—hair burned off, bleeding tongues, teeth falling out, skin curled up like charred paper? Where was the joke in all that?

Somehow, though, I started feeling defensive, almost guilty, so finally I shut up and finished my pancakes and hustled off to school. God, I thought, am I crazy?

———

But that didn't end it.

All day long I kept thinking about the shelter, figuring ways to improve on it, drawing diagrams, calculating, imagining how I'd transform that plywood table into a real bastion against total war. In art class, I drew up elaborate renovation blueprints; in study hall, I devised a makeshift system for the decontamination of water supplies; during noon recess, while the rest of the kids screwed around, I began compiling a detailed list of items essential to human survival.

No question, it was nuke fever. But I wasn't wacko. In fact, I felt fully sane—tingling, in control.

In a way, I suppose, I was pushed on by the memory of that snug, dreamless sleep in my shelter. Cozy and walled in and secure. Like the feeling you get in a tree house, or in a snow fort, or huddled around a fire at night. I'll even admit that my motives may have been anchored in some ancestral craving for refuge, the lion's instinct for the den, the impulse that first drove our species into caves. Safety, it's *normal*. The mole in his hole. The turtle in his shell. Look at history: the Alamo, castles on the Rhine, moated villages, turrets, frontier stockades, storm cellars, foxholes, barbed wire, an attic in Amsterdam, a cave along the Dead Sea. Besides, you can't ignore the realities. You can't use faggy-ass psychology to explain away the bomb.

I didn't need a shrink. I needed sanctuary.

And that's when the Pencil Theory hit me. I was sitting at my desk during the final hour of classes that day, daydreaming, doodling, and then bang, the answer was there like a gift from God. For a second I sat there frozen. I held the solution in my hand—a plain yellow pencil.

"Pencils," I said.

I must've said it in a loud voice, too loud, because the teacher suddenly jerked her head and gave me a long stare. I just smiled.

The rest was simple.

When the final bell rang, I trotted down to the school supply room, opened up my book bag, stuffed it full of No. 2 soft-lead pencils, zipped the bag shut, and hightailed it for home. Nothing to it. I didn't like the idea of thievery, but this wasn't a time for splitting moral hairs. It was a matter of live or die.

That evening, while my mom and dad were watching *I've Got a Secret*, I slipped down into the basement and quietly went to work reinforcing my shelter.

The theory was simple: Pencils contain lead; lead acts as an effective barrier against radiation. It made perfect sense. Logical, scientific, practical.

Quickly, I stripped the table of everything I'd piled on it the night before, and then, very carefully, I began spreading out the pencils in neat rows, taking pains not to leave any cracks or spaces. Wizard, I thought. I replaced the lumber and bricks and rugs, added a double layer of charcoal briquettes, and then crowned it off with an old mattress. All told, my shelter's new roof was maybe three feet thick. More important, though, it now included that final defensive shield of solid lead.

When I got upstairs, my father didn't say much. He just frowned and shook his head and told me to hit the sack.

"Sleep tight, tiger," he said—something like that. Then he closed his eyes.

Later my mother came by to tuck me in. I could tell she was worried. She kept clucking, smoothing down the blankets, touching me.

Finally she sat on the bed and hooked her fingers into mine and asked if things were okay, if I'd been having any problems.

I played it cool. "Problems?" I said.

"You know—" She smiled tentatively. "School problems, friend problems. You seem *different*."

"Really?"

"Really," she said. "What is it?"

What could I do? I couldn't just blab it all out, tell her I'd been having visions of the world blowing up. Mothers don't like to hear that sort of thing; they start blaming themselves. Besides, the whole business embarrassed me in a funny kind of way.

I shrugged and rubbed my eyes and told her everything was fine, no problems at all.

My mother patted my stomach.

"You're sure?" she said.

For a long time, nearly a minute, she gazed at me in that scary way mothers have of psyching you out, getting you to spill out your deepest emotions just by staring you down. It made me squirm. It was as if she were digging around inside my head, actually touching things, tapping the walls for trapdoors and secret passageways.

"I'm okay," I said, and smiled. "Perfect."

But she kept staring at me. I forced myself to look up to meet her eyes, but the next thing I knew she was pressing her hand against my forehead, checking me for a fever.

"You know," she said softly, "your father and I, we love you a great deal. Bunches and bunches."

"Yeah," I said, "thanks a million."

"You understand that?"

"Sure I do."

"Seriously. We love you."

"I *said* thanks."

"And so if things are bothering you, anything at all, you shouldn't be afraid to talk it out. That's what moms and dads are for."

She went on like that for several minutes, gently prodding, coaxing me to talk. Finally I couldn't take it anymore. Just to reassure her, to make her feel better, I manufactured a story about how I'd been getting weird flashes in my sleep, like lightning—bright zinging flashes—and I must've laid it on pretty thick, because my mother's face suddenly seemed to freeze.

"Flashes?" she said. "What kind of flashes?"

I shrugged. "The usual. Just flashes, the regular ones."

Her lower lip puffed out at me.

"Red flashes, white flashes?"

"All colors," I said. "Pink, mostly. And blue and green, you name it. It's sort of beautiful, really, like a rainbow, I guess, or like shooting stars with great big tails, and then they start mixing together, they mix up into one gigantic flash, a huge one, and then everything sort of blows apart. It's fun to watch."

"William," she whispered.

"But it's okay now," I told her. "I haven't had a flash in a long time. Two weeks, I bet."

My mother scanned my eyes. "William," she started. Then she stopped, touched her lip, then started again. "William, darling, I think it's time for a checkup."

"Checkup?"

"I think so, yes."

"The doctor, you mean?"

She nodded gravely. "Just to be safe."

Clucking her tongue, speaking in the softly modulated tones of a school nurse, my mother explained that there were all kinds of diseases around, polio and mumps and so on, and then she kissed me, a long kiss, and told me I wouldn't be going to school in the morning. "Right now," she said, "I want you to get some sleep. In bed. No creeping down to the basement, promise me? No Ping-Pong."

"God."

"William?"

I pulled the pillow over my face. "Ridiculous," I groaned, but I promised.

Next morning, first thing, Doc Crenshaw showed up with that black bag of his. I felt like an idiot. In the first place, I was perfectly healthy, not even a headache, and in the second place I hated Crenshaw with a passion you feel only once or twice in your entire life. He was a butcher. I don't want to exaggerate, and I won't, but there was something unmistakably foul about the man, almost evil. His breath: It was a mixture of formaldehyde and stale chewing tobacco and foot rot. And he looked as bad as he smelled. The simple truth—warts and wrinkles and liver spots and mushy yellow skin. Like a mummy. A walking stiff. And a personality to match. I despised the guy, and to be honest, Doc Crenshaw wasn't all that fond of me either. It went back a long way. A few years earlier, when I was seven or eight, I had this embarrassing bicycle accident, a bad spill, and the damned bike came down on top of me and I ended up with a mangled pecker. A huge gash, and it hurt like crazy. My mother almost had a seizure when she saw it—I guess she thought I'd be sterilized or something—so very quickly, almost in a panic, she stuffed a towel into my pants and drove me down to Crenshaw's office. The man had zero finesse. He laid me out on a table and cut off my underwear and started to sew me up, no anesthetic, no nothing, and naturally I squealed and squirmed around, and Crenshaw slapped my leg and told me to lie still, a sour-snappy voice, and then he jammed the needle in, and that's when I yelled and sat up and kicked the son of a bitch. I don't remember it, but my mother swears it happened, and apparently Crenshaw got fairly upset, because he put in these huge stitches, like railroad ties, and I've still got the scar on my pecker to prove it. Great big tread marks, as if I'd been sewn up by a blind man.

So there wasn't a whole lot of love lost between me and Doc Crenshaw. The man had messed around with my pecker, and besides, he didn't have what you'd call a gentle bedside manner.

"Well, well," he always said.

When he came into my room that morning, I beat him to it: "Well, well," I said.

He didn't smile.

All business. He unzipped his bag and pulled out some rusty-looking gadgets and began poking away at me. No reassurances, no preliminaries, no friendly little nod.

"Flashes," he grunted. "Never heard of such crap."

I took a breath and tried to hold it. Given our history, I figured tact was the best policy, and so, quietly, I tried to explain that the flashes were just minuscule things, barely worth mentioning, and that my mother and father tended to worry too much.

"Actually," I said, "if you want the truth, they might not be flashes at all."

"No?"

"Well, sure, what I mean is, I mean, it always happens late at night, you know, real late, so maybe I'm just dreaming or something. Just dreams. Or else—"

"Crap," he snapped.

A doctor, for God's sake.

I couldn't help it. Instantly, before I could stop myself, I was blabbering away about the flashes, elaborating, adding little flourishes here and there—how it always started with a high-pitched sizzling sound, like hot grease, like bacon on a skillet, and how my ears would start buzzing, and how I'd sometimes see an enormous silver-colored cloud spreading out for miles and miles. Weird rainbows, I told him. And a spectacular purple glow in the sky. Looking back on it, I'm not quite sure why I rambled on like that. To get sympathy, maybe. To give the story some credibility, to make him *believe* me. Or maybe, in some roundabout way, I was trying to clue him in on the real problem—real bombs, real danger. In any case, it went right over the old man's head.

"Well, well," he finally said.

Then he stared right at me.

I knew what was coming.

He started out by telling me that the flash stuff was total garbage, that I should be ashamed of myself for throwing a scare into my parents.

"Next time you hanker for a vacation," he said, "just go play yourself some honest hooky. No more flash crap. Understood?"

"I wasn't—"

"Understood?"

I nodded.

But he was dead wrong. I hadn't *tried* to scare my mom and dad. Exactly the opposite: I wanted to make them feel better, give them something to focus on. They couldn't understand the real issue—nuclear war and sirens and red alerts—and so I had to concoct the flashes as a kind of handle on things, something they could latch on to.

It was compassion.

But you couldn't tell Crenshaw that. You couldn't tell him anything.

When he was finished preaching at me, he packed up his equipment, went to the door, stopped, turned around, and looked at me for a few seconds.

Finally he smiled.

"By the way, young man," he said. "How's your penis?"

Then he cackled and limped away.

Murder, that's all I could think. For a while I sat there slugging my pillow, but it didn't help much, so I got out of bed and crept over to the doorway and listened in while he told my parents what a faker I was. I couldn't hear much, just laughter, but then my father said something about the Ping-Pong table, and a few minutes later they trooped down to the basement.

Barefoot, I moved to the top of the stairs. And that's when I heard my dad explaining to Crenshaw about the fallout shelter. Except he wasn't explaining it. He was mocking it. Mocking me.

"Note the briquettes," he said. "And the mattress. Safety cushion, right?"

Crenshaw laughed like hell, and so did my dad, and both of them kept making zippy little wisecracks. "Keep it down," my mother said, but then she joined the fun.

"Piss," I said.

I didn't understand it.

The shelter was no professional job—I knew that—but wasn't it better than nothing? Better than twiddling your thumbs?

"Right," I said. "So *piss* on it."

All that laughter, it hurt me. Partly embarrassment, partly anger. It hurt quite a lot, in fact.

The way I was feeling, I couldn't face my parents right then. I couldn't stop saying "Piss!" So very calmly, even though I wasn't calm, I got dressed and hopped on my bike and pedaled hard until I reached Main Street. For a time I just sat on one of the green benches out in front of the county library. I kept hearing my mother's giggle, Crenshaw's high cackle. It didn't make sense. What about the facts? The countdowns and silos—a question of simple jeopardy. Wasn't my father always telling me to be careful crossing the street? Safety first, he always said. It baffled me. I wanted to scream; I didn't know what I wanted.

Finally, to pass some time, I dragged myself into the library and moped around for half an hour, thumbing through back issues of *Time* and *U.S. News*, studying photographs of bona fide, real-life fallout shelters. They were made of steel and concrete and asbestos, very strong and sleek, and by comparison my Ping-Pong table seemed a little pitiful.

And that made me feel even worse. Miserable, in fact. I'm not sure, but I must've sighed, or maybe groaned, because the librarian began shooting edgy glances at me. Eventually the woman wandered over and stared down at my pile of magazines.

She made a soft breathy sound.

"Ah," she said. "Civil defense."

I shrugged and turned away, but she leaned in for a closer look at the photographs. A nice-looking woman. Smooth skin and greenish eyes and a thick tangle of black hair. As she bent down, one of her breasts accidentally pushed in against my neck.

She frowned and said, "Frightening business, isn't it? We tend to forget. I suppose we want to forget."

"Sure," I said.

"If you ask me, we should—"

The woman hesitated. I could almost feel her heartbeat.

"But anyway," she said, "I'm always pleased to see youngsters taking an interest in these problems. It's a rare thing. Very, very rare."

"I guess."

"War and peace. The issues of the day, it's important. You enjoy politics?"

"Sort of, maybe. There's other stuff I like better."

The woman laughed. It was a husky laugh, like a cow's moo, deep and throaty.

"No apologies," she said, "I'm impressed." She paused, straightening up, and I could feel that breast wobbling like water as it moved off my neck. "So then, here you are. No school today?"

It wasn't an accusation, just a question, and I had the answer. I told her I'd been excused to do some special research. "Civil defense," I said.

"Crucial topic."

"It is?"

"A top priority," she said, and nodded. "On my list it's number one. The future. Everything. Crucial isn't the word."

I was starting to like the woman.

No giggles, no jokes, and that soft chest. For a few seconds it seemed she was getting ready to sit down for a long talk—I *hoped* she would—but then she reached out and tapped my knee and said, "Good luck with the research. And if you need help, just pipe up. I'm always here."

Help, I thought, but I didn't say anything. Instead I watched her move back to the circulation desk, all hips and breasts and brains.

For another twenty minutes I skimmed through more magazines, wasting time, wondering if maybe I should head for school. It hardly seemed worth the effort. Besides, I didn't know if I could take it. There was a queasy feeling in my stomach, and my head hurt—not enough oxygen or something—and when I closed my eyes, things seemed to press in on me. My ears hummed. It wasn't really a sound, just a dense heaviness as if I were sinking deep under water, a pressurized silence, and then, in the empty center of that silence, I heard somebody whimper.

I nearly laughed, but I didn't, because I was sobbing.

I didn't actually cry. But the whimpering sound got louder, and I kept telling myself to shut the hell up, kept trying to swallow, and then I felt something break open inside me, like a water balloon, and then I was sniveling and carrying on like a baby, like a little kid.

There was a hand on my neck. Her hand, the librarian's.

"Say, there," she said. "You all right?"

"Of *course* I am," I told her, and I tried to laugh, and then it hit me.

A funny experience. Way down inside, I didn't feel all that terrible. I could hear myself sobbing, I could feel the thump in my chest, but I didn't have that crying urge.

The librarian hustled me into her office and sat me down and went straight for the telephone. She must've known my parents, because she didn't ask questions, she just dialed. Eyes closed, I listened as she told my mother the whole sorry tale. Dumbo, I thought. Sad and stupid. I could picture my mother's face, and my father's, and how their eyes would meet very briefly in panic, then separate, then slowly come together again.

I bawled until the librarian hung up, and then, like magic, it stopped. Just like that, it stopped. I was fine.

Stupidly, I wiped my forehead and then stared at the floor.

"There now," said the librarian. "Better?"

She brought over a glass of water, but she didn't make me drink, she simply sat there with the glass in one hand, the other hand lightly on my knee, and in that deep mooing voice of hers, cool and steady, she told me that things were under control, no problem. And she was right. Now and then I made a weak little moan, but not because I had to, not because I was feeling bad. I did it for her. So she'd know I wasn't wasting her time. So she wouldn't take that hand from my knee.

"There," she kept saying, "just relax."

When my parents showed up, they weren't laughing anymore. They weren't even smiling.

My mother kissed me, straight on the lips, and my dad took the librarian aside for a secret conference. I only heard one word: "sensitive." A while later he came over and clomped me on the back and said we'd better get home.

"I'm okay now," I told him.

"Hey, kiddo," he said, "I know you're okay." He locked his hands together, swaying back and forth on his heels. "Who says you're not? Who? Up and at 'em—toss your bike in the trunk, we'll give you a lift. Play her safe, right?"

He winked at the librarian.

It was one of those confidential, between-us-grown-ups winks, but, to her credit, the woman didn't wink back at him. In fact she frowned, then almost scowled. I loved her for that. I wanted to crawl into her lap and curl up for a long sleep, just the two of us, cuddling, that gentle hand on my knee. All I did, though, was sigh and take a last fond look at her chest, then I headed for the door.

––––––

The ride home was tense. Every so often my father fired quick glances at me in the rearview mirror, jittery and unsure, almost shy, and my mother wouldn't stop talking about how we really had to do something about that rattle in the car's engine. She went on and on about it.

Then a crazy thing happened.

Quickly, without warning, my father offered to buy me a chemistry set. It popped right out of the blue. At first I wasn't sure I understood him.

He was smiling.

"You know," he said, "one of those elaborate jobbies. Beakers and bottles and everything. A chemistry set. A good one."

I stared down at my fingernails.

Fathers, I thought.

His intention, I suppose, was to cheer me up, to get my mind off bombs and missiles, but even so it was hard to believe. I despised chemistry sets. I despised kids who played with them. Several years earlier, back in fourth grade, one of my ex-buddies used to own one, a chemistry set fanatic, and whenever you went over to his house you had to sit around and go gaga while he performed the dumbest experiments you ever saw—testing nails to see if they really contained iron. The guy was a turd. In fact, as far as I could tell, chemistry sets were originally invented for turds. Toy companies must've hired people to sit around and dream up ideas for goofballs like my ex-buddy—weirdos and losers and poor chumps who couldn't play baseball.

But my father was enthusiastic about the idea, and all the way home he kept talking it up. It was obvious he had his heart set on it. "First-class," he said. "A regular laboratory."

"Can't wait," I told him.

I couldn't hurt his feelings. By then I was mature enough, or wise enough, to understand that when your parents think you want something, they get upset when they find out you don't.

My father was smart, though.

"Look," he finally said, "what do you *really* want? Just name it."

"Anything?"

"Anything, cowboy. Say the word."

There was a short silence.

"A chemistry set," I said.

I probably choked, because my dad's eyes jerked up. He looked at me hard in the mirror.

"William," he said.

"Well," I admitted, "I *could* use a Geiger counter, too."

Immediately I knew it was the wrong thing to say. My father blinked and squinted into the mirror. He wasn't even watching the road.

The silence must've lasted thirty seconds.

"William," he said, "we need to talk."

I put it off as long as I could. For a while I holed up in the bathroom, which was the only place in the house where you could find any privacy. I locked myself in. I brushed my teeth and washed up and then sat on the can and read *The Saturday Evening Post* all the way through. Finally, though, I had to eat dinner.

Right away my parents started in.

"Here's what disturbs us," my father began. "It's this. It's the way you've been brooding. The Ping-Pong table, that episode at the library today. It's not healthy, William, and that's what we care about—your health."

"Fallout," I said. "I suppose that's healthy?"

My father released a long, terribly patient sigh. "Of course not. Dangerous, I know. Scary as hell. And we understand—we're on your side, got it? In fact ... Hey, now, *look* at me ... Your mother and I, we should've been paying closer attention to this—whatever you call it—this whole nuclear thing. Bombs and radiation, it's enough to scare anybody. I mean *anybody*. So like I say, we should've noticed. I'm sorry we didn't. Our mistake."

He looked across the table at my mother, who nodded.

"But here's the point," he went on, soft and serious. "You can't let these things get the best of you. You can't stew in the bad juices. Can't dwell on all the problems and dangers in this world.

When it comes down to it, we all have to keep the faith, just hang in there, because otherwise you end up—"

"I'm not crazy!" I said.

My mother's head snapped up.

"Darling," she said quickly, "we know you're not . . . disturbed. We worry, that's all."

"Well, I'm worried too," I told her. "I worry about getting roasted. Thermal burns and shock waves and who knows what all. That junk gives me the willies."

"Sweetheart—"

"And you guys act like I'm bonkers. Like I'm loony or something."

My father clicked his spoon against the chicken platter.

"Easy does it," he said.

"It's true! Laughing at me, telling stupid jokes. I *heard* you."

They were quiet for a moment.

"William," my father said gently. He closed his eyes, then opened them. "We weren't laughing at you. We weren't."

"Sure."

"We were amused," he said. "Fair enough? The Ping-Pong table, the charcoal. Just amusing." His eyes fastened on me. He didn't blink. "Think about it. Amusing, isn't it?"

"Ha-ha," I said.

"Come on, now. See the humor? A Ping-Pong table versus the bomb?"

"Right," I said, "except I fixed it up. The bricks and pencils and stuff. I'm not stupid."

My father almost smiled. I could tell he was trying not to.

"No," he said carefully, "you're not stupid. A bright boy, I'd say." He paused, absently tapping a spoon against his plate. He cleared his throat. "One thing, though—one thing I'm curious about. The pencils. What are all those pencils for?"

"Lead," I told him.

His eyelids fluttered. I could tell he didn't get it.

"Lead, it stops radioactivity. I bet you didn't even *know* that."

Again, my father tried to stop from smiling, but this time he didn't quite make it.

"Ah, yes," he said softly, "I see." He made a funny whistling sound through his teeth. "A smart, smart cookie."

I grinned at him. For an instant it seemed that I'd wrested an important admission from my father, almost an apology.

He gazed at me for a long time.

"Just one tiny problem," he said.

"Such as?"

"Nothing much. Tiny."

He looked at my mother. Something odd passed between them, a kind of warning. My mother got up and moved to the stove.

"Forget it," said my father.

"No, let's hear it. Like what?"

"Well," he said. His shoulders were rigid. His hands whitened against the tablecloth. "I hate to break the news, kiddo, but pencils don't contain real lead. They *call* it lead, but in fact it's graphite or something."

"Graphite?"

"Afraid so."

I took a bite of chicken and chewed and swallowed. It was the driest, most tasteless chicken I'd ever eaten.

"Well, sure," I mumbled, "I knew that all along."

"Of course."

"I *did.*"

Down inside, though, I felt like strangling myself. Graphite, I thought. Parents could be absolutely merciless. They just kept coming at you, wearing you down, grinding away until you finally crumbled.

"Graphite," I said. "I *knew* that."

My dad nodded.

He was a decent man—an ideal father—but for an instant I felt killing rage, the same venom I felt for Crenshaw. That stone-hard face of his. And those eyes, so smart and unyielding. I loved him, but I also hated him. I hated the whole grown-up world with its secret codes and secret meanings. As if for the sport of it, adults were always keeping important information up their sleeves, and then, bang, when you least expected it, they'd zap you right between the eyes: "Hey, dumbo," they'd say, "didn't you know that lead pencils are made out of graphite?" It was cruel and senseless. Why not come straight out with things? Bombs, for instance. Were they dangerous or not? Was the planet in jeopardy? Could the atom be split? Why wasn't anyone afraid? Why not clue me in? The truth, that's all I wanted. The blunt facts.

My father's hands came apart. Only the fingertips were touching. His lips curled: a smile or a smirk? How could you be sure?

"Anyway," he said.

It was bewildering and sad. Sitting there at the kitchen table, I suddenly didn't give a damn about fallout or nukes or civil defense. All I wanted was to get back to normal. The way things were going, I was afraid I might end up like that ex-buddy of mine, a chemistry set bozo, testing nails for their iron content.

"Graphite," I said. "*Piss* on it."

After supper I stayed away from the basement. I helped my mother with the dishes, knocked off some homework, watched the last ten minutes of *You Bet Your Life*, then went to bed.

Except I couldn't sleep.

I was afraid. For myself, for my prospects as an ordinary human being. It was like getting on a tightrope. You start tiptoeing across, very slowly, feeling your way, but you know you can't make it, you know you're going to fall, and it's only a question of which way you'll go, left or right. I could either end up like my ex-buddy, a screwball, or like my dad, a regular guy. No other options.

And the nuclear stuff. I was afraid of that, too.

Lying in bed, pillow tucked up against my belly, I couldn't push the terror away. I wasn't nuts. I wasn't seeing ghosts. Somewhere out there, just beyond the range of normal vision, there was a bomb with my name on it.

I tossed around in bed, curling up, uncurling, trying out different sleep positions.

Perhaps I did sleep. Not for long. A Soviet SS-4 whizzed right over the house. I almost died. There was a rumble, then a whine, then a shrill sucking sound. Far off, the earth's crust trembled; continental plates shifted in the night. The mountains above town, so solid and ancient, began to groan like the very deepest summer thunder. I held my breath. In the distance, a mile away, a trillion miles, I could hear the sizzle of a lighted fuse. I could smell hot bacon. Then suddenly the sky was full of pigeons, millions, every pigeon on earth—screeches and wings and glowing eyes. I jerked up in bed. I was stunned. I just watched. Against the far window a single fly buzzed and hissed. The planet tilted. Kansas was burning. Hot lava flowed down the streets of Chicago. It was all there, each detail: Manhattan sank into the sea, New Mexico flared up and vanished. All across the country, washing machines kicked into their spin cycles, radios blared, oceans bubbled, jets scrambled, vending machines emptied themselves, the Everglades went bone dry. Oddly, I felt no fear. Not at first. It was a kind of paralysis, the curiosity of a tourist. There were dinosaurs. The graveyards opened. Marble churches burned like kindling. New species evolved and perished in split seconds. Every egg on the planet hatched.

Clutching my pillow, I watched the moon float away.

And then the flashes came. I almost smiled—here it was. Continent to continent: red flashes and silver flashes and brilliant uncolored flashes, raw energy, the blinding laws of physics, green and gold flashes, slippery yellow flashes that fuzzed like heat lightning, black flashes in a chrome sky, neutrons, protons, a high pop fly that never quite came down, a boy in a baseball cap shielding his eyes, circling, waiting forever, pink flashes, orange and blue, powdery puffs of maroon and turquoise opening up like flowers, a housewife running for the telephone, a poet puzzling over a final line, a grounded submarine, a silent schoolhouse, a farmer frozen on his tractor, cobalt flashes, bronze and copper and diamond-white, and it was raining upside down—but the rain was burning, it wasn't really rain, it was wet and burning—loud noises, electricity, burning mountains and rivers and forests, and those flashes, all colors, the melted elements of nature coursing into a single molten

stream that roared outward into the very center of the universe—
everything—man and animal—*everything*—the great genetic
pool, everything, all swallowed up by a huge black hole.

The world wasn't safe.

I grabbed my pillow and ran for the basement. No time to
think. It was cold down there, mildewy and damp, silent as outer
space, but I crawled under the Ping-Pong table and hugged myself
and waited.

"Yo-yo," I whispered. "You poor sick yo-yo."

But even then I couldn't leave the fragile safety of my shelter.
I tried but I couldn't.

"Crazy," I said.

I said it loud. Maybe I even shouted it. Because right away
my father was there, he was there with me, under the table.

"William," he was saying, "it's okay, it's okay."

He held me tight, cradling me, arms around my shoulders. I
could smell the heat of his armpits.

"It's okay now," he purred, "no problem, you can *keep* the
shelter, honest, you can fix it up like a fortress—why not, why not?
Better than nothing, right? Right? Take it slow, now."

All the while he was massaging my neck and shoulders and
chest, cooing in that soft voice, warming me, holding me close.
We lay under the table for a long time.

Later, he led me over to the stairs and sat beside me. He was
wearing undershorts and slippers, and he looked silly, but I didn't
say anything. I just rocked against him.

"No kidding," he said, "I think it's a terrific shelter. Absolutely terrific."

Then the embarrassment hit me.

To cover up, I began jabbering away about the flashes, the
pigeons, the sizzling sounds, whatever came to mind, and my father held me close and kept saying, "Sure, sure," and after a time
things got very quiet.

"Well, now," he said.

But neither of us moved.

Like the very first men on earth, or the very last, we gazed at my puny shelter as if it were fire, peering at it and inside it and far beyond it, forward and backward: a cave, a few hairy apes with clubs, scribblings on a wall.

"Well, partner," he said. "Sleepy?"

I wasn't, but I nodded, and he clapped me on the back and laughed.

Then he did a funny thing.

As we were moving up the stairs, he stopped and said, "How about a quick game? Two out of three?"

He seemed excited.

"Just you and me," he said. "No mercy."

I knew what he was up to but I couldn't say no. I loved that man. I did, I *loved* him, so I said, "Okay, no mercy."

We unloaded the bricks and charcoal and pencils, set up the net, and went at it.

And they were good, tough games. My dad had a wicked backhand, quick and accurate, but I gradually wore him down with my forehand slams. Boom, point. Boom, point. A couple of times it almost seemed that he was setting me up, lobbing those high easy ones for me to smash back at him. But it felt good. I couldn't miss.

"Good grief," he said, "you could be a *pro.*"

Afterward he offered to help me rig up the shelter again, but I shrugged and said I'd get to it in the morning. My father nodded soberly.

It was close to dawn when we went upstairs. He brewed some hot chocolate, and we drank it and talked about the different kinds of spin you can put on a Ping-Pong ball, and he showed me how to grip the paddle Chinese style, and then he tucked me into bed. He said we'd have to start playing Ping-Pong every day, and I said, "It sure beats chemistry sets," and my father laughed and kissed me on the forehead and said it sure did.

I slept well.

And for the next decade my dreams were clean and flashless. The world was stable. The balance of power held. It wasn't until after college, on a late-night plane ride from New York to Miami, that those wee-hour firestorms returned. The jet dipped, bounced, and woke me up. I pushed the call button. By then I was a mature adult and it really didn't matter. The stewardess brought me a martini, wiped my brow, and then held my hand for a while.

3

Chain Reactions

I WAS ON FIRM GROUND. The nights were calm, and those crazy flashes disappeared, and the end of the world was a fantasy. Things were fine.

All through seventh and eighth grades, that most vulnerable time in a kid's life, I carved out a comfortable slot for myself at the dead center of the Bell-Shaped Curve. I wore blue jeans and sneakers. I played shortstop for the Rural Electric Association Little League team; I batted a smooth .270—not great, but respectable. I was popular. People liked me. At school I pulled down solid grades, A's and B's, mostly B's, which was exactly how I wanted it. I devoted long hours to the practice of a normal smile, a normal posture, a normal way of walking and talking. God knows, I worked at it. During the autumn of my freshman year, I hiked down to the junior high every Thursday night for dancing lessons—fox-trot and tango, the whole ballroom routine. I went out on hayrides with the Methodist Youth Fellowship. It didn't matter that I hated hayrides, or that I wasn't a Methodist, it was a question of locking in with the small-town conventions, hugging the happy medium.

So what went wrong?

Genetics, probably. Or a malfunction somewhere in the internal dynamics.

The problem was this: I didn't *fit*.

34

It's a hard thing to explain, but for some reason I felt different from all the others. Like an alien, sort of, an outsider. I couldn't open up. I couldn't tell jokes or clown around or slide gracefully into the usual banter and horseplay. At times I wondered if those midnight flashes hadn't short-circuited the wiring that connected me to the rest of the world. I wasn't shy, just skittish and tense; very tight inside; I couldn't deal with girls; I avoided crowds; I had trouble figuring out when to laugh and where to put my hands and how to make simple conversations.

I did have problems, obviously, but they weren't the kind a shrink can solve. That's the key point. They were *real* problems.

I gave up dancing lessons.

I also gave up hayrides and MYF.

By the time I reached high school, 1960 or so, I'd turned into something of a loner. A tough skin, almost a shell. I steered clear of parties and pep rallies and all the rah-rah stuff. I zipped myself into a nice cozy cocoon, a private world, and that's where I lived. Like a hermit: William Cowling, the Lone Ranger. On the surface it might've looked unwholesome, but I honestly preferred it that way. I was above it all. A little arrogant, a little belligerent. I despised the whole corrupt high school system: the phys-ed teachers, the jocks, the endless pranks and gossip, the teasing, the tight little self-serving cliques. Everything. Top to bottom—real hate.

And who needed it?

Who needed homecoming?

Who needed cheerleaders and football and proms and giggly-ass majorettes?

Who needed friends?

I was well adjusted, actually, in a screwed-up sort of way. During the summers I'd hike up into the mountains above town, all alone, no tension or tightness, just enjoying the immense solitude of those purply cliffs and canyons, exploring, poking around, collecting chunks of quartz and feldspar and granite. I felt an affinity for rocks. They were safe; they never gave me any lip. In the evenings, locked in my bedroom, I'd spend hours polishing a single slice of mica, shaving away the imperfections, rubbing the tips of my fingers across those smooth, oily surfaces. There was something reassuring about it, just me and the elements.

My parents, of course, didn't see it that way.

"Look," my dad said one evening, "rocks are fine, but what about people? You can't *talk* to rocks. Human contact, William, it's important." He stood nervously for a moment, jingling the loose change in his pockets. "Thing is, you seem cut off from the world. Maybe I'm way off base but I get the feeling that you're—I don't know. Unhappy."

I smiled at him. "No," I said, "I'm fine."

My father nodded and ran a hand along his jaw.

"What about—you know—what about girls?"

"Girls how?"

"Just *girls*," he said. He studied the palms of his hands. "This isn't a criticism, it really isn't, but I haven't noticed you out there burning up the old social circuit, no dates or anything, no fun."

"Rocks are fun," I told him.

"Yes, but what I'm driving at . . . I'm saying, hey, there's more to life than locking yourself up with a bunch of *stones*. It's bad for the mental gyroscope. Things start wobbling, they get out of synch. Just a question of companionship."

I nodded at him. "All right. Companionship."

"Fun, William. Get on the phone, line up a date or two. If you need cash, anything, just say the word."

"Will do."

"Fun."

"Fun," I said. "I'll get right on it."

He smiled and gave me a bashful pat on the shoulder. For a second I was afraid he might lean in for a hug, but he had the good sense to fold his arms and wink and back off.

He took two steps and then hesitated.

"One other thing," he said quietly. "Your mother and I—we love you. Love, got it?"

"Got it," I said.

I loved him, too. Which is why I didn't blurt out the facts. To protect him, to beef up his confidence. Say what you want about honesty and trust, but there isn't a father in the world who wants to hear that his kid has turned into a slightly warped ding-a-ling. All I wanted, really, was to give him the son he deserved.

So I kept the wraps on. A few fibs here and there. Quite a few, in fact.

Once or twice a week, for instance, I'd do a little trick with the telephone, dialing a random number, quietly breaking the connection, then carrying on fake conversations with fake friends. It was strictly a parental morale booster. Eyes closed, leaning back, I'd pretend I was calling up one of Fort Derry High's hot-dog cheerleaders, like Sarah Strouch, and I'd make up zippy little bits of dialogue, clucking my tongue, trying to imagine the sort of topics Sarah might want to talk about. There were problems at first, but eventually, once I got the hang of it, I was able to relax and enjoy myself. It was a form of human contact. "So what's happening?" I'd say, and she'd say, "Nothing much," and then for an hour or two we'd discuss politics and religion, the nature of cheerleading, anything that popped up. A spooky thing, but there were even times when I'd get the feeling that Sarah was actually on the line—I could almost hear that husky voice of hers, very sexy but also very tough. "You poor, fucked-up guy," she'd say, and I'd listen while she listed all my problems, then finally I'd say, "Okay, you're right, but it's just temporary," and then I'd hear a snorting sound and she'd say, "I'm all ears, Billy, tell me about it." So I'd lay it on the line. I'd talk about that alien feeling. How lonely I felt, how disconnected—lost in space.

It might sound strange, but those fake phone calls produced some of the most intelligent conversations I'd ever had. Absolutely no bullshit, no teasing. Sarah Strouch was my closest buddy.

A game, that's all.

And what was the harm?

On weekends I'd sometimes go out on trumped-up dates. I'd do my phone trick with Sarah and splash on some Old Spice and bum money from my dad and then head down to Jig's Confectionery for an evening of pinball and cherry phosphates and do-it-yourself fun.

It was a double life. Normal, but also shaky, and there were times when all the pressures took a toll. A weighed-down feeling: I couldn't function. Lying in bed at night, I'd hold my breath and pretend I was stone dead, no more troubles, a nice thick coffin to keep out the worms.

Other times I'd imagine a yacht bobbing in the South Pacific. Waves and sun and gentle winds. Sarah Strouch sunbathing on a teak deck, those tight muscles, all that smooth brown skin.

Or a tree house made of steel.

A concrete igloo in Alaska.

A snug spaceship heading for the stars.

In the middle of the night I'd get up and wander out to the living room and shake dice or play solitaire. I'd roam from room to room. I'd fill the bathtub with hot water and ease myself in and practice floating.

Once, around four in the morning, my mother found me there. I was half asleep, waterlogged.

"Darling," she whispered, "what's *wrong?*"

"Nothing," I said.

"William, please, it's almost daylight."

I smiled.

"No problem," I said. "I need a bath."

October 1962, and things got ticklish.

I looked at my father and said, "There, you see?" I wasn't being a smart aleck. It was a serious question: Did he finally *see?*

How did we survive?

We were civilized. We observed the traditional courtesies, waving at neighbors, making polite conversation in supermarkets. People counted their change. Vacations were planned and promises were made. We pursued the future as though it might still be caught.

My mother vacuumed the living-room rug, dusted furniture, washed windows, told me to buckle down to my schoolwork—there was college to think about.

"College?" I said, and my mother fluffed her hair and said, "We have to trust," so I buckled down.

We carried on.

By looking loved ones in the eye. By not blinking when Kennedy said: *The path we have chosen for the present is full of hazards, as all paths are.*

And we were brave. We went to church. We paid attention to our bodies—the in-and-out movement of lungs, the sweet pulse of a toothache. We masturbated. We slept. We found pleasure in the autumn foliage. There was much kissing and touching, and the name of the Lord was invoked at Kiwanis meetings.

My father made me get a haircut. "Shaggy-waggy," he said, playfully, but he meant it.

Birthdays were celebrated. Clocks were wound.

One evening, at twilight, my mother and father and I sat in plastic lawn chairs in the backyard, scanning the sky, a peaceful pinkish sky rimmed with violet. No words were spoken. We were simply waiting. When darkness came, my mother took my hand, and my father's hand, pressing them together. A modest gesture: Did she finally see? We just sat and waited. Later my father covered his eyes and yawned and stood up.

"Oh, well," he said. "Tomorrow's another day."

I didn't dream. I felt some fear, of course, or the memory of fear, but I had the advantage of having been there before, a kind of knowledge.

At school we practiced evacuation drills. There was bravado and squealing.

> *Hey, hey!*
> *What do you say?*
> *Nikita plans*
> *To blow us away.*

A convocation in the school gym. The principal delivered a speech about the need for courage and calm. The pep band played fight songs. Sarah Strouch led us in the Pledge of Allegiance, guileless and solemn, her hand teasing the breast beneath her letter sweater. The pastor of the First Baptist Church offered a punchy prayer, then we filed back to the classrooms to pursue the study of math and physics.

How?

By rolling dice. By playing solitaire. By adding up assets, smoking cigarettes, getting ready for Halloween, touching bases, treading water.

A dream, wasn't it?

Jets scrambled over Miami Beach and warships cruised through the warm turquoise waters off St. Thomas.

"How's tricks?" my dad asked.

"Fine."

"Flashes?"

"What flashes?"

He grinned. "That's the ticket. *What* flashes?"

We held together.

By pretending.

By issuing declarations of faith.

"They aren't madmen," my mother said.

"Exactly," said my father.

So we played Scrabble at the kitchen table, quibbling over proper nouns and secondary spellings.

"They know better."

"Of course."

"Even the Russians—they don't want it—politics, that's all it is. True? Isn't that true?"

"Oh, Christ," my father said.

I wasn't haunted by the nuclear stuff, I didn't lose control, and if it hadn't been for the headaches and constipation, I would've come through in good shape. Problem was, I couldn't shit. Which brought on the headaches, which led to other problems.

In any case, I spent the Cuban missile crisis squatting on a toilet. It was painful business, and embarrassing, so one morning on the sly I slipped down to Elf's Drug Store on Main Street and swiped the laxatives. Except nothing much happened. A slight bellyache, a throbbing at my temples. I doubled the dose and drank a couple of Cokes and dragged myself off to school.

That's where it hit me.

One minute I was sitting quietly in study hall, finishing up some geometry problems, then a dizzy-scrambly feeling came over me. A fun-house experience—topsy-turvy, no traction. In a way I felt very loose and relaxed, letting things spin, lying there on the floor while everybody yelled, "Give him air."

I almost laughed.

I didn't *need* air. I needed peace. I started to sit up, but then I felt a cool hand against my forehead. "God," someone said, and right away I knew who it was. All those fake phone calls. "Man alive," Sarah muttered, "just look at this, just look."

She unbuttoned my collar and began fanning me with a notebook.

I closed my eyes. The situation, I realized, was not romantic, but still I felt a sparky kind of human contact. That thick voice of hers: "God," she kept saying. A few seconds later, when I opened my eyes, the first thing I saw was one of her kneecaps, smooth and shiny. I could've licked it, or kissed it, but instead I jerked my arms and pretended I'd gone into a deep coma.

"Wow," Sarah whispered.

I ended up in the school nurse's office.

One thing led to another, thermometers and ice bags, and a half hour later I was ass-up on Doc Crenshaw's examining table. "Don't sweat it," I told him, "I'm all right," but Crenshaw didn't listen.

His eyes sparkled. "Well, well," he said.

I never saw a man enjoy his work so much.

He was a quack, though. He didn't cure me. A week later my insides were clogged up again and the headaches were worse than ever. I was even running a temperature. Crenshaw put me through every test in the book, but at the end, when the results were in, he just wagged his head and told my mother that it didn't seem to be anything physical.

"Not physical?" my mom said.

"You know. The opposite."

"Opposite."

"You know."

My mother allowed herself a half-smile.

"Yes," she said. "Yes, well."

Calmly, I tried to explain the situation. A huge mistake, I said. A plumbing problem, nothing else.

My mother stared.

"William," she said, "stop hiding it."

"What?"

"Please, I wish you'd—"

"Hiding *what?*" I said. "Go on, let's *hear* it."

Her eyes seemed to frost over. She was a thin, delicate woman, with tiny wrists and ankles. She hesitated, toying with her wedding band. "William," she said, "just listen to me." And then she rattled off the facts. Apparently she'd been doing some detective work at school, because she knew about the telephone gimmick and the fake dates, how unpopular I was, no friends or prospects.

When I denied it, my mother stiffened and crossed her legs.

"No arguments," she said. "There's someone we want you to see. Someone to talk to."

"Talk how?" I said.

"Just talk. A counselor up in Helena. A nice man, I think you'll like him."

"Jesus," I said.

"It might help."

"I don't *need* help. I don't need—"

"William."

"No way."

"We'll find a way," my mother said, very thickly, very decisively. "It's your future we're talking about."

It was hopeless.

I raised hell, of course, but two days later we made the drive to Helena. I didn't say a word the whole way. Arms folded, I sat there in the backseat, staring out at the mountains and trees and telephone poles. Treachery, I thought. Who could you trust in this screwy world?

"Piss," I muttered.

My mother turned: "*What's* that?"

"Bombs," I said.

We took two rooms in a Holiday Inn—one for me, one for my parents—and the next morning they drove me across town to a dingy office building a few blocks down from the state capitol. As we were riding up the elevator, my father stood behind me with his hands on my neck and shoulders, massaging them as if to warm me up for a big race. "Nothing to it," he said brightly. "Just level with the man, don't hold back. Whatever's on your mind."

"Suicide," I said.

"That's the spirit. Anything."

For ten minutes we sat around in a sterile little waiting room. My mother kept humming. Every few minutes she'd get up and go to the water fountain and then dab at her lips with a shredded-up Kleenex.

"Well, now," she'd say.

It took forever, but eventually the shrink came out and shook everybody's hand and led us down a tight corridor to his office.

Adamson was his name—Charles C. Adamson, that's what his diplomas said—but while he was pouring coffee he made a point about how we had to call him Chuck. "Chuck-Chuck," he said, "like in woodchuck," then he smiled to show off his big front teeth. I looked away. Bad omens, I thought. Bare tile floors, two old armchairs, a sofa, a gray metal desk, flaking paint on the walls and ceiling. The office had a sour, slightly brackish smell, like the men's room in a Greyhound bus depot, and right away, even before I sat down, I could feel the beginnings of a headache.

I stayed calm. There was some small talk, some nervous energy, but finally the shrink looked at his wristwatch and said it might be a good idea if he and I had a private chat. He blinked and gave me a tentative grin.

"Alone?" my mother said.

"I think so. For starters."

She took a deep breath. "Private," she chirped.

My dad winked at me, raised a thumb, then led my mother out to the waiting room.

Instantly, my whole body seemed to tense up. It was an itchy, clammy feeling—I couldn't get comfortable—but the odd thing was that Adamson seemed a little jittery himself. He hustled over to his desk, opened a manila folder, and began chewing the skin around his fingernails.

"So then," he said, "here we are."

He reached into his shirt pocket and pulled out a stick of Doublemint.

"Gum?" he said.

"No, thanks."

"You're sure?"

"Positive," I said. "I hate Doublemint."

Adamson nodded. "Right, who doesn't?"

He picked up a pencil and tapped it against the bridge of his nose. All nerves, I thought. He was a reasonably young man, maybe thirty-five or so, but he seemed old and weary-looking, especially the eyes. The saddest eyes I'd ever seen—very tiny, very timid, a moist copper color.

"So," he said.

There was a short pause, then he asked me to begin by telling him a few things about myself, a general self-description.

"Just the basics," he said. "Nothing fancy." He gazed out the window, studying the big golden dome on the state capitol building. "Hobbies. School. One small request, though. If it's possible, try not to bore me. Short and sweet. Make it peppy."

"Well, sure."

The man shrugged and showed me his front teeth.

"No offense," he said, "but you wouldn't believe the crap I have to tolerate in this job. Same old sob stories, day after day, and I have to—" He stopped and blinked at me. "Anyhow, do your best. Feel free to pull the lid off."

"Look," I said, "we can take a break if you want."

"No. Just keep it halfway interesting."

I was cautious. Briefly, as vaguely as possible, I outlined the bare facts of my life. I told him I was in good shape. An average kid, I said. Nothing unusual. Very sane.

Adamson folded his fingers around the pencil.

"Fine," he murmured, "but what about—" He paused, flicking his tongue out. "What about your parents, for example? You get along all right?"

"Of course."

"No tension areas? Squabbles?"

"Forget it," I told him. "You met them. They're terrific parents."

It was an obvious ploy, trying to pin the blame on my mom and dad, but I wouldn't let him get away with it. "Best parents in the world," I said flatly. "Nobody better. Period."

"I didn't mean—"

"The *best*," I said.

For some time we sparred back and forth like that, a polite little duel. I could tell it was wearing him down. He kept fidgeting, rubbing those sad little eyes. It was time, I decided, to let him know where I stood.

Very casually, I asked if he wanted my true feelings, and he said he did, so I leaned forward and told him that the whole counseling game was a waste of time. A racket, I said. It was for creeps and crybabies. I was strong; I knew how to deal with the world. A total charade, I told him—that was my honest belief.

Adamson shrugged.

"Charade?" he said. "How so?"

"It just is. Worthless. That's how I feel." I stared him in the eyes. I meant every word of it. "Take an example. Edgar Allan Poe: a disturbed guy. All those weird visions running through his head, fruitcake stuff. But I'll tell you something, he didn't go crying to some stupid counselor. He *used* his nuttiness. He *made* something out of it—those disturbed poems of his, those disturbed stories. He had willpower, like me. And besides, maybe there's nothing *wrong* with a little wackiness. Maybe it's a plus. An asset. You ever think of that?"

"Quite possible," Adamson said.

"Sure, it's possible. It's true. And there's plenty to be disturbed *about*. Real stuff, I mean. Realities. They don't shrink."

For a moment I wasn't sure if he'd even heard me, but then he frowned and said, "Which realities are these?"

"Just things," I said.

"Like?"

"Like everything. Turds. Assholes. The whole corrupt pecking order."

And then I gave him a quick lecture on the ins and outs of high school. No personal secrets, I just listed all the crap I had to put up with: the popularity game, hayrides and dancing lessons and sadism and petty cruelty. I told him how brutal it could get. How sometimes you had to turn your back on it, just walk away, ignore the bastards.

"The real world," I said, "it comes pre-shrunk."

Adamson nodded. "I know the story. High school. Fucking torture."

He snapped his pencil in half.

Outside, the sky had gone dark. There was thunder. No rain, just the feel of rain.

Adamson got up and closed the window and stood with his back to me. He seemed hypnotized, not quite there, staring out at the dense clouds beyond the capitol dome.

"High school," he said bitterly. "I *hated* it. Torture, that's the word. Snobs and bullies—those tough-guy letter jackets—who *cares* about letter jackets? Christ, when I think about it . . . Hate."

"Well," I said.

"Hate! Worst experience of my *life*."

His voice had a strange wound-up sound. He paused and touched the corner of his right eye.

"A nightmare," he said. "Start to finish. Just hate."

I looked out at the heavy sky. It could've been an act of some sort—I wasn't naïve—but what threw me off was the man's obvious passion. I couldn't be sure. I waited a moment and then changed the subject, rambling on about neutral topics like pep rallies and homecoming, but the more I went on, the gloomier he got.

"High school!" he suddenly yelled. "Should be *laws* against it. Hate, William. You know hate?"

There was lightning now, and hard thunder, but Adamson didn't seem to notice. He slouched forward, examined his fists, and then, in a low, soggy-sounding voice, nearly inaudible, he gave me the entire play-by-play description of his pitiful high school days. How he was low man on the totem pole. No friends, nobody to talk to. Eventually it got so bad, he said, that he began having fantasies about lacing the cafeteria food with arsenic, or rigging up dynamite and blowing the whole school sky-high. "No joke," he said, "I would've done it. Dust and bones."

I moved my head thoughtfully.

"Well, look," I said, "maybe you shouldn't dwell on it quite so much. You're an adult now, just forget it."

"Sure," he grunted. "Easy for you to say."

Pivoting, rolling his shoulders, Adamson stared at the far wall. I felt a strange jumble of emotions. Pity mixed up with contempt, sympathy with a kind of smug superiority.

I liked him. I despised him.

For a while neither of us said a word. The room was muggy and dark, and I could smell the rain coming. Finally, to fill up the time, I offered a few more horror stories. I described the cliques and teasing and practical jokes; I talked about terrorism and repression; I told him how inane it was and how hot-ass cheerleaders like Sarah Strouch wouldn't give you the time of day. "Nobody *cares* about anything," I said. "Just garbage. Turds and jocks."

"Jocks?" he said. He jotted something down on a note pad. "Jocks, they think they rule the *world*."

As it turned out, we spent the rest of that session comparing notes on how much we loathed the whole sports setup in this country. It was a coincidence, probably, but we'd experienced some of the same problems. Adamson talked about the trouble he'd had as a Little Leaguer—always dropping easy pop flies, booting ground balls—and so to make him feel better I admitted that I wasn't the world's greatest shortstop. "The thing is," I told him, "you can't let it get you down. That's life, that's how it works. No sense moping about it."

"I guess not," he said. There was a boom of thunder, then the rain came. He slapped his hands together. "Baseball, though. I'd like to ban it forever. Make it a felony just to play the game. Almost wrecked my *life*."

And there it was again.

That sullen, quavering voice. It was a relief when the session finally ended.

Five minutes later, in the elevator, my mother asked how things had gone, whether we'd made any progress, and I gave her a noncommittal shrug. "Too early to tell," I said. "The guy's a real sickie."

Except for his unhappiness, it seemed that Adamson and I had quite a lot in common. We were both intelligent. Both loners, both somewhat cynical. We even shared a certain defensive attitude toward the world. Despite myself, I ended up half liking the man, which was a good thing, because we spent six days cooped up together. Six grueling sessions. Each morning, my parents would drive me across town and drop me off in front of Adamson's office. "Go get 'em," my dad would say, and my mother would reach out and brush down my hair.

Always the same routine. As soon as I walked in, Adamson would take a look at his wristwatch and rub his eyes and gaze out at the shiny dome on the state capitol building. "So, then," he'd say, "how's my pal William?" Then he'd wag his head and start complaining. It was his favorite pastime. There were times when I wanted to bang him on the head, or shake him up somehow, but instead I tried finesse, using little incidents out of my own life as a way of putting things in perspective. When he mentioned insomnia, for instance, I recommended solitaire and hot baths. At another point, when he brought up the subject of nightmares, I told him about some of my own experiences in that area, the nuclear stuff, the sirens and pigeons and fires, the incredible reality of it all. I discussed the Cuban missile crisis and tried to get across that sense of quiet fear, nothing desperate, just a wired-up tightness.

"It's not mental," I said. "Kennedy and Khrushchev—I didn't make those guys up out of thin air. I just get worried sometimes."

For at least two full sessions we talked about how volatile and dangerous the world is, fragile as glass, no margin for error, and we agreed that the best strategy was to put a premium on avoiding unnecessary risks: stay alert, never take chances. I explained that my basic philosophy of life was to seal myself off from potentially threatening situations. Locked doors were essential. Solid walls and a solid roof—shelter.

"You can quibble all you want," I told him, "but it boils down to common sense. A matter of safety."

Adamson bobbed his head.

"I'm with you," he said. "Safety."

"That's right. And the same thing goes for how you deal with people. That Chuck-the-Woodchuck stuff, you have to be careful about it. Don't give away too much."

Adamson thought about it for a few seconds.

"Makes sense," he finally said. Then he hesitated and made an indefinite, sweeping gesture with his arm. "But doesn't it get a little lonely? A guy like you—you must have a million friends. You don't shut them out?"

"Well, no," I said. "I use the phone a lot. Safer that way."

"Safer?"

"Sure it is. No complications. Very clean."

Adamson's eyes thickened. "Lucky guy," he said. "Personally, I don't even *have* friends. Nobody to call up."

"Nobody?"

"Zero."

I crossed my legs and settled back. Once again, briefly, I wondered if he was putting me on. I wanted to trust him but I had to keep my bases covered.

"No friends?" I said, and for the next hour or so we combed through the man's balled-up social life, every sad detail.

In the evenings, after supper, my mother and father and I would usually kill time by strolling around the city, checking out shopwindows, trying to put a happy face on things. Except in the most general terms, they never asked about my meetings with Chuck Adamson, but still I knew they were going through a rough period.

Late at night I'd wake up and hear them talking in the adjoining room, soft hospital voices, hush-hush and serious. It was painful. I wanted to rap on the wall and tell them to stop worrying. "Take it easy," I wanted to say, "I'll make it." But they wouldn't have listened. When your parents think you've gone haywire, it's impossible to talk them out of it. So I'd lie there listening to those wee-hour motel sounds. Pacing footsteps, doors opening, doors closing, a television set blaring out *The Star-Spangled Banner*. My mother crying. My dad consoling her. "Relax," I wanted to say.

I was feeling terrific. The headaches were gone, and I slept well, and on the fourth or fifth day, right before my morning consultation, I squeezed out one of the sweetest movements in the annals of toiletry. Later, in Adamson's office, I couldn't resist bragging. "Well," I said, "it happened."

"What's that?" he asked.

He took a couple of guesses, way off the mark, so finally I blurted out the news. It didn't impress him. He turned away and shuffled through some papers.

I stopped him cold.

"Hey, listen," I said, "I'm *cured*. You're a doctor—*say* something."

Adamson frowned.

"Nice going," he mumbled, "good job," but he wasn't even listening.

Obviously the man wasn't cut out for that line of work. Later that morning, as subtly as possible, I suggested that he take some time off to reevaluate his career objectives. "You don't put out any effort," I told him. "You don't pay attention, you don't listen, you don't *do* anything. It's all me me me." I could see sweat stains at the armpits of his shirt, but I had to lay it out for him. I was crisp and clinical. "For openers," I said, "you're definitely the most depressing human being I ever met. How can you expect to help people? Even if you wanted to, which you don't, how could you cheer anybody up? I mean, those *eyes* of yours."

He touched his forehead. "Lay off, William. My eyes are fine."

"They're *not* fine," I said. "Look in the mirror, for Christ sake. Those sad, miserable little eyeballs. Think how your patients must feel. And it's dangerous. Sadness. It can actually kill people."

"Kill?"

"That's right. Kill."

I moved to his desk and picked up a wooden ruler and slapped it against the palm of my hand.

"I'm no expert," I told him, "but the first thing is to take a good look at yourself. Stop covering up. Stop pretending." I waved the ruler at him. "You might not believe me, but I've had some experience with this sadness stuff, and there's one thing I know for sure. Self-deception, that's the killer. You can't get well if you don't admit you're sick. You have to open up the gates. Cut out the complaining. Have some fun, for crying out loud. Find yourself a hobby."

Then I filled him in on the virtues of rock collecting. I told him how stable it was, how rocks never deserted you or let you down.

"Safety?" he said.

"There it is. Safety."

Adamson made a crisp, decisive motion with his jaw. "I get the message. Locked doors and rocks."

"For sure," I said. "The main thing, though, is to find something you're good at, something you enjoy. Just trying to help."

He nearly smiled.

"Yes," he said, "and I appreciate it, William."

"Rocks."

"Rocks. Thank you."

I shrugged and pretended to tie my shoe.

"No sweat," I said, "that's what friends are for."

Basically, that was the end of my therapy.

On the last day we got involved in a rambling, pointless conversation about the end of the world. Ridiculous, I thought, but for some reason Adamson was all fired up about the subject. It started out very innocently. I was giving him pointers on how to get set up in the rock-collecting business, listing the various tools he'd

51

need, and then, out of nowhere, Adamson brought up the fact that he used to own a toy telescope back when he was a kid. I couldn't shut him off. He kept chattering on and on about how much he'd loved that telescope. "Astronomy," he said, "now there's a magical hobby—astronomy." He gave the word a cushioned sound, as if it were somehow breakable, and that's when I made the mistake of asking a couple of questions. I did it to pep him up. To prove I cared. Right away, he was off and running, giving me the entire in-depth lecture on stars and galaxies and the chemical composition of Halley's Comet. I'd never seen him so excited. Almost smiling, almost happy. "Astronomy, that's terrific," I finally said, "but if you're so hepped about it, why not take some action? Buy yourself a new telescope."

Adamson wagged his head. "No," he murmured, "I don't think so. Too depressing."

"You were just telling me—"

"Super depressing." His entire posture seemed to change. It was back to suicide-as-usual. "You want to know the truth?" he said softly. "Why I gave up astronomy?"

I didn't, but I nodded.

"Doom," he said.

"I'm sorry?"

"Doom."

Then he almost shouted it: "Doom! End of the world, end of everything! You want a depressing hobby? Try astronomy—*doom!* Christ, you don't know the half of it."

He was right, I didn't, but he wasn't shy about laying it out for me: How someday the sun would begin cooling down, losing energy, and how our pretty little planet would freeze up into a shining ball of ice.

"Doom!" he yelled. "Nothing else, just doom doom doom! Frozen oceans! Frozen continents! *Doom,* that's the lesson of astronomy."

He rubbed his face.

For a moment he seemed lost, but then he took a breath and went on to explain how the sun would pull one final trick before it died. A terminal flash. Nothing left, he said. Not a tombstone. Not a mountain. Not a statue or a book. Nothing. No trees or grass or amber waves of grain. No bacteria. No people. Nothing. Not a single footprint. It was inescapable—a law of nature.

"Doom," he said. "And that's just the start. It gets worse."

Then he explained how the entire universe was scheduled for destruction. Not just our own puny planet. Everything. Every star, every speck of dust. It was hard to follow the technicalities, which had to do with whether we live in a collapsing or expanding universe, but his main point was that no matter how you cut it, whichever theory you believed, the end result was doom.

"The end of the world," he said flatly. "Don't kid yourself, it's in the cards. Can't prevent it, nowhere to run. Just a question of time."

He stared at me, half smiling. There was a smugness about it that touched a nerve.

Showdown, I thought.

I sat up straight and pointed a finger at him and told him I was fed up.

"The same old bitching day after day," I said. "It's a sickness. You're happy to be unhappy. That's how you get your kicks. Unhappiness. A disease."

He shook his head.

"Science," he said. "You can't ignore it."

"Here we go."

"Doom, William."

"So what?" I snapped. "We *all* die. You're a doctor, you should *know* that."

"Oh, I do know."

"And?"

"Nothing, I guess." He looked at me with an expression of intense disappointment. "Nothing. Except I thought you and I were on the same wavelength about this."

"About *what?*"

"All of it. Civilization. I mean, yes, we all die. But we have these . . . these ways of coping. Our children. The genetic pool.

53

The things we've made, books and buildings and inventions. Doesn't Edison still live in his light bulb? Switch it on and there he is. Immortality, in a way. A kind of faith. We plant trees and raise families, and those are ways of seeking—I don't know—a kind of significance. Life after death. That's what civilization *is:* life after death. But if you wipe out civilization—"

He stopped and waited. It was as if he were asking me to complete the sentence.

"See the sticker?" he said. "Nothing lasts. Doom, it means no children. No genetic pool. No memory. When the lights go out, Edison goes out. And what significance did his life have? Erased. Shakespeare and Einstein. You and me."

"But nobody—"

"Right, nobody realizes," he said. "Nobody cares. People just keep diddling on. A joke, they think. But it's not. It's our goddamn silhouette."

We sat facing each other, eye to eye, and for an instant there was something very much like a bond between us, as if we were touching, or embracing, shared knowledge and shared vision, two losers drawn together by the interlocking valences of terror.

"Imagination," Adamson said gently, "that's what you and I have in common. A wonderful faculty, but sometimes it gets out of control, starts rolling downhill, no brakes, and all you can do is hang on for dear life and hope you don't—"

"Crack up," I said.

I looked down at the ragged edges on my fingernails. And then suddenly, without planning it, I was talking about bombs and missiles and radioactivity and thermal blasts and the sound of a Soviet SS-4 zipping across the night sky. Real, I told him. The silos and submarines and launching pads. Things you could touch. Real things. It wasn't some theory, I said, it wasn't a ghost story, it was real.

My voice caught.

"Crazy," I said.

Adamson sat very still. "No, just special. Very special."

We were quiet again; that bonded feeling.

Adamson finally smiled at me and came across the room and shook my hand. It was an awkward moment. He kept squeezing, hanging on.

"Well," I said, "I hope that helps. Sometimes it's better to talk things out."

He laughed and said, "You bet, it helps plenty." He clapped me on the back, fairly hard, as if signaling something, then he led me out to the elevator. Funny, but I felt a little choked up, almost teary. We stood there in the hallway, not quite looking at each other, and then we shook hands again. *"Adios,"* he said. But a strange thing happened next. When the elevator doors opened, Adamson got in and rode down to the first floor with me and followed me all the way outside. Like an orphan, I thought, or a stray dog.

My mom and dad were parked across the street, ready to head home, but I couldn't just walk away. I thanked him for all the help. A good listener, I said, a good sharp mind. Adamson shrugged. He took out a pencil and a scrap of paper and jotted down a telephone number.

"Keep it in your wallet," he said. "Night or day. I'm here."

He looked away.

There was a short silence, then he laughed and said, "A charade, you were right."

He pointed up at the dome on the state capitol.

"Politics," he said. "A new racket. What the hell—run for governor."

"You're a shoo-in, Chuck."

"You think so?"

"Absolutely. I mean, hey, you've got the sympathy vote all locked up."

We smiled at each other.

"Friends?" he said, and I said, "Friends," and then my dad honked the horn and I turned and trotted across the street.

Those six days in therapy did not turn my life around. The headaches disappeared, and my plumbing problems cleared up, but otherwise things remained almost exactly the same. A wobbly gyroscope; a normal guy in an abnormal world. But now and then, when the pressures began to accumulate, it cheered me up to think about Chuck Adamson, remembering that dismal face of his, imagining his campaign for the governorship—anti–high school, anti-baseball, anti-social. A hard person to pin down. How much was acting, how much was real? Even now, in memory, it all blends together. Those moist, fearful eyes and that weary posture and the way he'd sigh and tap his pencil and gaze out at the bright golden dome on the state capitol.

I missed him.

That much was for sure. I did miss the man.

Except for a few postcards, I had no contact with him for the next seven or eight years, and yet there was still a certain consolation in having his phone number tucked away in my wallet, just in case. Like a safety valve, or a net. Often, during bad times, I'd take out that wrinkled scrap of paper and quietly rub my fingers across it, memorizing the numbers, and on one or two occasions I came very close to putting in a long-distance distress call, person to person. I'd dial and break the connection and then spend an hour or so in a nice relaxed conversation, almost real, as if we were back in his office again, discussing telescopes and loneliness and the powers of the human imagination, figuring out ways to cope with the end of the world.

4

Quantum Jumps

D IG, IT WHISPERS. Two weeks on the job, and my hole is nearly four feet deep, ten feet square. It's a beauty—I'm proud—but I've paid a terrible price. My daughter says I'm nutto. My wife won't speak to me, won't sleep with me. She thinks I'm crazy. And dangerous. She refuses to discuss the matter. All day long, while I'm busy saving her life, Bobbi hides in the bedroom, quietly cranking out those insinuating bits of verse. She uses silence like a blackjack; she withholds the ordinary courtesies of love and conversation. It hurts, I won't deny it. Those damned poems. Christ, she's baiting me—

THE MOLE IN HIS HOLE

Down, shy of light, down
to that quilted bedrock
where we sleep as reptiles
dreaming starry skies and ash
and silver nuggets that hold
no currency in life misspent.
Down, a digger, blind and bold,
through folds of earth
layered like the centuries,
down
to that brightest treasure.
Fool's gold.

I don't get it. Meanings, I mean. What's the point? Why this preference for metaphor over the real thing?

Fuck her, the hole says. *Dig!*

Bobbi doesn't understand. She's a poet, she can't help it. I've tried to talk things out. I've presented the facts. I've named names: Poseidon, Trident, Cruise, Stealth, Minuteman, Lance, Pershing—the indisputable realities. Trouble is, Bobbi can't process hard data. The artistic temperament. Too romantic, too sublime. She's a gorgeous woman, blond and long-legged, those shapely fingers and turquoise eyes, a way of gliding from spot to spot as if under the spell of a fairy tale, but she makes the mistake of assuming that her beauty is armor against the facts of fission. Funny how people hide. Behind art, behind Jesus, behind the sunny face of the present tense. Bobbi finds comfort in poetry; Melinda finds it in youth. For others it's platitudes or blind optimism or the biological fantasies of reproduction and continuity.

I prefer a hole.

So dig. I won't be stopped.

I'll admit it, though, these past two weeks have been murder, and at times the tension has turned into rage. This morning, for example. After a night of insomnia and celibacy, I came to the breakfast table a bit under the weather. It was hard to see the humor in finding another of Bobbi's snide ditties stapled to the Cheerios box. I wanted to laugh it off, I just couldn't muster the resources. Besides, the poem was cruel, an ultimatum. *Fission,* she called it.

> *Protons, neutrons.*
> *Break the bonds,*
> *Break the heart.*
> *Fuse is lit.*
> *Time to split.*

I can read between the lines. Split, it's not even cute.

Who could blame me? I lost my head for a minute. Nothing serious—some bad language, some table-thumping.

"God," Melinda squealed. "Crackers!"

Bobbi remained silent. She lifted her shoulders in a gesture that meant: Yes, crackers, but let's not discuss it in front of your father.

"Daffy Duck," said my daughter. "Hey, look at him! Look, he's eating—"

I smiled. It was a mark of sanity, the cheerful face of a man in tip-top health—I smiled and chewed and swallowed *Fission*— and then I asked if they'd kindly put a lid on all the name-calling stuff, I was fed up with wisecracks and Mother Goose innuendo. "A little respect," I said. "Fair enough? Time for some understanding."

Melinda stared at her mother.

"You see that?" she said. "He ate your poem."

My wife shrugged.

"I think he's flipped!" Melinda yelled. "He did, he *ate* it, I saw him."

"Now wait a minute—"

"Daddy's flippo!"

"No," I said, "Daddy's smart. He's a goddamn genius."

Melinda snorted and flicked her pale eyebrows.

"Selfish Sam," she said. "What about *my* feelings? What happens when everybody at school finds out? God, they'll think I've got the screwiest family in history."

"They laughed at Noah, princess."

"God!"

I tapped the table. "Eat your Cheerios," I said. "And cut out the swearing."

"*You* swear."

"Hardly ever."

"I just heard it, you said—"

"Hustle up, you'll be late for school."

Authority, I thought. Don't bend. Don't crack. I ignored their coded mother-daughter glances. I made happy chitchat, humming, stacking the dishes, buttoning Melinda's coat and then marching her out to meet the school bus. A splendid morning, despite everything. That smooth blue sky, wildflowers everywhere, the wide-open spaces. And the Sweetheart Mountains—beautiful, yes, but also functional, a buffer between now and forever. Shock absorbers. Heat deflectors.

But Melinda had no appreciation for these facts. She wouldn't look at me. We stood a few feet apart along the tar road.

"Well, Flub-a-dub," she finally said, "I hope you enjoyed your breakfast."

I reached out toward her, but she yelped and spun away. Again I offered extravagant apologies. Too much tension, I told her. Too little sleep. A lot on my mind.

"Holes," Melinda said, and glanced up for a moment, soberly, as if taking a measurement. "God, can't you just stop acting so screwy? Is that so hard?"

"I suppose it is sometimes."

"Eating *paper*."

She closed her eyes.

"You know what Mommy says? She says you're pretty sick. Like a breakdown or something."

"No way, baby."

"Yeah, but—" Melinda's voice went ragged. She bit down on her lower lip. "But you always act that way, real flippy, and it makes me feel . . . You know what else Mommy said?"

"What else?"

"She says if you don't stop digging that hole, she says we might have to go away."

"Away where?"

"I don't *know* where, just *away*. That's what she told me, and she means it, too. That poem you ate—that's what it was *about*."

I nodded. "Well, listen, right now your mother and I have this problem. Like when the telephone doesn't work. Like a busy signal, you know? But we'll get it fixed. That's a promise."

"Promise?"

"On my honor."

Later, when the school bus came grinding up the road, Melinda generously offered me her cheek, which I kissed, then I watched her ride away. A beautiful child. I love her, and Bobbi, too.

Isn't that the purpose? To save those smooth blond hides? Split?

Doesn't make sense.

Dig.

That makes sense. All day long I've been at it, sweat and calluses, and my back hurts, but there's pleasure in the pain. It's duty-doing; taking charge. Tension translates into doggedness, anxiety into action, skittishness into firm soldierly resolve.

I feel a nice tingle as I rig up the dynamite.

Ollie Winkler taught me—I learned from a pro.

Two sticks and the primer. Wire it up. Crimp the blasting caps. Take shelter behind the tool shed. Think about Ollie and his Bombs for Peace.

"Fire in the hole!" I yell.

The kitchen windows rattle. A muffled explosion, just right. Bobbi comes to the back steps and stands there with a mystical smile on her lips. In the backyard, like smoke, there's a light dusting of powdery debris, and my wife and I stare at each other as if from opposite sides of a battlefield. Bobbi bites her thumb; I smile and wave. Then it's over. She goes inside, I go back to digging.

The dynamite, that's what disturbs her. She thinks I'll miscalculate. Crazy, but she thinks I'll blow the house down, maybe hurt someone. Dangerous, she thinks. But what about the bomb, for Christ sake? Miscalculations? If that's the stopper—miscalculations—I'll be happy to show her a few. Four hundred million corpses. Leukemia and starvation and no hospitals and nobody around to read her miserable little jingles.

Screw it. Dig.

A pick, a garden spade, a pulley system to haul out the rock.

When Melinda returns from school, I'm still on the job. I straighten up and smile over the rim of the hole. "Hey, there," I say, but she doesn't answer. She kicks a clod of dirt down on me and says "Nutto" and scampers for the house.

I don't let it rattle me. At dusk I plug in the outdoor Christmas lights. I skip supper. I keep at it, whistling work songs.

It isn't obsession. It's commitment. It's me against the realities.

Dig, the hole says, and I spit on my hands. Pry out a boulder.

Lift and growl and heave. Obsession? Edgar Allan Poe was obsessed.

At ten o'clock I tell myself to ease off. I take a few more licks at it, then a few more, and at midnight I unplug the lights and store my tools and reluctantly plod into the house. No signs of life, it's eerie.

In the living room, I find only the vague after-scent of lilac perfume—a dusty silence. I stop and listen hard and call out to them. "Bobbi!" I shout, then "Melinda!" The quiet unnerves me, it's not right.

Melinda's bed is empty. And when I move to Bobbi's bedroom—my bedroom—I'm stopped by a locked door.

I knock and wait and then knock again, gently.

"All right," I say, "I know you're in there."

I jiggle the knob. A solid lock, I installed it myself. So now what? I detect the sound of hushed voices, a giggle, bedsprings, bare feet padding across oak floors.

Another knock, not so gentle this time.

"Hey, there," I call. "Open up—I'll give you ten seconds."

I count to ten.

"Now," I say. "Hop to it."

Behind the door, Melinda releases a melodious little laugh, which gives me hope, but then the silence presses in again. It occurs to me that my options are limited. Smash the door down—a shoulder, a foot, like on television. Storm in and pin them to the bed and grab those creamy white throats and make some demands. Demand respect and tolerance. Demand *love*.

I kiss the door and walk away.

Supper is cold chicken and carrot sticks. Afterward, I do the dishes, smoke a cigarette, prowl from room to room. A lockout, but why? I'm a pacifist, for God's sake. The whole Vietnam mess: I kept my nose clean, all those years on the run, a man of the most impeccable nonviolence.

So why?

There are no conclusions.

Much later, at the bedroom door, I'm pleased to discover that they've laid out my pajamas for me. A modest offering, but still it's something. I find a sleeping bag and spread it out on the hallway floor.

As I'm settling in, I hear a light scratching at the door, then a voice, muted and hoarse, and Melinda says, "Daddy?"

"Here," I say.

"Can't sleep."

"Well, gee," I tell her, "open up, let's cuddle."

"Nice try."

"Thanks, sweetie."

She clears her throat. "I made this promise to Mommy. She said it's a quarantine."

"Mommy's a fruitcake."

"What?"

"Nothing," I murmur. "We'll straighten things out in the morning. Close your eyes now."

"They *are* closed."

"Tight?"

"Pretty tight." A pause, then Melinda says, "You know something? I'm scared, I think."

"Don't be."

"I am, though. I hate this."

There's a light trilling sound. Maybe a sob, maybe not. In the dark, although the door separates us, her face begins to compose itself before me like a developing photograph, those cool eyes, the pouty curvature of the lips.

"Daddy?"

"Still here."

"Tell the honest truth," she whispers. "I mean, you won't ever try to kill me, will you?"

"Kill?"

"Like murder, I mean. Like with dynamite or an ax or something."

I examine my hands.

"No killing," I tell her. "Impossible. I love you."

"Just checking."

"Of course."

"Mommy thinks . . . Oh, well. Night."

"Night," I say.

And for several minutes I'm frozen there at the door, just pondering. Kill? Where do kids get those ideas?

The world, the world.

I groan and lie down and zip myself into the sleeping bag. Then I get jabbed in the heart. Another poem—it's pinned to the pajama pocket.

THE BALANCE OF POWER

Imagine, first, the high-wire man
a step beyond his prime,
caught like a cat,
on the highest limb,
wounded, wobbling,
left to right,
seized by the spotlight
of his own quick heart.
Imagine, next, the blue-eyed boy
poised on his teeter-totter
at the hour of dusk,
one foot in fantasy,
one foot in fear,
shifting, frozen—
silly sight—
locked in twilight balance.
Imagine, then, the Man in the Moon,
stranded in the space
of deepest space,
marooned,
divorced from Planet Earth
yet forever bound to her
by laws of church
and gravity.

> *Here, now, is the long thin wire*
> *from Sun to Bedlam,*
> *as the drumbeat ends*
> *and families pray:*
> *Be quick! Be agile!*
> *The balance of power,*
> *our own,*
> *the world's,*
> *grows ever fragile.*

Horseshit of the worst kind. Bedlam—unbalanced, she means. Marooned, divorced—a direct threat, nothing else. At least it rhymes.

Lights off.

Sleep, I tell myself, but I can't shut down the buzzings. The issue isn't bedlam. Uranium is no figure of speech; it's a figure of nature. You can hold it in your hand. It has an atomic weight of 238.03; it melts at 1,132.30 degrees centigrade; it's hard and heavy and impregnable to metaphor. I should know, I made my fortune on the stuff.

We were all in on it, Sarah and Ned and Ollie and Tina—we followed the trail and plundered those ancient mountains and now we're left with the consequences, that old clickety-clack echoing back. It's history. It can't be undone.

There's a soft tapping at the bedroom door.

"Hey, Goofy," Melinda whispers, "stop talking to yourself."

5

First Strikes

UTUMN 1964, AND THERE was a war on, and people were
dying. There were jets over the Gulf of Tonkin. There were
bombs and orphans and speeches before Congress. It was
a season of flux: leaves were turning, times were slippery. And it
was real. No paranoia, not this time. At night, in bed, I detected a
curious new velocity at work in the world, an inertial zip; I could
hear it in the rhetoric, in the stiff battering-ram thump of the
music. Unwholesome developments, I thought. The Chinese de-
tonated their first nuclear device. Khrushchev was on the skids.
Call it prescience, or a sensitivity to peril, but I could not shake
the hunch that things were accelerating toward the point of hazard. In Da Nang the Marines were digging in, and in Saigon the
generals played their flamboyant games of hopscotch, and at
home, at random spots across the North American continent, in
back rooms, in the dark, there were the first churlish rumblings of
distemper.

Nothing mutinous, not yet. Abbie Hoffman was a nobody.
Jane Fonda was a starlet. By daylight, at least, Vietnam was still a
fairy tale.

We were at peace in time of war.

And at Peverson State College, in September of 1964, we did
the peaceful things. We crammed for exams and talked sex until
four in the morning. We were kids, after all, and the future

seemed altogether probable. It was a bridge between two eras, a calm, old-fashioned time, and on the nation's campuses, certainly at Peverson State, football was still king and booze was queen and raw physicality was the final standard of human excellence.

To be sure, Pevee was not a distinguished institution. More like a health resort, I decided, or a halfway house for the criminally vacuous. Mostly ranch kids—hicks and dullards. Even after my experience at Fort Derry High, I had to admire the way my new classmates so daringly refined the meaning of mediocrity. A dense, immobile apathy. Ignorance on a colossal scale. There was something ambitious about it, almost inspired. No one cared. No one tried. On the surface, of course, the place could seem deceptively collegiate, with the usual tweedy teachers and wimps with slide rules, but even so, beneath the cosmetics, Peverson State College was a student body without student brains. In a note to my parents, composed near the end of freshman orientation, I outlined the major difficulties. Stereos that blew your brains out at 3 a.m. Coeds who pondered the spelling of indefinite articles. Elaborate farting contests in the school library, with referees and formal regulations and large galleries of appreciative spectators.

Cynical, maybe, but true. The college had been founded back in the early fifties in anticipation of the coming wave of baby-boomers, millions of us, children of the age. To educate us, or at least to contain us, Montana's state legislature had appropriated several million dollars for the construction of a large, fully modern facility along the banks of the Little Bighorn, ten miles from the famous battlefield, forty miles from SAC's northern missile fields. It was a danger zone, to put it mildly, and this circumstance was clearly reflected in the campus architecture, a kind of Neo-Pillbox, forty acres of solid concrete. Dorms and parking lots and fences, all cement: Ready-Mix University.

The place wasn't ugly, exactly. It wasn't anything, exactly. Just bland and boring, like an East German housing development.

A zoo, some people called it, but that wasn't quite the case. It was jungle. So I kept a low profile during the fall and winter of my freshman year. I avoided parties and mixers. Fortunately, I had no roommates, which kept the socializing to a minimum, and I was scrupulous about steering clear of the bull sessions and nonstop horseplay in the dorms. I installed a special lock on my door. I took my showers late at night to ensure privacy, no towel-snapping shit, no comparing penis sizes.

My theory, essentially, was the old standby. Cover your flanks and watch out for morons.

I wasn't lonely, just careful.

On the plus side there was the fact that I was smarter than the typical Pevee underclassman, more mature, and in class I didn't mind showing off those qualities. A little arrogant, I suppose, but there was a real world out there, a serious world, and I cared about it, I knew what the stakes were. I enjoyed chemistry, for example—learning about quantum mechanics and the periodic table, how atoms worked, how fractional errors could produce massive consequences. I studied history, too, and political science. I liked the certainty of absolute uncertainty. I liked reading about Winston Churchill and Davy Crockett: obsessed people, but real dynamos when the chips were down.

And of course geology. That was my main love, and from my first day at Peverson I knew I'd be majoring in rocks.

The geology lab was my true home on campus. Some evenings, when the dorm became unbearable, I'd take my pillow and blankets over to the lab, lock the door, turn out the lights, and lie there watching the brilliant twinklings all around me, like a jeweler's showcase, flakes of silver and gold, ruby reds, fluorites and diamonds and foliated talc, those glowing prisms. *Terra firma*, I'd think. Back to the elements. A hard thing to explain, but for me geology represented a model for how the world could be, and should be. Rock—the word itself was solid. Calm and stable, crystal locked to crystal, there was a hard, enduring dignity in even the most modest piece of granite. Rocks lasted. Rocks could be trusted. The covalent bonds were tight and sure, and the electrons held fast from hour to hour, age to age. Sometimes I'd pick up a chunk of uranium dioxide and just squeeze it. I'd press it to my cheek. I'd study its properties, the purply-black coloration, bits of red and yellow, slightly greasy to the touch, dull and opaque and brittle. And it was safe; it did not explode. Not in the world-as-it-was, not in the world-as-it-should-be. I'd put my tongue against it, tasting, thinking about Ping-Pong and Chuck Adamson and collapsing stars, thinking doom, but the uranium was a friend. It had staying power. Man was goofy but the earth was tolerant. In geology, there was always time.

I wasn't crazy. I didn't unravel. Over that long freshman year, 1964 and 1965, I stuck it out alone. I had my own table in the cafeteria, my own good company. At times I felt a little frazzled, but I was blessed with the mental equipment to keep a firm fix on the moral priorities.

Imagination, that was my chief asset. Not fantasies, exactly, just vivid home movies of the world-as-it-should-be.

At night, in my room, I carried on internal dialogues with important world personages. I was perfectly sane. I'd set up meetings with LBJ and Andrei Gromyko and Ho Chi Minh, informal summit conferences at which I would preside as an instrument of moderation and compromise, a peacemaker. "Just relax," I'd say, and Gromyko would say, "Man, I *can't* relax, these fucking Texans," so then I'd come up with suggestions about ways to cope with anxiety and stress, anything to prevent twitches in the trigger finger.

Mind games, but nothing freaky. I pretended I was a corpse. I saw myself as a member of Custer's lost command.

And Sarah Strouch.

Sarah was Fantasy Number One.

Ever since high school, our relationship had been a classic love-hate affair, and at Peverson State there was no change. Two different people, two different worlds. She was a campus superstar—a cheerleader, of course—vapid, vain, cruel, and beautiful. The combination intrigued me. During our first year at Peverson, we crossed paths fairly often, in the cafeteria, or walking to class, but Sarah's eyes would always slide over me with a kind of queenly indifference. She didn't nod or wave. She didn't smile. The signals,

I thought, were not encouraging, so naturally fantasy took over. There was Sarah-as-she-was and there was Sarah-as-she-should-be.

At certain hours of the night she would slip into my room and put her arms around me and say, "Well, now, here we are. Just you and me."

Or she'd sit quietly on the bed, smiling a secret smile while I finished my homework.

Not crazy.

Not mere whimsy.

To the contrary, those feats of imagination kept me sane. They were a means of connecting the dots, locating the hidden scheme of things. Who could become a surgeon, for instance, without first visualizing the surgical event, slicing open a human breast and prying apart the ribs and dipping into blood and gore? Our lives are shaped in some small measure by the scope of our daydreams. If we can imagine happiness, we might find it. If we can imagine a peaceful, durable world, a civilized world, then we might someday achieve it. If not, we will not. Therefore Sarah Strouch would say, "Imagine *this*, William—I'm all yours." And it was somehow real. Or at least a kind of reality, the reality of what could be and might still be. Lying back, smiling with her eyes, she would perform uncommon acts of generosity and understanding. She would allow liberties—holding, touching. "Very nice," she'd whisper, "just keep squeezing, don't stop."

It's true, I lived in my head, but my head was a secure residence. There were no fracture lines. Sometimes I'd feel a little slippage, even some inexplicable sorrow, and yet with luck, with immense willpower, I made it through my freshman year.

I put up No Trespassing signs outside my door.

I papered my walls with obituaries.

No problem, I was fine.

Strange goings-on, however.

January 1966, a sophomore slump, and there were some disconcerting nighttime occurrences.

I watched a missile rising from the plateau beyond the Little Bighorn. Yes, a rocket, bright white with blue markings and a silver nose cone. "Ah me," I said mildly. But there it was, sleek and conspicuous against the night sky. I could read the letters USA on its midsection; I could see the tail fins and the peeling paint at its rear quarters. This was not, I realized, a dream. This was a missile. At the time, which was well after midnight, I was situated in a reclining position at the riverbank. I was alone. I had no future. "Ah me," I said, then came a high whining sound. The missile rose at a slight northward angle. It passed across the face of the moon. For a moment I feared the flashes might come, but there was just the missile climbing against gravity, beyond the football stadium, toward Canada and the Arctic Ocean, a smooth, graceful parabola that was not without mystique and beauty.

The omens were obvious. It occurred to me that the world's mainspring had tightened up a notch. Much later, when I looked up, the missile had vanished and there was a light snow falling, soft and deadly.

"No sweat," I said.

Imagination, that was my strong suit. I pretended nothing had happened.

But it happened, and it kept happening.

In February I watched thirteen marines die along a paddy dike near Chu Lai.

I recall an encounter with napalm.

Voices, too—people shouting. In the hours before dawn I was awakened by Phantom jets. I saw burning villages. I saw the dead and maimed. I saw it. I was not out of my mind. I was *in* my mind; I was a mind's eyewitness to atrocity by airmail. There were barricades before public buildings. There were cops in riot masks, and clubs and bullhorns, and high rhetoric, and Kansas burning, and a black bomb pinwheeling against a silver sky, and 50,000 citizens marching with candles down Pennsylvania Avenue. I heard guns and helicopters and LBJ's nasal twang: *This will be a disorderly planet for a long time . . . turbulence and struggle and even violence.*

Disorder, I reasoned, begets disorder, and no one is immune. Even Chicken Little got roasted.

But I held tight.

Day to day, I waited it out. February was dreary, March was worse. Delusion seemed optional. I couldn't quite choose; I couldn't unburden myself. In the bathroom, pants at my knees, it was easy to envision a set of circumstances by which I would ultimately expire of unknown causes in the confines of some public toilet stall—in a Texaco station outside Tucson, or behind a door marked "Gents" in a Howard Johnson's along the road to Cleveland. It made a poignant image. A night janitor would find my corpse; the autopsy would be brisk and businesslike. For a month, perhaps, my remains would lie unclaimed, and afterward I would go to a pauper's grave, in an aluminum box, and there I would present my modest tribute to the worms.

No question, I was depressed. Scared, too. One evening I picked up a scissors and held it to my throat. It was a ticklish sensation, not unpleasant. I drew the blade upward. No blood, just testing.

The time had come, I decided, to seek help.

Quickly, I dropped the scissors and walked down the hallway to a pay phone and put in a call to Chuck Adamson.

No answer, though.

So while the phone rang, I talked about the facts of the case. I told him I was boxed in by disorder. I described the pressures. "I swear to God," I said, "it's like I might explode or something. I keep *seeing* things." Then I told him about that missile over the Little Bighorn. Nothing mystical, I said. It was there. I went on for some time about napalm and Phantom jets, how things were accelerating toward crack-up, high velocity, how I couldn't cope, how I couldn't make any headway with Gromyko and LBJ, how it was down-the-tubes time, the scissors, the temptation to call it quits, how I couldn't shit, couldn't sleep, couldn't find my place in the overall pattern of events. "Otherwise," I said, "I'm doing pretty well." Then I pressed the phone tight to my ear. There were cracklings on the line, long-distance buzzings, but I paid attention while Adamson explained that he'd gone through the same experiences back in college, a tough time, and that it was finally a question of maintaining mental traction, keeping purchase on slippery winter roads.

"The first step," he said, "is to stop talking to yourself."

I nodded and said, "What else?"

There was a pause.

"These visions of yours. You have to figure out what's fact and what's—"

"It *is* fact," I said sharply. "The war, it's a fact."

"True."

"So?"

Adamson seemed pensive. "Imagination," he said, "that's your special gift, but you have to *use* it. Take charge. And stay away from scissors."

There was a sharp clicking sound. The phone kept ringing, no answer, but for a few moments I was back in his office again. He winked at me. His eyes were clear and lucid. Smiling, he swiveled in his chair and stood up and went to the window. And there it was: the shining dome on the state capitol, buffed and golden. "Politics," he said, "give it some thought."

I was no radical, not by a long shot.

But what does one do?

I recovered. I spent the next six months seeking traction. Finally, though, what does one *do?*

By the autumn of my junior year, October 1966, the American troop level in Vietnam exceeded 325,000. Operation Rolling Thunder closed in on Hanoi. The dead were hopelessly dead. The bodies were bagged and boxed. In Saigon, General Westmoreland called for fresh manpower, and at the State Department, Dean Rusk assured us that rectitude would soon prevail, a matter of attrition. Yet the dead remained dead. For the dead there was no rectitude. For the dead there was nothing more to die for. The dead were silent on the matter of attrition. So what does one do? Among the living, Richard Nixon peeled his eyes and bided time. Robert Kennedy waffled. Richard Daley ruled a peaceful city. Beneath the surface, however, premonition was evolving toward history. I was a witness. Like déjà vu in reverse, lots of backspin. In Los Angeles, Sirhan Sirhan came into possession of a .22-caliber Iver Johnson revolver. I watched the transaction. In Minnesota,

Eugene McCarthy reviewed his options; in Washington, Robert McNamara entertained misgivings; in Hollywood, Jane Fonda began setting an agenda. Hawks were at the throats of doves. It was a fitful, uncertain autumn, but the dead kept dying. They died on the six o'clock news, then they died again at midnight, and now and then I could hear the shearings of a great continental fault, I could feel the coming fracture.

In a time of emergency, the question will not be begged: What does one do?

I made my decision on a Sunday evening.

Politics, I thought.

On Monday morning I purchased some poster paper and black ink. The language came easily. In simple block letters I wrote: THE BOMBS ARE REAL.

Trite, I realized, but true.

At the noon hour I took up a position in front of the cafeteria. The place was crowded but there was the feeling of absolute aloneness. I lifted the poster with both hands. As people filed by, nothing much registered, just background noise, a brisk wind and giggles and wisecracks. That was the price. I knew it and I paid it.

Weird William, I thought.

In hindsight, it might seem silly, a kid holding up a sign that announced the obvious, but for me it represented something substantial. I felt proud. Embarrassment, too, but mostly pride.

I'm not sure how long I stood there. Twenty minutes, a half hour. I remember how bright the day was, no clouds, very crisp and clean, that wind off the river. I remember the sound of clanking plates in the cafeteria. There was laughter, but it didn't bother me. In a sense, I suppose, I wasn't entirely there. Drifting, maybe. The faces seemed to blend and dissolve. There was a war on—they didn't know. There was butchery—they didn't know. "Shit," someone said, but they simply did not know, they had no inkling, so I smiled and let my sign speak sign language: the blunt, trite, unarguable truth. Real. The guns were real, and the dead, and the silos and hot lines and Phantom jets. The war was real. The technology was real. Even that which could not be seen was real, the unseen future, the unseen letting of unseen blood—and the bombs—the fuses and timers and tickings—and the consequences of reality, the consequences were also real. But no one knew. No one imagined. "What this brings to mind," a voice said, "is shit." And that, too, was real. And Sarah Strouch, who paused at the cafeteria doors, watching me with cool black eyes. Real, I thought. She wore blue shorts and a pink T-shirt scooped low at the neck. There was a hesitation, then she tilted her head sideways and said, "Such true shit."

I was in control. Over the next two months, every Monday, I stationed myself at the same spot in front of the cafeteria. It was a feeble exercise, I realized that, but in conscience what does one do? Take a stance—what else?

I was alone until early December.

A frigid Monday, another noon vigil, then Ollie Winkler tapped me on the elbow and said, "Bombs."

I knew the voice.

A couple of years earlier, back in chem class, we'd shared a Bunsen burner, but that was the full extent of it. Ollie was not my kind of person. Very short, very plump. A Friar Tuck facsimile in a white cowboy hat and fancy high-heeled boots.

He gestured at my poster with fat fingers.

"This bomb shit," he said, "a catchy tune. Who do we assassinate?"

He straightened up to his full height—maybe five foot two. His smile seemed thin. "Just narrow it down for me. Plastic explosives? Time bombs? You got to name some names."

I was candid with him. I told him to fuck off.

Ollie flicked his eyebrows. "A sense of humor, ace, it goes a long way. Bombs, though. I guess you could say I'm halfway intrigued." He winked and tipped up his cowboy hat. Circus material, I thought. Not quite a midget, but there was obvious evidence of a misplaced chromosome. "What I mean," he said, then paused again. "I mean, you've had your one-man show out here, but maybe you could use a helping hand, so to speak. If I'm interested, that is."

I nodded.

"That's wonderful," I said, "just don't get interested," then I turned and left him standing there.

But ten minutes later, in the cafeteria, he waddled over to my table and put his tray down and made himself at home. The wise thing, I decided, was silence. I opened up a book called *Minerals of the Earth* and studied the cubic structure of thorianite.

"The problem," Ollie said cheerfully, "is nobody likes you."

Thorianite had a specific gravity of 9.87. It was soluble in nitric and sulphuric acids. It had a hardness factor of 6.5.

"I mean, you prance around with this holier-than-thou outlook. Don't even *talk* to nobody. And this bombs-are-real bull— people just laugh. You want results, you best retool your whole piss-poor attitude."

I took a sip of lemonade.

Thorianite, I noted, often contained traces of cesium and lanthanum. The largest deposits occurred in Ceylon and the Soviet Union.

"You want to be laughed at?" he asked. "You *want* that?"

"Morons," I said.

Ollie rubbed his nose. "Don't I know it? Hayseeds. But like I said, results is the bottom line."

"And?"

"Kick ass. Find yourself some allies and start punching tickets. Riots, maybe. Whatever's necessary."

"Allies," I said. "Like you, I bet."

"Maybe. First we talk."

I snapped the book shut. The cafeteria was jammed with the usual lunchtime crowd. Behind me, a radio was booming out *House of the Rising Sun*, and there was the clatter of silverware and triviality. No one knew. At the next table Sarah Strouch was showing off her thighs to a linebacker named Rafferty.

I folded my arms and said, "So talk."

"Straight?"

"However," I said. "Quick would be nice."

Ollie straddled his chair and spent the next several minutes outlining my character flaws. Too conceited, he said. Too wrapped up in myself. Too smug and pompous and high and mighty.

"I could go on," he said, and smiled, "but you get the drift. And now this bomb nonsense."

"The truth," I said.

"Oh, yeah. Truth. The war, right?"

"Partly. Other items, too."

He shrugged. "Shrapnel, I know. You made your point, that's why I'm here."

"The point, Ollie."

"Action. We team up." He waved a pudgy hand at me. "In case you haven't noticed, you and me got a lot in common. Two birds of the same fucked-up feather. Losers, that is. But I'll tell you a basic fact. Losers sometimes get pissed. They get impolite, sometimes. That's how revolutions happen."

I put my coat on.

"Well," I said, "it's been fun."

"Like in Moscow, 1917. Losers banging on winners. They didn't wave no signs, they cut throats."

"I'll remember that."

"Losing sucks," he said. "Losers *lose*."

He removed his cowboy hat and brushed the brim with the back of his hand. His voice had a squeaky, hollowed-out sound, like an old 78 recording.

"So anyway," he said, "let's brainstorm a minute. Let's say, for instance, we drop this peaceful-protest crud. Winning-wise, it don't create the right impression. You got to wake people up—get their attention, basically—which means you blow a few socks off. Rig up some ordnance. Let the wreckage speak for itself."

"Not interested," I said.

"You don't *talk* bombs. You *show* bombs. Scorch City. I guarantee, nobody laughs. Don't hear jack."

Then he listed some recent developments.

He talked about C-4 explosives and white phosphorus and the killing radius of a Claymore mine. A technical whiz, I thought, but what impressed me most was his little-man ferocity, and that gremlin voice, and the way he managed to present his own freakiness in a fairly convincing context. Sitting there, half listening, I was reminded of those old B movies with midgets dressed up as cowboys—the hero and the outlaws and the Shetland ponies—all midgets, but they play it straight, so after a while you begin to think that's how the world is, it's pint-sized, it comes at you in small doses. With Ollie Winkler, however, there was the added dimension of danger.

I finally stood up.

"One personal question," I said casually, smiling at him. "When you were a kid, I mean, did you ever fool around with chemistry sets? Like testing nails for their iron content?"

He gave me a stare.

"Maybe so," he said. "What if?"

"Just a question."

"Yeah, but so what?"

"Fine," I said, "don't get defensive."

"I'm *not* defensive. What *if*, though?"

I nodded soberly and picked up my tray.

"Those nails," I said. "I've always wondered. Iron or no iron?"

Ollie slapped a fork against the palm of his hand. There was a pause, then he chuckled and rolled his shoulders.

"Super wit," he said. "Chemistry sets, I like that, very shitty-witty. And here's another funny one: What'd the chef say to the terrorist? There's this chef, see, and there's this jerkoff terrorist—real namby-pamby, can't get no results—so the chef says, he says: Listen up, asshole. You don't make a revolution without breaking a few legs."

A week later he joined me on the line. He was carrying a home-made model bomb. "Audiovisual device," he said, "like in show-and-tell."

It wasn't friendship, just an alliance. Two of us now—me with my poster, Ollie with his bomb—and together we established a makeshift front against the war. It was entirely my show. No broken legs, I told him, and although there were complaints now and then, he generally played along.

"You're the boss," he'd say softly, "but the time'll come. You can mark it on your calendar."

I didn't let it influence me.

Slow and steady, I thought.

It was a routine. All through December, then time off for Christmas vacation, then the brittle cold of January. Long hours on the line, stiff fingers and tenacity. There was schoolwork, too, and exams and humdrum classes, but there was also a subtle new sense of command. I slept well. Fluid sleep, smooth and buoyant, a plush new laxity in my bowels. I was healthy. I was almost happy.

The only drawback, really, was Ollie Winkler.

"Letter bomb?" he'd say. "All I need's a zip code. Send it COD."

"No."

"Yeah, but Jesus, we're not *getting* anywhere."

"Negative."

"No, you mean?"

"I do. I mean no."

By temperament, obviously, I was not inclined toward violence, and therefore even his mock-up bomb made me a bit queasy. A demo model, Ollie called it, but it had the heft and authority of the genuine article. A steel frame with nasty appendages at each end, bright copper wiring, a soft ticking at its core.

"The bombs are real," Ollie said, and tapped the hollow casing. "Say the word, I'll arrange some surprises."

I just shook my head.

In a way, though, he was right. The bomb had credibility. People made wide turns as they entered the cafeteria. The power of firepower: it delivered a punchy little message.

"What I could do," Ollie said, "I could—"

"No."

He grinned. "Oh, well," he said, "live and learn."

Mostly it was drudge work. We doubled our picket time— Mondays and Fridays. No theatrics, just moral presence. We were *there.* All around us, of course, the apathy was like cement, hard and dense, and to be honest there were times when I came close to chucking it. Goofy, I'd think. And futile. I was no martyr. I hated the public eye, I felt vulnerable and absurd. Fuck it, I'd tell myself, but then I'd remember. Headlines. A new year, January 1967, and eighteen GIs died under heavy mortar fire outside Saigon.

Goofy, perhaps, but the goofiness had an edge to it.

So what does one do?

Hold the line and hope. My dreams were honorable. There was the golden dome on the state capitol; there was the world-as-it-should-be.

When I look back on that period, it's clear that my motives were not strictly political. At best, I think, it was a kind of precognitive politics. Granted, the war was part of it, I had ideals and convictions, but for me the imperative went deeper. Sirens and pigeons. A midnight light show. It occurred to me, even at the time, that our political lives could not be separated from the matrix of life in general. Joseph Stalin: the son of a poor cobbler in Tiflis. George Washington: a young neurotic who could not bring himself to tell a modest lie. Why does one man vote Republican, another Socialist, another not at all? Pure intellect? A cool adjudication between means and ends? Or more likely, does it have to do with a thick tangle of factors—Ollie Winkler's garbled chromosomes, my own childhood, a blend of memory and circumstance and dream?

I wasn't a fortune-teller.

Vision, nothing more. Dim previews of coming attractions. The rest was trial and error.

In the first week of February, we set up a formal organization on campus. The Committee, we called it. We took out an ad in the *Pevee Weekly*, calling for volunteers, and three days later, on a Saturday afternoon, we convened our first meeting in a small conference room in the basement of Old Main.

I presided, Ollie sat to my immediate left. At two o'clock, when I called the meeting to order, it was clear that we had a severe manpower problem. The only other body in the room belonged to a large, tent-shaped coed who brooded in total silence at the far end of the table.

"This is Tina," Ollie said, "I'll vouch for her."

The girl gazed fixedly at her own stomach; she seemed fascinated by it, a little overwhelmed.

Tina Roebuck: two hundred pounds of stolid mediocrity. A home-ec major. A chronic overeater. She was not obese, exactly, just well spread out. Generous hips and sturdy thighs and big utilitarian breasts. Like a Russian hammer-thrower, I decided—the poor girl obviously could not tell day from night without a sundial.

I smiled and shuffled some papers.

"Floor's open," I said, and shrugged. "I think we can dispense with parliamentary procedure."

Then I settled back.

Ollie Winkler did most of the talking. For ten minutes the discussion revolved around petty organizational matters. Ollie slipped his boots off, resting a foot on the edge of the table. "What we got here," he was saying, "is a troika situation, like in the USS of R, three horses pulling the same big sled. Which means we best divvy up the power, keep the reins straight so to speak, that way we don't get tangled up or nothing . . . Like with—"

I stood up and opened a window. The room had a stale, dirty-sock smell.

"Like with electricity," Ollie said. "Power lines, I mean. One person can't hog the amps and volts. Power, that's where it's at, we got to spread it around equal. The troika idea. Equal horsepower." He paused to let this concept take shape, then massaged his toes and went on to talk about the virtues of shared leadership, how we had to be a democracy.

I slapped the table.

"Democracy's fine," I said. "Put your goddamn *boots* on."

Ollie blinked.

"A case in point," he said.

There was laughter at the end of the table. Tina Roebuck reached into her purse and pulled out a giant-sized Mars bar and placed it on the table directly in front of her.

She folded her hands and stared at it.

"Democracy," Ollie sighed, "a lost art."

"Next item," I said.

Ollie hesitated. "Well, hey. Can't we at least assign jobs, sort of? Like sergeant at arms. Where's the fun if you don't get special jobs?"

"Sergeant at arms," I said. "You're elected."

"We didn't *vote*."

"One-zip, a landslide."

"But we got to—"

"Unanimous. Congratulations."

He grinned and tipped back his cowboy hat. "Sergeant at arms, it's right up my alley. Jeez, maybe I should get myself an armband or something—I saw that on TV once, they always wear these nifty black armbands. Like a symbol, you know?"

"Fine," I murmured.

"Armband. Write it down, man."

"What?"

"On *paper*. Armband, put it in writing."

I jotted a quick note to myself.

There was a disconcerting absence of dignity in the room. Shallow, I thought. Sad and stupid. Across the table, Tina Roebuck was still examining her Mars bar, hands folded. It was a test of willpower, apparently, a curious exercise in temptation and denial. At one point she reached out and nudged the candy with a thumb and then shuddered and quickly folded her hands again.

The world, I realized, was a frail and desperate place.

"Tina," I said gently, "eat it."

She frowned and looked up.

"Eat?" she whispered.

"Don't be bashful."

"But I'm not . . . I mean, I'm not hungry."

"Go ahead, though," I said. "Treat yourself."

She glanced at the Mars bar. "No, I just like to look at it. Window-shop, sort of." She swallowed. Her voice was soft, almost sexy, a surprising Deep South lilt to the vowels. "Anyway, I'm not hungry."

"Well, good."

"I'm *not*."

"But if you get the urge—"

"Fuck off!" she yelled. The softness was gone. She shifted weight and stared at me. "All this bullshit! The *war*, that's why I'm here. People getting *killed*."

Ollie smiled.

"Give it to him," he said. "Open up, kid—both barrels."

"Killed dead!" said Tina.

"More."

"Dead," she repeated. She poked the candy bar. "Talk-talk, no *action*. When do we start raising hell?"

Again, Ollie smiled at her, fondly.

"There's the question," he said. "When?"

Strange people, I thought. The incongruities were beguiling. I couldn't help but take notice of Tina's white ballet slippers, Ollie's cowboy shirt with its fancy embroidery and brass studs. Here was the new order. A midget in the White House, a Mars bar on every plate. Almost funny, except there was some emotion in the room.

"Shock waves," Ollie was saying. "We cut out this pussyfoot stuff. Apply some heat, that's my vote."

I shook my head.

"We've been over this," I said. "No bombs."

"I'm not *talking* bombs. Noisemakers. Don't hurt nobody, just decibels. Sit there, thumb up your ass, but sooner or later it's smash time. The chef and the terrorist, remember?"

"I do."

"And you know the moral? The moral's this. Heat. You bring it to bear. And if you can't stand the heat . . . Understand me?"

Tina Roebuck chuckled.

"The frying pan," she said softly.

"That's it exactly," said Ollie. He smiled at me, but it was a grim smile. "Fuckin' sizzle. That's what the chef says. He says you better learn to tolerate extremes."

I'd had enough.

I stacked my papers, stood up, and moved to the door.

"Carry on," I said. I nodded at Tina. "Let me know how it turns out with that candy bar."

At the time it all seemed hopeless, but in the end that meeting represented a pivot of sorts, a classic confrontation between the either-ors. The choice was there. I could've backed out with honor. Shrug and walk away—I could've dismissed the complications. Was it a correct war? Was it a civil war? Was Ho Chi Minh a nationalist or a Communist, or both, and to what degree, and what about the Geneva Accords, and what about SEATO, and what is worth killing for, if anything, and what is worth dying for, and who decides? I could've done without these riddles. I could've pursued my studies and graduated with distinction and spent the next decade lying low. Hedged my bets. Closed my eyes. Nothing to it, a slight change of course. Let the gravediggers do their work, I could've managed quite nicely. A snug mountain retreat. Or a cave, or a hole. No armies, no social milieu, no drafts to dodge, no underground strife. True, you can't rewind history, but if I'd recognized the pivot for what it was, things might've followed a different track. I could've avoided some funerals. A choice, and I chose, but I could've avoided the rest of my life.

Amazing, how the circuits connect. One minute you're all alone and then suddenly it just happens. The wires touch. A Friday evening, February 1967, and Sarah glared at me.

"You," she said.

It was an affair called Winter Carnival. Like a prom, basically: an all-night party to ward off the midterm blahs. First a dance, then a buffet, then a movie, then finally a dawn breakfast. I'm not sure what made me go—premonition sounds phony—but around eight o'clock I put on a clean shirt and hiked over to the gymnasium.

For a while I just stood at the doorway letting my eyes adjust. Pitiful, I thought. Penny loafers and spiffy sweaters. No one knew. The theme for that year's Carnival was "Custer's Last Stand," and the gym had been decorated to resemble a large and very gory battlefield, a mock-up of the Little Bighorn, with cardboard cutouts of dead horses and burning wagons and arrows and tomahawks and wild-eyed Indians and mutilated soldiers. At the center of the dance floor was a big papier-mâché dummy of Custer himself—

very lifelike, except he was obviously dead. The body had been propped up against a wagon wheel. It was shot full of arrows and the hair was gone and the whole corpse was wet with ketchup-blood. The idea, no doubt, was to make everyone feel a swell of state pride, or a sense of history, but for me it was the creeps. Especially the scalps. Greasy and convincing—scalps every-where—dangling from the basketball hoops, floating in the punch bowl.

Custer's Last Stand, it was insane and juvenile. It was Montana, 1967.

At the front door a kid dressed up as Crazy Horse used a scissors to perform a symbolic scalping. Ned Rafferty, a big-shit line-backer—I recognized him through his war paint. Dumb as bread, of course, but very presentable in the muscle department.

Rafferty dipped some of my hair into a bowl of ketchup.

"Careful now," he said. He gave me a long look. "Like your poster says. A violent world, white man."

I nodded and edged away.

Jocks, I thought. Linebackers and bacteria. Try, but you couldn't escape them.

Up at the far end of the gym, a band was playing *Stranger on the Shore*. The place was dark and noisy. Like a cattle show—everybody sweating and swaying and grinding up against each other. Right then I nearly called it a night. No dignity, I thought, but I moved over to the punch bowl and stood around drinking scalp for the next half hour. No knowledge, no vision. Wall-to-wall morons. At one point I spotted Ollie and Tina out on the dance floor. They were snuggled up close, like lovers, and in a way I envied them. Just the closeness. They weren't my kind, though, and when Ollie waved at me I turned away and watched the band.

I could feel my stomach cramping up. Maybe it was the punch, maybe loneliness, but I was on the verge of walking out when the circuits connected.

Partly luck, partly circumstance.

It began as a silly party game called Pevee Pair-Off. The idea was for the women to line up in a single long row at one end of the gym, all the men at the other, and then when the signal was given, the two rows were supposed to march toward each other like opposing skirmish lines in old-fashioned warfare. A lottery of sorts. Whoever you bumped into became your partner for the evening. Again, for me, it was one of those mysterious either-ors—I could've headed for the door—but for some reason I took the risk.

Once the rules had been explained, and once we'd lined up in our parallel formations, the band struck up a jazzy version of *Moon River* and someone blew a whistle and we started out across the floor. It was a ticklish experience. Exciting, I suppose, but scary. The lights had been turned off to prevent people from taking aim, and there was the strange, somewhat dizzy sensation of moving blindfolded toward a steep drop-off. Finally I closed my eyes and let the momentum take over.

I almost knocked her down.

When the lights came on, she was bent forward at the waist, drawing shallow little breaths. It took a few seconds before she recognized me.

"Oh, shit," she said. "You."

It was not instant love. We danced a few numbers, watched the limbo contest, then sat at one of the tables near the bandstand. She seemed a little sullen. But gorgeous—the body of a gymnast, like hardwood, and black eyes and black eyebrows and black-brown hair. And the skin. Miracle skin, I thought. Even there, in winter, it had a rich walnut gloss, smooth and flawless against a white blouse and a crisp white skirt.

For some time nothing much was said. She kept fidgeting, very ill at ease, so finally I began chattering away about various cheerleading matters, megaphones and culottes, whatever I could dream up.

"Culottes?" she said absently. "What about them?"

I glanced over at Custer. "Nothing, really. Mysterious. Tantalizing, I guess."

"Tacky," Sarah mumbled.

"Exactly right."

"You, I mean."

I smiled. "Maybe so," I said, "but I always thought you looked fabulous in culottes. Super kneecaps. Culottes and kneecaps, they *go* together."

"No shit?" she said. Her eyes shifted out toward the dance floor.

It was not going well, I knew that, but I couldn't seem to settle down. I told her how I used to sit up in the bleachers during high school football games, how much I admired her cartwheels and backflips. Stunning, I said. A real athlete. I even confessed that I'd always been somewhat in awe of her—in awe of cheerleaders in general.

Sarah nodded and looked at her wristwatch.

"Well," she said, "I can understand that. We're special people."

She paused and massaged her temples. When she spoke again, her voice had a plaintive quality, mournful and bleak.

"I know what you're thinking," she said. "Fluffhead. All beauty, no brains. People think we're just glitz and glitter, nobody realizes how much crap we have to put up with. Christ, if—" She stopped and stared at me. Complex things were happening in her eyes. "I mean, just *think* about it. You ever see a cheerleader with fat thighs? All that cruddy cottage cheese—God, I *hate* cottage cheese, it's like eating chalk—but do you hear me complaining? No way, because I care. Because I'll go that extra mile."

"A martyr," I said.

She gave her head a quick, violent shake.

"Don't mock me, man. Straight A's, you can check it out. I'm *smart*. Body and brains, the whole package."

"I didn't mean—"

"Smart," she said.

There was a silence.

"What I despise," she said quietly, "is condescension. I'm a human being."

"For sure," I said. "A smart one."

"Yes?"

"It's very clear."

Sarah frowned at me. For the first time there was some warmth in the eyes, tiny flecks of orange and silver floating in the deep blackness.

The band was playing *My Girl*.

"Well," she said, still frowning, her voice cool and wary, "maybe you're not such a creep after all."

"Maybe not."

"But still—"

Again, there was that softening. She looked at her hands.

"Anyway, this is strictly a one-night shot. We're stuck with each other—*c'est la vie*, et cetera—but to be perfectly honest I'd rather be down in Brazil munching on maggots. No offense. Just so we have an understanding."

I nodded, then Sarah stood up and hooked a thumb toward the dance floor.

"All right, let's jiggle it," she said. "Hands off, though. I know every gimmick in the book."

She looked like a starlet. Sleek and lean and smart. She danced with her eyes closed, ignoring the crowd and the music, ignoring me. Luck, I kept thinking. Between dances we talked about the old days at Fort Derry High, the time I'd passed out in geometry class, the way she'd cradled my head and fanned me with her notebook. "Bizarre," Sarah said, and I smiled at her and admitted that I'd gone through a rough period back then. I described the headaches and constipation, that out-of-synch sensation, my sessions with Chuck Adamson.

Sarah listened carefully.

"In other words—" She waited a moment. "Bats? Breakdown?"

"Not quite. Ancient history, back to normal."

"Right," she grunted. All around us people were dancing hard to drums. "And this thing at the cafeteria? The bomb scare—that's normal?"

"No," I said. "Necessary."

"Which means?"

"Nothing. Just necessary."

Sarah made a vague motion with her shoulders.

"Maybe so, but it seems a little—what's the word?—preten-
tious. Mr. Prophet."

"War," I said. "Vietnam. In case you haven't—"

She stepped back. "I *told* you, I'm not stupid, so you can cut
out the condescending crap. The prophet with his poster, it's all
very cute, I suppose, but very half-assed."

"Just a symbol," I said.

"Oh, lovely." Sarah snorted and shook her head. "Take a look
around. You think these idiots care about symbols? Fireworks,
that's all they understand. Bang for the buck. It's a bad new age—
symbols don't make it."

"And you could do better?"

"No worse. At least you'd see some pyrotechnics. Not that I'd
ever get involved."

Her eyes moved sideways. She started to add something, then
thought better of it.

The music had gone mellow.

"Symbols," she muttered, then reached out and slipped her
arms around me and came in close. There was a new openness in
her posture: legs separated, a subtle tilt to the pelvis.

For the next hour things were fine. No talking, just motion. It
all seemed appropriate. The scalps and arrows and twinkling
lights, and the way she moved, athletic but graceful, and the
mood, and the romantic expression in Custer's wide blue eyes.
I recognized the compatibilities. When we danced slow, I could
feel her breasts against me, the give and take. There were skin
smells, too, and a perfume of roses sprinkled with spice—clove or
cinnamon.

The perfume was what did it to me.

First a prickly stirring below my belt, then the inevitable
laws of hydraulics. I shut my eyes and tried to force it down, but
Sarah suddenly jerked away.

"What the hell's *that?*" she said.

"Nothing, it's a—"

"I know what it *is!* Just keep it *away* from me!"

I was already wilting.

"An accident," I said.

"Accident!"

"Look, I'm sorry, it's like chemistry or something, those things happen. You shouldn't take it quite so personal."

Sarah winced.

"Never fails. Same old garbage—put on a letter sweater, guys automatically assume you're Little Miss Easy Squeezie. Little Miss Huff and Puff."

"Not me. I don't think that way."

"I've got *feelings!*"

For a second it seemed she might spin away. Her eyes moistened. It was real anger, and a kind of sadness, but then she gave me a resigned half-smile, almost tender, and locked her hands around the small of my back. She kept dancing even after the music stopped.

Here, I realized, was a very troubled young lady.

After a time Sarah sighed and put her cheek against mine. "All right, you couldn't help it," she said. "Chemistry. You're not such a bad guy, really. Under other circumstances—who knows? It's just too bad about your rotten personality."

"My mistake."

"A queer duck, aren't you?"

"Unique," I said. "One of a kind."

She smiled. A volatile person, I thought, but it was a genuine smile, crooked and friendly.

We danced flat-footed, barely moving.

"You know what I remember?" she said. "I remember back in high school—even junior high—you had this tremendous crush on me. Remember that? Not that I blame you. Thing is, you never made a move. Didn't even try, for God's sake."

"A little bashful," I said.

"Maybe. But it was like I wasn't quite good enough for you. I mean, did you ever smile at me? One lousy little smile?"

I thought about it.

"I guess not," I said. "I didn't know you were all that interested."

Sarah laughed. "Of *course* I wasn't interested. I would've shut you off like a light. All I'm saying is you never gave yourself a chance. Gutless, et cetera."

But again she smiled.

It was tempting. Partly a dare and partly something else. Sarah looked straight at me.

"The problem," she said softly, "is I'm bad news. Too hot to handle. You'd get burned."

"I suppose."

"Seriously. Don't mess with it."

There was still that intriguing half-smile, like an invitation, it seemed. At the corner of her mouth was a small red blister, which inspired me, and there was that hard acrobat's body, and that perfumed skin.

I was working my way toward an act of great courage when Ned Rafferty tapped me on the shoulder and stepped in and glided away with her.

It was too quick to process. No words, just a wave, then she was gone.

"Sure," I said, "go right ahead."

I felt the fuses blowing. Scalped, I thought. First my father, now me.

Hard to find meaning in it.

When the music ended, I began weaving my way across the floor, but things were jammed, and by the time I got there it was too late, they were dancing again.

That fast—every time. It just happens.

I moved off to a corner and stood watching. Painful, but I had to admire Rafferty's style, all the dips and fancy footwork. He was handsome, too—curly brown hair and gray eyes—but his greatest strength, I decided, was strength. He had that Crazy Horse power: feathers and war paint and big killer shoulders. It was pure hate. And what I hated most was the way Sarah smiled at him, that same inviting half-smile, except now it was aimed elsewhere.

Which is how it always happens.

That fast.

You get all revved up for somebody, ready to take the plunge, and the next thing you know you're diving onto concrete.

There was a moral in it. Never underestimate the power of power. Never take chances. Because you end up getting smashed. Every time—crushed.

Safety first, that was the moral.

A half hour later Sarah found me sitting at a table near the buffet line.

"Back in the fold," she said cheerfully, but I ignored her. I was busy twisting a scalp around my fists.

There was a hesitation before she sat down.

"You're excited," she said, "it's obvious."

At her forehead was a smudge of Rafferty's orange war paint. I turned sideways and crossed my legs and began braiding the scalp into two neat pigtails.

For a few minutes Sarah sat watching.

"All right, listen, I'm sorry," she finally said. She studied the scalp for a moment, then smiled. "Shouldn't have gone off like that. The call of the wild, I guess. Fickle me. But it's not like we're engaged or anything. We're barely friends."

"Right," I said, "barely friends. Take a walk."

Sarah's lips compressed.

"That old green devil. Jealousy, it gives me goose bumps." As if by accident her hand dropped against my wrist. "Apologies, then? I didn't mean to mess up your super ego. I was just—you know—just letting loose. Just *dancing* with the guy. No big deal."

"He's a turd," I said.

"If you say so."

"Fuzzball."

Sarah laughed.

"Absolutely," she said. "That's why I'm here. Fuzzballs get boring. They tend to stick to your sweater."

She liked me. She almost said so.

It was like riding ice, things seemed to skid by. I remember a saxophone. I remember Sarah leaning up against me. Not love, exactly, just intense liking. And it cut both ways. I liked her, she liked me. Late in the evening there was a Hula Hoop contest, which Sarah won, and afterward we ate sandwiches and potato salad, then danced, then sat in the bleachers and watched the party and talked about little things, our lives, which led into bigger things. Now and then she'd touch my arm. She'd look at me in a fond sort of way. At one point, I remember, she said she admired what I was doing at the cafeteria. It took guts, she said; it was honorable. I shrugged and said, "Half-assed?" and she was silent for a while, then said, "Well, listen, I've got this big mouth." I told her it was a beautiful mouth. Then later we talked politics. It was soft, serious talk, not romantic, but it implied something. She said she hated the war as much as anyone. She had principles. She knew a thing or two about death—her father was a mortician—the stiffs stayed stiff—they didn't wake up—she couldn't see any reason for the killing. She put her hand on my arm. Her only quibble, she told me, was tactical. It was a real war, wasn't it? Real bombs? Which required a real response. Posters were fine, but too passive, not enough drama.

She kept smiling, I remember. She kept that hand on my arm.

"What I'm trying to explain," she said, "is you have to get people's passions involved. Like with cheerleading. Politics and passion, same thing."

And so then we discussed passion.

For me, I said, it wasn't a question of right or wrong. It was a kind of *seeing*. "Crazy," I said, but she didn't laugh, so I told her about the flashes, and she nodded—she cared—she listened while I went on about Phantom jets and napalm and Kansas burning, how it wasn't a dream, or not quite, or not entirely, just seeing.

Even then she didn't laugh.

"Well," she finally said, "I guess that's one kind of passion."

At two in the morning there was a final dance, then we

trooped over to the student union to watch an old Jane Fonda movie.

But it was hard to concentrate. Sarah sat with her legs in my lap, knees cocked up like targets near my chin.

"You can touch," she whispered.

So I touched. And later she chuckled and said, "Kneecaps—who would've thought it? You're a sly puppy, aren't you?"

Then she fell asleep.

For a long while I simply sat there in the dark. Up on the screen, Jane Fonda was busy seducing a basketball team, but I couldn't keep my mind on it. I watched Sarah's sleeping face. Real, I thought. It was no fantasy. Those pulsing places at the throat and inner thigh, the connectives, the curvatures and linkages. I considered my good fortune. There was a curious flow of warmth between us, as if we were exchanging blood, and the rest I imagined.

Much later, Sarah nudged me.

"Hey, there," she murmured.

"Hey," I said.

She sat up and stared at the screen. There was fatigue in her eyes, a lazy blankness.

"Kiss?" she said.

I kissed her, and she nodded. She moved closer. "You were aching for it, weren't you? I can always tell. And now I suppose you want more?"

"I suppose so."

"No future in it. No tomorrow."

"We'll see."

"I do see. Nothing." She eyed me for a moment. "You're a virgin, no doubt?"

"Sort of," I said. "With you, I used to pretend."

"Pretend?"

"You know. Make-believe."

There was a short silence. "Well," she said, "glad I could help." Then she sighed. "All right, permission granted, but just kisses. Nothing else. Don't even pretend." She slipped her head against my shoulder. "A little intensity this time, it's good for the complexion."

And later—maybe four in the morning, maybe five—later, when the lights came on, Sarah tucked her blouse in and looked at me with level eyes and said, "I wish it could work out. I really wish that."

"But?"

"Let's walk."

We skipped the pancake breakfast.

Outside, there was a bright moon. Not quite dawn, but I could feel the stirrings.

"Be a gentleman," Sarah said. "I'm *très* bushed. Too late for nookie."

She hooked my arm.

We walked past the science building, across a parking lot, down a gravel path tha*t* led to the Little Bighorn. Our shoes made crunching sounds in the snow.

"What it comes down to," she said, "is we're different people. Complete opposites. Nobody's fault."

"Right," I said. "Opposites."

Sarah stopped at the riverbank.

She lay down and made an angel in the snow, then shivered and stood up and took my hand.

There was a slight droop to her eyelids.

"It's like a jigsaw puzzle, like when the pieces don't fit. Miss Razzle-Dazzle. Mr. Gloom-and-Doom. We've got our images to protect."

"Images. I never thought of that."

"I wish you'd—"

"Fucking images."

I was moving on automatic. The river curled eastward, through white birch and pine, and things were very still.

"Besides," Sarah said, "we had an agreement. A brief encounter. Didn't we decide that?"

"I guess we did."

"There you are, then."

"Of course," I said. "A deal's a deal. Very tidy."

She stopped, removed her gloves, put her hands on my cheeks, and held them there. We were the same height, almost exactly.

"It's for the best," she said. "I told you before, I'm dangerous. Too raunchy, too bitchy. Everything. You'd get hurt."

"Sarah—"

"Enough."

Crossing campus, we didn't say much.

I was a gentleman.

Now and then, by chance, we brushed up against each other, and I could smell her skin, the skin itself, and there was that moment of hurt and panic, the urge to try something desperate, something gallant, like rape, a blow to the chin and then drag her off.

It made a nice picture.

At her dorm door I swallowed and said, "Well."

Sarah kissed me.

"Passion," she said, "good luck," then she shook her head and backed away.

It was a rough weekend. Hard to envision a happy ending. Complete opposites—she was right.

On Monday morning I confronted the facts. It wasn't love, after all. It wasn't anything.

Getting out of bed was a major enterprise.

I showered and shaved and examined myself in the mirror. The eyes were bloodshot, the expression empty.

"No problem," I said.

At noon I picked up my poster and walked over to the cafeteria. Ollie and Tina were already there. It was a dull winter day, bare and frozen, and no one cared, no one understood, and when I took my place on the line it all seemed trivial and small and dumb. Three clods in the cold. The poster, the model bomb—a bad joke. Not love, I thought. Not passion either. A joke, but it wasn't funny.

For a long while I just stared down at my shoes, shoulders hunched, pondering the world-as-it-should-be.

When I looked up, Sarah was there.

Which is how it always happens—that fast. She was simply *there.*

We stood inspecting each other. Her hair was pulled back in a businesslike ponytail. She wore blue culottes and earmuffs and a silver letter sweater.

"What you remind me of," she said after a moment, "is tooth decay. No sleep, I'll bet. Bad dreams."

"Surprise," I said.

"You could've called."

"I could've. I didn't."

Her lips brushed across my cheek.

"Well," she said quietly, "a girl likes to be chased. Hot pursuit. The feminine mystique, I guess." She looked over at Ollie and Tina, then at my poster. "So this is it? The famous Committee?"

It was all I could do to nod. There was an absence of symmetry, a strange new tilt to the world.

Sarah shrugged. She made a low sound, not quite a sigh, then took a step forward and turned and stood beside me. She was carrying a megaphone and red pom-poms.

"Don't expect miracles," she said. "You and me. A trial period, understand?"

"Of course."

"And there'll be some changes. New tactics. New leadership."

"Agreed," I said. "It's only natural."

Sarah lifted her megaphone.

"All right, that settles it," she said. "Two weeks, maybe three, then we shut this rathole down. No more bullshit. There's a war on."

6
Escalations

L IKE HIDE-AND-GO-SEEK—the future curves toward the past,
then folds back again, seamlessly, always expressing itself
in the present tense.

The year is 1969, for example.

If I concentrate, if I stop digging for a moment, I can see
Sarah sitting at a kitchen table in Key West. She wears a black bikini. She's oiling an automatic rifle. "Terrorism," she tells me, "is a
state of mind. No need to hurt people, you just give that impression."

Or it's 1971. She's famous. She's on the cover of *Newsweek*.
She smiles and says, "I warned you, William. Years ago, I told you
I was dangerous. Remember that? And now I belong to the ages."

Or it's 1980, or 1985, and the war is over, and she's one of the
last of the die-hard rads. Her skin is leathery. Her eyes show the
effects of windburn and fatigue. "Terrorism," she repeats, "is a
state of mind, but nobody gets terrified anymore."

And now it's late in the century, it's 1995, and I'm digging,
and I see sharpshooters and a burning safe house and the grotesque
reality of the human carcass. The dead won't stop dying. Ned and
Ollie and Tina, all of them, they die in multiples, they can't call it
quits.

Then 1967.

Mid-March, a Sunday afternoon, and Sarah slips into my

dorm room. She takes off her clothes and does a handstand at the center of my bed.

Even then, I suppose, she was something of a terrorist.

"Lucky William," she'd sigh. "This relationship can't last, you know. A law of nature, I'm just a higher form of life."

At times it seemed she was right. Different species, almost, certainly different social classes, and yet over the final months of our junior year at Peverson State, as cause led to effect, Sarah and I somehow managed to make it work. We studied together, ate together, eventually slept together.

Even now, with the advantage of hindsight, I'm not sure what she saw in me. Maybe a counterpoint to her own charm; maybe a challenge. Cute, she'd sometimes call me, but I knew better—too skinny and angular and gawky. I had no poise, no presence. I'd often glance into windows or mirrors, obliquely, trying to catch myself unawares, to see myself as Sarah would, but the results were always depressing. I couldn't find the cuteness. It was a strained, almost haggard face, blond hair gone sandy brown, blue eyes set back in deep dark sockets—grim-looking, I thought.

Still, she liked me. Not quite romance, just an intense collaboration of spirit. She kept me on my toes. Sudden shifts in mood, a heavy emphasis on coercion.

Extremism, after all, was her specialty and those were extreme times. There was a nip in the air. The music was militant. In Vietnam, more than 400,000 Americans were at war, and at home, even in Montana, apprehension had come to discontent.

"No more bullshit," Sarah said, "there's a war on," then she went to work.

At the end of March, she orchestrated a series of teach-ins and classroom boycotts; in the first week of April she led a torchlight parade along the Little Bighorn—a pep rally for peace—half protest, half party.

How she did it, exactly, or why, I'm not sure, but by May Day politics had become respectable at Peverson State College, trendy and stylish. Again, the images blend and collide, but I remember pom-poms and cartwheels and barricades in front of Old Main. I can see Tina Roebuck silhouetted against a bonfire along the river. And I can see Ollie Winkler, who grins and spits on his hands as he wires up a stink bomb in the school auditorium. His eyes are nasty. "You don't make a revolution," he tells me, "without breaking a few legs."

Mostly, though, I remember Sarah. She made things happen. Glamour, yes, and a flair for the dramatic, but she was also tough and practical, no tolerance for abstraction. "It's combat," she'd say. "Philosophy's fine, but you don't hem and haw on the front lines. You haul in the artillery."

Intelligence, that was part of it. And she also had a rare intuitive gift for the process of push and shove. She brought glitter to bear, and at times a certain ruthlessness.

Cheerleader to rabble-rouser: It was a smooth, almost effortless transition. Surprising, maybe, and yet the impulse was there from the start. In a sense, I realized, cheerleaders *are* terrorists. All that zeal and commitment. A craving for control. A love of pageantry and crowds and slogans and swollen rhetoric. Power, too. The hot, energizing rush of absolute authority: *Lean to the left, lean to the right.* And then finally that shrill imperative: *Fight— fight—fight!* Don't politicians issue the same fierce exhortations? Isn't sex an active ingredient in the political enterprise? Pressing flesh, wooing the voters, stroking the Body Politic—aren't these among the secret lures of any cheerleader?

Too simplistic, no doubt, but during the spring of 1967 the parallels seemed uncanny.

Sarah had the touch.

Her generalship was impeccable. Her demands were unqualified.

In public, but also in bed, she was a born leader.

"Passion," she'd say. "Make me squirm."

She'd use the bed like a trampoline. She'd lock her legs around me, tight, keeping the pressure on until I begged her to ease off.

Then she'd snort.

"Caution-caution," she'd say. "No zip or zing. Can't cut loose."

"It's not that."

"It *is* that. I mean, here I am—perky Sarah—show me some sizzle, man. A girl wants to feel *wanted.*"

"But I can't just—"

"Sizzle!"

She'd kneel beside me. Coyly, without shame, she'd do a little trick with her breasts, an expanding-flattening thing.

She might smile.

"Now *that*," she'd say, "is what I call perkiness. Mona Lisa with muscles. And besides, I'm fond of you. God knows why—opposites attract, I guess—but it's all yours. Everything. The entire perky package."

"Nice," I'd say, "it's a nice package."

"So what's the holdup?"

"Nothing. Time, that's all."

"I'm *loyal*, William. I won't desert you. I've got sticking power, you know? High fidelity."

"I know that."

"So?"

I'd shake my head and say, "Give it time."

Sometimes she'd nod, sometimes not.

"Well, that's very prudent," she'd finally say, "but see, here's the problem. Life has this weird quality called shortness. Places to go, minds to blow. It's *love* I want. Worship."

And then she'd straddle me.

She'd twirl her tongue against my throat.

"Don't be bashful," she'd whisper. "Yank out the cork, man, let's go steady."

The human heart, how do you explain it?

I was gun-shy. I didn't trust her. Too temperamental, I thought. Too flashy.

A campus celebrity, wasn't she?

That whole aura—the rattlesnake eyes, the pink polish on her toenails, the plucked and penciled eyebrows—an exhibitionist, a compulsive show-off. In the warm weeks of late spring, it wasn't uncommon to find her sunbathing out in front of the student union, oiled up and elegant, flaunting her assets in a string bikini and high-heeled sandals. She'd come to class in spangled red shorts; she'd show up for dinner in pearls and mesh stockings and a fake fox coat. When I asked about all this, Sarah would only shrug: "The Age of Image," she'd tell me. "Project or perish, it's that simple."

But it wasn't simple. The psychological contradictions were stunning. An intelligent girl, she played the coquette; a dignified girl, she played vulgar. And yet she was also oddly vulnerable, even little-girlish at times. She could be gentle; she could be vicious. It wasn't a split personality, it was fractured.

How could I take the risk?

In part, no doubt, I was held back by the old doomsday principle, an unwillingness to expose myself. But it was more than that.

Politics, too—she was aggressive in the extreme. True, she had a conscience, and tremendous charisma, but even so I could detect the intimidating shape of things to come. In May, I remember, she led a midnight raid on the ROTC offices in the basement of the humanities building—no damage done, just a statement of intent, but a day or two later she began pushing for even more drastic measures. She had no interest in compromise. She knew where the screws were.

"Either you're serious about this," Sarah told me one morning at breakfast, "or you're a twit. There's no halfway. Like your poster says, real bombs, you can't hide your head. Pain leads to pain. Ask the kids in Saigon."

I nodded.

"Fine," I said, "but sometimes it seems just a little excessive."

"You think so?"

"A little."

Sarah gazed at her coffee cup. Complicated events were occurring along the surfaces of her eyes.

"Well, that's a pity," she finally said. "Excessive. Tell it to the White House. Go lay it on the Joint Chiefs, I'd be real interested in some professional feedback." Then her voice went low. A husky, mocking tone. "You're something else, pal. You want this nice happy world, all roses, except you get all squeamish when somebody goes out and tries to make it happen. The jellyfish mentality."

"Forget it. You win."

"I do," she said softly, "I win."

She finished her coffee and stood up.

"And one more thing. So far you haven't seen diddly. Excessively speaking, I mean."

An unpleasant tone, I thought.

Culottes to sansculotte—a radical realignment. The question, though, was why. There were many such questions: Why politics? Why so sudden? Why so rabid? And why me? Why stick with a jellyfish?

Except in the most superficial sense, I didn't really know her. Even the facts seemed unsubstantial.

A cheerleader, of course.

But why?

A history major. Pre-law. Brains, obviously, but not legal brains.

A birthmark below her right breast.

Thick blackish brown hair freshened by modern chemistry.

A small, recurring fever blister at her lower lip. I'd often catch her toying with it, applying ointments. "It's a fatal flaw," she'd say, "for the femme fatale."

Flippant.

Sarcastic to the point of wise-ass. But it was almost certainly a kind of camouflage, like her cosmetics, the gaudy nail polish and lipstick and mascara. At times, I thought, it was as if she were hiding herself, or from herself.

Reticence, maybe.

Maybe fear.

A splay-footed way of walking, like a deer. A certain stiffness in her posture. As a kid, she told me, she'd had polio, a mild case. But no details. When I pressed her about it, Sarah smiled and tapped her chest. "Nothing serious," she said. "Iron lungs."

Her mother was dead.

Her father was a mortician.

Does it matter? She wasn't gloomy, and she rarely talked about it, but I often found myself imagining what it must've been like to grow up in that big white funeral home on Main Street. How did it feel? What was the emotional residue? I was curious, of course, but she wouldn't respond to even the most basic questions.

"Don't be a ghoul," she'd say.

Or she'd say, "No big mystery. Luscious me, sugar and spice. Don't analyze it, William, just adore it."

A playful, uninhibited girl.

And yet there were also moods of complete withdrawal. It could happen instantly. In bed, she'd peel off her clothes, clowning, then suddenly her whole face would freeze. She'd slide away. She'd pull a pillowcase over her head and crawl up on my desk and squat there like a statue. Tempting, I'd think. Not lewd, not immodest, just the white pillowcase and that awesome nakedness. "Sarah," I'd say quietly, but she wouldn't budge. There was something chilling about it, something desperate. Why the mask? Why, sometimes, would she clamp the pillowcase at her throat and whisper, "I want to be *wanted*. Get reckless, William. Go for broke—*love* me."

And in my own way I did.

Granted, it was a judicious sort of love, one step at a time, but over the spring of our junior year I discovered the great pleasures and bondings of a political romance. I was part of something. I belonged. At our Committee meetings, I was perfectly content to let Sarah take charge; I admired her poise and control; I got a kick out of watching how she kept Ollie and Tina under tight rein. I liked the closeness. I liked being seen with her. In the geology lab, late at night, I liked it when she'd come up behind me and turn off my microscope and say, "For Christ sake, man, stop playing with your *rocks*." Endearment, I liked that, too. How she held my arm walking to class, how she always stood beside me during our noon vigils at the cafeteria. Many things. The times I'd wake up to find my hands tied to the bedposts. The way she'd sleep with one knee hooked tenderly around my neck.

And the sex.

Congress, she called it.

"All rise!" she'd cry. "Congress is in session!"

In a way, naturally, I was grateful for this, but there were times when I thought she took it too far. It was the rah-rah side of her personality, too flamboyant, and one evening I asked if she'd mind toning it down.

Sarah gave me a hard look.

"Down?" she said. "Discreet, you mean?"

"Well, no, I just wish you'd—"

"Demure? Candy and flowers? A nice little Southern belle— sit around batting my eyes?"

She twisted away.

It was a warm spring evening, very humid, and she was naked except for a chrome bracelet. She got down on the floor and began a furious set of exercises, sit-ups and leg-lifts. I could see goose bumps forming in the flesh at her nipples.

After a moment she laughed.

"Discretion," she said bitterly, "is for *dead* people. Am I *dead?*" Her tone surprised me. The anger was real. "I grew up in a goddamn mortuary, remember? Organ music day and night. Flowers up the bazoo. You wouldn't believe how discreet a stiff can be. Very modest. They're *dead*, get it? Tickle them, they don't budge—real coy, real *dead.* You don't get deader. You know what *dead* is? It's *dead.*"

Then she gave me a brief synopsis of life and death in a funeral home.

The various odors. The comings and goings. How her father's workshop had been located directly beneath her own bedroom, one floor down, and how at night she used to lie there with a pillow pushed up to her face. Like a gas mask, she said. Wonderful fragrances—just what a kid needs at bedtime.

She paused in mid-sit-up. There was a soft, faraway look in her eyes.

Then she shrugged.

"Anyway, I know what discreet is," she said. "Plain flat *dead.* You take demure, I'll take rigor clitoris any time."

"I didn't mean—"

"Besides," she said tightly, staring at me, "you better consider the alternatives. Who else would go near that mincemeat pecker of yours? Like a battle zone."

"A bike accident, I explained that."

"Oh, sure, a fine story." She shook her head. "Scars and stitches. Looks like you tried to poke a blender."

"Sarah—"

"Discretion!" she said. "Go paste Band-Aids on your weewee, Congress is adjourned."

A troubled girl, that much was clear.

Part iron, part mush. Neurosis maybe. But how far can you dig into a personality? How much do you finally accept at face value? Do motives matter?

Politics, for example.

Why ask why?

Clearly, in Sarah's case, the war deeply offended her. The pain was genuine. I remember how she closed her eyes during those made-for-TV combat clips; I remember the casualty count she kept on a bulletin board in her dorm room. "The thing about a corpse," she once told me, "is you can't fix it. All that formaldehyde, but nothing *moves*. Poor fuckers just lie there." Psychology seemed superfluous. From my own experience, I'd learned to distrust the easy explanations of human behavior; it's all too ambiguous; the inner forces ricochet like pinballs. John Reed: a Harvard cheerleader. How do you draw conclusions? The real world, I thought, is unresponsive to Rorschach tests. You can't shrink a warhead. Ultimately, you take things as they are, you accept the imponderables, you find harmony in the overwhelming incongruity. Sarah Strouch: schizophrenic, perhaps. Unpredictable. But there was a war on, people were dying, and the realities conditioned consciousness, not the reverse. Issues of personality became trivial. Was Noah paranoid? Who sank and who swam? In a crowded theater, if someone yells "Fire!" do you respond by inquiring into matters of the mind? If a madman holds a knife to your throat, if a butcher goes berserk, do you pause to administer a character inventory? And if the bombs are real. If you see a missile rising over the Little Bighorn. If you can conceive of last things. If there's a war on. If you care.

She was a mystery.

Only one thing for certain, Sarah Strouch understood the critical dynamic of our age. It was all escalation.

On May 21, 1967, two weeks before summer break, she gave Ollie Winkler the green light. Once more, there's that time-space slippage—the beginning mixes with the end, effect becomes cause—but I can see Sarah commanding a bonfire rally down at the river. She's wearing her silver letter sweater and blue culottes, she's got the crowd leaning left and right. There's a flush at her cheeks. And I see Ollie Winkler bending over a set of bomb blueprints. "Not big bombs," he says, "just attention-grabbers," then he slips on a black armband and says, "Sergeant at arms! It takes *arms*, like in deadly force." There were occupied offices. Picket lines went up in front of Old Main. My own role was limited, but I remember the sound of breaking glass, a jimmied lock, how we effected entry into the Dean of Students' office on that last warm night in May. I remember holding a flashlight while Ollie set up the ordnance. It was well after midnight, and there were echoes and creakings, and I remember the rubber gloves on my hands, the reflections, the sudden thought that things had passed into a vicious new dimension. The flashlight plucked out random objects in the dark. A typewriter, I remember, and a vase of lilacs, and a slender white fuse. There were numerous shadows. There was ambiguity. And there was also, briefly, the image of terrible waste. I could see gunfire. Then the flashlight wobbled—it seemed greased and heavy. Behind me, or off to the side, there was a whisper, then someone laughed and Tina Roebuck appeared and pried away the flashlight and said, "Poor boy." But it didn't matter. The present was firmly fixed to the future; the pattern was evident. This, I realized, would surely lead to that. There would be wastage, no doubt, and breakage, and abbreviation by force. My thoughts were precise. I remember the moment of stealth when Ollie struck the match. And the yellow-red glow against Sarah's face, the way she hesitated and moved to a window, then smiled, then came back and touched my arm.

"Here," she said softly, "is how it goes. You know?"

I made an indefinite motion with my shoulders. I was inclined toward silence.

Tina Roebuck giggled.

"William?"

I remember backing off. I remember thinking: What do I think? There was that delicate white fuse, like dental floss, and the burning match, and the metallic, curiously amplified sound of my own breathing. "From now on," Sarah said, "it's rough-and-tumble. Question is, do you understand?"

I did not.

The human heart, I thought, how do you explain it?

But I shrugged and said, "Of course."

"Of course what?"

"This."

"You're sure?"

"Like black and white," I said.

The summer went fast. Fort Derry seemed smaller now, and dead, but Sarah gave it motion: a Fourth of July picnic, nights at the drive-in theater. "If you love me," she said, "you'll steal that speaker. Do you love me?" Cruising up Main Street in my father's big Buick. Windows open, *Revolution* on the radio, Sarah tapping time against the dashboard. Root beers at the A&W. Pinball and cherry phosphates at Jig's Confectionery. Sex in any number of places; she loved the risk of it. "Don't be a lame duck," she'd say, "you've got congressional responsibilities." Sarah sunbathing—a hammock and sunglasses and deep brown skin. In midsummer we took a tent and sleeping bags up into the Sweethearts, just the two of us, and for nine days we eased the time away, exploring, walking the canyons, trading secrets late at night. A campfire, I remember . . . She said she loved me. Quite a lot, she said. I asked why, and Sarah said, "Who knows? Chemistry," and I said, "The big explainer." I remember stars and crickets. One night, very late, she told me about a crazy three-legged dog she used to have. Got hit by a car, she said. Lost a leg. Still fast, though, kept chasing cars, kept running away, and how one day it started running and never stopped. "That rotten crippled dog," she said, "I hated it, but I loved it. That's chemistry for you." Things were quiet. Sarah poked the fire and talked about the first time she ever kissed a boy. She told me about a vacation to Chicago. She told me her dreams. "Stupid, I know," she said, "but sometimes I dream I'm—you know—I'm sort of dead, I'm in this dark closet, I can smell these mothballs, and then, bang, somebody knocks on the door—I don't know who, just this guy—and he asks me what it's like, being dead, what it feels like. And you know what I tell him? I tell him it feels real *alone*. Alone, I tell him. That's the worst part." Sarah looked at me, then looked away. There were pines, I remember, and those jagged mountains, and we had our sleeping bags zipped together. "I want you to want me," she said, "like real love." Then she smiled. She said she was fertile, she could feel it. She wanted children someday. There was the war, of course, things to do, but when it was over she wanted all the peaceful stuff. Babies, she said, and a house and a family. But she wanted to travel first. She wanted to see Rio. "You and me together," she said, and her hands wandered. I could smell smoke and mosquito repellent. "You and me, William, we could do it, couldn't we? Have babies, maybe? I mean, we'd probably have to get married first, blood tests and so on, but it's possible, isn't it? And Rio, too. I've always had this wild fantasy about Rio. The sun and everything. All the tight brown bodies, those weird masks they wear at Carnival time. Sounds like I'd fit right in. A good life. Adventure, I want that, but I want . . . I don't know what I want exactly. I want you to tear down those walls. Does that make sense? You build these *walls*. And, God, sometimes I can't get through, I try but I can't. Just walls, and you hide there, and I can't break through. My own fault, maybe. Sometimes I act pretty rough, I know that. But I'm not rough. Down inside I'm not so rough. And I get afraid sometimes, I need you to say things, like you care about me and you won't ever . . . That damned dog. You believe that? Muggs, that was her name, that crazy rotten dog. Three legs, but lickety-split, she wouldn't listen, she wouldn't stop chasing those goddamn cars . . . Am I rambling? I guess I am. But I don't mean to act so rough. I hate myself sometimes, I really do, I'd like to rip my tongue out, but it's like self-defense or something. Anyhow, I do have these feelings. Rio and a billion babies. It's possible, don't you think?"

I couldn't find a great deal to say.

The nights were slippery, but the days were fine. I remember Sarah in her alpine climbing hat. Sarah swimming under a waterfall. A box canyon, a secret cave, a stream where I found the uranium.

We were barefoot, I remember, and the water was fast and cold. I bent down and scooped up a rock and showed her the purple-black crystals.

"A souvenir," I said.

"It isn't—?"

"Harmless."

Sarah squeezed the ore with both hands, deliberately, the way a child might handle modeling clay. There was a bright sun. I remember the heat and the cold water and the red polish on her toenails. Squinting, she looked at the stream, tracing its course toward the violet ridges.

"You don't suppose . . . I mean—"

"Maybe."

"Up there?"

"Chemistry," I said.

With her thumb, she flicked the ore away.

"What we'll do," she said after a moment, "is we'll pretend it's not there. Leave it be."

"Sure. That's how it's done."

"William—"

"Wish it away," I said, and smiled. "No sweat."

But there was a dynamic at work.

It was all around us. In our lovemaking, in the mountains. It was there in the music that summer.

On August 9, 1967, President Lyndon Johnson lifted the old

restrictions on U.S. bombing policy. Warplanes were now unloading over the city limits of Hanoi and Haiphong.

On August 20, the United States Air Force flew more than two hundred combat sorties—a new record for the war.

On August 23, a plane bearing nuclear weapons crash-landed at Edwards Air Force Base.

The world, I reasoned, was not entirely sane.

The dynamic was permissive.

On August 27, during Custer Days, Sarah and I sat up in the grandstand at the county fairgrounds. It was no big thing. We held hands and watched Crazy Horse gallop away with my father's hair.

"Kids," she said afterward. "They just can't take a joke."

At the end of August, on a humid afternoon, Sarah took me on a tour of the Strouch Funeral Home—her own home, actually—a lived-in place with bright kitchen curtains and family photographs. It did not smell of death. Even her father's workshop, I thought, seemed warm and cheery, the walls painted in bright pastels. At the center of the room was a white porcelain table with slightly raised edges. "So anyway," Sarah said, "home, sweet home." She held me lightly by the arm, just in case. There was a faint hospital odor—nothing terrible. An oversized sink, a few cabinets, a closet, a coil of orange tubing, a second table mounted on rubber rollers. "Hop aboard," she said, but I declined. Later she showed me the viewing room, which *did* smell of death, then she led me up a wide staircase to her own bedroom. "I don't want pity," she said. She undressed and pulled the shades. In bed, despite the muggy afternoon, we lay with a quilt up to our necks, side by side, only our arms and ankles touching. "Not pity," she said, "but love would be nice. You can try, can't you?"

"It's not a question of love."

"Time?"

"I don't know. I guess." I thought about it for a few minutes. "Screwed up, probably. It's like I can't take the jump. Can't believe in miracles. I don't know."

Sarah pulled a pillow over her face.

We lay there quietly, without moving. After a time I pried the pillow away and kissed her.

"What I'm saying," she murmured, "is I don't want to be alone. Not ever. You had your Ping-Pong table, I had this."

The rule of thumb was acceleration. During our senior year, 1967 and 1968, Sarah led us toward new occupations. History had finally caught up with itself. On November 30, 1967, Eugene McCarthy announced his presidential candidacy. Robert Kennedy sorted through the scenarios. In the city streets, there was organized disorder, and at Berkeley and NYU, even at Peverson State, the writing was on the wall in big black letters. Evolution, not revolution. Abbie Hoffman was now a somebody; Jane Fonda was making choices; Sirhan Sirhan was taking target practice; LBJ was on the ropes; Richard Nixon was counting noses; Robert McNamara was having second thoughts; Dean Rusk was having bad dreams. By the turn of the year, the American troop presence in Vietnam had approached 500,000. Bad omens, I thought, but General William Westmoreland declared that "we have reached an important point when the end begins to come into view." And he was right, of course. The silhouette was there. The end revealed itself as an ending that would never quite end. When I look into my hole, allowing for distortion, I can see the end all around me. I can see Sarah leading the rallies at Peverson State. A baroque cartwheel, a fingertip handstand, a pair of identical somersaults—like the tracings of a compass, like school figures in skating. "We're *all* cheerleaders," she says, "you and me and Nelson Rockefeller. High fidelity, William. No switching sides at half time."

There are fracture lines in the continuum from past to present. Are the dead truly dead?

Dig, the hole says, but I'm watching Sarah and Tina and Ollie in action at a Friday-night football game. I can see the American flag at stiff-flutter beyond the goalposts. I'm up in the bleachers. I know what's coming. The score is deadlocked, the teams are at midfield, it's a punting situation—imagine it—that brown ball spiraling through the bright yellow floodlights, the crowd, the stadium, the artificial greenness of the grass—and the ball never comes down—it's still up there, even now, it's still sailing high over Canada and the Arctic Ocean—and there's a distant sputtering sound—Sabotage, I think, it's the work of Ollie Winkler—then the floodlights flicker and the stadium goes dark. At the fifty yard line Sarah lights a sparkler. Tina, too, and later Ollie, and then I join them. "Spine straight," Sarah whispers, "show me some class." The pep band plays peace music. It's all orchestrated. The sparklers and the music and the blackout and people standing and locking arms and singing and swaying under a huge autumn sky.

Impressive showmanship, but what disturbed me was the outlaw mentality. Too reckless, I thought. Those sabotaged floodlights: there was a cost involved, and over the next months it kept rising.

In January they seized the campus radio station. A year of decision, 1968, and Tina manned the microphone, and Sarah and Ollie took turns issuing demands. My own contribution was minimal. Five minutes into the operation I excused myself and found a men's room and sat there for a long while, just reflecting, tracking goofiness toward sorrow.

Afterward Sarah said, "Well."

Ollie laughed. "He's not tuned in. Too shy, maybe. Hasn't got that on-air personality."

"Poor boy," said Tina.

Recklessness, that was one thing, and there was also secrecy. Sarah had undesignated irons in the fire; she wouldn't always confide in me. Security, she called it, but the variables seemed to graph out as conspiracy. On three occasions during our senior year, Sarah took off on extended trips to various unspecified locales. She came back tan and silent. There were late-night phone calls and coded conversations with anonymous personages. In February, after one of her trips, I came across a packet of twenty-dollar bills in her book bag. The currency still smelled of mintage, stiff and unwrinkled, two thousand dollars in all. And there were other such discoveries. There was an airline schedule. A Spanish-English dictionary, a travel brochure with photographs of Key

West by moonlight, a set of house keys, a snapshot of two imposing black gentlemen dressed in berets and fatigues and combat
boots. Unhealthy, I thought. I didn't like the way things were
trending. "Loose lips, leaky ships," she'd tell me. "What you have
to bear in mind is that this college crap won't last forever. Pretty
soon we graduate. Commence, et cetera."

"Et cetera?"

"You know," she'd say, and smile. "Apply our educations."

The drift was disquieting. It put a crick in my dreams, I could
sense the conclusion, but the real bitterness came in March when
Ned Rafferty joined the Committee.

"He's *not* a fuzzball," Sarah said.

"I know."

"Not a son of a bitch."

"Sure, I *know*."

"And we need him," she said.

There was no subtle way to express it. Chemical, I suppose—
just hate. It was irrational, in a way, because on the surface Rafferty was a genuinely nice person, friendly and courteous, almost
formal in the way he'd call people "sir" or "ma'am" without irony
or affectation, as if he meant it. He had a solid handshake. He
looked you in the eyes. A jock, of course, but he didn't brag about
it, he kept it in reserve, a certain power that was there in his shoulders and arms and gray eyes. It was a modest sort of strength,
which is why I hated him. I hated the goddamn modesty. I hated
the good manners and the firm handshake and the body mass and
the quiet confidence and the way he'd stare at Sarah until she
blushed and looked away. Partly, I think, it was the Crazy Horse
connection—I couldn't dismiss the feathers and war paint—but
there were other factors too. His obvious affection for Sarah, for
instance. They had a history between them, something more than
friendship, and although she insisted it was over, I could read the
subtext in their body language.

It wasn't paranoia. A truly nice guy—that's what I hated
most.

When he walked into our strategy session that afternoon, I stood up and let him shake my hand and then backed off. For the next half hour I didn't say a word.

The meeting, I remember, was in Tina Roebuck's dorm room, which was small to begin with, and the place was cluttered with empty Coke bottles and dirty dishes and diet books. The air had a sweet oily smell, like scorched butter. For me, though, the really peculiar thing was the room's décor: All the walls were papered with photographs of fashion models—trim, well-tailored girls out of *Vogue* and *Seventeen,* shapely specimens out of *Cosmopolitan*—and beneath the pictures were little hand-printed notes:

THIS CAN BE YOU!

TINY TINA—THINK LEAN!

SIZE 8 OR BUST!

It was somehow touching. Leaning back, I found myself measuring the vast distance between reality and ambition. Tina with her Mars bars and anorexic dreams, Ollie with his short fuse and high-heeled boots. Even Sarah. Or especially Sarah, who wanted to be wanted and soon would be.

And there was Ned Rafferty, too, whom I hated, but whose strength and modesty I would one day come to admire.

That afternoon, however, my thoughts were unkind.

I remember Rafferty sitting on a window ledge, quiet and composed. The conversation had come to departure points. Unfinished business, Sarah was saying. College was one thing but the world was something else. We had to grow up. Time to make commitments. Turning, she looked straight at me. Bombs, she said. The war—did we care? Active or passive? Were we in for the duration? Were we serious? Then she smiled and looked at Rafferty. Her voice was low. She had access to certain resources, she told us. A network. Connections: people and places. First, though, we had to resolve the basic question. In or out?

A stirring little speech, I thought. The ambiguities alone carried weight.

I was considering the risks when Ned Rafferty cleared his throat.

"I'm new at this," he said. "Correct me if I'm wrong, but what you're saying is we have to put up or shut up. Make a choice. That's the gist, right?"

And then for the next five minutes he completely dominated the proceedings. A smooth talker, I thought, slow and deliberate, but there was a glibness that made me uneasy. Like grease. The whole time he kept his eyes fixed on Sarah.

"So anyhow," he'd say, "here's the gist of things."

The gist of things: that was his favorite expression. The same phrase over and over, like dripping water. This gist, that gist. It was amazing how long I kept my composure. No doubt I was looking for an opening, some flaw in all that niceness, but the sheer enormity of it surprised me. The gists kept piling up. Whenever Ollie or Tina made a comment, he'd mull it over for a while and then smile and say, "I see what you're driving at, but what you *really* mean is this—here's the gist of it." A couple of times I almost laughed. I couldn't understand why Sarah kept nodding and taking notes.

Finally I had to cut him off.

"Hey listen," I said, "you lost me somewhere. I see what you're *driving* at, but what's the *gist* of it?"

"Gist?" Rafferty said.

"The nub. The nutshell. I need the goddamn gist."

A little muscle moved at his jaw. "William," he said slowly, "I just *gave* you the gist."

"You did?"

"Yes, sir. I did."

For a moment I came close to backing down.

"Well, fine," I said, "you gave me the gist, but I need the *absolute* gist. The gist of the gist. You have to step back and boil it all down for me."

"Now listen—"

"Sum it up, put it in perspective."

Rafferty's eyes fell. There was puzzlement in his face, even hurt. I wanted to stop but I couldn't.

"Nail it down solid," I said. "The bottom line. I need the ultimate, final gist."

Sarah stood up.

"Enough," she said.

"Let's get to the *heart* of it. Real fundamental basics."

"William."

Something in her voice stopped me. Apparently Ollie felt it, too, because he laughed and then busied himself with a fingernail clipper. Tina Roebuck studied the fashion models across the room.

After a moment Rafferty shrugged.

"A comedian," he said. "Humor, I can appreciate that."

"It wasn't humor," said Sarah. She looked at me for a long time. "Unnecessary. Whatever it was."

"A joke," Rafferty said. "No harm."

"Harm, bullshit," she hissed.

I felt some tension. There were things I could've said, and wanted to say, but I was already out the door.

That night, in bed, Sarah faced the wall.

"I'm sorry," I said.

"You're not sorry."

"All right, I'm not. Slimy bastard. The way he looks at you, it's almost like—" I waited a second, then said, "Are you sleeping with him?"

Sarah rolled sideways.

"And what does that mean?"

"What it means."

"Cry wolf, William."

"The truth."

There was a long quiet. She leaned on her elbow and stared down at me. Her eyes, I thought, were a little puffy.

"Am I sleeping with him?" she said softly. She made it sound like a problem in mathematics. "Well, it's not something a nice girl talks about, but let's hypothesize. He likes me, I like him. It's mutual. I said it before, life has this weird built-in factor called shortness. All this time I've been waiting and waiting, for *you*, just

waiting, but the joyride never showed up. So maybe—it's all hypo-
thetical—maybe I decided to stick out my thumb and pull up my
skirt and see if I could stop a little traffic. Conjecture. But what
if?"

"I'm asking."

"Ask."

"Are you?"

Sarah closed her eyes.

"You know what it is, William? It's a sickness."

"Yes or no?"

Again, there was silence.

"Funny thing," she finally said, "I thought I was sleeping
with *you*. Appearances deceive." She lay back and watched the
shadows. "I care about you, William. A whole lot—too much. But
this sickness I mentioned. There's a name for it. Shall we call it by
its name?"

"No," I said, "let's not."

"But you know?"

"I know."

Sarah touched me.

"So then," she said. "Imagination time. Am I sleeping with
him?"

"You're not."

"Sure?"

"Pretty sure."

"I'm *not*," she sighed. "More's the pity."

Then she turned away.

It was a bad night. I kept turning the unnamed name over in
my head, just letting it tumble. I thought about pigeons and
bombs. Crazy, I thought, but that wasn't quite the name.

In the morning Sarah got dressed and sat on the edge of the
bed.

"Rafferty," she said. "He's in. You realize that?"

For a few moments she looked away, then she shrugged and
pulled the bedspread over me. "The strange thing about it, William, is he likes you. Thinks you're extraordinary. Extraordinary—

his word. The bombs-are-real stuff, that poster of yours, he says you started it all. Says he respects you."

"Well," I said, "that's very genuine."

"Yes, isn't it?"

"Very sweet."

"He is."

"A nice guy," I said. "I'll bet that's the gist of it."

We graduated on May 27, 1968.

There were hugs, I remember, and slapped backs and promises, and on May 28 there were departures. In a way it was sad, in a way it wasn't.

Ned Rafferty headed for his father's ranch in Idaho.

Ollie Winkler and Tina Roebuck went west to hook on with the McCarthy campaign in California.

Sarah had appointments in Florida.

I knew better than to ask for details. She'd be in touch, she said, but for now there were numerous housekeeping chores, loose ends to attend to. At the bus station she put her hand on my cheek. She said she loved me. She told me to pay attention to my dreams. "It's a tough call," she said, "I know that, but you can't straddle fences forever. In or out. Let me know."

"Maybe it won't come to that."

"Oh, it'll come," she said. "No neutrality."

For me it was a holding pattern.

I spent the summer in Fort Derry, a terrifying summer, a split between black and white. I couldn't decide. Like sleepwalking, except I couldn't move, the dynamic was paralyzing.

The war, of course.

The world as it clearly was.

There was violence in Grant Park. There was Sirhan Sirhan, who shot Robert Kennedy, and there was Robert Kennedy, who died. I saw it in slow motion, as we all did, but I also imagined it, and still do, how it can happen and will happen, a twitch of the index finger, a madman, a zealot, an aberration in human history, Kennedy's wide-open eyes, a missile, a submarine off Cape Cod, a fine bright expansive day in June when the theater of things becomes a kitchen, and there's a chef and there's a terrorist, so it happens, a twitch, or it's a balmy evening in midsummer and a finger comes to rest on a button in that cruising submarine—is it malice? spite? curiosity?—just a trigger finger that comes to perfect rest, then twitches, it's reflex, it's Sirhan Sirhan, and Kennedy blinks as we might blink, a sudden flash and a blink and then wide-open eyes. Which is the dynamic. Which is how it happened and will happen. We are immortal until the very instant of mortality. I imagined dying as Kennedy died, and as men died at war that summer.

But no decisions. Vaguely, stupidly, I was hoping for a last-minute miracle. In Paris they were talking peace, and I wanted the miracle of a decision deferred into perpetuity. I wanted resolution without resolve.

One evening Sarah called.

"So?" she said.

It was a long-distance connection broken by static, and I could hear coins clicking somewhere in the tropics. I told her I was frightened. I talked about the pros and cons and the shadings at the center. Like a teeter-totter, I said, or like a tightrope, I couldn't make up my mind.

"Time," I said.

In the background I heard someone laugh—the operator, maybe—then Sarah whispered, "Teeter-totter," and hung up.

But mostly it was just waiting. During the days I'd drive up and down Main Street in my father's Buick, watching the small-town silhouettes. I thought about Paris; I thought about Canada. There was Vietnam, too, and Uncle Sam, but I tried not to think about those things. Around dusk, sometimes, I'd stop at the A&W for french fries and a Papa Burger. I'd push the intercom button and place my order and then sit back listening to the radio. Peace, I'd think. Then I'd think: What does one *do*?

At night, with my parents, I'd watch the news on television.

"Whatever happens," my mother said, "we're with you all the way. A thousand percent."

"Two thousand," said my father.

He stared at the TV screen.

There were flags and limousines at the Hotel Majestic. Averell Harriman was shaking hands with Xuan Thuy.

"Assholes," my father said, very quietly. "Shit or get off the pot."

My mother nodded.

"Your decision," she said.

But it was not my decision. The dynamic decided for me.

When I think back on the summer of 1968, it's as though it all occurred in some other dimension, a mixture of what had happened and what would happen. Like hide-and-go seek—the future curves toward the past, then folds back again, seamlessly, and we are locked forever in the ongoing present. And where am I? Just digging. The year, for instance, is both 1968 and 1971, and I see Ollie Winkler tipping back his cowboy hat, squinting as he kneels down to rig up a bomb. I can hear the whine in his voice when he says, "You don't make a revolution without breaking a few legs." But the bomb is real. Legs get broken. And I see Tina Roebuck storming a radio station, except she's older now, and meaner, and there is an impulse toward bloodshed. I see Robert Kennedy's wide-open eyes, a twitch, a flash, Sarah oiling an automatic rifle, sharpshooters and a burning safe house and the grotesque, inexpungible reality of the human carcass. Odd, how the mind works. It goes in cycles. The year is 1968, and 1958, and 1995, and I'm here digging, I'm sane, I'm trying to save my life.

What can one do?

Safety first.

It was no surprise when I received the draft notice in late August. "Run," Sarah said, and I did. First by bus, then by plane, and by the second week in September I was deep underground.

7
Quantum Jumps

MY WIFE THINKS SHE'S leaving me. Already the suitcases are packed, and in the bedroom, behind a locked door, Bobbi spends the afternoon sorting through old letters and photographs. Her mood is truculent. Two months since she last spoke to me. When necessary—today, for instance—she communicates by way of the written word, using Melinda as a go-between, dispatching fierce warnings like this one:

RELATIVITY

Relations are strained
in the nuclear family.
It is upon us, the hour
of evacuation,
the splitting of blood
infinitives.
The clock says fission
fusion
critical mass.

"Mommy's not too happy," Melinda tells me. "Pretty upset, I think. She *means* it."

"Mommy's not herself," I say. "Off the wall."

"Off what?"

"The wall, baby. She's a poet, we have to expect it."

Melinda sniffs. She sits at the edge of the hole, legs dangling, peering down on me as I study *Relativity*. Her expression is grave. She tugs on her ponytail and says, "We're going away. Real soon, like tomorrow, she told me so."

"It won't happen, angel."

"Tomorrow. In the morning."

"Won't happen."

"I *heard* her," Melinda says. "I'm not deaf, that's what she said—she already called the stupid goddamn *taxi*, I heard it."

"Don't say goddamn."

"Goddamn," she mutters.

It's no use lecturing. I pocket the poem, spit on my hands, and go back to digging. Later I say, "This taxi business. What time?"

"Can't tell you."

"Early?"

Melinda nods. "Real early. We have to sneak out so you can't get crazy and try to stop us. It's a secret, though. I'm not supposed to talk about it."

"Better hadn't, then."

"I already *did.*"

"You did, yes. Thanks."

Shrugging, Melinda kicks some dirt down on me. Her position is precarious. I tell her to back away—it's a fifteen-foot drop—but she doesn't seem to hear. Those blue eyes, they're wired to my heart.

What can one do but dig? Mid-June now, two months on the job, and I've got myself one hell of a hole. Fifteen feet and counting. No tricks—solid walls and solid rock. Amazing, I think, what can be done with a spade and a jackhammer and a little dynamite. I bend down and lift a chunk of granite.

"Daddy," Melinda yells, "we're *leaving!*"

But it doesn't stop me.

I put my spine to the spade and lean in. Relativity, for Christ sake. Metaphor. Poets should dig. Fire and ice—such sugar-coated bullshit, so refined and elegant. So stupid. Nuclear war, nuclear war, no big deal, just a metaphor. Fission, fusion, critical mass . . .

"Daddy!" Melinda cries. I look up and smile. The world, I realize, is drugged on metaphor, the opiate of our age. Nobody's scared. Nobody's digging. They dress up reality in rhymes and paint on the cosmetics and call it by fancy names. Why aren't they out here digging? Nuclear war. It's no symbol. Nuclear war—is it embarrassing? Too prosaic? Too blunt? *Listen*—nuclear war—those stiff, brash, trite, everyday syllables. I want to scream it: Nuclear war! Where's the terror in this world? Scream it: Nuclear war! Take a stance and keep screaming: Nuclear war! Nuclear war!

"Daddy!" Melinda wails.

She drops a clod of hard clay from fifteen feet, a near miss. The real world. It gets your attention.

"Do something!" she shouts. "God, we're *leaving! Do* something!"

"Baby," I say.

"Now!"

She smacks her hands together. She's crying, but it isn't sadness, it's fury. She pushes a wheelbarrow to the lip of the hole. "Do something!" she yells. And then she shoves the wheelbarrow down. Frustration, that's all. She doesn't mean to kill me. "I don't *want* to leave," she cries. She's on her hands and knees, bawling. I scramble up the ladder and try to hold her, but she rolls away and kicks at me and says, "Please!"

I clamp on a bear hug.

Melinda squirms but I press close, and for a long time we lie there at the edge of the hole, father and daughter. I can feel her heartbeat. A warm afternoon, a Friday, and there are puffy white clouds above us. Melinda's eyes are closed.

"Better now?" I ask.

She stiffens, wipes her nose, puts her head in my lap. She doesn't understand. Twelve years old, how could she?

"You'll do something, won't you?" she whispers. "Tomorrow, you won't just let us go away?"

"Can't happen."

"Mommy said so."

"She's wrong," I say firmly. "Nobody's leaving."

Later, in the house, we take turns using the shower. I go first, then Melinda. There was a time, not long ago, when we'd do our showering as a team, a real family, but now she's at the age of modesty. I love that little girl. I love my wife. Standing in the hallway, toweling off, I can hear Melinda singing *Billy Boy* behind the bathroom door.

"Nobody's leaving," I murmur. "I won't allow it."

I know what must be done.

It's ugly, but it's also a relief. In the kitchen, I'm whistling *Billy Boy* as I prepare a lunch of sausage and salad.

"That song," Melinda says, "I hate it."

She comes to the table wearing a pink robe and pink slippers, a white towel wrapped turban style around her head. She tells me she's sorry about the wheelbarrow. I nod and say, "A bad time." Nuclear war: I want to scream it. But instead I tell her we'll find a solution. Back to normal, I say, and then, out of the blue, I hear myself asking if she'd like to have her own pony someday. It's a preemptive tactic, I suppose. Or maybe an apology. Melinda thinks about it for a moment and says, "I guess that'd be okay. A pony. Except you'd probably blow it up with dynamite."

"I wouldn't."

"You *would*. Boom—dead pony. No, thanks."

Composure, I think.

I shrug and fix up Bobbi's lunch tray and carry it to the bedroom door. I knock twice but there's no response. For a few seconds I listen with my ear to the door. Packed suitcases, things neatly folded and tucked away. A walkout.

I put the tray down and head back to the kitchen.

"See what I mean?" Melinda says. "She's serious. It's all planned, so you better hurry up and *do* something."

"Done," I say.

"What?"

"Relax, princess. All under control."

The afternoon goes by peacefully. Bobbi has her plans, I have mine. While she's busy tidying up the loose ends of our marriage, I go about my business with confidence and dispatch, a disconnected calm that seems to nudge up against sadness.

Two things are clear.

I won't stop digging. I won't lose my family.

The trick now is to avoid arousing suspicion. I'm canny. I stick to the routines: wash the dishes, sweep the floor, lace up my boots, and then march back to the hole.

I know what must be done, and I'll do it, but for now I just dig.

Squeeze the spade. Concentrate on kinetics. The downward drag, it's a solid feeling. All motion.

I was born to this sort of labor, a jackhammer and a spade. There are no metaphors. There is only science when I say, "Nuclear war." Why, I wonder, is no one explicit? Why don't we stand on our heads and filibuster by scream? Nuclear war! Nuclear war! Why such dignity? Why do we shy from declaring the obvious? Why do we blush at our own future? And why, right now, as I save her life, does my wife think I'm crazy? Why would she leave me? Why separate?

Dig, the hole says.

A light echo, then it chuckles and says, *Nuclear war, man. Just dig.*

All afternoon I keep at it. I weigh progress by the pound. I count the inches.

You're sane, the hole says. *Dig-down-dead!*

I won't be blackmailed.

This running-away garbage, I won't tolerate it.

Dig—it's my life.

Late in the afternoon I climb out of the hole and slip into the tool shed and make a few quiet preparations. Some measuring, some easy arithmetic.

Oh, yeah, the hole says.

I pile up a stack of two-by-fours; I go to work with a saw and hammer and nails. Specifications. I know what I'm doing. There's nothing funny about it, but at one point I start giggling—it hurts, my eyeballs sting—and I have to step back and take a breather. *Child's play*, the hole purrs. *Follow the dotted lines: fission, fusion, critical mass.*

"Love," I say.

An hour later, when I leave the tool shed, the afternoon has become twilight. There's a soft rain.

I switch on the outdoor Christmas lights and the backyard glows in reds and greens. The rain is warm and steady, not quite real, like a movie set. If Sarah were here she'd squeeze my arm and tell me to calm down. "Step by step," she'd say, "one thing at a time."

I cut the telephone line.

I trudge over to the Chevy, open the hood, remove the battery, lug it across the yard and hide it in the tool shed.

"Good work," Sarah would say.

I pause at the edge of the hole, wavering. There is something burdensome in the night. I hear myself reciting aloud the names of my wife and daughter, then other names, Ollie and Tina and Ned and Sarah.

What happened to them? All of us? I wonder about the consequences of our disillusion, the loss of energy, the slow hardening of a generation's arteries. What *happened?* Was it entropy? Genetic decay? Even the villains are gone. What became of Brezhnev and Nixon and Curtis LeMay? No more heroes, no more public enemies. Villainy itself has disappeared, or so it seems, and the moral climate has turned mild and banal. We wear alligators on our shirts; we play 3-D video games in darkened living rooms. As if to beat the clock, the fathers of our age have all passed away— Rickover was buried at sea, von Braun went quietly in his sleep. Sarah, too, and the others. Left for dead. And who among us would become a martyr, and for what?

The hole seems impatient.

So then. Get on with it.

It's an era of disengagement. We are in retreat, all of us, and there is no going back.

I return to the tool shed.

I arm myself with hammer and nails. I pick up the two-by-fours and make my way toward the house.

In the kitchen I try for stealth. Past the stove, a left turn, down the hallway to the bedroom door. There I stop and listen.

The sounds are domestic. Muffled but still comforting—Bobbi's hair dryer, Melinda's radio.

"You guys," I say, "I love you."

I perform each task as it comes.

First a wedge, which I tuck between the knob and the door's outer molding. I drive it tight with the hammer.

Next the two-by-fours.

Speed is critical.

I feel sorrow coming on, but I push it back and carefully check the measurements. I don't want mistakes. We are dealing, I remind myself, with the end of the world. Nuclear war: I am not crazy.

When I begin hammering, the hair dryer clicks off and Melinda says, "What's going *on?*"

I nail a board flush to the door.

"Daddy!" she shouts.

I am sane. Yes, I am. Sane—I hit the nails square on.

"God!" she yells.

Bobbi hushes her, and I hear bedsprings, sharp voices, but I know what bombs can do, I've *seen* it, I'm willing to call it nuclear war, and I do, I cock the hammer and say, "Nuclear war." There's justice involved. It's love and preservation. It's shelter. It's carpentry. I nail down the second two-by-four, then the third, an overlapping system that anchors on the hallway wall.

"Hey, you!" Melinda says. Her voice is closer now, a bit shaky. "Stop that racket! Can you *hear* me! Stop it!"

Finally the braces. Six of them. Door to molding: I've figured the angles. As an afterthought I remove the knob and use a screwdriver to jam the inner workings.

I kneel at the door.

The shakes have got me, and for a moment or two it nearly spills over into sentiment.

Melinda jiggles the inside knob.

"Well," she says, "I hope you're happy."

"Almost," I say.

"The *door* doesn't work."

"No, it doesn't."

She gives it a sharp tug. I hear a squeak but it's solid. For a time the house seems impossibly silent, as if a furnace had shut down, then from behind the door comes the sound of a latch turning, a window sliding open. There's a conference in progress. No doubt about the topic. Bobbi's a poet, Melinda's a child. It adds up to a paucity of imagination.

"Forget it," I say gently, "I'm years ahead of you."

My pace is brisk.

Not rushing, not dawdling either.

When I step outside, the night has become treacherous. A heavy rain now, and the Christmas lights seem blurry in the dark, almost mobile, like the lights in a dream, fluid and shapeless. There is an absence of clarity.

I find the ladder, place it against the house, climb nine rungs to the bedroom window. I take great care. I don't want broken legs, not mine, not theirs.

The window is wide open. The gauzy white curtains billow inward, and through them I watch my wife and daughter. It's a touching scene. Bobbi stands at the center of the room, in profile, her lips drawn in concentration as she ties the bedsheets together. She wears green cords and sneakers and a yellow cotton sweater. Poignant, I think. The bedsheets make me smile; it would be funny if it were not so poignant. A gorgeous woman—the breasts beneath that cotton sweater, the places I would touch, the things I would say. But now she tests the knot, frowning, and I can't let it go on. Behind her, wearing a raincoat, Melinda sits on a blue suitcase, waiting, her eyes excited with thoughts of escape.

I feel sadness in my backbone.

If I could, I would climb through the window and take them to me and crush them with love.

If I could, I would.

Softly, though, I close the shutters. If there were any other way. But I pull the hammer from my belt and drive in the nails.

"Hey!" Melinda shouts.

It's a two-minute job. If I could, I would do otherwise, but I can't. I seal up the window with two-by-fours. Guilt will come later. For now it's just heartache.

"We'll starve!" Melinda screams, but of course they won't, I'll figure something out in the morning.

The rain seems hot and dry.

There are no shapes, the night has no configuration.

The hole says, *Beautiful!*

Inside, I take a bath, then shave, then busy myself with little household chores. I'm optimistic. I'll reason with them. I'll explain that it's love and nothing else. I'll be logical. Bowl them over with my own sanity. I'll show them photographs of an armed nuclear warhead—that's what I'll do—I'll do mathematics—I'll slip the equations beneath the door.

Yes, I'll *do* it, and they'll understand.

But now I find comfort in vacuuming the living-room rug. I'm domestic. I have duties. I dust furniture, defrost the refrigerator, scrub the kitchen floor. Ajax, I think, the foaming cleanser . . . I sing it. The house seems empty around me. In the basement I toss in a load of laundry and sit on the steps and sing, *Clean clear through, and deodorized too, that's a Fab wash, a Fab wash, for you!* I watch the clothes spin. My voice is strong. In Key West we'd sit out on the back patio and one of us would start singing, maybe Tina, and then Ned and Ollie . . . Are they dead? What happened? They knew the risks, they indulged in idealism. There was evil at large. Vietnam: the word itself has become a cliché, an eye-glazer, but back then we recognized evil. We were not the lunatic fringe. We were the true-blue center. It was not a revolution, it was a restoration. And now it's over. What happened? Who remembers the convoluted arguments that kept us awake until five in the morning? Was it a civil war? Was Ho Chi Minh a tyrant, and if so, was his tyranny preferable to that of Diem and Ky and Thieu? What about containment and dominoes and self-determination? Whose interests were at stake? Did interests matter? All those complexities and ambiguities, issues of history, issues of law and principle—they've vanished. A stack of tired old platitudes: The war could've been won, the war was ill conceived, the war was an aberration, the war was hell. Vietnam, it wasn't evil, it was madness, and we are all innocent by reason of temporary insanity. And now it's dropout time . . . *Be young, be fair, be debonair . . .*

We pat ourselves on the back. We marched a few miles, we voted for McGovern, and now it's over, we earned our rest. Someday, perhaps, we'll all get together for a bang-up reunion, thousands of us, veterans with thinning hair and proud little potbellies, and we'll sit around swapping war stories in the lobby of the Chicago Hilton, the SDS bunch dressed to kill in their pea coats and Shriner's hats, Wallace in his wheelchair, McCarthy in his pinstripes, Westmoreland in fatigues, Kennedy in his coffin, Sarah in her letter sweater. We'll get teary-eyed. We'll talk about passion. And I'll be there, too, with my hard hat and spade. I'll lead the songfest. I'll warm them up with some of the old standards, and we'll all get soppy with sentiment. We'll remind ourselves of our hour of great honor. We'll sing, *Give peace a chance,* then we'll drink and chase girls and compare investment portfolios. We'll parade through Lincoln Park singing, *Mr. Clean will clean your whole house, and everything that's in it . . .*

The world has been sanitized. Passion is a metaphor. All we can do is dig.

I put the laundry in to dry.

Upstairs, I smoke a cigarette, stand at the bedroom door. It's not a pleasant thing.

If I could, I think. If there were no Minutemen. If we could somehow reverse the laws of thermodynamics.

Around midnight I lie on the sofa. Can't sleep, though. I get up and clean the oven. Scour the sinks, apply Drano, carry out the garbage, make coffee, plan the breakfast menu.

It's nearly dawn when Melinda begins banging on the bedroom door.

"Daddy!" she cries, and I'm there in an instant. I tell her to calm down, but she won't, she keeps yelling and thumping the door. "Have to *pee!*" she says. "Real bad—I can't *hold* it!"

It's a dilemma. I ask her to hang on until I've had time to work out the arrangements.

"Wait?" she says. "How long?"

"Not long. You're a big girl now, go back to bed."

"*Wet* the bed. One more minute and—"

"Use a bottle, then."

"What bottle?"

"Look around," I say. "Check Mommy's dresser."

"Gross!"

She hits the door. I can picture the droop in her eyelids, the tightening along her jaw.

"Bottle," she says, "that's stupid. I'm a *girl!* God, I can't even believe this." Then she moans. "Daddy, listen, don't you think maybe something's *wrong?* It's not too nice, is it? First you lock us in here, like we're prisoners or something, and then you don't even let me go to the *bath*room. How would you feel? What if I did all that stuff to you?"

"Bad," I tell her. "I'd probably feel terrible."

"So there."

Leaning against the door, rocking, I listen to a silence that seems to stretch out forever.

"Daddy?" Melinda says.

"I'm here."

"You know what else?"

"What else?"

"I'm scared, I guess. And real sad, too. If you were me, you'd get so sad you couldn't even stand it."

"I know, honey."

"Like right now. I'm sad."

"Yes."

"Let me out," she says.

It's a rocky moment, the most painful of my life. I hesitate. But then I tell her it can't be done, not yet. "The hot-water bottle," I say quietly. "Wake up your mother, she'll handle it."

"Please, can't you—"

"I'm sorry, angel."

She's right, I can't stand it. When she says she hates me, I nod and back away. I turn off the hallway light and move to the kitchen and drink coffee and try to patch myself together.

It's a splendid sunrise. No more rain. The mountains go violet, then bright pink.

Just after six o'clock a taxi pulls up the long driveway.

Willpower, I think, and I write out a handsome check. "Tip?" the driver says. He's just a kid, granny glasses and a sandy beard, but he clearly knows what it's all about. He takes a twenty without blinking. "Could've called," he says. "Six o'clock, man, no fucking courtesy."

And that's it.

Inside, I roll out my sleeping bag before the bedroom door. I strip to my underwear and curl up like a watchdog.

What more can I do?

Melinda hammers on the door.

"Daddy," she shouts, "you're crazy!"

FUSION

8
The Ends of the Earth

"**I**F IT WERE UP TO me—" my father said, but he had the courage not to finish. Instead he said, "What can I do?"

"The money, that's all."

"Cash? Play it cozy?"

"Probably so."

"And you've got a place to—you know—a place to go?"

"It's being set up," I told him. "I'll know tonight."

"That's good, then. Fine. So what about the basics? Toothbrush, clothes. A new wardrobe, what the hell."

"Not necessary."

He smiled and touched his jaw. "On the house. Any damned thing you want, just say it."

"A wig," I said.

"Right. What else?"

"I'm kidding. No wig. Nothing, just the cash."

"A coat, though. You'll need a coat. Definitely. And new shoes—some decent leather."

"It's not a funeral," I said.

"No?"

"It's not."

My father jiggled his car keys. "Shoes," he said, "let's not argue. Shoes, then a coat, then we'll see about a haircut."

At the shoe store on Main Street, my father sat beside me, draped an arm across the back of my chair, and told the clerk he wanted the best. Leather soles and rubber heels, no plastic. The clerk said, "Yes, sir," and hustled off to a back room. My father lit a cigarette. For a few minutes he sat watching the smoke, legs crossed, and then he shook his head and said, "Christ."

"If you want," I told him, "I'll call it off."

"I don't want."

"If you do, though."

"No," he said. "It's a crime, that's all I mean. Just a sick rotten crime. No other possibilities, right?"

"Except to call it off."

He nodded. "Except that. And there's Doc Crenshaw."

"Yes, but I can't——"

"Who knows?" he said. "A heart murmur maybe. I read somewhere—I think it was in *Time*—I read how heart murmurs can do the trick, or else asthma, a hundred different things. You never know."

"I won't beg."

"Of course not. But we can hope, can't we? Heart murmur, we can damn well hope."

"Or cancer," I said.

My father laughed and clapped me on the leg.

"That's the spirit," he said. "Cancer."

He bought me shoes and a wool overcoat and shirts and jeans and a big green Samsonite suitcase. In the barbershop, he smoked cigarettes and flipped through magazines, keeping his hands busy. "Lop it off," he told the barber. He made a slicing motion across his neck. "Amputate. Major surgery. The kid's growing corn up there." The barber chuckled and my dad went back to his magazine while I watched myself in the mirror. September 1968, and there was a thinning out in progress, a narrowing of alternatives. The scissors felt cool against my ear. The smells were good, I thought, all those lotions and powders. I closed my eyes for a few moments and when I looked up my father was studying me in the mirror. He turned away fast. "What we need," he told the barber, "is one of those heavy-duty lawn mowers. Scissors won't hack it."

After dinner that night, when the dishes were done, I modeled my new clothes. An off-to-camp atmosphere, jokes and smiles, a nervous twitter when my mother said, "Well, it's not the end of the world, is it?"

We avoided specifics. There was great courage in what was not said. We listened to records, made small talk about neighbors and old times, and then later, on the spur of the moment, my father challenged me to a game of Ping-Pong. "Two out of three, no mercy," he said, and he winked, and I said, "You asked for it," and we moved down to the basement and set up the net and played hard for almost an hour.

At eight o'clock I asked for the car keys.

"Right," he said. "Absolutely."

There was a clumsy moment when he handed the keys over. He followed me outside and stood on the steps as I backed the Buick down the driveway, then he waved and held up two fingers.

A good man, I thought. A veteran of foreign wars and a good man.

Twenty minutes to kill, so I drove up Main Street to the railroad tracks at the east edge of town, then circled around and came back again, slowly, elbow out the window. The air was warm and calm. A big red moon presided over the mountains, a Friday night, and the shoppers were out. There was commerce and goodwill. I drove past the Ben Franklin store, the Thompson Hotel with its old hitching post, my father's real estate office, the courthouse and the library and Doc Crenshaw's little three-room clinic. The streets were safe. It could've been anywhere, small-town America.

Nobody knew.

I turned on the radio. Rhythms, I thought, *Surfin' Safari*, and I tapped the steering wheel and watched the mountains above town, the safe streets and storefronts. I was afraid, of course, but it was mostly homesickness. I thought about the things I'd be losing. Little things, like backyard barbecues, but big things, too, family and history, all of it. For me, at least, it would not be an act of high morality. My father understood that. "It's a mess," he'd said, "it's all upside down, a real hornet's nest. If it were up to me . . . It's not, though. What can I tell you? That damned war. What the hell are we fighting *for*? That's the bitch of it, I guess, but I don't know. I wish I knew."

Certain blood for uncertain reasons.

It was a phrase I'd picked up in college, one of Sarah's favorite lines, and now, as I turned past the A&W, I said it aloud. I whistled *Surfin' Safari*.

I did not want to die, and my father understood that.

It wasn't cowardice, exactly, and he understood that, too, and it wasn't courage.

It wasn't politics.

Not even the war itself, not the coffins or justice or a citizen's obligation to his state. It was gravity. Something physical, that force that keeps pressing toward the end.

Certain blood, uncertain reasons, but finally you have to choose.

At eight-thirty I stopped at a pay phone outside the State Bank building. Sarah was all business. "On or off?" she said.

"On," I said, "I'm pretty sure."

"Pretty?"

"Yes, I think so."

There was a pause before she said, "Class dismissed. Call me back if—"

"On," I said.

"Louder, man. Bad connection."

"It's go, almost positive. A couple of things to take care of first."

"Medically, you mean?"

"My dad thinks it's worth a shot."

Sarah seemed pensive. In the background, barely audible, I could hear a tinkling sound, ice cubes or wind chimes.

"Flat feet," she said, and sighed. "Or cold feet. What you should do, maybe, is buy yourself some cute pedal pushers. Have Congress with a butcher knife—works every time."

"That isn't quite fair."

"Maybe not," she said. "Stick an ice pick up your weewee. Tell them you're two months pregnant."

There was a moment of problematic silence. I watched a tractor turn left off Main, a big John Deere painted green with yellow trim. I was hurting. When the tractor was gone, I told her how sick I felt. Turned around, I said. Lost, too, and trapped, and I needed something more than smart-ass bullshit.

Sarah chuckled.

"You're not pregnant?" she said.

"I'm not pregnant."

"Pity."

"Sick," I said. "Lost."

There was that wind-chime sound again.

"All right, then, you're lost," she said, and her voice seemed to back off a bit. "That's understandable. Problem is, we need a commitment, something firm. These things get complicated. Heat's on, I'm sorry, but you'll have to—I hate to press—but you'll have to . . . I *am* sorry."

"Okay," I said.

"Okay what?"

"Okay, on. Tomorrow night."

"That translates to Saturday?"

"Saturday."

"Firm?"

"Yes," I said, "I guess so."

Sarah cleared her throat. "That's what I admire. All that boldness and fire." She waited a moment, then told me to take notes. "Number one, you'll have to bus it to Chicago. Number two—write this down—TWA, flight 233, Chicago to Boston, nine o'clock Monday morning. Nine sharp. Miss that flight, the whole deal's off."

"Tickets?" I said.

"At the check-in counter. Your name's Johnson, L. B."

"That's comic."

"We thought so. Anyhow, nine o'clock Monday. You've made financial arrangements?"

"My parents."

"They know?"

"Not the details."

"But they know?"

"A little. I couldn't just walk away."

Sarah snorted. "I thought it was clear. Mouth shut, I said. Didn't I *say* that?"

"I was careful. No names."

"Careful, shit," she said. There was a brittle sound on the line, a clicking, as if someone were transmitting in code. Voices, too. I heard a whisper, or thought I heard it, then a soft buzzing. After a moment Sarah said, "So where was I? Number three. We'll have a watchdog waiting in Boston—TWA, main lobby. Find a comfy chair and sit tight. Simple enough?"

"Like cloak-and-dagger."

"You think so?" Her tone was perfectly neutral. "Because, listen, we can call it a bust right now. You think that?"

"Trans World," I said. "Sit tight."

"Exactly."

"And?"

"Bring a book or something. The watchdog, he'll find you."

"Who?"

"No can say. A familiar face." She made an indistinct sound, almost motherly, but her voice remained firm. "It's not easy, we both know that. But flat feet don't cut it. Sooner or later you have to walk."

Breakfast was a ceremony. There was great decorum in the scrambling of eggs, cups on saucers, pourings and stirrings and fussings over fresh-squeezed orange juice.

"Socks," my mother said.

"Plenty," I told her, "no more socks," but she smiled and shook her head and added socks to the shopping list. "Towels," she said, "you could use towels."

We spoke in ellipses.

My father stirred his coffee, glanced at the clock, yawned,

stretched, folded his arms, and said, "Goddamned idiots. The whole jackass crew—the Pentagon, the jackass diplomats—give me a chance, I'd strangle the whole crew, one by one, line them up and start—" He strangled his napkin, then shrugged. "I *would*. My own two hands. March in and murder the sons of bitches, all those whiz-kid bastards. You think I'm not serious? Westmoreland, I'd nail him first, and then Bundy and Ho Chi Minh. I swear to God, I'd do it. Just like that. I'd do it."

"Towels," my mother said.

"Towels, right." My father winked at me. "Towels, to mop up the gore."

At noon they dropped me off at Doc Crenshaw's office.

It was hopeless but I went inside and stripped down and closed my eyes while Crenshaw searched for flat feet and asthma and disturbances in the heart. I felt drowsy. Lying there, I wanted to curl up for a decade-long nap, an iron lung breathing for me, fluids flowing in and out through rubber tubing. I held my breath as the old man listened through his stethoscope.

"Thump-thump," Crenshaw said. "Always the same old tune. Just once I'd like to hear *Rhapsody in Blue*."

Later, when I was dressed, he took me by the arm. He squeezed hard, his eyes sliding sideways.

"You could go mental," he said. "Start seeing flashes."

"No," I said.

"Just a thought."

He released my arm and stepped back.

"I'm a doctor," he said, "I can't—"

"No problem."

"A crazy world, but I can't fake it. Tell your dad I'm sorry. Don't blame him for asking—leaning hard. I'd do the same myself. Tell him that."

"Sure," I said, "you're a doctor."

In my bedroom, as I finished packing, there was the feel of a performance gone stale, too many rehearsals.

"Bag money," my father said. He slipped a thick envelope into my pocket. "Tens and twenties, hard to trace."

"Unmarked, I hope."

"Slick as a whistle. Ran it through the scanner, it's clean."

My mother folded shirts; my father sat on the edge of the bed, head down, hands carefully pressed to his knees. Now and then he'd take a quick peek at his wristwatch.

"You know what this reminds me of?" he said. "That TV show—*I Led Three Lives*. Herb Philbrick, remember? That trench coat of his. Always pulling up the collar and ducking into phone booths, sweating to beat holy hell. Remember that?"

"Richard Carlson," I said.

"Yeah, Richard Carlson. Subversives everywhere. FBI agents, too, all over the place, in the closet, under the bed. And that poor slob Philbrick, the way he'd slink around in that damned spy coat, just sweating up a storm—like a flood, I mean *gallons*—the guy couldn't turn it off."

"I'll go easy on the sweat," I told him. "No trench coats, either."

My father smiled.

"Comrade," he said.

Late in the afternoon I took a shower and dressed up in my new clothes. There was a short picture-taking session, fierce smiles straight at the camera, then my father said, "Ready, comrade?"

The ride down to the bus depot was almost jolly. We talked about David Janssen in *The Fugitive*, how it was the greatest TV program in history. My mother said she'd start looking for me in the next episode.

We were tough people. Scared, a little dazed, but we followed the script.

When the bus rolled up, my parents took turns hugging me.

"Postcards," my mother said. "Don't forget."

"Invisible ink," I said.

"Microdots under the stamps."

My father turned away. It was a wobbly moment but he didn't lose control.

"One favor," he said. "Keep that hair trimmed."

"For sure."

"What I mean is, we're proud of you. Not a single thing to be ashamed about."

He kissed me on the forehead.

"Pride," he said, "and love, that says it all, cowboy."

I made Chicago at six o'clock Monday morning. Thirty-five hours on the run, and already I was feeling the side effects. Stomach problems and a crushing headache. I splurged on a cab out to O'Hare, ate breakfast, spent a half hour in the men's room, then popped an aspirin and made the hard walk up to the TWA counter. "Johnson," I said, and felt a telltale grin coming on. The girl didn't look up. Her lips moved as she counted my tens and twenties, then she cranked out a ticket and waved me on. It was almost a disappointment. Over and over, during that long haul through North Dakota and Minnesota, I'd played out the various scenarios. A cop asking for my driver's license, a Herb Philbrick sweat, then handcuffs and fingerprints.

"Gate Twelve," the girl said. "Safe trip."

Too ordinary, I thought. The effortless takeoff. Tweedy seats and canned music, the flight attendants with their rubber smiles and toasted almonds. It was unreasonable, of course, but I felt cheated. I wanted something more. A clot in the fuel lines. An instant of daffy panic. I wanted contact with my own emotions.

But the plane nosed up through a pale morning sky, banking eastward, leveling off at thirty thousand feet.

Automatic pilot, no pain.

I levered back my seat and slept through to Boston. It was a purring sleep, like the engines, not even a bad dream.

At Logan, Ollie Winkler was there to meet me at the gate.

"Well," he said, "you look like snot. Green and rancid."

There was no hugging or handshaking. We collected my luggage, took an elevator up to the main ticketing area, dropped quarters into a vending machine, and sipped our coffee standing up near a window.

"I kid you not," he said, "you look sick. Like fried oysters.

Real nice haircut, though." He grinned and put his nose to the window and watched a plane lift off. "So anyhow, welcome to the depths. Depths—underground, get it? I'm real keen on the lingo."

"Watchdog," I said, "that's another good one."

Ollie shrugged. "Sarah, she goes in for the spook stuff. You ask me, it's too James Bond-y, slightly paranoid, but I guess that's her style. Like right now—today—I'm not even supposed to talk to you, just drop messages. Screw it, though. I figure you got to go with the normal flow, otherwise you start . . . Listen, maybe you better sit down."

"Maybe," I said.

"Worse than sick. *Dead* fuckin' oysters."

I let him lead me over to a bench in the main lobby. Jet lag, I thought. I closed my eyes and leaned back while he filled me in on his doings since graduation. Most of it I already knew. He explained how the McCarthy business had gone bust after California. Clean-cut candidate, clean-cut defeat. "Tidy Bowl Politics," he said, "it makes you yearn for the pigpen. Crack a few skulls, you know?"

"I do know. Like RFK."

"Right, Bobby. Messy shit. Didn't do much for morale."

"But you stuck?"

"Oh, sure, me and Tina both. The holy wars."

Ollie was silent for a time. He'd lost some weight, and he seemed taller now, and stronger, and a little more subdued. He wore a buckskin jacket and boots, but no cowboy hat. At the crown of his head, I noticed, there was evidence of aging. After a moment he sighed, snapping his fingers, and talked about life on the campaign trail, mostly the disappointments. "The Windy City," he said, "that was an eye-opener for all of us. Yippies here, Dippies there. Turns out clean-cut isn't trendy. No offense, I do love that haircut."

"And now?"

"You know. Politics as usual."

"Meaning?"

He looked at his fingernails. "The chef, remember? I said it before, you got to break some legs. Three years ago. Nobody listened, but I said it."

"You did."

"Now they're listening."

"Sarah?"

"Oh, sure," he said, "especially Sarah. Sometimes I almost wonder . . . Anyhow, you'll see. She's got some rude new friends."

"Who—"

"Three fucking *years* ago, I said it. You heard me, right? I *said* it."

"Yes. What about these friends?"

Ollie stood up. He unwrapped a stick of Juicy Fruit, folded it twice, placed it on his tongue, and chewed vigorously. "Just pals," he said. "Concerned citizens, you might say."

"Bad-weather types?"

"Sure," he said, shrugging, "you might say that, too. Vigilantes. Various shades of dread. The network, it's your basic franchise principle, like Kentucky Fried Terror. Independently owned and operated, but you can always count on the Colonel."

"Happy arrangement," I said.

"I guess. Let's eat."

We ordered sandwiches at a stand-up counter. Ollie reviewed my itinerary and told me the hard part was over. Like when a little kid starts walking, he said, the first few steps were tough, he understood that—sort of seasick, everything moving at weird angles—but in a week or two I'd get the hang of it. A month, max. He said to treat it like a business trip, a vacation, whatever. A big country, he said. Not to worry about Uncle Sam. Don't start seeing ghosts. Paranoia, that was the killer. Just follow the rules of the road, he said, then he listed them for me, how I should avoid strangers, stay cool, keep my nose clean. Never jaywalk, he said. Be a good citizen. Then he laughed. "There's nothing like crime," he said softly, "to keep you honest."

I was not feeling well. Disconnections, I thought, or maybe the sandwich.

Ollie's voice seemed to be coming from the far end of the terminal.

"What you have to remember," he was saying, then came a short hum. "See what I mean? Right now you're on the ultimate guilt trip, just ride it out. You know?"

We took our time heading down to the TWA gate area. It was a thirty-minute wait. When the flight was announced, Ollie went over to a pay phone, placed a quick call, then came back and handed over a packet of tickets.

"Okay, you're off," he said. "The Big Apple. Another layover at La Guardia then a straight shot down to Miami. Pure gravity the whole way." There was a soft, almost compassionate expression on his face; he paused and held out a stick of Juicy Fruit. "Don't dwell on it. Put her on cruise and just coast for a while. The gum, too. Keeps the ears unplugged, helps decompress. No problem, you just got caught in a draft."

There was turbulence all the way to New York. I didn't crack. I put myself on glide, breathing deep, imagining I was aboard a one-man spaceship tracking for the stars. Far below, the home planet spun on its axis, a pleasing vision, those lovely whites and blues, the fragile continents, and as I sailed away, as the world receded, I felt a curious measure of nostalgia, desire mixed with grief. Here, in space, there was just the smooth suck of inertia.

At La Guardia I dozed off for an hour, then roamed around the terminal, then called home.

It did not matter that the line was busy. I just kept talking, very quietly, picturing my mother's face, and my father's, explaining to them that I was running because I couldn't envision any other way, because the dangers exceeded the reach of my imagination. Safety, I said. Nothing else. Not honor, not conscience. All I wanted for myself was a place to ride out the bad times.

"It isn't cowardice," I said, "it's my life."

And then I chuckled.

No big deal, I told them, because none of it was real. If you're sane, that is.

I put courage in my voice. I told them how alone I felt, how much I missed them, but how it was all a daydream. There are no bombs, I said. We live forever. It's a steady-state universe. I told them about the spaceship sensation, warped time and high velocity, as if I were traveling through some strange new dimension, another world, no maps or landmarks, no right or wrong, no ends to the earth.

It was Trans World from there on.

A clear night sky, like glass, and I could see it all. I could see the lights of Atlantic City, the scalloped edges of Chesapeake Bay, the tidewaters of Virginia. The clarity was amazing. Telescopic breadth and microscopic precision. I could see Baltimore and Richmond and Washington, the glowing dome on the nation's Capitol, the Lincoln Memorial, the dark Carolinas, Cape Hatteras and Cape Fear, the quiet suburbs of Norfolk, the rivers and inlets, the Jersey shore, north to Maine, south to the Keys, all of it, the whole profile, the long sleeping silhouette of midnight America.

I was in orbit. The eye of a satellite. A space walk, and I was tumbling at the end of my tether.

There were lights in the Kremlin.

I could see a submarine in the shallows off Cape Cod, like a fish, and I could see Kansas, too, where there was a harvest moon and vast fields of corn and wheat, and men in blue uniforms beneath the translucent earth. The men wore silk scarves and black boots. They were not real men, of course, for none of it is real, not the blue uniforms and not the boots and not the Titan II missile with its silver nose cone and patriotic markings. I could see Los Alamos, too, where nothing real had ever happened; I could see across the ocean to Bikini; I could see the Urals and the Sweethearts; I could see all of what cannot be seen, because it's beyond seeing, because we're sane.

The Trans World engines made a lullaby sound. People slept, the flight attendants chatted in the galley.

There was nowhere to land.

Below, in the dark, I watched ball lightning strike Georgia: a conspicuous white fireball that rolled toward Atlanta. The jet was on low-hum cruise. There was comfort in knowing it could not be real. Later, I fell asleep, and later yet, as we passed over Charleston and Savannah, I could see how it might happen, if it could, though it can't—crisscrossing threads of color in the great North American dark, bright flashes zigzagging from sea to sea. It was not a dream. One by one, all along the length of the eastern seaboard, the great cities twinkled and burned and vanished. A half-dream, I thought. I felt no fear. I buckled my seat belt. I knew what was next, and when it came, I watched with a kind of reverence. There were flashes of red and gold. There were noises, too, and powdery puffs of maroon and orange and royal blue, fungal arrangements in the lower atmosphere, the laws of physics. But it was not real. When it happens, I realized, it will not happen, because it cannot happen. It will not be real.

The jet dipped, bounced, and woke me up.

I pushed the call button.

Just a nightmare, the stewardess said, and I nodded, and she brought me a martini and wiped my brow and then held my hand for a while.

Over Miami we went into a holding pattern. I was sick, but I fell in love.

When I told her so, the stewardess smiled and said it was the martini, or altitude sickness.

We circled over the Everglades at ten thousand feet.

She said my skin was green—pale green, she said, like a Martian. Then she gave my hand a squeeze. She asked if I was feeling better. I said I felt fine, I was in love.

The stewardess crossed her legs. She was tall and slim, with space-blue eyes and yellow hair and a pair of wings on her collar and a name tag at her breast that said Bobbi.

"Bobbi what?" I asked, but again she smiled, and after a moment she told me names didn't matter. There were company policies, and private policies, too. But in any case names didn't matter, did they? I thought about it as we banked over the Atlantic. No, I decided, names did not necessarily matter. But without names, I asked, how would we get married? I told her we had to be practical. Bobbi smiled at this and said it seemed a bit sudden. I agreed with her. Things sometimes happened suddenly, I said, even things that could not happen. Passion, for instance, and commitment. Her eyes were cryptic. Was this a line? she asked. It was not a line. She took the olive from my martini and fed it to me, saying I needed vitamins, I should find a nice beach somewhere and stretch out and bake away the bad dreams. She told me to close my eyes. I was sick and the plane was circling through fog. What about love? I asked. Could we run away together? How many children would she want? Over the Everglades she looked at me and said, You're crazy, you know that? I knew. Bobbi nodded. Then I told her as much as there was time to tell. I told her about the dynamic. It was crushing, I said. How much was real? Was *she* real? I told her I was caught up by current events. I couldn't separate right from wrong. I needed a hideout. Would she mind saving my life? Could we find an island somewhere?

"Bobbi *what?*" I asked, but she only smiled.

The plane seemed to wobble for a moment, then stabilized. The fog was gone and there were stars and blinking lights. I listened to the engines.

Later, very softly, Bobbi talked about flight and books and travel and poetry. Poetry, she said, that was her first love. Would I care to hear a poem? Very much, I said. And she recited one about a violet sunset over Hudson Bay. A remarkable piece of work, I thought; I asked what it meant. She gave me a long secret look and explained that poems do not *mean*, that art is like grass and dreams, like people holding hands in the sky, that meanings are merely names, just as grass is a name, but that grass would still be grass without its name. I did not fully understand this. What I understood was love, and I asked if we could go away to Hudson Bay. Watch the sunsets? Live happily? Build a cabin in the woods? She said no, but she touched my face. She recited Auden and Frost and Emily Dickinson, then several of her own poems, and I thought about Sarah, and how sick I was, and lost, and in love.

I drifted away for a time. Just hovering, on hold, and when I looked up I was alone.

To what extent, I wondered, was it real?

A hard landing—too much torque. There was again the problem of gravity.

At the ramp, I waited for the plane to empty out. She was gone. But when I put my coat on, I found a poem pinned to the pocket—*Martian Travel*—and it was signed Bobbi. That much was real. The words didn't matter. It had to do with flight and fantasy and pale green skin, which was hard to follow, but it seemed meaningful despite the absence of meaning. There was some grass tucked into the fold. Plain dried grass, yet fragrant, and a postscript which explained that the grass expressed her deepest feelings for me.

We spent two days in a motel on the outskirts of Miami. The grass, I kept thinking. I couldn't match it to the real world. When I was well enough to travel, Sarah rented a van and fixed up a bed in back, pillows and blankets.

"Home free," she said.

We made Key West in just under four hours. There was blue water and sickness and jungly greens and a fierce sun that made my eyes burn. What did it *mean?* The pieces wouldn't fit. A white stucco house, I remember, and Ned Rafferty said, "Hang tight," and he helped me inside, where it was cool, and then I felt the disease. Chills turning to fever. It was true illness. Emotional burnout, too, but the rest was physical. I remember a ceiling fan spinning over my bed. A heavy rain, then dense humidity; faces bobbing up—Tina Roebuck peeling an orange, Ned Rafferty wringing out a washcloth and folding it across my forehead. There were voices, too. Some I recognized, some I didn't. And cooking smells. And intense heat, and doors swinging open, and a radio at low volume in another room. The smells were tropical. At times I'd seem to float away on one of those leisurely space walks. Nowhere to land, I'd think, and I'd be circling over the Everglades, airborne, all flight and fantasy.

"It's done," Sarah kept telling me.

She was patient. At night, when the chills came, she would come close and whisper, "End of the road."

*   *   *

Key Wasted, Tina called it. There was no war here, and no clamor, just the tropical numbs.

Over that first month we took things slow. Hour by hour, quiet meals and quiet conversation. The patterns were entirely domestic. Tina did the shopping and cooking, Rafferty tended a small garden out back. For me, it was recovery. Safe, I'd think. A safe house, a safe neighborhood, and the underground seemed tidy and languid. There were no choices to make; the killing was elsewhere. Our little bungalow was situated at the edge of Old Town, near the cemetery, on a narrow, dead-end lane that was prosperous with window boxes and sunlight. No one talked politics. If this was the movement, I decided, the movement was fine, because nothing moved. Our neighbors were property owners and retired naval officers and widows and watercolorists. The houses were painted in pastels. In the yards were many flowers and pruned shrubs. During the day, from my bedroom window, I'd watch people passing by in their bright clothes, and at night I could hear radios tuned to the Voice of Havana.

I'd hear myself thinking: Where am I?

On the lam, I'd think. Then I'd smile. What, I wondered, was a lam? And why did it sound so corny and sad?

"There now," Sarah would say. "Sleep it off."

But my dreams were unwholesome. Criminal and outlandish. One night I was Custer. Another night I was chased through a forest by men with torches and silver badges—"Shame!" they were yelling—but I put my head down and ran. I dreamed of dishonor. I dreamed of dragnets and posses and box canyons and dead ends. "Shame!" my father yelled, but I couldn't stop running. And then, dreaming, but also awake, I came to a country where there was great quiet and peace. It was a country without language, without names for shame and dishonor. Here, there was nothing worth dying for, not liberty or justice or national sovereignty, and nothing worth killing for. It was a country peopled by apostates and mutineers, those who had dropped their arms in battle, runaways and deserters and turncoats and men with faint hearts.

Just a dream, like everything, but the nights were disjointed.

I'd wake up dizzy—uncertain whereabouts. A malfunction of compass. I couldn't get my bearings; I felt open to injury.

"Easy," Sarah would say, "give it time."

She was tender with me. Uncommonly careful, and caring. In the mornings, before the heat set in, she would often lead me on long winding strolls through Old Town. The pace was slow. She was tactful, never pushing. Along the way she pointed out the local flora and fauna, many gulls and flowers, exotic trees, fish bones bleaching on white sand. We'd go arm in arm down Margaret Street, then left on Caroline, past Cuban restaurants and conch houses, then right on Duval, where there were crowds and drinking establishments and young girls in halters and headbands and young boys with long hair and bruised arms, then down to the waterfront, just walking, often resting, watching the shrimp boats and fishermen and tourists. Mildew smells, I remember. And salt and gasoline. There were jugglers and magicians at Mallory Square. There was an old man with an iguana on a leather leash. There was no war here, but there was bright sunlight and water, so we'd walk until we were hungry, then we'd stop for fish cakes at one of the outdoor cafés. We'd hold hands under the table. We'd be silent, mostly, or else talk around things, admiring the temperature and the shadings of color in the sky. Later, at the house, we'd nap or read, then take a swim, then oil up our bodies and hide behind sunglasses and spend the late afternoon soaking our toes in the Gulf of Mexico.

On the surface, at least, it was a holiday. R&R, Sarah called it, but she skirted the hard topics. She did not mention her new friends. She did not venture information as to why we were here or what her plans might be or where the trends might take us. Except for a few late-night phone calls, there were no contacts with any outside network. There was an odd passivity to it all, an absence of endeavor. Too lush, I thought. Too remote. The immense quiet and the afternoon heat and the slow island tempo. Where, I wondered, was the resistance? And why Key West? And what next? There were these questions, and others, but I was not yet prepared to frame them.

I concentrated on convalescence. Day to day, just idling. A good time, mostly—a family feeling.

Tina Roebuck performed home economics, toiling over casseroles and desserts that flamed. "Health begins with nutrition," she'd say. Then she'd chuckle and tap her belly: "Balanced diets make balanced minds." So we'd sit down to nutritious meals, Tina in a brightly colored muumuu, Rafferty in gym shorts, Sarah in almost nothing. The talk was family talk—Tina told McCarthy stories, Rafferty went on at length about his garden. After supper we'd play Scrabble or Monopoly, or watch television, or go dancing down on Duval Street, and although I'd sometimes feel myself slipping away, space walking, the others were always there to give comfort.

September was neither here nor there.

On October 1, my birthday, Tina baked a cake. There were candles and songs, and it was a happy occasion until I felt the grief. I excused myself and went out to the back patio and watched the sun go down.

Later, at twilight, Ned Rafferty joined me. He was still wearing his party hat. He smiled and showed me a bottle of rum and two glasses. For some time we just watched the dark. Ocean smells, and a breeze, and we drank the rum and listened to the crickets and tree frogs.

"Anyway," he said.

But then he shrugged and fell silent.

Behind us, in the kitchen, Sarah and Tina were doing dishes. I could hear a radio somewhere. When the moon came up, Rafferty took off his party hat.

"You know," he said softly, "we've always had this tension between us, you and me, but I wish—I mean, it's too bad—I wish we could be friends. A treaty or something. Here we are."

"Wherever here is," I said.

Rafferty stirred his drink with a thumb. He seemed pensive.

"I know the feeling. Hard to connect sometimes, but you shouldn't think—you know—you shouldn't feel alone or anything. You shouldn't. The Benedict Arnold disease, it's one of the hazards. We all grew up saying the Pledge of Allegiance."

"I'll live," I told him.

He nodded. "No doubt. But if you need to talk, I'm not such a terrible guy."

"You're not."

"Just a fuzzball," he said, and smiled.

He filled my glass.

A nice person, I thought. I wanted to tell him that, but instead I shifted weight and examined the sky. The radio seemed closer now, and louder, and for a while Rafferty hummed along with the Stones . . . *just no place for a street-fighting man*.

Then he stopped and looked at me.

"You'll learn to live with it," he said. "Guaranteed. At first you get the jumps, that's normal. You feel like J. Edgar Hoover's on your tail, Feds and G-men and all that, but after a while you realize, shit, it's a huge country—a *free* country, right?— and they can't track down every Tom, Dick, and Harry. They just can't. Not if you follow the rules of the road."

"Don't jaywalk," I said.

Rafferty smiled at me.

"That's one rule. Don't jaywalk. Don't ask a cop for directions. Not all that difficult. If a guy wants to get lost, he gets lost. Easy."

I contemplated this. The rum was doing helpful things.

"Fine," I said. "Lost-wise, I'm shipshape."

"It gets better."

"Sure it does." I looked at him. "What about you? How's your lostness?"

Rafferty laughed. "So-so," he said. He picked up the party hat and put it on his head. "A goof, man. What do I know? Dumb jock. Long line of fuzzballs."

"Not so dumb."

"Dumb," he said, and rubbed his eyes. "Hick. Grew up on a ranch. Like where the buffalo roam. All I ever wanted—that old home on the range. Deer and antelope. Dumb, you know? And now this."

"Why?"

"Why what?"

"Here," I said. "How come?"

He was silent. He stood up and moved over to his garden, peeing with his back to me, then turned and came back slowly and lifted the bottle and said, "Motives. Who knows? Real jumbled."

"Sarah?"

"Oh, sure," he said. "Sarah. Classy lady. Much love, but that's not . . . This rad shit, it's not me. Politics, I hate it. Humphrey, Nixon—who cares? But here I am. Sarah, sure. The right thing, I guess. The war. Not a nice war. Very tangled. So do the right thing . . . Dumb jock. The right thing, I think. Dumb. So what's the right thing? Down inside I'm all red, white, and blue. Fucking Republi-can, you believe that? True. Many misgivings. What's *right?* Mo-tives, man, I don't know. I walk away. Real brave, real dumb. No more home on the range. My dad says, 'Hey, where you going?' so I tell him, I tell him it's the right thing, and my dad gives me this long look—he's got these eyes you wouldn't believe, like Gary Cooper or somebody, these no-bullshit eyes—he looks at me and he says, 'Pussy.' That's all he says. My old man, he wasn't pleased. Didn't think it was the right thing."

"Parents," I said.

Rafferty rolled his shoulders. "Oh, yeah," he said, "parents."

We proposed a toast to parents. I told him how my mother kept packing socks and towels, how we couldn't really talk about it, not straight on, just the logistics, socks and towels and haircuts. Like a game, I told him. Like it wasn't real.

"Right," Rafferty said, "like that."

"Parents."

"Unreal. That's the thing."

The radio was playing calypso now. We drank to our parents and birthdays and the right thing. Rafferty told me to stay loose. So far, he said, so good. Then he grinned and said, "Like the army, sort of. Hurry up and wait." For the time being, he told me, no need to worry. Sarah had resources. There was no shortage of wherewithal.

Vaguely, a little drunk, he talked about the competing factions within the movement, how scrambled it was, the cliques and cabals and petty conspiracies.

"The political thicket," he said, and shook his head. "Tangled, you know? Classic worm can. Slimy creatures, very messy. Panthers here, Weather guys there. Shades of red—like with blood, all types, you need a goddamn flow chart—SDSers and Quakers and the CPA and the PLP and God knows what all— let me think—the People's Coalition for Peace, Dwarfs for a Nonviolent Solution. You name it. Lots of moral hairs to split. Head-smashers, ass-kickers. Hard-core weirdos, Liberation fronts. The League of Concerned Dieticians. If I had my way, I'd wipe out the whole rat's nest. There it is, though. The famous network."

There was a pause, then Rafferty shrugged and raised his glass.

"Screw it," he said, "let's drink. To the nonviolent dwarfs."

We drank and refilled our glasses.

It wasn't friendship, exactly, but it was something. We drank to moral hairs and split ends.

"Anyway, that's the gist," he said. "Where we fit in, I don't know. Unaffiliated, I guess. Sarah wants to run her own little show. A ma and pa operation, whatever that means. Big dreams."

"Franchise," I said. "Kentucky Fried Terror."

"Yeah, well. Forget the terror part. I'm not in this to bust skulls. Just a nice little subway system for guys like you and me. Fast and efficient."

"Crack-ups?" I said.

Rafferty smiled. "No crack-ups. One thing about draft-dodging, it's hardly ever fatal."

"I meant—"

"Yes, I know," he said. "Mental hygiene. Go with the shuffle, that's all. Just flat-fuck *live* with it. Pretend it's the right thing."

"I suppose," I said. "But sometimes—"

"Lost, right?"

"Pretty lost."

We were quiet for a few moments.

"All right, then, lost," Rafferty said. He smiled. "I guess we'd best drink to it."

There were mobile shapes in the dark, rustlings and penetrations. We drank to the League of Concerned Dieticians. Later, after Sarah and Tina had gone to bed, we went inside and ate birthday cake and proposed toasts to mental hygiene and low profiles and safe houses and reformed fuzzballs and treaties of peace. We drank to Crazy Horse and Custer.

"To Herb Philbrick," I said.

Rafferty seemed puzzled. Apparently the name didn't ring a bell, but he shrugged and drank anyway.

By mid-October the cure was solid. Flat on my back, I basked away the daylight hours, staring up at a huge blue sky, alert to contrails and the whine of passing jets. There was an alternating current at work. A kind of giddiness at times, almost elation, and I'd hear myself laughing at the unlikely melodrama. Jesse James, I'd think. I could imagine my hometown draft board saddling up for the chase, that hide-and-go-seek feeling, fully revved, like a little kid paying grown-up games—slip under the bed and cover your eyes and giggle. Other times, though, it was grim. Shipwrecked, I'd think. Lying there, watching the sky, I'd seem to drift outside myself, outside everything. The law and history and the precedents of my own life. It wasn't anything fanciful—I wasn't ill—it was just disengagement. How much, I wondered, was real? I'd sometimes find myself hovering at thirty thousand feet. I'd contemplate the flight patterns and violet sunsets over Hudson Bay. I'd study *Martian Travel* for hidden meanings, sniffing the dried grass, smiling as I visualized the Trans World possibilities.

I'd tease the name, saying "Bobbi."

Bobbi who? I'd wonder.

And there was Sarah, too, whose love and ministrations speeded recovery.

In the evenings, before bed, she gave me long professional back rubs, attending the vertebrae one by one, taking each toe to her mouth and sucking out the poisons and wickedness. There was some guilt, of course. There were unsaid things. Our lovemaking was often quick and formal. Bobbi, I'd be thinking, which was silly, and Sarah would regard me with flat eyes, just waiting, and eventually I'd find reason to look away. But even then she showed patience. Quietly, without sarcasm, she said she was proud of me. I'd done the proper thing. She knew how difficult it was, she knew about the pain.

"We all want to be heroes," she said one afternoon. "That's the constant. Nobody wants a bad rep. Ducking out, the big blush, I know. But I'll tell you a true fact—you can't die of embarrassment. Doesn't happen that way."

I watched the clouds.

A seashore scene, and we were beached up side by side. The blues were startling. It was an afternoon of repose, just the wide-open stratosphere and those long rhyming wavelengths of water and light.

For a time Sarah watched me through her sunglasses. There was a hesitation, then she reached into her beach bag and pulled out a new leather wallet.

"Yours," she said, and passed it over.

Inside, under clear plastic, was a Social Security card made out in the name of Leonard B. Johnson. There was a driver's license, too, in the same name, with my face affixed, and two credit cards, and a snapshot of Sarah in her Peverson cheerleading outfit. At the bottom of the photograph, in black ink, she'd written: *With high fidelity, Sarah*.

"The credit cards," she said. "Don't use them. ID stuff, just for show."

"Leonard?" I said.

"You don't like it?"

"Not much."

Sarah sat up and massaged cocoa oil into her calves and thighs. Her skin was deep brown with good muscle definition. A hard act, I thought, in a hard world.

She laughed.

"Ah, well," she said brightly, "what's in a name? No real meaning. Know what I mean?"

"No, I don't."

"Names and names, William. Meanings. Names don't matter." She rolled onto her stomach. Overhead there were sea gulls and wispy white clouds. "Anyway," she said, "I hope it's not an identity crisis. Leonard, I mean, it'll grow on you. Very wishy-washy as names go. Tomorrow, maybe the next day, I'll have your passport."

"And then?"

Absently, Sarah traced a design in the sand.

"Nothing, really. New papers, new citizenship. We're all émigrés here."

She wiped the sand clean and started over, drawing an airplane, wings tilted at a steep downward angle. Her eyes, I thought, were wired.

"One of these days," she said slowly, "you'll have to stop grieving for the old country. It's gone. Not there anymore."

"A new world," I said.

"Believe it."

"New friends, too?"

She gave me a sharp look.

"Friends, too," she said. "Who do you think *pays* for all this? Those papers—the house, the groceries—somebody has to pick up the tab. They aren't bad people."

"I didn't say that."

"You implied."

"All right," I said. "Generous people. What I'm curious about, though, is the repayment schedule. The fine print, the terms of agreement and all that."

"A few favors. Odd jobs here and there."

"I'll bet."

"Complaints?"

I shook my head. "No, just apprehensive. The law."

"Well," she said, "it takes some savoir-faire."

Sarah studied her airplane in the sand. It wasn't what she wanted, apparently, because she hit it with her fist and then flipped onto her back and watched the circling gulls.

"Savoir-faire?" I said.

"You know."

"I don't know. I'm stupid."

She made an impatient movement with her chin. "Survival skills. How to cope. How to avoid handcuffs. Like grad school except it's strictly pass-fail. Anyway, you're enrolled."

Her voice trailed off. She kept fidgeting, tight and restless.

Presently she sighed.

"You're right," she said, "there's always a price. But listen, you made the decision, you *walked*, so pretty soon you'll have to get off your butt and start showing me some involvement. You do or you don't."

"A war," I said.

"True enough." She took off her sunglasses and looked at me. "Things change, William. All that pom-pom garbage, it's history, I'm in this for keeps. I'm *in*. And what I mean is, I mean you have to grow up. Crawl out of your goddamn hidey-hole."

"Black or white," I said. "Sounds so simple."

"It *is* simple. Pull your own weight or pull out. I need a commitment."

For a moment she was silent, letting it hang, then she tapped the wallet.

"Commitment," she said softly. "Know what it means?"

There was a subtle undercurrent. She shook out her hair and stood up and waded out into the Atlantic.

Commitment, I thought.

Two different value systems. She was out to change the world, I was out to survive it. I couldn't summon the same moral resources.

I dozed off for a time, and when I looked up, Sarah was standing over me, toweling off, the sun directly behind her head.

"Who's Bobbie?" she said.

Her face was all angles. She knelt down, opened the wallet, and pulled out *Martian Travel*.

"Found it this morning. Naïve Sarah. Went to reload your billfold. Switch papers—some switch. What do I find? I find this. All about airplanes and safe landings. Maybe I should read it out loud."

"No," I said, "don't."

But she went ahead anyway, in a soft, measured voice, and at the final line she nodded and placed the poem in my lap.

There was some stillness.

"Snazzy stuff," she said shortly. "Mars and stars. Dah-dee-dah, et cetera. Nice metrics. Content-wise, it seems a little ambiguous, but I guess that's literature for you."

"Sarah, it's not—"

She shook her head and laughed.

"Fidelity?" she said. "Offhand I can't think of a decent rhyme. True? Blue? Shit." Her eyes were closed. "I guess I'm just hypersensitive. The whole thing, it strikes me as—how do I say this?—a little cheesy. And there's that cute P.S., too. Something about grass. The regular cow kind. She says it expresses her deepest feelings for you."

"Yes," I said, "I know."

"Cheesy."

"I know."

After a time, Sarah put on her sunglasses and stretched out beside me.

The afternoon was hot. A fine clean sky, and for a long while nothing more was said. All whimsy, I thought. It wasn't what it seemed. Out on the horizon a white cruise ship was toiling south, and we lay quietly until it disappeared over the rim of the world.

Sarah touched my arm.

"I'm not poetic, William. You and me. I thought we *had* something. Remember?"

"I remember."

"Love. Rio and babies. That was the plan, I thought."

"It still is. A good plan."

She sat up.

"Fucking Martians," she said. "Fucking grass. I don't get it."

"No meaning," I said. "All air."

"I *love* you."

"Just air."

"*Love,*" she said, then paused. "So who's Bobbi?"

I gazed out at where the cruise ship had been, but there was just the thin, unbroken edge of things.

"Bobbi who?" I said.

9

Underground Tests

NOVEMBER 6, 1968, A DISMAL DAY in paradise. Dark and drizzling and steamy hot. After breakfast Sarah dressed in mourning. She wore a black hat and a black bikini and a long black widow's veil.

"Nixon's the one," she said. "Let's walk it off."

Outside, there was fog and thunder. We unfurled an umbrella and strolled past bait shops and boutiques, along the waterfront, down to a deserted beach at Land's End. The rain was steady. Sarah lifted the veil and spat and said, "Not that it matters. We needed a classy new villain."

She lay down and made angels in the sand, then stiffened and folded her arms.

"Go ahead," she said. "Bury me."

"Deep?"

"Use your judgment."

I dug a shallow grave and rolled her in and tamped down the wet sand. At the end, only the hat and veil were visible.

She nodded.

"A prayer might be appropriate. Talk about my free spirit, how much you adored me."

I knelt down and uttered a blessing.

"Beautiful," she said.

There was gloom at Land's End, and the day smelled of salt and mildew and troubled times.

Sarah's eyes were dark behind the veil.

"Our beloved, misgoverned Republic," she said. She attempted a smile. "And me, William? You do care?"

"A lot. Don't be silly."

"Silly me."

"That's right."

"And Bobbi?"

"I explained that. Just this thing."

Her head shifted slightly in the sand.

"Heavenly bodies," she said.

It was a day for sobriety. I propped up the umbrella and leaned back and studied the rain. Things were pasty-gray. The ocean was part of the land and the sky was part of the ocean. Far off, there was lightning.

"The thing that gets me," Sarah said, "is the broad's guile. I'd give anything to watch her work a singles bar: 'Hi, there, my name's Bobbi. Here's a delicious little poem I wrote just for you.' A huckster, William. And you fall for it."

"I didn't fall."

Sarah grunted. "Fall, flip, what's the difference? I mean, Christ, I can knock out my own little beddy-bye rhymes. The grass, the grass! Bobbi, baby, kiss my ass!"

"Talent," I said.

"Talent. You bet."

"It's not what you think."

"No?"

"I told you, we barely even . . . Nothing."

The rain was vast and undramatic. America had misstated itself—Nixon was the one—and at Land's End there was only Real Politic.

Sarah made a clucking sound.

"Nothing," she said. "Like Mother Goose. Now you see her, now you don't."

"Stop it."

"The competition, man, it's too celestial."

"No competition. I'm here."

"Oh, yes."

"I am."

She laughed.

"Half here, half there," she said. "A little of both. The *Martian Travel* trick."

Then she cried.

There was definite slippage. Along the surface of the grave I could see bits of brown flesh where the rain had made fissures in the sand. Sarah cried quietly, inside herself, then closed her eyes and lay still. "You never *look* at me," she said. "Not really. When you love somebody, you keep looking, you can't help it. But you never do that. You never look at me or ask questions about how I feel or . . . Just things. You know? I'm a real person."

"You are," I said.

I looked at her, then looked away.

She was not, I realized, beautiful. Hard and pretty but not beautiful. I pulled the veil up and kissed her and told her it was just circumstance. A random encounter, I said. Nothing to hold on to. A martini, a voice without language: I couldn't remember *words.*

Sarah cradled her legs and began rocking. For some time she just watched the weather.

"It's foolish," she finally said, "but I need promises. You have to promise me things."

"Things?"

She shrugged. "Whatever seems possible. The future. We keep doing this evasive dance together, all kinds of intricate footwork, but just once I'd like to stop the waltz. Just once. Tell me there's a future for us. You have to *promise.*" She removed her hat and veil. "Do you love me?"

"Yes," I said.

"Promise?"

"I do. I promise."

"Say it."

"I love you," I said.

"More."

"I don't know more."

"Make it up, then. Tell me we'll be happy. Tell me it's perfect love, it'll last forever."

"It will."

"Swear it, though."

"I swear. Forever."

"Forever," she said, and nearly smiled. "I like that."

The next evening Ollie Winkler hit Key West aboard a sleek thirty-eight-foot Bertram cabin cruiser. He was in the company of a slim, mustachioed Cuban without a name. Compadre, Ollie called him. The man did not speak English. He touched his cap and stepped back while Ollie gave us a tour of the boat. It was brand-new and expensive-looking.

"A real attack vessel," Ollie said proudly. "*Fast*, you know? All we need's a torpedo or two."

"And depth charges," said Tina.

"You got it, kid. Charges for the depths." Ollie beamed as he showed us the galley and the teak decks and the two big Evinrude engines. He was wearing Bermuda shorts and a sequined T-shirt that said MOON IN MIAMI. "No joke," he said, "these babies cost a pretty penny. Had to shop around almost a week."

"But?" Sarah said.

"Yeah, but."

"A steal, I'll bet."

Ollie's smile was modest. "You know me. Mr. Thrift."

"Problems?"

"Zero problems. Compadre and me, we drove a hard bargain. You like it?"

Sarah pecked his cheek.

"It'll float," she said.

Then it was all action.

We had a quick dinner, packed our suitcases, locked up the house, and headed down to the boat. We spent the night on board. It was a reunion of sorts, and there was champagne and comradeship, but there was also the certainty that we had come up against departure. I slept badly. Late in the night I woke up and took a pee over the bow and then stood there for a long time. Coward, I thought. I watched the water and stars. I thought about the things I valued. I valued the love of my father and mother. I valued peace. I valued safety. I did not want to kill, or die, yet I did not want to do this thing we would now be doing. I had no zeal. For me, it was just a ride, and there were no convictions beyond sadness.

At dawn Tina Roebuck served omelets and orange juice.

"I won't make speeches," Sarah said. "Anyone wants out, now's the time."

Ollie reached for the jam.

"Love it!" he said.

"William?"

"I heard."

"What I mean is—" She looked at Tina. "Go on, tell him what I mean."

"Business," Tina said, smiling at me. "Get with the program, she means. We're tired of jump-starting your conscience."

Ollie laughed and said, "*Love* it!"

It was a smooth seven-hour crossing.

Too smooth, I thought: a weekend boating party. The young Cuban manned the helm, and there was a polished sky and fair winds and the Gulf Stream running green to blue. A radio boomed out calypso. When the Keys sank away, I took off my shirt and pondered ticklish points of international protocol. It occurred to me that our passage held historical hazard—the Monroe Doctrine and piracy on the high seas. Also, in these same warm waters, the world had once squared off in preparation for expiry, causing prayer and the contemplation of final causes. What, I wondered, had happened to memory? *Here*, I thought. Idle musings, perhaps, but I couldn't shake the sense that there was a pursuit in progress. The fugitive jitters, obviously. I imagined a helicopter high off our stern. A warning shot, and demands would be issued, and we would go eyeball to eyeball, and then it would happen as it nearly happened and finally must.

But no one knew.

Among the sane, I realized, there is no full knowing. If you're sane, you ride without risk, for the risks are not real. And when it comes to pass, some sane asshole will shrug and say, "Oh, well."

Events had their own track.

At noon we established radio contact. A half hour later a small gray pilot boat pulled alongside. There were guns and khaki uniforms.

Ned Rafferty touched my arm.

"You okay?" he asked.

"Just fine."

"That's good, then. Steady as she goes." He squeezed my arm. "Clear sailing. Just us and the wild red yonder."

We made Havana in time for a late lunch.

Afterward there was paperwork, then our hosts arranged for a bus that took us along a coastal highway, past poverty and palms and vast fields of sugarcane. The ride lasted four hours. We stopped once for water, once for fuel, but otherwise it was exactly as Rafferty predicted, clear sailing, just us and the wild red yonder.

For six days, which I marked off on a pocket calendar, we lazed away the time at an orientation compound situated beachside a few miles west of Sagua la Grande. It was an old plantation house that had been converted into a combined resort and training facility, with colorful flower beds and neatly tended grounds sloping to the sea. The rooms were spacious, the tennis courts lighted for night play. Plush, to be sure, but there was also menace. The watchtowers and barbed wire and armed cadres.

"Mix and match," Tina said. "Half Che, half JFK. Two stars for originality."

Then six relaxing days.

We devoted our mornings to the sun, swimming and snorkeling, idling. Tina built elegant sand castles; Ollie demolished them; Sarah snoozed behind sunglasses; Ned Rafferty taught me the elements of killer tennis, yelling encouragement as he fired cannon shots from point-blank range. A languorous time. Rum punch at sunset, dinner by lantern light in the villa's pink-tiled courtyard, linen tablecloths and Russian wine and Swiss crystal. The service was cordial and efficient. Why? I'd sometimes wonder. Then I'd think: Why not? A holiday, I'd tell myself, but late at night I'd hear machine guns, or voices counting cadence, and on those occasions I'd find myself engaged in serious speculation.

No answers, though, just questions.

"Play it by ear," Sarah advised. "Mouth shut, eyes open. That's all I can say right now."

It was no use pressing. I was afraid of the answers, no doubt, and I was also a little afraid of Sarah herself. She seemed cool and distant. Small, subtle things that added up to large, obvious things. The way she moved; her silences; a tactical precision to her lovemaking.

The hardness factor, too.

A power disequilibrium. She had it, I didn't.

"You know something?" she said one evening. We were in bed, windows open, and there was the nighttime rustle of wind and ocean. "I was born for this, William."

"This?" I said.

"Right here, right now. The whole decade. Like destiny or something. I honestly believe it couldn't happen without me." She made a pensive sound, then ran her tongue along my hipbone. "The cheerleading and the funeral home—all that—when I look back, I think, God, it was all *planned,* it was like a ladder up against a high wall, and I couldn't see the top, but I started climbing, I had this incredible drive, I didn't know why, I just *had* it, so I kept climbing, and here I am. It was planned *for* me."

"Destiny," I said.

She shrugged. "Laugh. It doesn't bother me."

"I'm not laughing. Wondering."

"All I know is what I feel," she said. "It's in the stars, somehow. The DNA. I can't explain it any better. This goddamn war. I hate it, I *do* hate it, but it's what I'm here for. I hate it but I love it."

She swiveled out of bed and went to an open window. For several minutes she simply stood there, framed by the future, whatever it was.

Then she sighed, squatted down, and pulled a pillowcase over her head.

"A long time ago," she said, "I told you something. I want to be *wanted*. By you, by Interpol. Those handsome dudes on the FBI—doesn't matter, just wanted. Do you see? I need that."

"Of course."

"Here, too. They *want* me." She made a broad gesture with her arm. "What I'm trying to say is, I mean, I'm not the strongest person in the world. I get overwhelmed by all this. You know, this Red connection, Cuba and all that. I don't know where it's headed. Guns or jail. I'm committed, though, and it's necessary, but sometimes I get the creeps, I get scared. You understand? Part of me wants to run away. Like to Rio, or anywhere. Have babies and clip coupons. Be your wife, maybe—something normal—anything."

I smiled at the pillowcase.

"Except?"

"Yes," she said. "Except there's still that ladder I told you about."

"And me?"

"You."

"No grand destiny, Sarah. A guy on the run."

"Agreed."

"So where do I fit?"

She waited a moment. Outside, there were crickets and night birds.

"Difficult question," she said. "There's always Sweden or Hudson Bay, right? Hide your head. Cover your eyes and wish the war away."

"I didn't say—"

"William, listen to me. I love you, you know that, but sometimes—lots of times—I can't help wondering about your backbone. All that bullshit about a dangerous world. The bombs are real, la-di-dah, but you don't ever *do* anything, just crawl under your Ping-Pong table. That jellyfish attitude, I despise it. Despise, that's the only word. I love you, but the despising makes it hard."

Sarah turned and made her way toward the bed. She was attractive, I thought, in her chrome bracelet and white pillowcase.

For a few moments we lay still.

"Involvement," she said. "In a day or two, I'm afraid, it'll get very rough around here, and if you can't hack it—"

"A warning?"

"No, just a statement. Love and war. Sooner or later you have to choose sides."

Six splendid days.

On the seventh we were roused a half hour before dawn.

A bell, a shrill whistle. "Up, up!" someone yelled, and then another voice, much louder: "Haul ass!"

We assembled in the courtyard.

A single rank, stiff at attention. All around us were khakied soldiers with heavy boots and bad tempers. "Freeze!" someone shouted, and we froze.

Dream time, I decided.

I concentrated on the sounds. Across the courtyard, in shadows, a door slammed shut. There was the squeal of a bullhorn.

We stood with our backs to a tile wall.

At noon we were still there.

Near midnight Tina said, "Wow," then smiled and collapsed. But infirmity was not allowed. After a moment one of the soldiers hoisted her back to a standing position. No explanations, just blood in the feet. Speech was prohibited. Eighteen hours, I thought, then later I thought: twenty hours. Mostly, though, I tried to keep from thinking. Don't think, I'd think. Then I'd think: this world of ours. But I refused to think about it. A matter of moral posture. Shoulders square, spine stiff. I calculated the precise specifications of pain, quantifying things, squaring off the roots, letting the numbers pile up as a kind of insulation.

And then the zeros came. Blank time, nothing at all. When I looked up, it was full daylight.

Two men stood staring. They were dressed identically in

combat fatigues, jungle boots, and black berets. Their skin, too, was black, and their eyes.

"Oooo, lookie," one said, and smiled.

The other did not smile.

They surveyed us for a time, then the first man—the smiler—stepped forward and said, "Hi, there, kiddies. Welcome to camp."

His companion snorted.

The smiler kept smiling. It was an extraordinary smile, sharp-toothed and wolfish. He prowled back and forth, gracefully, stopping once to wipe sweat from Ollie's forehead, once to inspect the fat at Tina's stomach.

"These campers," he said gently, "are in sore need of outdoor recreation."

"Bullshit," said the second man.

The first man chuckled.

"Pitiful, I concur." He smiled and made a tsking noise. Stooping, he ran his hand along the surface of Tina's stomach. Then suddenly he stopped smiling.

"My name," he said, "is Ebenezer Keezer. This here gentleman is Nethro." He paused to let these facts take shape. "So let's everybody get acquainted. Real loud an' happy. Say hi to my pal Nethro."

"Hi," we said.

"Loud, children."

"Hi!" we shouted.

"Bullshit," said Nethro. "Can't hear nothin'."

"Volume, people. Blow it out. On three—ready?"

On three we yelled, "Hi!"

Nethro shook his head. He was a large, unhappy man. "Fuckers forgot my name. They s'posed to say, Hi, there, Nethro."

"Legitimate truth," Ebenezer said. "Repeat them your name."

"My name," said Nethro, "is fuckin' Nethro."

"Again," said Ebenezer.

He counted to three, and on three we shouted, "Hi, there, Nethro!"

Nethro seemed unimpressed.

"Nobody waved."

"Beg your pardon?" said Ebenezer.

"Didn't *wave*," Nethro said. "Not one wave in the whole bullshit crowd. My ego's hurt."

Ebenezer Keezer sighed. Carefully, he took off his beret, inspected it for dust, put it on again, then stepped up to Ned Rafferty and stared at him with an expression of solemn perplexity. His nose was a half inch from Rafferty's forehead.

"A level answer," he said softly. "You forget to wave?"

"I guess."

"Oh, you guess," Ebenezer purred, smiling again. "First day at camp an' you don' display no fundamental politeness. Where's your salutations, shithead?"

"Sorry," Rafferty said, and grinned.

"Oooo! Man's sorry, Nethro."

"I overheard."

"Man claims sorryhood."

Nethro shrugged and scuffed the toe of his boot against the courtyard tiles. He seemed genuinely aggrieved.

"Sorry don' do it," he said. "Don' help the hurt none."

"Shitheads," said Ebenezer Keezer. "What they require, I submit, is politeness practice."

"Let's practice 'em," said Nethro.

There was distress in the courtyard. Reality, I surmised, was passé. Here was a new dimension. Over the morning hours we engaged in supervised waving practice. "Hi, there!" we yelled, and we waved with both hands, vigorously. The courtesy was painful. I could feel it in my throat and shoulders. Nethro counted cadence, Ebenezer Keezer smiled and offered instruction in matters of form and posture, schooling us in the complexities of camp etiquette. It was a kind of basic training, clearly, but with numerous innovations. Standing there, waving, I recognized the diverse and intricate plenitude of a world on tilt.

At noon Ebenezer Keezer clapped his hands and said, "Recreation time, people. Fun an' games."

Single file, we marched through the courtyard and down a long grassy slope to the tennis courts. There were no rackets or balls. The game was called Fictitious Tennis, and the rules, I thought, were capricious. "Advantage, Shithead!" Ebenezer cried—"Quiet, please!"—and then we pantomimed the mechanics of serve and volley, rushing the net, backpedaling in pursuit of high phantom lobs. "Out!" Nethro would yell. Or he'd yell, "Let! Two serves!" There were no disputed calls. For me, at least, it was hard to maintain a keen competitive edge.

The match went five sets. An awards ceremony, a quick lunch, then we convened on the volleyball court.

"No net," said Ebenezer.

"No problem," said Nethro.

In the late afternoon they led us on a nature hike. The pace was brisk, mostly running, and by dusk, when we trooped into the villa's courtyard, things had approached the point of shutdown.

We ate supper standing up.

Afterward we were escorted into a small lecture hall. The room was bare except for a podium and five metal chairs.

Ebenezer Keezer smiled at us.

"This concludes," he said, "our first day at camp. I trust we're all relaxed."

His beret was gone. He wore a dark blue suit, a blue tie, a crisply starched white shirt with gold cuff links. His voice, too, had changed. There were no dropped consonants, no ghetto slurrings; it was the precise, polished voice of a corporate executive. Smoothly, referring now and then to notes, he outlined the program that lay ahead. He stressed its rigors. The idea, he said, was to stop a war, which would require certain skills, and certain qualities of a physical nature, among them stamina and strength and the capacity to resist hardship. "Resistance," he declared, "entails resistance." Then he discussed the particulars of Vietnam. It was a firsthand account, largely anecdotal. He talked about the effects of white phosphorus on human flesh. He talked about anatomy. He described the consequences of a foot coming into contact with the firing mechanism of a Bouncing Betty, the reds and whites, the greenish-gray color of a man's testicles in bright sunlight. He smiled at this, and winked. He leaned forward against the podium, adjusting his tie, and spoke quietly about a morning in 1966 when his platoon of marines had gone on a buffalo hunt in Quang Ngai province, how they'd entered the village at dawn, and burned it, and how, afterward, with the village burning, they had moved out into a broad paddy where the buffalo were—big slow water buffalo, he said, maybe a dozen, maybe twenty—and how the platoon had lined up in a single rank, as if on a firing range, and how without hunger or provocation the platoon had gone buffalo hunting—like the Wild West, he said, like Buffalo fucking Bill—how they put their weapons on automatic, M-6os and M-16s, how it was slaughter without aim, just firing to fire, pistols, too, and M-79s, and grenades, and how those slow stupid water buffalo stood there and took it broadside, didn't run, didn't panic, just *took* it, how chunks of fat and meat seemed to explode off their hides— how the horns exploded, and the tails and heads—but those ignorant damned buffalo, he said, they *took* it, they didn't make sound, and how there was the smell of a burning village and munitions and those buffalo that wouldn't run or die, just took it. Ebenezer paused and shuffled his papers. "That's the Nam," he said softly, "and it's unbecoming. I've seen my share of buffalo. And you folks—you nice folks have not seen shit. Understand me? You have not *seen* shit." There was conviction in the room. There was also, I thought, anger. Ebenezer Keezer folded his hands and smiled and went on to discuss evil. He was specific about atrocity and saturation bombing. The war, he told us, was a buffalo hunt, and we would be wise to disabuse ourselves of romantic notions regarding the propriety of peaceful protest and petitions of grievance. We were soldiers, he said. Volunteers one and all. It was an army. "Like in wartime," he said, and his smile was cool and pleasant. "When there's evil, you learn to absorb it. You build up your resistance. This here's buffalo country."

He studied his notes, then nodded at Tina.

"Young lady," he said, "front and center."

Tina moved to the podium.

Deftly, with the tip of his thumb, Ebenezer lifted her yellow T-shirt. "Yummy," he whispered. Tina's stomach was conspicuous under the white fluorescent lighting. Fish-colored, it seemed, bloated and pale and slightly bluish. She wore a white bra. Her breasts, too, were large, but Ebenezer ignored them.

He chuckled and dipped a finger into the belly fat.

"Now, then," he said, "let us discuss obesity. You porkers gross me out."

He grasped Tina's stomach with both hands.

"Piggies!" he said.

Tina squirmed but he held tight.

"Fatsos! Grease!"

Still smiling, Ebenezer bent down and put his mouth to her stomach and licked the flesh.

"Pigs!" he yelled. "Pigs and pork chops—I want to *eat* it! Gobble it up, all those good juices. Can I eat your fat, girl?"

Tina whimpered.

"Say the word, I'll definitely eat it. Yes, I will. I'll *swallow* it."

"No," said Tina.

"One bite?"

"No."

She tried to back away, but Ebenezer Keezer had her by the fat. Oddly, I found myself thinking about Mars bars, the relations between fantasy and gluttony. Eyes half shut, Ebenezer was nibbling at her belly.

"Oink!" he said. "Go oink, babe. Give me a piggy squeal."

"Oink," Tina said.

"Louder!"

"Oink!" she cried.

"Oooo, good! Oink it up!"

Tina oinked and wept.

Later, when it was over, Ebenezer's tone became philosophical. He dwelled on the need for physical fitness. Soldiers, he told us, are neither pigs nor pork chops. Resistance required resilience.

"For the next sixty days," he said, "you lardballs are my personal property. I say oink, you definitely oink. I say don't oink, you definitely abstain from oinking. Same applies with Nethro. We own you. Questions?"

There were no questions.

"Wunderbar," he said. "Sleep tight, kiddies. Tomorrow's a weird day."

That night, as in many nights, I indulged in fantasy. It was a means of escape, a way of gliding from here-and-now to there-and-then, an instrument by which I could measure the disjunction between what was and what might be. I imagined myself in repose beneath a plywood Ping-Pong table. I imagined my father's arms around me. I imagined, also, a world in which men would not do to men the things men so often do to men. It was a world without armies, without cannibalism or treachery or greed, a world safe and undivided. Fantasy, nothing else. But I pressed up against Sarah, stealing warmth, imagining I was aboard a spaceship sailing through the thin, sterile atmosphere of Mars, and below were the red dunes, the unmoving molecular tides, and I smiled and stroked Sarah's hip and whispered, "Bobbi." There was guilt, of course, but I couldn't stop myself. Stupid, I thought, all fluff and air, but then I remembered *Martian Travel*, and the grass, and the great calm as we flew high over the darkened seaboard of North America. I remembered that Leonardo smile—eyes here, lips there, the blond hair and soft voice. I imagined embarking on a long pursuit. Pick up the airborne scent and track her down and carry her away. A desert island, maybe, or the planet Mars, where there would be quiet and civility and poetry recitals late at night. Peace, that's all, just a fantasy.

Over the first month it was all physical fitness. Reveille at dawn. Formation, inspection, waving practice. Then down to the beach for warm-up exercises. "Move it!" they'd yell. "Agility! Hostility! Make it hurt!" And it did hurt. Even Sarah felt it, even Rafferty. It was the kind of hurt that comes to visit and rearranges the spiritual furniture.

Unreal, I'd think, but I couldn't ignore the pain.

There were jumping jacks, I remember. We ran and climbed ropes and took nature hikes at full speed. We learned to say "Yes, sir!" and "No, sir!" and little else. No use complaining, because the penalty was pain. There were push-ups and sit-ups and hot afternoons on the obstacle course. There was tear gas, too—I remember the sting. I remember Tina crying. All night, it seemed, she cried, and in the morning there was more pain.

"Maniacs," I told Sarah. "Psychosis. Deep in the crazies."

In the second week I came up hard against the barrier of self-pity. Here, I thought, was everything I'd run from. But you couldn't run far enough or fast enough. You couldn't dodge the global dragnet. The killing zone kept expanding. Reaction or revolution, no matter, it was a hazard to health either way.

Day to day, I did what I could. Arms and legs, just the bodily demands. The days seemed to skid by, and even now, looking back, I remember very little in the way of detail.

The fierce sun.

Mushiness in the extremities.

Ollie huffing, Tina straining under the forces of fat and gravity, Sarah's lip swelling up in reaction to the tropical heat.

I remember intense thirst. Intense hunger, too. Yearnings for Coca-Cola and the air-conditioned wonders of a Holiday Inn. America, I'd think, but this was somewhere else. We were tutored in hand-to-hand combat. We ran mock relay races up and down the white beaches. Often, at night, we were awakened and made to stand at attention against the courtyard wall.

"A good waver," Ebenezer Keezer told us, "is a rare cat in this day an' age. Everywhere I go, I see half-ass waves that don' truly emanate from the inner soul. A sorry commentary. Collapse of the social fabric, that's what it is."

"God's word," said Nethro. "Ebenezer and me, we just missionaries out to spread the wavin' gospel."

"Tell it."

"I did. I tol' it."

A sunny afternoon, and Tina Roebuck sat in the sand and folded her arms.

She did not move.

Squatting down beside her, Ebenezer Keezer frowned and said, "Oh, my. Tuckered Tina. El mucho fatigo?"

She did not move and she did not speak.

Ebenezer lifted her shirt, very gently.

"I'm famished," he murmured.

But even then she was silent. Arms folded, she gazed straight ahead, northward, where the sea curved toward the Straits of Florida.

Ebenezer pinched her stomach.

"Let me eat it," he said softly. "Be a good girl now, let me eat that yummy tummy."

But she did not move.

A drugged, dreamy expression. Her eyes were empty. It was the emptiness that follows upon surrender, and one by one it happened to all of us.

In mid-December, as we moved into our second full month, the curriculum turned increasingly technical. We learned the craft of crime: how to break and enter and spot surveillance and plant a bug and sweep a room and untap a telephone. The platitudes of felony, spoken straight, had the sound of wisdom. "Always travel first-class," Nethro said, " 'cause the law goes coach." There were many such maxims, lessons passed on from Jesse James. The best disguise is a crowd. The best weapon is brain-power. "In God we trust," said Nethro, "but don' forget to frisk him."

There was also a formal side to our training. Most evenings, after dinner, we would assemble in the lecture hall for a series of so-called political education seminars. Indoctrination, I suppose, but there was no haranguing; if anything, Ebenezer's presentations had a low-key, almost professorial quality. In one instance he outlined and analyzed the ideological underpinnings of the American Revolution. He reviewed constitutional doctrine and explicated key passages from the *Federalist* papers and the Virginia Statute of Religious Liberty. He reminded us that our republic had been born in disobedience, even terrorism, and that the faces which decorate our currency had once appeared on English Wanted posters.

"The line between sainthood and infamy," Ebenezer said quietly, "is the line between winning and losing. Winners become statues in public parks. Losers become dead."

There was a pause.

"Dead," he said.

Then another pause, longer, after which he smiled.

"*Dead*, children. Losers get embalmed. Our purpose here is to produce winners."

Over the course of those evening seminars, it became clear that both Nethro and Ebenezer were true professionals. They never preached or proselytized; there was no evidence of ideology. Combat veterans, of course—nothing theoretical. They were mechanics. Turners of nuts and bolts.

"A guerrilla-type war," Ebenezer told us. "Which means we take a page from our good brethren Uncle Charlie. No trenches, no battle lines."

"Tell it," said Nethro.

"Ghost soldiers. Invisible. Like in the Nam, we hit here, hit there, then beat sweet feet."

"Oooo!" Nethro said.

"During the day we wear our civvies. We melt away, we nowhere to be found. And then at night—"

"Ooooo!"

"At night we do our business. Slick little operations. In an' out, like surgery, then presto, we vanish, we *gone*. Nothin' but boogiemen. *Ghost* soldiers."

It was important stuff, I suppose, but I had a hard time digesting the implications.

Ghosts, I'd think.

Tombstones and cemeteries, all the consequences of ghosthood.

I wanted out.

A motivation problem, I told Sarah. Not enough mobility or

hostility. A shortage of spirit. Turned around, I said. I'd walked in blind, I hadn't understood the terms.

Sarah stepped out of the shower.

She toweled off, dusted herself with powder, examined her breasts in a mirror, and stood on the bathroom scale. One hundred and twelve pounds, but each ounce carried authority.

"Well," she said, "you're crawling up on a conclusion."

"Hard to say."

"Say it."

I wiped off a damp spot at the small of her back.

"Everything," I said. "Start with treason. And this boot camp thing—those two zombies. Like a death squad. Can't tell the good guys from the bad guys, they're all gunslingers. Completely scrambled. But it's lethal. I know that much, it'll kill somebody."

"Lethal?" Sarah said. She stood facing the mirror. Her skin was a glossy brown, freckled at the shoulder blades. I wanted to touch her but it seemed inappropriate. After a moment she turned. "Funny coincidence, William, but that's exactly what the folks in Da Nang keep saying. When the artillery comes down. Kaboom. Lethal, they say."

"Granted."

"Lethal times. Take it or leave it."

"Yes," I said. "Leave it."

"Walk?"

"Maybe."

For a moment she looked at me without expression. Then she smiled. It was a neutral smile, not angry, just dense with indifference.

"Sissy-ass," she said. "A sad case, man." She aimed a hair dryer at me. "Anyhow, you wouldn't last ten minutes out there on your own. What about cash? Connections? And this minor legal hassle with Uncle Sam—you guys had a date, remember?"

I nodded. "There are places I could go, maybe. Hibernate for a while. Wait for things to quiet down."

Sarah dropped the hair dryer.

"Fucking hibernate! *Animals* hibernate, people *act.* That's why we're here—to stop the goddamn *killing!*" She slapped her hip. "No lie, you amaze me. William the victim. Fuck conscience, fuck everything. Vietnam, you think it was cooked up just to ruin your day. That's how you *think*. All the big shots, all the world leaders, they got together at this huge summit conference, and LBJ jumps up and says, 'Hey, there's this sissy-ass creep I want to fuck over,' and Ho Chi Minh says, 'I got it! Start a *war*—we'll *nail* the son of a bitch!' A persecution complex. Almost funny, except it's so contemptible."

"My error," I said.

"Terrific. That's your only comment?"

"Not quite. I get the feeling we're growing apart."

We stood facing each other.

The shower curtain was bright red. There was some steam in the room.

Sarah turned away. "This conversation," she said slowly, "has outlived its utility."

If you're sane, you see madness. If you see madness, you freak. If you freak, you're mad.

What does one do?

I froze. Couldn't sleep, couldn't move my bowels. At night I'd roam the villa's hallways, thinking this: If you're sane, you're not completely sane.

By daylight, too, the bombs were real. Nethro explained the physics. He showed us how to make big bangs out of small household appliances. How to bait a booby trap and adjust the tension on a pressure-release firing device. All around us, for three days, there was the smell of cordite and gasoline.

Down on the beach, taking turns, we pitched grenades at mock enemy bunkers. We learned how to set up a Claymore mine—the angles of aim, a geometry lesson. If you're sane, I decided, you can calculate the effects of petrochemicals on bone and tissue. If you're sane, but only then, you understand the profundity of firepower.

"Blammo!" Ollie yelled.

Nethro folded his big arms. "Shit, man," he said softly. "You don' know shit."

But Ollie did know shit.

And Sarah, too, and Ned and Tina. They knew the whys and wherefores of deadly force.

So I froze.

It happened first on the weapons range, where I locked and loaded, taking aim, pressing my cheek to the rifle's plastic stock. I closed my eyes and drew a breath and squeezed the trigger. Then I froze. Full automatic—twenty rounds.

The rifle seemed to pick me up and shake me.

I heard myself squeal. I heard Sarah say, "Christ." Behind me there was laughter.

I tried to release the rifle—drop it, throw it—but I couldn't, because then the freeze came, and the panic, and I turned and watched the bright red tracers kick up sand all around me.

The black rifle kept jerking in my hands, I was part of the weaponry.

Then silence.

A soft, watery sound. The blue Caribbean, wind and waves, Sarah looking down and saying, "Christ."

I was smiling. I dropped the rifle and squatted in the sand.

"Audie fuckin' Murphy," Ebenezer said.

Ollie giggled.

Ned Rafferty put his hand on my head, just holding it there, and there was still that silence.

Strange, but I didn't feel shame. Emptiness and relief, but not shame. Later, when the jokes started, I thought: If you're sane, you don't feel shame. You feel helpless. You feel a stickiness at the seat of your pants. But not shame.

Rafferty helped me up.

"This development," said Ebenezer Keezer, "gives scared shitless a whole new meaning."

"Ain' roses," said Nethro.

"Let him be," Ned Rafferty said.

"Yeah, but that *smell*."

Rafferty held my arm and said, "Let him be."

And again that same night.

A final exam, Ebenezer called it. He was grading on the pass-fail system.

At midnight we formed up in the courtyard. We smeared our faces with charcoal. We wore black sweat pants and black cotton jerseys. On our backs and belts, we carried C-4 explosives, wire cutters, Claymores, blasting caps, fuses, electric firing devices, rifles, and rucksacks.

"Tonight," said Ebenezer Keezer, "we baptize the Christians. You people *will* get shot at. You will *not* commit messies in your shorties."

He looked directly at me.

"Shitpots," he said, smiling. "Regulation panty-poopers."

Nethro briefed us on the details.

A simulated commando raid. The object, he said, was to make our way across a two-hundred-meter stretch of open beach. To move with haste and silence. To attack and destroy a twenty-foot wooden tower that had been erected that afternoon. Along the way, he told us, we would encounter certain obstacles. Barbed wire and booby-traps and tear gas. Then he grinned and snapped his fingers. "Oh yeah, an' two machine guns. M-6os—live ammo." Nethro opened his hands in a gesture of reassurance. "No sweat, we aim high. Four feet, more or less. Just don' take no leaks standing up."

Then we moved out.

We crossed the tennis courts and followed Nethro down to the dunes.

The darkness was something solid. There was fog, too, which carried the scent of brine and seaweed, and the night seemed to slide beneath itself. Ahead, I could see the green phosphorescent glow of a wristwatch. I reached out and put a hand on Rafferty's rucksack and moved by touch. If you're sane, I thought. Then I laughed and thought: Ghosts.

"Hush," Rafferty said. "Cerebral slack, man, just spin it out."

The starting line was a shallow trench in the sand. Quietly, we knelt down to wait. There were spooks in the dark but I imag ined I was elsewhere. Mars, maybe. A deep cave. I breathed from the bottom of my lungs. Forty minutes, a full hour, then the fog lifted and I could see moonlight on barbed wire, the outline of a rickety tower two hundred meters up the beach. No panic, I thought. Just this once, I would perform with dignity. I would not wail or freeze or befoul myself.

There was movement in the dark.

"On your bellies!" Nethro called. "Stay flat, kiddies!"

At the far end of the beach there was a sharp splatting noise. A green flare exploded high over the tower.

Rafferty tapped my arm.

"Stick close," he said. "I'll run the interference."

Behind us, Nethro fired up a flare and yelled, "Hit it!" and we were moving. Sarah went first, then Ollie and Tina and Rafferty. Nethro kicked me and said, "Anytime, darlin'."

The first twenty meters were easy. Up and over, out of the trench, snaking motions, part wiggle, part crawl, rifle cradled across the elbows. I was a commando now. Anything was possible. Push-glide, no thinking. Off to my right I could make out the peaceful wash of waves where the sea touched land. Dignity, I thought, then I said it aloud, "Dignity."

When we hit the first wire, Rafferty used his cutters and mo tioned for me to slip through.

We bellied forward.

"Easy," Rafferty said, but it wasn't easy. There was confusion, and my rucksack caught, and I felt a cool slicing sensation on my forehead. Concertina wire—looped and tangled—and when I twisted sideways I was cut again at the neck and cheek.

A white flare rocketed up over the beach.

There was a soft whooshing sound and then the guns opened up. Red tracer rounds made edges in the night. "Move," Rafferty said, "just *move*." But the wire had me. High up, almost directly above us, another flare puffed open, and the two machine guns kept up a steady fire. A game, I reminded myself, but then I flopped over and watched the red tracers unwind through the dark. That much was real. The guns were real, and the flares and muzzle flashes. No terror, just the absence of motor control. I felt Rafferty's big arms around me, and then came a clicking sound, and we rolled through the wire.

I pressed my face into the sand. I found myself posing foolish questions. Why were my eyelids twitching? Foolish, but why?

Later, when I looked up, Rafferty was gone.

I lay flat and hugged my rifle. It was all I could do, hug and twitch. Gunfire swept the beach. This, I deduced, was how it was and had to be. If you're sane, if you're in command of the present tense, you dispense with scruples. You recognize the squirrel in your genes. You sprawl there and twitch and commit biology.

The night whined with high velocities.

Lazily, I got to my hands and knees. It occurred to me that the danger here was mortal. A tracer round ricocheted somewhere behind me—blue sparks, a burning smell—then a succession of flares lit up the sky, yellow and red and gold, and for a moment I seemed to slide back to the year 1958, a balmy night in May when I jerked up in bed and waited for the world to rebalance itself. I was a child. A Soviet SS-4 whizzed over my head. Far off, the earth's crust buckled and there was the sizzle of a lighted fuse. The sky was full of pigeons. Millions of them, every pigeon on earth. I watched the moon float away. There was horror, of course, but it was seductive horror, even beautiful, pastels bleeding into primaries, the radioactive ions twinkling blue and purple, the pink and silver flashes, charm mixing with childhood.

If you're sane, I thought, you come to respect only those scruples which wire to the nervous system.

I surprised myself by crawling forward.

It was a crabbing kind of movement, without dignity. I heard myself saying, "Sorry," then saying, "Stop it!" Squirrel chatter. I was thinking squirrel thoughts: There is nothing worth dying for. Nothing. Not dignity, not politics. Nothing. There is nothing worth dying for.

I reached a miniature dune and stretched flat. The guns kept firing, raking the beach, swiveling left to right and back again.

Nothing, I thought.

A tracer round corkscrewed over my head. I was twitching, but the twitches were strictly amoral. I was lucid. I understood the physics: If there is nothing, there is nothing worth dying for.

I blinked and looked up and swallowed sand. There were no ethical patterns. Ahead was another tangle of barbed wire, and beyond the wire was more wire, then flat beach, then the two droning machine guns. There was fog, too, and tear gas, and familiar voices. In the distance, Ebenezer Keezer was shouting through a bullhorn, "Life after Lenin! Revolution, people! Ollie-Ollie in free!"

Then amplified laughter.

Briefly, near the tower, a human form rose and took shape against a yellow flare. Sarah, I thought, and I scrambled forward. Gunfire snapped close by. "Please," I said, and lunged into the wire. The pain surprised me. I was bleeding from the nose and lips. The tear gas was heavy now, and the tremors took hold, but I clawed through the wire and rolled along the beach and whimpered and thought: Nothing. The thought was perfectly symmetrical, because if there is nothing, there is nothing worth dying for.

I sobbed and listened to Ebenezer Keezer's bullhorn laughter. He was engaged in philosophy.

"Terrorism," he shouted, "is a state of mind! A state of mind is a state of bliss! Extremism in the pursuit of bliss is no bummer!"

There was a harsh electronic squeal. A lavender flare exploded without sound. The guns were on automatic and the night shimmied in bright greens and reds.

Odd, but I also heard music.

Out on the margins, Buffalo Springfield was singing . . . *a man with a gun over there . . . tellin' me I got to beware.*

The bullhorn buzzed and Ebenezer cried, "States of mind! States of bliss! Down with the states!"

With effort, I detached myself.

It all seemed fanciful, the mix of guns and rhetoric, the Bea-

tles now insisting on revolution. Belly-down, I crawled toward the
sea.

"Ain' no mountain high," Ebenezer sang.

I bled from the lips and nostrils. Numerous clichés came to
mind. Missing in action, I thought. Lost in space. My gyro had
gone, I couldn't locate the scheme of things, but I kept moving
until chance brought me to the fringe of the sea.

It was the maximum reach. This far, no farther.

I composed myself in a respectable posture, faceup, heels sea-
ward, hands folded at my belly, and I lay back and watched the
lights.

"Day-O, Day-O," Ebenezer sang, "dee daylight come an' I
want to go home."

A dud flare fizzled overhead.

Tracers skipped across the Caribbean, toward Miami, and the
sound track had become sentimental. Mellow music, smooth and
wistful . . . *Those were the days, my friend, we thought they'd
never end.*

"In time of terror," Ebenezer declared, "there is no objection
by means of conscience. There is no alternative service."

I didn't budge.

I watched the sky do sleight of hand. Awesome, I decided,
miracles of form and color. Dangling from its parachute, a nearby
flare sailed upward against gravity. The twin machine guns kept
firing their steady fire, and Mary Hopkin sang persuasively in the
dark, achingly, *we'd fight and never lose, those were the days, oh
yes . . .*

The bullhorn crackled.

"Hide an' go seek," Ebenezer cried. "You're it, shitpot. Peek-
aboo! I see you!"

His inflection carried mockery, but it wasn't enough to make
me move. I had strong convictions. There was nothing worth
dying for. Not for this, not for that. If you're sane, you resign
yourself to the tacky pleasures of not dying when there is nothing
worth dying for.

I knew my limits. I also knew my heart.

Up the beach there were battle cries. I heard Sarah shouting out commands. She had the knack, I didn't.

"Too bad," I said, but I didn't move.

Again there was that time-space slippage. I was back under my Ping-Pong table, under layers of charcoal and soft-lead pencils, and all around me, inside me, there were those powdery neural flashes lashing out like heat lightning. I watched it happen. The equator shifted. New species evolved and perished in split seconds. Every egg on the planet hatched. And then my father was there, holding me, saying, "Easy now, take it slow, tiger." He rocked me and said, "It's okay, it's okay." I could smell the heat of his armpits. "It's okay," he said, "just a dream," but it wasn't a dream, and even then, even now, there was still the glowing afterimage, the indelible imprint of things to come.

I am not crazy, I told myself. I am sane.

Gunfire swept the beach. The music now was martial, piccolos and snare drums. Ebenezer Keezer was doing impressions.

He did Groucho and Martin Luther King.

"Shane!" he cried. "Shane! Shane!"

It was coming up on a finale. A dozen quick flares made the sky tumble, and the machine guns kept firing and firing.

I pressed low into the sand.

"The darkest hour," Ebenezer intoned solemnly, "is just about now. But bear in mind, people, you'll find a jive light show at the end of the tunnel."

He did Woody Woodpecker and LBJ and Porky Pig.

"This is your life," he said. "Terror tends to terrorize, absolute terror terrorizes absolutely. Th-th-that's all, folks!"

A dull explosion turned me over.

When I looked up, the wooden tower seemed to be reconstituting itself. A second explosion blew away the tower's foundation. The structure stood legless for an instant, then toppled sideways and burned. "Fire in the hole!" Ollie Winkler shouted. Fine, clean work, I thought. And in the future, no doubt, there would be other such operations, the Washington Monument or the Statue of Liberty.

Immediately the gunfire eased off. A final flare colored the circumstances in shades of violet.

"Terrorism," Ebenezer Keezer declared, "is the subtraction of the parts. Back to zero."

Then I began digging.

I scooped out a shallow hole at the edge of the sea and slipped in and carefully packed wet sand against my legs and hips and chest. I apologized to my father. I jabbered away about the flashes and pigeons and sizzling sounds, and my father said, "Sure, sure," and he was there beside me, with me, watching me dig. I told him the truth. "There's nothing to die for," I said, and my father thought about it for a time, then nodded and said, "No, nothing." His eyes were bright blue. He smiled and tucked me in.

"Am I crazy?" I asked.

"That's a hard one."

"Am I?"

There was a pause, a moment of incompletion, but he finished it by saying, "I love you, cowboy," then he bent down and kissed my lips.

Pass or fail, so I missed graduation. I spent nine days cooped up in a hospital on the outskirts of Havana. The diagnosis had to do with acute anxiety, a stress reaction, and I was too canny to argue. I lay low. There were nurses, I remember, and they were sticking me with sedatives. But I was fine. I recited *Martian Travel* in my head. I carried on dialogues with Castro and Nixon, offering sage advice and psychological support. I urged caution above all else. If there is nothing, I told them, then there is nothing to kill for, not flags or country, not honor, not principle, for in the absence of something there is only nothing.

I had a firm grip on myself. On occasion I felt a sudden lurching in my stomach, as if a trapdoor had opened, and at night I dreamed barbiturate dreams—gunfire and flares. But I played it cagey. I didn't cry or carry on; I gave up speech; I smiled at the nurses and watched the needles without fear or protest. If you're sane, there's no problem.

I thought about escape.

I contemplated suicide.

No sweat, though, because I was on top of things.

I was released in mid January 1969. A week later we were back in Key West.

Things were the same now, but different.

"Believe me," Sarah said, "I'm not making judgments."

"Of course not."

"You understand?"

"Yes," I said, "pass or fail."

It was early morning, and we were having coffee at the kitchen table. The house had a stale, musty smell.

"No rough stuff," she said. "Strictly behind the lines. A courier maybe."

"Fine."

"Different thresholds, different boiling points. It's not a criticism."

"Sure, I know."

"William—" Her eyes skittered from object to object. She finished her coffee, stood up, and smiled. "So then, a passenger pigeon? Lots of exotic travel. Maybe Rio. Glamour and beaches, all those tight brown bodies. You can scout it out. Make reservations for after the war."

"Fine."

"Rio," she said, "it's a date."

I nodded and said, "Fine."

Which is how we left it.

Bad luck, I never made Rio. But for the next two years, while Sarah and the others pressed the issue, I found some peace of mind in my capacity as a network delivery boy. I was out of it. On March 6, 1969, when the Committee pulled its first major operation—a night raid on a Selective Service office in downtown Miami—I was buckled in at thirty-two thousand feet over the Rockies, heading for a pickup in Seattle. By all accounts they acquitted themselves well. Four days later, when I checked into my hotel in San Francisco, there was a message from Sarah: "I'm famous. *Newsweek*, page 12. I'm wanted."

10

Quantum Jumps

"**I**F I WANTED TO," Melinda says, "I could bust out of here."

"How?"

"Simple Simon."

"Go on, then, tell me. It's a dare."

She laughs. "Don't be so condescending. I mean, God, if I *told* you, then it wouldn't *work*."

"True."

"I'm not a dunce," she says.

Another laugh, then I hear a clatter behind the bedroom door. Midmorning cleanup—dishes being stacked, the transfer of waste products. It's all part of our new domestic order.

Stooping down, humming *Billy Boy*, I open up the service hatch at the foot of the door.

"Ready in there?"

"Just hold your horses," Melinda says, "it's not like we're going anywhere."

I smile at this. A fair statement: No one's going anywhere. It's a lockup. For two weeks now, nearly three, we've been living under conditions of siege at these bedroom barricades—an investment, so to speak, in the future—and the service hatch, though small, has functioned quite nicely as a means of communication and supply, a lifeline of sorts. I'm proud of it. It's a brilliant piece of engineering: a rectangular hole in the door, nine by twelve inches, wide enough to permit the essential exchanges, narrow enough to deflect foolish thoughts of flight. As an extra safeguard, the hatch is fitted with its own miniature door and lock—a door within a door.

Melinda's face appears at the opening. She slides out a tray piled with dirty breakfast dishes. The chamber pot comes next.

"Yunky to the max," she says.

"Yunky?"

"It means *stink*." She gets to her hands and knees and stares out at me. "Anyway, I could do it, you know. If I wanted to, I could escape easy."

"Oh, sure, absolutely."

"You don't think so?"

Her face is framed by the opening. Behind her, near the bed, I can see Bobbi's bare foot tapping out the meter to a poem in progress.

Melinda's eyes shine.

"Okay, here's a question, smartie," she says. "What if I got sick or something? You'd *have* to let me out. If I caught some disease like—you know—like that time I had my stupid tonsils out. Then what?"

Bobbi's foot stops tapping. This intrigues her, I can tell.

"Well," I say.

"So then what? What if I said, 'Daddy, I'm *dying*'?"

I smile at Bobbi's curled toes.

"I guess you'd be fibbing, princess."

"Well, sure," she says, "but how would you *know*? I could cry and scream and stuff, just like this—" She makes a twisted face and shouts, "Agony! Polio!"

Bobbi's toes stiffen.

"Agghh!" Melinda yells. "Can't breathe! God, I'm choking!"

"Knock it off."

"Help!"

Her face goes red. She jerks sideways and rolls out of my field of vision. Ridiculous, but I feel some discomfort. "Agghh!" she cries. And then it's instinct—I reach through the hatch and grope for contact.

"God," Melinda says, "talk about gullible." She reappears at the hatch. "You get the idea now? I could *do* it, couldn't I?"

"Maybe so."

"Not maybe. I scared you."

She wiggles her nose and says, "Agghh!" and then laughs. What are the limits? I wonder. What can be done? Such love. That cool, unblemished skin of hers, it makes me question my own paternity.

"So you see how it works," Melinda says. "Get sick, that's one plan, but I've got about six zillion *better* ones. I mean, boy, if I had to, I could—" She pauses, rubbing her eyes. There's a tentative quality in her voice when she says, "Daddy, what if I *did* get sick? I mean, really sick? It's not impossible."

"Nothing is."

"But what if?"

"Too iffy," I tell her.

"You're afraid to answer, aren't you?"

"Melinda, I can't—"

"You're afraid."

I shrug and try to finesse it, but she knows where I'm vulnerable.

"Tell the truth," she says. "You'd at least take me to the hospital, wouldn't you? You wouldn't just sit there and let me die?"

"Never, baby."

"Never what?"

"Can't happen that way."

"*What* can't?"

"You know," I say softly, "it can't happen."

"You're afraid."

"Not that."

"Afraid," she says.

For a few moments we just gaze at each other. Her eyes are like one-way mirrors; she sees out, I can't see in. If it were possible, I would end it here. I would break down the door and take the consequences.

Melinda knows this, and keeps pressing.

"If something happened to me," she says, "something real bad, it'd be like murder almost. Kidnapping your own family, keeping us prisoner, it's like . . . What if there's a fire? We couldn't even get out, we'd burn up in here, and it'd be just like murder."

"Sweetheart, don't talk that way."

"Why not?"

"Just because."

She wags her head sadly. "Because you're afraid. Because stuff can happen, like fires and stuff, or else you might blow me to smithereens with dynamite."

"Melinda, don't—"

"Murder," she says.

It's no use.

What all this represents, ultimately, is an erosion of the traditional family structure. Cohesion and trust, we've somehow lost it. A little faith, for God's sake—why can't they see the obvious?

Quietly, I close the hatch and secure the lock.

"Loony!" Melinda shouts, but I walk away.

I do the dishes, make coffee, empty the chamber pot, set out a pound of hamburger to thaw for dinner. Murder, though. It eats at me. I think about Sarah and Tina and Ned and Ollie, all that wasted blood, and the thought makes me squeamish. I'm no killer, I never was, I never had that terrorist nerve.

Besides, what about love?

Good intentions?

I'm saving their lives. An act of mercy. The year, after all, is 1995, and we're coming up on the millennium.

I return the chamber pot and change clothes and then trudge out to the hole. For a time I just stand at the edge. I've been at it nearly three months now, April to July, and the results are gratifying. Nineteen feet deep, twelve feet square. No need to justify. The hole speaks for itself. *Dig*, it says. At times I'm actually cowed by its majesty. It has a kind of stature—those steep walls plunging to shadow, the purity of line and purpose, its intangible holeness. There it *is*, you can't dismiss it. It's real.

Be safe, it says.

It says, *Survive.*

I'm not losing my marbles. Just a hole, of course, and when it speaks I rarely listen.

I know better.

Down the ladder, grab my spade, go to work. A hot day, but the earth smells cool and moist. I'm at home here. This is where it ends. *Hey, man,* the hole whispers. *Here's a riddle: What is here but not here, there but not there?* Then a pause. "You," I say, and the hole chuckles: *Oh, yeah! I am the absence of presence. I am the presence of absence. I am peace everlasting.*

There's a giggling sound, high and crazy, but I don't give it credence.

Discipline, I think. Mind and body. I work steadily, pacing myself. The key to progress, I now realize, is gradual accretion, routine and rhythm; that's how monuments get built. Today it's mostly a repair job. There was a light drizzle during the night, barely enough to dampen the grass, but it produced a thick coat of slime at the floor of the hole, slick and treacherous, and smelly, too, as if a toilet had backed up, and for the first hour I concentrate on tidiness. I'm alert to the possibility of a cave-in. Carefully, I check the four granite walls for signs of stress, those hairline fractures that can cause conclusion. You never know. Two weeks ago I was fortunate to be topside when a quarter-ton boulder sheared off along the north wall. It taught me a lesson: You can die saving yourself. Even safety entails risk. Which was the upshot of a poem Bobbi slipped through the service hatch a few days later. *Backflash,* she called it, and even now several lines still stick with me—

> *Here, underground, the flashes*
> *are back, filaments of history*
> *that light the tunnels*
> *beneath the mind*
> *and undermine the softer lights*
> *of love and reason.*
> *Remember this*

as though in backflash:
A bomb.
A village burning.
We destroyed this house
to save it.

There's more—it was one of her longish efforts—but I'm spared by a faulty memory. To my own ear, at least, there's something rather glib about the way those metrics goose-step off the tongue. Bad poetics compounded by bad logic.

How does one respond?

With tenacity and daring. Spit on the hands and bend down and put muscle to it.

Dig. Nuclear war.

If you're sane, you don't fuck with the obvious. You know what MAD means. It means there is nothing to live for. Which means bedlam. So who's crazy? True or false: The world can end. Multiple choice: Fire or ice or nuclear war. The realities are with us, Pershing and Trident and the kitchen sink, it's all throwweight, it's buried nose-up under the flatlands of Kansas and North Dakota. A radical age requires radical remedies. The *world*, for Christ sake—biology!—so don't call me crazy. I'm digging. You're diddling. You, I mean. The heavy sleepers. The mealymouthed pols and hard-ass strategists who talk so reasonably about containment and deterrence. Idiots! Because when there's nothing, there's nothing to deter, it's uncontained.

Sane, I think. I've got it together.

The hole snickers and says, *Sure, man, you're straight as an arrow.*

I nod.

At noon I rig up a charge of dynamite, crouch behind the tool shed, hit the button, wait for the dust to settle, then begin the hard chore of piling the debris into pulley baskets and hauling it to the surface. When in doubt, dig. Abnormal, yes, but what's the alternative? Plan a dinner party? Chalk it up to the existential condition? If that's normal, I'm proud to call myself deviant.

Reality, it tends to explode.

I've got eyes. I can see.

I've got ears. I can hear.

And because I'm sane, because I can imagine an unpeopled planet, because life is so precious, because I've seen the flashes, I am willing to recognize the facts for what they are, pared to the bone, unrhymed and unmusical.

Is it uncouth to speak plainly?

Nuclear war—am I out of key with my times? An object of pity? Am I comic?

Here, now, digging, my wife and daughter locked away, the hole egging me on, am I crazy to extrapolate doom from the evidence all around me, Minuteman and Backfire, a world stockpiled with 60,000 warheads? Are the numbers too bald, too clumsy? Am I discreet to say it? Nuclear war.

If you're sane, you're scared; if you're scared, you dig; if you dig, you deviate.

If I could—

You can't, the hole says. *If you could, but you can't. Keep the faith—you're my main man.*

"Right," I mumble.

Speak up!

"Right," I say.

The hole laughs.

Oh, yeah, you'll show 'em, brother. When the shit comes down, they'll sing a real different tune. Amazing grace! Sweet melodies! Your wife's a grasshopper, man—you and me, we're the ants. Yo-ho-ho and a bottle of blood! Ding dong bell! Pussy's gone to hell! Can you dig it, man? Can you truly dig it?

There's a quaking sound. The granite walls seem to shrug.

Dig, dug, dead! Bobbi's in her bed!

I'm perfectly calm. I ignore the chortling.

At two o'clock I knock off for the day. A cold shower, fresh clothes, then I sit down to prepare a shopping list. When it's finished, I rap on the bedroom door.

"Get lost," Melinda says.

"I am."

"What?"

"Nothing." I bend down and open up the service hatch. Melinda's hair is in curlers. She lies on the floor, belly-down, peering out at me with the smartest eyes on earth.

"Well," she says, "I guess you're here to kill me."

I treat it as a joke.

I smile and tell her I'm heading into town—is there anything she needs?

"Poison," she says

"Anything else?"

She thinks for a moment. "Yeah," she says, "I could use a new *father*."

"Sure, princess. I'll see what I can do."

"A *good* one this time. Get me one that's not so goddamn screwy."

The swearing disturbs me but she's out of spanking range. I tighten my smile and tell her to check with her mother.

"Final call," I say. "You want it, you name it."

Melinda slides away. Through the open hatch I can hear the soft tones of Bobbi's voice; it's a blond voice; the voice of art, or the inexplicable mysteries of art; the voice of a flight attendant, calm and calming in the high turbulence. The words, of course, don't register. The meanings don't mean. Like the grass she once gave me, like her poetry, Bobbi's voice is pure timbre. She doesn't make sense.

Still, I can't help listening. In a way, she's right, the meanings don't matter, it's the voice that counts.

But why would she leave me?

Why a separation?

"Hey, you," Melinda says, "wake up."

She passes a slip of notepaper through the hatch, a requisition in my wife's neat, left-leaning script: mouthwash, asparagus, Raisin Bran, olives, gin, vermouth, spaceship, husband.

It tickles me.

"Yes," I say gently, "I love you, too."

Outside, as I hook up the Chevy's battery, I'm feeling

pinched and out of touch. A little dizzy. Anything can happen. Eventually, given time, anything will happen.

No guts, no glory.

I fasten my seat belt and honk twice and point the car toward town. It's a twenty-six-minute drive, all downhill, and I let my mind unwind with the road, curling west along the spine of the Sweetheart Mountains, through rock-collecting country, the canyons and shaggy stands of birch and pine, then south to the foothills which open into meadow and dusty ranchlands, then straight west to Fort Derry. Off to the left, beyond the new K Mart, I can see the grandstand and floodlights at the fairgrounds where my father used to die—once too often; he no longer dies. At the east edge of town I cross the railroad tracks and turn down Main Street. Here, nothing much has changed. My father's real estate office is under new management, but otherwise the year could be 1958. Slowly, just tapping the accelerator, I cruise down a corridor of hitching posts and weathered storefronts, past the courthouse and the Strouch Funeral Home and Doc Crenshaw's little clinic at the corner of Main and Cottonwood. The old fart won't let loose. Over ninety now, and he's out of the doctoring business, but he hangs in there like the town itself, cantankerous and stubborn. He doesn't know his days are numbered. No one knows.

Grasshoppers! the hole hisses. *The wolf is at the door! These jerks don't know the score!*

I pull into the parking lot behind Gordy's Piggly Wiggly. I'm exhausted. A strange spinning. For several minutes I lean forward against the steering wheel.

"Christ," I groan, but the hole tells me to snap out of it.

Sin and din! Lemme in! Not by the hair of my chinny-chin-chin! Time to pay the piggy!

Odd thing, but I'm dealing with disorder as I do the grocery shopping. Some sorrow, too.

I can't find the fucking Raisin Bran.

Entropy and dissolution, it's all around us.

I want to loot this place. But I don't. I smile at the stock boys and fill my cart with imperishables. Powdered milk for Melinda's teeth. Frozen carbohydrates and vacuum-sealed proteins. Asparagus, olives, mouthwash. I know what I'm doing. I'm a sly fox. And the hole says, *You betcha, you're no dummy. Just look at these assholes—smug motherfuckers! Don't know doom from canned goods. Nitwits! They think it's a joke. Can't happen, they think. Won't happen. Ding dong doom!*

It requires some effort, but I locate the Raisin Bran.

Who's crazy?

Who's lost whose perspective?

Not you, the hole says. *You're a sharpie. This little piggy went to market. Those little piggies perished.*

In the checkout line I'm all business, cool and sober.

Higgily wiggily bang!

I don't pay attention. The mental operations are strictly rote. Later, after I've stashed the groceries in the car, I check my lists and then cross the street to the Coast to Coast store.

I go down the agenda item by item.

One electric drill. One crowbar. Two sleeping bags. Two hammocks. Rope. Nuts and bolts. In a moment of inspiration I do some impulse buying—four strings of outdoor Christmas lights from last winter's stock.

Up front, at the cash register, a young clerk gives me a wise-ass smirk. He looks at his calendar and says, "Smart decision, sir. Only six more shopping months."

"Time flies," I tell him.

The kid grins. "Plan ahead—I'll bet that's your motto, right?"

The question contains a subtle commentary, but I show him my brightest smile. Plan ahead, I think. If the poor cocksucker only knew.

"Merry Christmas," I say.

The next part is difficult.

I hate to contemplate what might go wrong. Love, it's my only defense. Purity of mind and motive. Outside the drugstore I stop to give it some final thought, then I shrug and walk in and present my prescription. My voice sounds reedy. It's like listening to myself on a tape recorder, that same distance and surprise, unexpected squeakiness in the higher registers, but I keep up a running banter while the pharmacist does his duty. Not a decent night's sleep in weeks, I tell him. The man makes sympathetic noises and sends me away with a month's supply of Seconal.

Not murder, I tell myself.

I won't hurt anyone. A legitimate means to a noble end. Time capsules.

The idea, simply, is to live forever.

Next the liquor store—vermouth and gin—then down to the A&W for a quart of root beer.

The ride home is smooth. I lean back and floor it. If there were any other way—*Hush*, the hole says, *just go with the rhymes. High diddle diddle.*

"They'll thank me," I whisper. "When the time comes, they'll wake up and thank me."

Yeah, tiger, when they wake up. You bet your life.

It's a gorgeous afternoon, windless and warm, cattle grazing under a yellow sun, not a cloud, wheat and wildflowers growing in patches along the road. Here is the world-as-it-should-be. A constant universe. Harmony among all things, unchanging, without dynamic, just the unaging ages.

From now on it's all black holes.

Twenty miles later, when I pull up the driveway, I'm feeling clearheaded. I remove the Chevy's battery, hide it behind the tool shed, then lug my purchases into the kitchen. The house seems undisturbed. For a few seconds I stand there, watching bits of dust play in the late-afternoon window light. It's a house at peace—the drowsy hum of deep July. I put the groceries away and move to the bedroom door.

"Hey, Flub-a-dub," Melinda says, "is that you?"

"Safe and sound, baby."

"Too bad. Thought you might get arrested." Laughter rattles up against the summer quiet. Melinda's tone is aggressive when she says, "So did you *buy* me anything?"

"Lots," I tell her.

"Like what?"

"Raisin Bran. Asparagus. All kinds of stuff."

"Wonderful."

"And root beer."

"Root beer," she mutters, but I can tell she's tempted. There's a pause. "All right, then, I'll try some, but you can't bribe me. Pretty soon I'll have to do something drastic." Another pause, then a squeal. "Agghh! Can't breathe—I'm a *goner!*"

"Good show, kiddo. Very impressive."

She snorts and says, "Okay, I'm thirsty now."

In the kitchen I become a chemist. A martini for Bobbi—a double, no holding back—a tall root beer for Melinda. I break open six sleeping pills, sprinkle in the white powder, stir gently, taste for bitterness, wipe my forehead, top off the glasses, and carry them on a tray to the bedroom door.

Radical times, radical remedies.

There is only the slightest hesitation before I open the hatch. "For you," I say.

And then, for perhaps an hour, I lie flat on the hallway floor. I smoke a cigarette. I pay heed to the passing shadows.

A fleet of bombers circling over Omaha.

A burning safe house.

A planet lighted by glowworms and fireflies.

As if through Chuck Adamson's toy telescope, faraway yet close, I see my father's scalp floating in a punch bowl, my mother weeping at graveside, all the dead and dying, Tina and Ollie and Nethro and Ned, and there is no one left to grieve.

Outside, but also inside, the hole rumbles—

I am Armageddon.

I am what there is when there is no more. I am nothing, therefore all. I am the before and after. I am the star which has fallen from the heavens. I am sackcloth, the empty promise, the undreamt dream, the destroyer of worlds.

"Safe?" I ask, and the hole chortles and says, *You bet your booties! That, too—I am safe.*

When dusk comes, I make my way to the backyard. The stars

are out; the night is receptive. At the horizon, a crescent moon climbs over the mountains and the laws of nature insist: *Now*.

I strive for objectivity. Lucid, yes, and tingling-alert, but vertigo intrudes as I descend into the hole and begin rigging up the two hammocks. Familiar presences appear—Sarah's silhouette flowing along the south wall, my mother and father holding hands in the dark. Rattling sounds, too, and a voice I can't quite place until I realize it's my own. "No sweat," I'm saying. Then Sarah calls out to me—"Please!" she screams. But I concentrate on the operations at hand. Bolts into rock—ropes—attach the hammocks—lay out the sleeping bags. A deep breath. Step back. Survey the arrangements. A pity, I think, that the shelter will go unfinished, without roof or creature comforts, but for now I've done all I can.

"William!" Sarah shouts.

It's unreal, though, like everything.

I climb the ladder and stand for a moment at the rim.

If I could, I tell myself, I would find another way. If I were a believer, if the dynamic were otherwise, if we could erase the *k* factor, if Fermi had failed physics, if at the nucleus of all things we might discover an inviolate, unbreakable heart.

The hole groans at this.

Poetry! Hop to it, man! Time is short, can't abort! Holy night! Dynamite! What a sight!

Reluctantly, I go back to work. I string up the new Christmas lights in the trees and shrubs, along the roof of the tool shed, and when I push the switch, the backyard swirls in brilliant greens and reds and blues. I'm in awe. The night seems touched by something supernatural.

And now, the hole whispers. *The family hour.*

I return to the house with my crowbar and drill.

The bedroom door can't stop me. Board by board, I tear down the two-by-fours. I plug in the drill and blow away the lock in a single shot.

I'm in tears when I lift Melinda from her bed.

"Daddy," she slurs.

Her eyes come partly open, a lazy blink. She has no weight. Warm and flannel-smelling, she curls against me and says, "What's happening?"

"There, now," I say.

"Where's Mommy?"

"Right here, baby. We're all together."

Melinda's eyelids flutter. "Daddy?" she asks, but she's sleeping.

I press my cheek to hers. I feel powerful. My daughter, I think, and I cradle her in my arms and carry her down the hallway and through the kitchen and out to the hole. I'm strong. I'm capable of anything. A one-arm hold, then down the ladder—it's easy—and I zip her into a sleeping bag and kiss her and place my fingers at her throat and smile at the steady pulse, then I take her to a hammock and tuck her in and say, "Sleep tight, princess."

And now Bobbi.

It's a struggle but I manage it. She doesn't wake. She's a poet. Two arms this time, with great care, down the ladder face-forward as if descending a steep staircase. Risky, but it's a time of risk. The night is deep and mysterious, and there is no limit to man's appetite for atrocity.

I place Bobbi in her hammock, kiss the soft lips, then climb the ladder and pull it up after me. "Done," I say, and the hole belches and falls silent.

And here at the edge I sit down to a nightlong vigil. The Christmas lights give me courage. I will not compromise; I'll defend what I have. The moon is out and the stars are stable, and below, in the earth, my wife and daughter sleep without nightmares, and all around us there is the blessing of stillness and safe repose.

If I could, I would join them.

I would slip into a sleeping bag and let the epochs take me down. If it were reasonable, if it were only sane, I would give credence to the proposition that ours is a universe without beginning or end, that mortality itself is relative, that the dead never die.

If it were believable, I would believe.

I would have faith. I would take my family from this hole in the conviction that we might live happily upon the earth. I would fly the flag and pooh-pooh the prophets. Yes, I would.

But the hole chuckles at me.

If you could, it says. *Too bad, though, because you know better. Dynamite! Blow my mind! Fission, fusion, critical mass!*

I shake my head.

"No," I say.

Ain't no sin to lock 'em in! T minus eight, the century's late! Dynamite, man!

"No," I say firmly. "Never."

The hole widens around me, I can smell its breath.

Higgily wiggily doom!

11

Fallout

O VER A TWO-YEAR PERIOD, from early March 1969 to late April 1971, I logged something on the order of 200,000 miles in my capacity as a network passenger pigeon. Shuttle diplomacy, Sarah called it. Hectic but safe: Wake up in Key West, eat breakfast over the Gulf, do business in Tampa, fly on to New Orleans, make my pickups and deliveries, see the sights, then hop a night flight for Denver or Chicago. Typically, I'd be on the move for a week at a time—mostly college towns—and then back to the Keys.

In theory, I suppose, it might've seemed a decent way to spend the war. "Mr. Jet Set," Sarah liked to say. "Join the revolution and see the world."

But it wasn't that rosy.

What she didn't understand, and what sometimes gets lost in my own memory, is that constant tickle in the backbone, the Herb Philbrick sweats. I could never relax. Even during the most monotonous times I'd find myself tensed up and waiting, imagining a knock at the door, then a cop asking questions.

It was a delicate daily balance. Betrayal, informants, random accident. The variables were complex.

I was on the run, after all.

Implausible, I'd often think, but my crimes were punishable by lock and key. The draft was one problem. Contraband was another. Routinely, even on the easy campus runs, I was ferrying hot goods through hot channels: money, of course, and the various ways and means of un-American activity.

The situation required vigilance.

Whom to trust? How far? How often?

Early on, I established certain SOPs and then stuck to them without exception. I avoided strangers. I took my meals alone. I dictated the terms for all transactions. If a drop looked questionable, if instinct instructed caution, I'd simply walk away and go about the tedious chore of setting up new arrangements. Granted, paranoia was a factor, but when you're deep in the shit, you can't help turning slightly anal.

Loneliness, too. Clerks and bellhops and crowded lobbies, but no human intercourse.

And also exile. It sounds trite but I longed for America. Out on the fringe, alone, there wasn't a day when I didn't feel a sense of embarrassment nudging up on shame. Unhinged and without franchise, prone to odd daydreams, I had trouble sleeping. I'd get the midnight chokes. I'd sit on my bathroom throne and close my eyes and ask, "Where am I?"

Two years, but they were long years.

1969—Jane Fonda was on the stump and Kissinger was calling trick shots and Hoffman and Rubin and Dellinger were raising hell in public places. In Vietnam the American troop presence peaked at 540,000, and in Paris the peace talks idled along from hour to hour with high formality, many limousines, frequent adjournments for tea.

At home there was riot gas. It had come now to fracture.

In August a small bomb exploded in a janitor's closet outside the offices of a Manhattan draft board; in early September a somewhat larger bomb caused untidiness in a Houston National Guard armory. Headlines, of course, and deadlines, and three weeks later, on September 24, a consignment of two hundred M-16 automatic rifles disappeared at a truck stop along Interstate 84 near Hartford.

I was on the road at the time of these events, but it was no surprise to find a celebration in progress when I reached Key West on the evening of September 28. There was cheap wine and laughter. At the appropriate moment Sarah led us up into the attic and pulled back a canvas tarp to display the goods.

"What you see before you," she said, "is the product of man's search for meaning."

The guns were still sealed in plywood crates bearing the Colt logo. At the rear of the attic, where the eaves narrowed, twelve cases of ammunition were lined up neatly along a bare wooden beam. There was the faint smell of oil and carbonized steel.

"Disarmament," said Ollie Winkler. "No treaties or nothin', we just flat-out disarmed the fuckers."

"Unilateral," said Tina.

Ollie blushed and smiled at her fondly. "Smart lady," he said.

Ned Rafferty was silent.

This, I surmised, was where it had to go. The future was firepower. Obliquely, half smiling, Sarah looked at me as if waiting for some secret acknowledgment—a sign of conviction, perhaps—then she shrugged and covered the guns.

"What this calls for," she said, "is ritual."

Tina produced champagne and we sat on the attic floor and passed the bottle. To me, it didn't mean much, only late-hour collegiality. I was out of it now. They were fine as friends but it was hard to show enthusiasm when Tina described the hijacking operation: How it had gone like tick-tock—like shoplifting, she said—Ebenezer and Nethro had set it up—a map and a timetable and duplicate keys—a cinch—hop in the truck and drive away.

Tina laughed and shook her head.

"Broad daylight," she said, "that's the amazing part. This Howard Johnson's, you know, real clean and friendly, traffic zipping by, and we just take off with the ordnance. Put it in gear and wave bye-bye."

"Simple," said Ollie. "Unilateral piece of cake."

There was obvious pride and good feeling. Later, when the champagne was gone, we went out for ice cream and then sat drinking at an outdoor café along the waterfront. The night was tropical with stars and a warm wind. I was tired but I listened attentively while Sarah brought me up to date on current events. There was movement now, push alternating with shove. It had gone beyond mere protest.

"The guns," I said, "I suppose that's one indicator."

"I suppose," Sarah said.

"They don't stay in the attic?"

"No," she sighed, "probably not."

Behind us, a jukebox was playing old Temptations and people were getting up to dance.

Sarah yawned and kicked off her sandals and arranged her feet in Ned Rafferty's lap. Her hair had been cropped Peter Pan style, tight to the head, and she was wearing yellow camp shorts that called attention to the shapely integrity of her legs. There was distance between us. Opposite extremes, I thought. The conclusion was foregone—she had her code, I had my own—but even so I felt some sadness.

After a moment Sarah smiled.

"Anyway, don't fret about it," she said pleasantly. "You play possum, we'll handle the politics. No objections, I hope."

"I guess not."

"But?"

I watched her feet move in Rafferty's lap.

"But nothing," I said, "except it seems a little out of proportion. Those guns. I keep thinking people could get hurt."

"Hurt?"

"Just one opinion."

Sarah glanced across the table at Tina. "Hurt, he thinks. He's got opinions."

"I heard," said Tina.

"No scruples, lots of opinions."

"Sad boy."

"No doubt," Sarah said, "very sad."

Ned Rafferty seemed uncomfortable. He looked down at Sarah's pink toenails, then shifted in his chair and examined the night sky.

Ollie and Tina got up to dance.

For a time things were quiet. Sarah picked up her glass and drained it and rattled the ice. Not drunk, I thought, but close. Her eyes had a hazy, indefinite shine.

"Just one item," she said thickly. "Those guns you're so worried about, you know where they were headed? Here's a hint—not Iowa. Not South Dakota. Guess where."

"I know where."

"Oh, you know. That's the bitch, man, you really *do* know. That's the sin. Right and wrong—real perceptive. Bombs and jets and shit, you know it all. But there's this neuter problem. Huff and puff but you can't get it up—conscience-wise, pecker-wise—can't perform. Just can't. You *know* but you *can't.*"

"Whatever you say."

Sarah nodded and reached for Rafferty's glass.

"Neuter," she murmured, "that's what I say. Emasculation Proclamation."

"All right, then."

"*Not* all right. That people-might-get-hurt bullshit—dead wrong. Go count the bodies, check out the stats, then tell me who's hurting who. Mull it over for a while. Ask yourself this: What's it like to have Congress with a jellyfish?"

I folded my hands and said, "Fine."

Sarah laughed.

"Fine, fine," she mimicked. "Bury your head, it's always fine." She turned unsteadily toward Ned Rafferty. "I've said my piece. Anything to add?"

Rafferty kept his eyes down. It occurred to me that he wasn't entirely unsympathetic. All evening, especially up in the attic, he'd been watchful and silent. A jock, to be sure, but he was no gunman.

"Final thoughts?" Sarah asked.

Rafferty tried to smile.

"No," he finally said, but gently, as if to suggest apology. "I guess that's pretty much the gist of it."

He wiped his forehead with a napkin and looked straight at

me, not without kindness, then shrugged and stood up and took
Sarah's hand and led her toward the music.

Too bad, I decided. They made a handsome couple. Fluid and
fitting. Partners in dance and crime and bed. That was the kicker.
The ultimate gist—just too damned bad.

There was nothing to be done.

I left some cash on the table and took a short walk up Duval
Street and headed back to the house. Endings, I thought. It
seemed conclusive. I sat up reading for a while, then turned off the
light, but the various gists kept accumulating.

The kinetics, too.

Escalation: G-forces and dizzy spirals. Ho Chi Minh was
dead. Others were dying. In the Republic of Vietnam there was
the weekly butcher's bill to pay. There was demolition and priva-
tion. There was duplicity. In New York, before the General As-
sembly of the United Nations, Richard Nixon spoke eloquently of
peace, of raising a "great cathedral" to the human spirit, but even
then, in Cambodia, the secret bombs were falling on the secret
dead. What was unknown could not hurt us, yet somehow it did
hurt. There was uncommon distress. Buildings were burning.
Harsh words were exchanged. Autumn 1969—the scheme of
things had come undone—councils of war, guns in the attic.

I was in it, yes, but I was not part of it.

I just watched.

On the first day of October, my birthday, Ebenezer Keezer
and Nethro flew in for a daylong planning session. The meeting
convened at 10 a.m. around the kitchen table. I kept my distance,
of course, serving coffee, washing the breakfast dishes, but even so
I heard enough to feel the dynamic at work. I remember the
sounds of shuffling chairs and a briefcase snapping open, the sing-
song inflection in Ebenezer's voice when he said, "Hurricane season," pausing a beat before smiling—"Stormy climate, kiddies,
that's what the Weatherman tells me."

He was wearing tweeds and sunglasses, a crimson tie loosened
at the neck. A professor's voice, I thought, cool and well waxed as

he analyzed recent developments—a situation report, he called it—stressing the convergence of certain historical factors. His smile was steady. "The Feds and the Reds," he said lightly, "they're on a collision course. We just aim to lend a helping hand."

Nethro grunted at this.

"No bullshit," he said. "Let the good times roll."

Ebenezer glanced across the table at Sarah, who nodded, then at Ned Rafferty, who looked away. I tried not to listen. I scoured the frying pan and hummed *Happy Birthday*, pretending I was back home again, my father outside raking leaves, my mother in the bedroom wrapping gifts. October, I thought, a splendid month, but then I was listening again. Knockout time, Ebenezer was saying. He discussed the meaning of moratorium—how it derived from the Latin, as in dilatory. His tone was contemplative as he talked about a pending coast-to-coast mobilization. The pieces were in place, he said. A nationwide coalition. Parades and pickets and fireworks of assorted caliber. The general thrust, he explained, would be nonviolent, but there was always room for maneuver.

Tina Roebuck looked up from the banana she was peeling. Her skin was sallow, her eyes small and beady.

"Maneuver," she said, "you mean guns?"

"A possibility," said Ebenezer.

Tina nodded. "You don't do shit with parades. Guns, that *does* it. People tend to notice."

Ebenezer crossed his legs professionally.

"Guns," he said, smiling. "Now there's a thought."

I'd heard enough.

When the dishes were done, I excused myself, moved out to the living room, and turned on the television. I was feeling a little fuzzy. The midmorning fare of game shows seemed wanton and ill conceived—mostly static—happy winners and plucky losers, prizes for everyone. It all rang up as tragedy. There were automatic weapons in the attic, and out in the kitchen my colleagues were discussing crimes against the state, but here on the magic box was a contestant in a clown suit squealing over an Amana self-cleaning oven. Where was the rectitude? And where, I mused, did comedy spill over into sadness? Hard to impose clarity. No theorems, no proofs. Just a war. And the clown-suited contestant bounced and danced in claim of a brand-new self-cleaning oven. Passions were stirred—laughter and greed, the studio audience found it amusing—and Bob Barker rolled his eyes, winningly, as if to absolve: Here it is, America, the fruit, the dream, and the price is right.

Happy birthday, I thought. Johnny Olsen's deep baritone: William Cowling—*come* on down!

Curtain Number One: Rio! Cha-cha-cha!

Curtain Number Two: Shine on, William! A trip to the *moooon!* Samsonite luggage and deluxe accommodations along the unspoiled shores of the Sea of Tranquillity— Shine on!

Curtain Number Three: Hold tight now, because here it is— You'll never *die!* That's right! Never! A blond stewardess and the northern lights and life ever after. It's all yours . . . *iffff* the price is right!

But no consolation prizes.

Which made it hard. Risky choices, and if you guessed wrong the real-life game left you unconsoled.

I closed my eyes and dozed off.

At noon, when they called me in to prepare lunch, the table talk had turned toward acrimony. The issue, apparently, was guns. Tina and Ollie favored force, Ned Rafferty was urging restraint. At the head of the table, his eyes behind sunglasses, Ebenezer Keezer seemed to be enjoying the democratic ironies.

Tina's face was flushed.

"Nobody ever *listens* to me!" she was saying. "Fat Tina, stupid Tina. I'm *not* stupid, though, I've got *brains.*"

"Look," said Rafferty, "I didn't—"

"You *did.* Ridiculous, you said, I heard it, you said fucking *ridiculous.*"

"The guns, I meant. The shoot-'em-up stuff."

Tina crushed a napkin in her fist.

"There, you see? Nobody pays attention. I didn't say anything about shoot, I never once *said* that. I said action. Action, that's all I ever said."

"Gun action," Rafferty muttered.

"And so?"

"So I object." He looked warily at Ebenezer. "This quick-draw business. I don't go for it. The rifles, they're just a symbol, right?"

Tina hooted.

"Symbols," she said fiercely. "What about Nixon? Our chief executive, he doesn't *grasp* symbols. Power. That's all he grasps. Just power. Symbolize all you want—sit on your ass and sing *If I Had a Hammer*—but I'll tell you something, somebody has to drive home the *nails.*"

Ollie Winkler clapped.

"Nails! Beautiful!" He got up and circled around the table and ran a hand through Tina's thin greasy hair. Lovebirds, I thought. I could imagine their children: midgets and Mars bars. "Pure beautiful," Ollie said. "Isn't she beautiful?"

"Charmer," said Nethro.

Ollie eased his fingers down the slope of her neck. "Nails, baby—say it again."

"Nails!" Tina said.

Nethro yawned and said, "Fun couple."

For two or three minutes the only sounds were my own, clanking plates and silverware.

Then Rafferty pushed his chair back.

Very gently, almost in a whisper, he said, "No guns."

He started to add something, but stopped and tapped the table with his fingernails.

I admired him. Go for it, I thought. Curtain Number Three.

I sliced the sandwiches and laid them on a platter.

After a moment Rafferty pushed to his feet.

There was no movement in his face when he looked down on Ebenezer Keezer.

"The guns," he said, "stay in the attic."

"That so?"

"It is."

Ebenezer lounged back in his chair. His eyes had a lazy, hooded quality.

"My friend," he said politely, "take a seat."

"No, thanks."

"Be cool, child. Sit down."

"No," Rafferty said, "I don't believe I will. If you want, we can settle it right here."

Ebenezer kept smiling.

I delivered the sandwiches and went back for the mustard and mayonnaise. The price, I was thinking. You play, you pay. I admired him, and I wanted to say something, but it wasn't my game.

Rafferty's eyes were flat. He seemed perfectly at ease.

"I'm serious," he said. "No gunplay."

"Or else?"

"However you want it."

"Oh, my."

"Right here," Rafferty said. "You and me. We settle it."

Ebenezer seemed delighted. He stroked his tie and removed his sunglasses and winked.

"Violence," he said mildly. "Love to oblige. Real pleasure, in fact."

Rafferty shrugged.

"Pleasure an' honor," said Ebenezer. He glanced at Nethro. "Me, though, I'm nonviolent."

"Peacenik," Nethro said.

"God's word. The nick of peace."

Even then Rafferty did not move. Briefly, his eyes swung in my direction, but I busied myself with the coleslaw and potato chips.

There was a dead spot at the center of the kitchen.

"That'll do," Sarah said.

"I just want—"

"Point taken, Ned. We hear you." She reached out and put her hand on Rafferty's waist. "Let's just table it."

"The guns. I need an answer."

"Ned—"

"Yes or no," he said. "Do they stay in the attic?"

Sarah shrugged.

"The attic. For now."

"And later?"

"Don't press it," she said, "later's later." She looked over at me and made a motion with her free hand. "Let's do food."

No problem, I served the sandwiches.

It wasn't heroism or cowardice. Just noninvolvement: potato chips and coleslaw and iced tea.

After lunch I did up the dishes and slipped out the back door. Nowhere to go, really, so I hiked down to the plaza off Mallory Square and sat watching the gulls and sailboats. The first of October, approaching tourist season, and the Key was crowded with youth and polyester. Things seemed very clean. There was a war on, but you wouldn't have known it, because there were happy faces and jugglers and shrimp boats and enterprising girls in halters and flowered skirts, blue sky and blue water, everything so pretty and polished and clean.

At midafternoon I drank a beer under one of the umbrellas at the Pier House.

Happy birthday, I thought.

Then I thought about Sarah and Rafferty. The signs were obvious. Sad, but there it was. They made a splendid match. I thought about the various comings and goings of age, how nothing ever lasted. Not romance. Nothing. I called the waiter and had another beer and then circled back to the house and sat on the porch and listened through an open window while my comrades mended fences.

I wasn't a party to it.

At one point I heard Rafferty say, "All right, it's settled. We don't play with guns."

I heard Tina Roebuck whine.

"Same old bullshit," she was saying. "Tina-do-this, Tina-do-that, but who ever *listens* to me? Dumb fat ugly Tina. Here's a fact, though—I've read my Chekhov—and if there's a gun in the story, it better go bang at the end. Better happen. Sooner or later."

I heard Ebenezer's mellow laughter.

"Tell it," he said. "Sooner or later."

"Nobody *listens*."

"No matter, girl. Just keep tellin'."

That night, while the others were out dancing, I baked a cake and opened a bottle of brandy and celebrated my birthday alone.

By midnight I was riding a chocolate high. I proposed toasts to my health and prosperity, to the stellar flight crews of Trans World Airlines. I was drunk, no doubt, but I was emotionally solvent. I retched and had a nightcap and fell asleep on the sofa.

It was a bouncy sleep, in and out. There was turbulence and disorder. "Fire!" someone screamed.

Late in the night I heard a door slam. Voices rose up, and then footsteps and darkness and silence again.

Nethro draped a blanket over me.

His face was calm and kind, almost brotherly. He put a hand on my forehead and held it there.

"Rockabye, babe," he whispered. "Don' mean nothin'."

Then I was back in the turbulence.

"Fire!" someone yelled, and I dreamed the attic was burning. There were projectiles in the dark. Intense heat and gunfire. Holes opened in the walls and ceiling, then other holes, and the wallpaper curled and burned. I smelled flesh. I heard Tina calling the fire department, but the line was busy, and the attic crackled with red tracers and flame. "I'm dead!" Sarah screamed. She leaned out a window and screamed, "I *told* you so! I'm dead!" The house was unsafe. Smoke and calamity. Tina crawled into a burning refrigerator. Ollie Winkler danced on the roof, which was also burning, and Ollie danced and burned along with it. "Dead!" Sarah cried. She was gone from the window—the glass was burning and the beams and timbers were silver-blue like bones lighted by X ray— but even then, though the fire had her, Sarah was still yelling,

"Dead!" I couldn't move; I was snagged up in long rubber hoses. "Alone!" she screamed. There were fire trucks now, and helicopters, and firemen wearing armored vests and silver badges, but the firemen were firing fire at the fire, it was cross fire, and the hoses hissed and shot fire, and Sarah screamed, "Dead!"

The sirens woke me up.

For a long while I lay there waiting for the dream to burn itself out. Not foresight, I thought. Just a preview. It was nearly dawn when I made my way to the bathroom. No sirens, and no smoke, but I could still feel the heat.

I showered and brushed my teeth and moved down the hallway to Sarah's bedroom.

I undressed without thinking.

Outside, there were morning birds, slivers of pink light playing against the curtains, and when I slipped into bed, softly, trying not to wake her, Sarah curled alongside me and smiled in her sleep, her arms bare, the soles of her feet cool and dry, and after a time she turned and came closer and said a name that wasn't mine.

It didn't matter. I knew anyway.

"No," I said, "just the birthday boy."

In the morning there was little to say. By fortune I was scheduled to fly out that afternoon, and at one o'clock I finished packing and called a cab.

We were adult about it. At the front door Sarah handed me my itinerary, and we smiled and said our goodbyes, and even hugged, but when the cab pulled up she decided to tag along out to the airport. It was a pleasant eight-minute ride. She wore white shorts, and her feet were bare, and I noticed how nicely engineered the heels were, so narrow and elegant, and the unshaved legs, the ankles and arches, the exact relations among the toes. These details seemed important.

At the boarding gate, we sat in plastic chairs and made grown-up conversation.

I wished her luck with the moratorium.

Sarah rubbed her eyes.

"The truth is," she said, "I did send out signals. Distress and so on. It isn't as if I didn't warn you."

"Often. You did."

"Your own damned fault."

"I understand."

"All those years, William, but you were never really there. Not totally."

"And he was?"

"Oh, yes. Yes, he was."

Again, briefly, her hand went to her eyes. There was the need to simplify things.

"Do you love him?" I asked.

"Such a question."

"Do you?"

"Love," she sighed. "Who knows? He cares about me. And he's present. No qualifications."

"Noble of him," I said. "A nice guy."

"Yes, that, too. He sticks. Completely there."

I nodded. "Wonderful, then, he sticks, that must be a great satisfaction. Do you love him?"

"I get by."

"That's something, I suppose."

"It is. Quite a lot, in fact."

"Happy you," I said.

When my flight was called there was a moment of regret and bitterness. My own fault, though. I kissed her lightly on the forehead and walked down the ramp, then came back and kissed her on the lips and said, "I'm sorry," which were the truest words I'd ever spoken.

It was the era of Vietnamization. The war, we were told, was winding down, peace through transfer, and to date our government had turned over to the ARVN more than 700,000 rifles, 12,000 machine guns, 50,000 wheeled vehicles, 1,200 tanks, and 900 artillery pieces. For some, however, it was not enough. President Nguyen Van Thieu proposed that the United States equip his nation with a modest nuclear capability. Others disagreed. Among them, Senator George McGovern took a fresh look at his options, and Senator Charles Goodell was legislating in behalf of final withdrawal. Others disagreed violently. Viet Cong flags flew over Sioux City. In Chicago, Judge Julius Hoffman presided over a discomposed courtroom, and in the streets, within shouting distance, the Weathermen went hand to hand with riot cops. There were gag orders and troop deployments. It was the year of upsets, and at the World Series, Gil Hodges and his fabulous Mets took Baltimore up against the center-field wall.

In Quang Ngai, the monsoons had come.

There were footprints on the moon.

Ronald Reagan governed California.

The Stones sang *Let It Bleed.*

On October 15, 1969, the moratorium came down on schedule. I checked into a Kansas City motel and watched it on television with the help of Magic Fingers. I'm not sure what I felt. Pride, on the one hand, and rectitude, but also a kind of heartache.

Big numbers—

In Boston, 100,000 people swarmed across the Common. New York City, 250,000; New Haven, 40,000; Des Moines, 10,000 plus tractors. At Whittier College, and at Clemson, and at a thousand other schools, you could hear the National Anthem mixing with hymns and folk songs and services for the dead. There were oratorical declarations by Hollywood dignitaries. Church bells, too, and torches and suspended commerce and pray-ins at national shrines. Wall Street was wall-to-wall with citizenry; the Golden Gate Bridge was stopped to traffic. At the University of Wisconsin a crowd of 15,000 carried candles and umbrellas through a heavy rain. At UCLA, 20,000. At Chicago's Civic Center, 10,000. In Washington, with a bronze moon over the White House, 50,000 constituents came with flashlights to petition their chief of state for peace.

Around midnight I went out for a hamburger. I played some pinball, took a short walk, and returned to the room.

It was hard to find the correct posture. I thought about the flow of things. Ping-Pong to Chuck Adamson to Peverson State, and also Sarah, her culottes and letter sweater, and now the guns, and how you couldn't nail down the instant of turn or change but how small actions kept leading to larger actions, then the inevitable reactions. The late-night CBS wrap-up showed Lester Maddox singing *God Bless America*. In Sacramento, Ronald Reagan talked about the perfidious nature of the day's events, which gave "comfort and aid to the enemy," and in the nation's capital Barry Goldwater and Gerald Ford harmonized on the grand old themes. Then came a closing collage: the American flag at half-staff in Central Park, a graveyard vigil in Minneapolis, Eugene McCarthy reciting Yeats, Coretta King reciting Martin Luther King, 30,000 candles burning in the streets of Kansas City.

I couldn't sleep.

I slipped my last quarter into the Magic Fingers and lay there in the twentieth-century dark. It was all kindling. "Save us," I said, to no one in particular, just to the forces, or to the 39,000 dead, or to those, like me, who needed Magic Fingers.

When the time expired, I picked up the phone and called home. It seemed appropriate. The ringing itself was a kind of shelter. That soft, two-beat buzz—like a family voice, I thought, indelible and yet curiously diminished by the phonics of history and long distance—older now, depleted and somewhat fragile. I lay very still. I pictured my father's Buick parked in the driveway; I could see the shadows and reflections of household objects: a chrome-plated toaster in the kitchen, windows and mirrors, the old rubber welcome mat at the front door. Silhouettes, too, and familiar sounds. The doorbell chiming off-key. The way the refrigerator would suddenly kick in and hum. Home, I thought. The shapes and smells, all the unnoticed particulars.

My mother answered on the seventh ring. Her voice was low and sleepy-sounding, not quite her own. I didn't speak. Eyes closed, I pictured her face, how she would frown at the silence, that impatient squint when she said, "Yes, hello?" I wanted to laugh—"Guess who," I wanted to say—but I held my breath and listened. There was a long quiet. I could see her wedding band and the veins running thick and blue along the back of her hand. I could hear the kitchen clock. Long-distance sounds. I imagined a tape recorder turning somewhere in the dark, a tired FBI agent tuning in through headphones.

Then my mother's voice. A hesitation before she said, "William?"

I was silent. I held on a few seconds longer.

"William," she said.

Then she repeated my name, several times, without question, softly yet absolutely.

"It's you," she said. "I *know*."

Like sleepwalking, the inertial glide.

I spent Thanksgiving in a Ramada Inn near Reno. On Christmas Eve I treated myself to oyster stew at a Holiday Inn outside Boston. My goals were modest—to stay unjailed, to keep the biology intact.

Crazy, I'd think.

On New Year's Day 1970, a new decade, I built a snowman in the parking lot of my motel in Chicago. Then I went haywire. I butchered it. I committed murder. I gouged out the eyes and smashed the head, and when it was done I took a shower and washed off the gore and lay in bed and watched the Rose Bowl.

Stability was a problem. You could only keep running for so long, then the odds caught up and you got mangled like a snowman.

If you're sane, I thought, you're fucking crazy.

Over the dreary months of January and February I performed my duties and nothing more. Inertia. Town to town: I delivered the mail and watched my step and looked for a way out. I focused on routine and ritual. Once a week I'd get a haircut. Twice a month I'd receive an envelope containing expense cash and a typed itinerary. Now and then I'd find a short note from Sarah. *Be well*, she'd write. Or she'd write: *William—I feel unwanted.*

In March there was no note at all.

In April she wrote: *I miss you. It hurts. Whatever happened to Rio?*

In May I began looking for Bobbi.

Madness, I realized, had now become viable. Fantasy was all I had. Something to hang on to—that one-in-a-million possibility—so I went after it.

Passively at first, then actively.

In airports, between flights, I stationed myself near the Trans World gate area, a stakeout, sitting back and scanning the crowds for blue uniforms and blond hair. Impossible odds, I'd think, but even so I'd feel a tingle at each arrival and departure. I'd listen for her name over the airport loudspeakers. Bobbi, I'd think. I'd rehearse bits of dialogue. Sure, I'd tell her—obsession—imagination—but those were my great assets. I knew how to dream. I'd win her over. Yes, I would. I'd recite *Martian Travel* from memory. I'd charm her with love and practicality. Money was no problem—I knew where the money was, it was in the rock, it was there in the Sweethearts to be found and dug up and spent without thought of consequence—I'd buy her furs and perfumes, whatever the ore could buy, and we'd have a family, and the world could go to hell, but we'd go in style, we'd live as others live, in fantasy, happily.

In mid-May I began making direct inquiries. There was little to go on, a first name and a vague description, but luck was the governing factor—a TWA flight, Denver to Salt Lake.

I picked up the trail at thirty-two thousand feet.

"Bobbi," the stewardess said, and she looked at me with grave eyes. "Sublime smile? Lots of rhythm?"

"It sounds right," I said.

The woman shook her head.

"Pity," she murmured. "This way."

She led me down the aisle to the galley area. We were somewhere high over the Rockies, a fresh spring sky, and there were troops in Cambodia and ceremonies at Kent State, but it didn't mean a thing to me. The stewardess mixed a pair of drinks and motioned for me to sit down in the last row.

She lighted a cigarette and blew smoke rings at the ceiling. Her name tag said Janet.

After a time she sighed.

"Bobbi Haymore," she said. "The Skywriter, we called her. Bobbi the Haiku Haymore. Let me guess—she pinned a poem to your shirt?"

"Coat."

"Coat, then. Fill in the blank."

"Haymore?" I said.

"Like Hey-more. Care less. Not my favorite person." She took out a pen and wrote down the name for me. "The golden bard. Very mystical. Those poems of hers, she'd pass them out like peanuts. Passengers loved it. Especially male types. You, too, I suppose."

"Yes," I admitted, "she had an effect."

"The full treatment, no doubt?"

"Not a treatment. She was—it's hard to describe—she was completely *there*. No qualifications."

The woman nodded. "I've heard it before. A spiritual experience."

She snuffed out her cigarette.

"All right," she said slowly, "let's see if I can set the scene. A night flight, I suppose. Very cozy. Dark cabin. Soft voice. Classy legs. Martini or two. Sound familiar? This leads to that, lots of spirituality. Next thing you know you're getting the complete unabridged works, sweet and sexy. A day later you find a sonnet pinned to your undies. I miss anything?"

"Grass," I said.

"I'm sorry?"

"Just grass, it came with the poem. She said it expressed her deepest feelings for me."

There was a pause.

"Yes, well," the woman said, "I think we're obviously talking about the same person."

For a time I was silent, just reflecting. I watched the passing atmosphere. It occurred to me that the events of imagination are never easily translated into the much less pliant terms of the real world. Too damned inflexible, I thought, but then I shrugged.

"So," I asked, "how do I find her?"

The stewardess grunted.

"Sucker," she said. She pulled a tube of lipstick from her handbag and dabbed grimly at the corners of her mouth. "Listen, I know the girl. I *crewed* with her. Tone-deaf little tramp. Doesn't *talk* to people—she *recites*. That so-called poetry of hers—rushing tides and dappled dunes—garbage, you know?—but the guys, though, they all fell for it, they just ate it up. Putrid. Men, they're all suckers."

She turned and half smiled at me.

"All I want," she said, "is to help. Forget it, that's my advice."

"Well, thanks."

"A word to the wise."

"I appreciate it," I said. "Where is she?"

The stewardess closed her eyes and leaned back. Her smile seemed bitter.

"Bailed out," she said. "The great blond beyond."

"In other words—"

"Departed. Thin air. Ran off with some navigator. New York, I think. Hey-more. Care less."

"Navigator?"

"Andy Nelson. Cute guy. Sucker, though."

"For sure," I said gently, "aren't they all?"

I borrowed her pen and jotted down the name Andy Nelson.

The facts came slowly, but in the end I had what I needed. Back in the early fall, Bobbi had retired to pursue her muse full-time. Grad school, apparently. A creative writing program at Columbia or NYU—New York City, that much was certain. The navigator had gone along for the ride.

I studied my notes. Sketchy at best, but at least there were options.

"Last warning," the stewardess said, "she's a bloodsucker, she'll eat your heart out. Crush it, I mean. Drain it dry."

I smiled and said, "That's the risk."

In Salt Lake I changed my travel arrangements.

Go, I thought. Curtain Number Three. There was time for a cup of coffee and then I was airborne again.

Fallout

The next few days were chaotic.

In New York, I took a room at the Royalton and started making calls. The phone book listed thirteen Haymores, no B's or Bobbis, but I tried anyway. No luck, just bad tempers. I spent a restless, tumbling night, and the next morning I was up early. Alarming developments on the *Today* show: the Kent State aftershocks. There was violence in Little Rock. In St. Paul, 80,000 people stormed down Summit Avenue, and there was public mayhem in the streets of Philadelphia. It was epidemic. Arson in Tallahassee, a bombing at Fort Gordon. Surreal maybe, or maybe not, but I imagined the Committee's contribution to all this. Sarah calling shots, Tina quoting Chekhov. I could hear Ollie Winkler's squeaky giggle: "The chef and the terrorist—they're finally cooking!"

No matter, though. I was disengaged. I turned off the television and closed the curtains and began dialing.

At Columbia, the registrar had no record of a Bobbi Haymore. I tried NYU, then Brooklyn College, then several others. All dead ends. At noon I went out for a walk down Sixth Avenue. Vaguely, without dwelling on it, I realized I was chasing air. Bobbi, I'd think, but the name was more than a name. Its meaning—the crucial *meaning*—was like grass. She was real, yes; the hair and the eyes and the voice; but the reality was also an emblem. "Bobbi," I'd say, which meant many things, possibility and hope and maybe even peace.

A pipe dream, I knew that.

But the future is always invented. You make it up out of air. And if you can't imagine it, I thought, it can't happen.

I ate a hearty lunch.

Afterward I returned to the room and opened up the phone book: N this time, as in Nelson or navigator. The trick was confidence. There were eighteen Andrews, five Andys, but I hit it on the second shot.

"Bobbi?" he said, as if puzzled.

Then he laughed.

There was some belligerence before he sobbed and hung up on me. I gave him ten minutes and tried again.

It was not a cheerful conversation. Mostly silences, then quick gusts of misery; the man was obviously navigating without charts or compass. Split, he said. She'd walked out in January. Left him for a poet-translator named Scholheimer. Scholheimer, he said bitterly—big-shot Nazi. Very famous. Her teacher at NYU. Admired her poetry—midnight office hours—claimed she had promise. At the word *promise* there was weeping and the man excused himself and dropped the receiver. In the background I heard a toilet flush. Ditched, I thought, and I pictured a 727 floating belly-down in the mid-Atlantic, the navigator strapped in and struggling, much panic, Bobbi smiling and waving and paddling toward the horizon in a bright yellow life raft.

I tried not to take pleasure in it. I wrote down the data on a note pad: Ditched. Scholheimer. Nazi. NYU—question mark.

Later, I commiserated as best I could. Sad, I told him. A general ungluing of things. It was the fundamental process of our age: collapsing valences and universal entropy.

Then I cleared my throat and asked where to find her.

No luck at NYU, I explained. Urgent business—I had to make contact.

The man blew his nose.

"You, too," he said.

"Not necessarily."

"No?"

"Just urgent. A personal matter."

"Personal," he said. "I'll bet."

He laughed.

There was a conspiratorial, almost friendly note to his voice when he said, "Fuck you."

It didn't matter. The last act was easy.

Scholheimer: only one listing.

There was no answer all afternoon but I enjoyed the dialing. That was the *pleasure*. A kind of pre-memory, dialing and listening and anticipating the rest of my life. "William," she'd say, instantly, without hesitation.

And then what? A dinner date. An Italian restaurant. Pasta and checkered tablecloths. Quiet talk. A ferry ride past the Statue of Liberty. A twinkly night sky. She'd smile and hold my arm, not clinging, just holding, and she would nod with full understanding when I confessed to the possibility of madness. I'd tell her everything. I'd start with the year 1958, when I first went underground, that night in May when I grabbed my pillow and blankets and ran for the basement and slept the one great sleep of my life. "Am I crazy?" I'd ask. I'd tell her about Chuck Adamson and the Cuban missile crisis and unevacuated bowels. I'd look her in the eyes and ask it bluntly: "Am I crazy?" Everything. Exile, dislocation, Key West, the events at Sagua la Grande, flares and tracers and guns in the attic. "How much is *real?*" I'd ask. "The bombs—are they *real?* You—are *you* real?" Quietly, in graphic detail, I'd tell her about ball lightning striking Georgia; I'd tell her about a Soviet SS-18 crossing the Arctic ice cap, how I could actually see it, and hear it, but how no one else seemed to notice, or if noticing, did not care, how no one panicked, how the world went on as if endings were not final. "Am I crazy?" I'd ask. All afternoon, as I dialed and waited, I worked my way through the scenarios. A rooftop bar with piano music and dim lighting. The way we'd dance, barely moving. Her steady blue eyes. Then a taxi ride through Central Park. The clicking meter. Her hand coming to rest on mine. I imagined rain. There would be rain, yes, and umbrellas and fuzzy yellow streetlights and the sound of the taxi tires against wet pavement. And she'd smile at me, that secret smile, which would give me the courage to suggest a lifelong commitment. I'd ask her to save my life. I'd say, "Bobbi, I'm crazy. But *save* me." And she'd listen to all this with grace and equanimity. At the Royalton we would no doubt undress and move to the bed and lie there listening to the rain. Maybe sex, but maybe not. And then later, near dawn, I would issue proposals. I would promise her happiness, and fine children, and a house with sturdy locks and heavy doors. No more running, I'd say. No nightmares. A happy ending in which nothing ever ends. "It's possible," I'd tell her, "it's almost *plausible*, we just have to imagine it," and after a time Bobbi would turn toward me and smile without speaking, placing her hand against my heart, holding it there, mysteriously, shaping the possibilities, and that shining smile would mean Yes, she could imagine these things and many more.

The dialing, that was the true pleasure. It was almost a disappointment when she finally answered.

Not grief, really, just an empty place where all the pretty pictures used to be. She was kind about it. She quoted Yeats: *We had fed the heart on fantasies, the heart's grown brutal from the fare.* She wished me luck. She was flattered, she said. She didn't laugh when I told her about the chase, how much she meant to me, how foolish I felt, how crazy, but how I had to go with my dreams. She said she admired that. She was smiling, I could tell. She said dreams were important. Then she told me her own dreams. She needed space, she said; NYU was fine but there was no space; she'd dropped out in April. She was happy, though. She was going to Germany— Bonn, she said—and there was a married man she was going with, Scholheimer, and the married man was her husband. She laughed at this, lightly. Dreams were lovely, she said, but they could be dangerous, too, which is when she lowered her voice and quoted Yeats: *We had fed the heart on fantasies, the heart's grown brutal from the fare.*

But it wasn't grief. Not even sadness. If you're crazy, I now understood, you don't feel grief or sadness, you just can't find the future.

I spent a few days reassembling myself, and on the evening of May 29 Sarah met me at the Key West airport. Understandably, her mood was dark. I'd been out of contact for some time; I'd skipped out on my responsibilities. "Globe-trotter," she muttered, "back from his magical mystery tour."

In the cab she applied irony.

I wasn't ready for it. I took her by the wrist and dug in with my fingernails.

"Don't push," I said quietly. "Don't even nudge. Just this once—total silence, I mean it."

Sarah nodded.

And for two weeks she treated me with something just short of respect. I went my way, she went hers. It was unlived-in time. Like blank film, no images or animus, no pretty pictures. At the dinner table, Ollie and Tina would keep up a nonstop banter about the current political situation, the screw-turnings and incipient terror, but none of it really registered. I couldn't make visual contact. I'd stare at my plate and try to construct the contours of a world at perfect peace: Bobbi's smile, for instance; binding energy; things to hope for and believe in; the city of Bonn with its spires and castles. But nothing developed. Blank film—I'd lost the gift. If you're crazy, it's a lapse of imagination. You stare at your dinner plate. You can't generate happy endings.

The postulate was obvious. If you're crazy, it's the end of the world.

Which is how it felt. Just nothing.

When there's nothing, there is no sadness. There was a war on, but it didn't matter, because when there's nothing, there is no outrage.

One evening Ned Rafferty knocked on my door.

For a moment he stood there waiting, then shrugged and came in and sat on the bed. He wore a beard now, and wire-rimmed glasses, but he still had strength.

Nothing was said.

It was late and the house was quiet. Rafferty leaned back against a pillow. He was simply *there*. At one point he got up and turned off the light and then came back and touched my shoulder and held it for a while and then sat down again and waited. His glasses sparkled in the dark. A humid night, dense and oppressive. I took a breath and tried to keep it inside, but it came out fast, and then I was choking and telling him everything I could tell. The tears surprised me. I didn't feel any great emotion. Ding-Dong, I thought, but I couldn't stop choking and saying, "Crazy." Rafferty was silent. He didn't move or speak, but he was there. I told him how crazy I was. The fucking Ping-Pong table, I said. The flashes and missiles and sirens, and the fucking war, the fucking draft, the bombs and shrapnel and guns and artillery and all the shit, the fucking *sun*, it would fucking fry us, I said, or we'd get fried by the fucking physicists, or else the silos and submarines and fly-boys and button-pushers—all the assholes out to kill other assholes— fucking Nixon, fucking Brezhnev, fucking Ebenezer Keezer and Nethro and Hitler and Crazy Horse and Custer, my father, too, yes, my father, the way he died out at the fairgrounds every sum- mer, just died and died and died, how he wouldn't stop dying, every fucking summer, all the heroes and corpses, the fucking Alamo, fucking Hiroshima and Auschwitz—No survivors!—every- body killing everybody else—yes, and the so-called peace move- ment, the fucking underground with its fucking slogans and riots, the fucking dynamic—what *good* was it?—those guns in the attic and Ollie with his fucking bombs—where was the *good*?—No sur- vivors!—it was all so crazy, I said, just absolute fucking crazy— and then I laughed and shook my head and told him about Bobbi.

Pie in the sky, I said.

I quoted Yeats.

I told him about obsession and fantasy.

I told him you had to believe in something; I told him how it felt when you stopped believing.

"It feels fucking crazy," I said, almost yelled, then I caught my breath and said, "That's what craziness *is*. When you can't be- lieve. Not in anything, not in anyone. Just can't fucking *believe*."

I was sobbing now, but it wasn't sadness. It was nothing. For a few minutes I lost my balance—I'm not sure what happened ex- actly, a kind of fury, thrashing around and yelling "Crazy!"—and then Rafferty had me pinned down by the wrists and arms. I could smell his sweat. He was leaning in hard, saying, "Slack now, lots of slack, let it unwind."

Then the quiet came.

"There," he said, "let it go."

I closed my eyes and cried.

"Just let it out," he said.

———

A nice guy. Nice, that was all I could think, and I told him so. "Nice," I kept saying, "you're a nice, nice, nice guy. You *are.* You're nice."

"A prince," said Rafferty.

"For sure. Fucking prince."

"Don't say fucking."

"I apologize. Not fucking at all. But *nice.*"

Rafferty filled my glass.

"What we should do in a situation like this," he said, "is drink to how nice I am."

We finished the brandy. The hour was late but Rafferty suggested a sea voyage, which seemed fitting, so we hiked down to the Front Street marina and exercised the right of angary over a handsome wooden skiff and aimed the vessel Gulfward. A mile out, we cut the engine. We drifted and breathed the air and looked back on the sad white lights of Key West.

I felt much improved. A quiet sway, and the skiff rode high and neat.

Rafferty laughed at something.

"Nice guy," he said. He lit up a joint and passed it across to me.

I wasn't a smoker but I liked the ritual of it. I liked him, too. And the smells and water sounds. There was largeness around us. When the joint was gone, Rafferty asked if I wanted more, and I said I did, so we smoked that one and then another, letting the currents take us, and presently I was made aware of numerous unique perspectives. It was all in the angle. The moon, I noticed, was without third dimension. I was intrigued by the concept of hemispheres. I detected a subtle crease at the horizon where the global halves had been stitched to perfect the whole.

Ned Rafferty nodded when I explained these matters.

"Nuts," I said. "Haywire. I warned you, didn't I?"

"I believe it was mentioned, yes."

"Loose screws. Did I say that? Sometimes I feel—you know—I feel—there's a word for it—not depressed, not just that. Like when you can't cope anymore."

"Desperate," Rafferty said. "I know."

"That's it. Desperate. Did I tell you about Bobbi?"

"You did."

"Married. Off to Bonn in Germany."

"You told me."

"Scholheimer."

"A turd. You told me."

"Desperate," I said.

"Desperadoes."

"That's *it*."

Rafferty sighed and removed his glasses. Funny angle, the dark and the Gulf and the dope, but it looked like he'd pulled out his eyes and placed them in the pocket of his shirt. The shine was gone. He leaned back and looked at me without his eyes.

"One thing," he said. "To clear the air."

"Anything."

"About Sarah. This relationship we had, Sarah and me. It's over. Never really got started. I love her. She loves you."

"You don't have to—"

"No, I want it out," he said. "She *loves* you. Breaks my heart, but there's the fact. Understand me? Loves you. Wants you back. Rio, that's all she talks about." He reached overboard, splashing water to his face. The skiff was gently fishtailing with the tide. "I do care for her, you know. Emotional thing."

"I'm sorry."

"Rio, for Christ sake. What the hell's Rio?"

"Nothing," I said. "A fantasy."

There was silence while Rafferty reflected on this. After a time he issued a complex noise from the bottom of his lungs.

"Fantasy, I can respect that," he said. "Obsessions, too. You're obsessed, I'm obsessed. Look at Tina—big fat killer obsessions. Our Lord Jesus Christ, the man was obsessed, who isn't? Ollie Winkler—walking obsession. Thing is, you have to respect people's obsessions. Like with me. You want to know my obsession?"

"What's your obsession?"

"Will you respect it?"

"I will."

"My obsession," he said gravely, "is Sarah. I'm a nice guy, you're right, but you know something? I'd do anything for her. Drown your ass. Right here, if I thought it would do any good, I'd just drown your ass. Can you respect that?"

"I certainly can."

"Maybe we should have another smoke?"

"Yes," I said.

"I *am* a nice guy."

"Of course. But you'd have to drown me."

"You understand, then."

"Completely and absolutely," I told him. "Obsession, it's nothing personal."

Rafferty laughed and stood up to light the joint. He seemed stable enough. The boat was sliding sideways to the current but he kept his balance, passing the smoke and then turning and staring out at the sad lights across the water.

"Stoned," he said, "but not all that stoned. You want to hear my fantasies?"

"Very much," I said.

"Get the hell out of here. That's the A-one deluxe fantasy, just split. With Sarah. Drown your ass and kidnap her—drugs or something—a sea voyage—take her away." He paused a moment, shook his head violently, then pointed at the town lights. "I *hate* this place. Key West, it sucks. Everything we're doing, the gangster shit and the guns and Ebenezer Keezer, everything, I hate it. Don't believe in it. Got to believe, man, and I don't. Never did. Ranch kid—I ever tell you that? Grew up on a ranch. Dumb cowboy. Home on the range. All I ever wanted, some cows and dope and git along little dogie. And Sarah. Not a damned thing else. That's why I'm *here*. No other reason. Just Sarah."

"A good fantasy," I said.

"Nifty lady, Sarah."

"She is."

"Different fantasies, though. I want her, she wants Rio. That's the thing, nobody has the same fantasies."

Rafferty swayed and sat down heavily.

"Anyway, there it is," he said. "Obsession. You and me, two peas in the same dipshit pod."

"Crazy," I whispered.

There was a short silence. When he spoke, his voice seemed firm and exact, fully sober.

"Not crazy," he said, "but here's a word of advice. Sarah, she's *real*. Take it and run. Get out. This whole situation—the guns and shit—we both know how it ends. Badness, that's all. Graveyards. Forget the dreams, man, do something positive. Grab her and start running and don't ever stop. The world-famous gist: Go with reality. Take off."

"And you?"

"Gone. First chance, I'm gone. Home on the range."

"What about—"

"Just *go*."

He smiled and held up a hand, palm forward.

"Peace," he said, "the gist of the gist."

There was a feeling of comity and goodwill. A fine human being, I thought, and we sat back and smoked, and for a long while I concentrated on the hemispheres. I watched the scheme of things, the constellations, the moon veering toward Europe, peace with honor, Bobbi and Bonn and Rio and Vietnam and the violet glow of uranium dioxide in the Sweetheart Mountains. I was not afraid. I knew where the future was. Later, as Rafferty slept, I watched without alarm as a black submarine surfaced to starboard, its conning tower cutting like a fin through the placid dark. I felt no dismay, only wonder. Here, I deduced, was how it would be when it finally came to be. It would be quick. Out of the blue, a blink and a twitch, here then gone. I could see it. I could hear the sonar. The submarine rose up in profile, buoyant, circling the skiff, and I nodded and closed my eyes and gave myself over to how it had to be. There was a slight trembling. A shower of yellow-white sparks, then the missiles ascended, but to my credit, I stood fast. I studied the ballistics. I admired the gleamings—reds and pinks spilling in the Gulf. There was grace in it, I thought, and the beauty that attends resolution, as fire is beautiful, and nuclear war, things happening as they must happen and always will. I was brave. I'd seen it all before, many times, and now there was just gallantry.

The question declared itself: Who's crazy?

Not me.

When the submarine slipped away, I was smiling. Imagination. I had the knack again.

For the next year, up to April 21, 1971, the casualties kept piling up on all sides. People were dying. In Vietnam, there was steady concussion; in Paris, the peace talks dragged on into the third year of stalemate; in Georgia, Lieutenant William Calley went on trial for murder; in Cambodia, there were fires. There was a war on, yes, but for me it was mostly blank time. Which is to say I can't remember much—the present never quite became the past.

What happened? How much is memory, how much is filler?

If I close my eyes, if I ignore the hole, I can see Sarah reclining in a lawn chair on the back patio at Key West. We're lovers again, though not exactly in love; we're both waiting, though for what I don't know. She just lies there in sunlight. She wears a blue bandanna and a white muslin blouse. Her skin is dark brown. The hair at her calves is bleached silver, and at the corner of her mouth is a lumpish blister—herpes simplex, but the complications will prove unhappy. In her lap is a copy of *Newsweek*. A celebrity now, she smiles at me from the magazine's cover, or seems to smile, and says or seems to say, "I warned you. Years ago, I told you I was dangerous, big dangerous dreams, and here's the proof. Now I belong to the ages."

Blank time, but great speed, too. I can see Sarah's eyes going cold. "I'm dead," she whispers.

Mid-November 1970, and a butchered pig was deposited on the steps of the FBI building in downtown Washington.

There was a bombing in Madison.

A startling image—is it real?—but I can see Ollie Winkler in a rented airplane. He's wearing his cowboy hat and aviator goggles, a yellow scarf flapping behind him, and he's squealing and dumping homemade ordnance on the nation's Capitol. It did not happen that way, but it could've happened, and still can, and therefore I see it.

"I'm dead!" Sarah cries. That much did happen.

In December they redecorated the Lincoln Memorial.

In January 1971, they released a dozen skunks in the carpeted hallways of the Rockefeller Foundation.

Not quite terrorism.

"Skunks," Sarah said, "that's a prank. TNT, that's terror. You have to know where to draw your nice fine lines."

I remember nodding.

Pathetic, I thought, but things were clearly moving toward misadventure.

The guns, for instance.

When I look back, I can see those plywood crates stacked in the attic. One night I heard noise up there, so I investigated, and I found Ned Rafferty sitting cross-legged before a candle, alone. Just cobwebs and guns. "How's tricks?" I asked, and Rafferty snuffed the candle and told me to get the fuck out. "Just go!" he said, and he sounded angry.

What else?

A minor hurricane named Carla.

I can hear the wind, I can feel Sarah up against me in bed. Maybe it's then when she says, "My God, I'm dead."

Slow time, but it seems fast.

I remember Ollie eating grapes at the kitchen table. The seeds make plinking sounds in a metal wastebasket; he talks about hitting banks; he seems serious; he doesn't laugh when he says, "Why not?" A seed goes *plink* in the wastebasket and he says, "Why not?"

Tina Roebuck on a crash diet.

She's determined. She papers the refrigerator with photographs from *Vogue*. "Just once in my rotten life," she says grimly, "just this once, a lean mean killing machine."

But it doesn't happen. The pressures intervene and she checks out as a heavyweight.

Are the dead, I wonder, ever dead?

The hole laughs and says, *Believe it.*

I believe it. The dead, perhaps, live in memory, but when memory goes, so go the dead.

There is no remembering when there is no one to remember. Hence no history, hence no future. It's a null set; the memory banks are wiped out; there is no differentiation—all the leptons look alike—believe it.

For now, though, I have a dim recollection of Ebenezer Keezer briefing us on coming attractions. Volatile stuff, no doubt, because I remember the brittle sound to his laughter. There was talk about crime. At one point, when Ned Rafferty brought up the subject of penalties, jail and so on, Ebenezer removed his sunglasses and looked heavenward for some time. Then he shrugged. He grinned at Nethro. "Freedom," he said, "is just a dependent clause in a life sentence. Don' mean nothin'." There was a pause before he entertained suggestions as to how the guns might be most properly used. "Let's discuss climax," he said, which is all I remember, except for walking away.

And Sarah.

Sarah in a cotton nightgown with lace and blue ribbons, her hair in curlers, puffy booties on her feet. Sarah sunbathing. Sarah baking cookies. In late January, I remember, she put on her old Peverson letter sweater to watch the Super Bowl, and afterward we went out for dinner, the two of us alone. It was a terrific time. We had some drinks, then several more, and on the way home she giggled and leaned up against me and asked if I believed in dreams.

She seemed a little unsteady.

"Dreams," she said, "can they come true? Like with a crystal ball or something? Can you dream your own life?"

"Well," I said, "let's hope not."

"No, I'm serious. Is it possible?"

I smiled and took her arm.

It was near midnight and we were walking through a park of some sort and I could smell flowers and cut grass. After a time Sarah stopped and looked at me.

"What I mean is . . . I mean, there's a dream I keep getting. Not a dream, really, just this wacky idea. You won't laugh?"

"Of course not."

"Promise?"

I nodded.

There was a hesitation while she thought it over. Her eyes, I remember, were like ice; you could've skated on them.

"All right, then, but you have to use your imagination." She bit down on her lip. "War's over. No more battles, it's finished, we all pick up and go home. You and me, we get married, right?"

"Right," I said.

"Babies. Lots of travel. Settle down. But then what? I mean, I'm still young, I'm famous, I've got certain skills. So what do I *do* with myself?"

"The dream," I said gently, "let's hear it."

Sarah sighed.

"You'll think I've flipped. It's like—I don't know—just weird." She giggled again, then swayed and kissed me. There was the smell of gin and lipstick. Drunk, I thought, but something else, too.

She shivered and hugged herself.

"Don't laugh," she said. "Pretend it's Super Bowl Sunday. Like today, sort of. Packed stadium. Bands and floats and celebrities. National holiday. Bigger than Easter, bigger than Christmas. Hospitals shut down. Nixon's got his phone unplugged. All across America—people adjusting the color on their TV sets, opening up that first beer. Whole country's tuned in. Showdown time—Dallas versus Miami. You have to close your eyes and just picture it."

I closed my eyes.

When I looked up, she was sitting on a park bench. She gazed at the sky for several seconds.

"Super Bowl," she said. "Greatest show on earth. There I am. I'm a Cowgirl."

"Cowgirl," I said.

"War's over, I'm bored, I need the spotlight. That's *me*, isn't it?—the glitter girl—this huge appetite—I just *need* it. Goose

bumps. All the noise and dazzle and music. Very warm and mysterious, like having sex with ninety thousand people. Can't explain
it. Just Cowgirl magic—I'm wearing the blue and silver. Those lit
tle shorts, you know, and those sexy white boots. I'm *there*."

I sat down and put my arm around her.

A hot night, but she was still shivering, and it occurred to me
that this was a very desirable but very frightened woman.

Presently she laughed.

"So there I am," she said. "Super Bowl. All the pre-game stuff
goes as usual—welcoming ceremonies, lots of color and excite-
ment—but then a funny thing happens. The *teams* don't show up.
Overslept or something—who knows?—they just don't show. Two
hundred million people waiting. No teams."

"Nice," I said.

"No teams. No football."

"A good dream."

Sarah shrugged.

"True," she said, "but here's the stunner. Nobody cares. Nobody *notices*. Because yours truly is out there blowing their dirty
little minds with cartwheels. Cartwheels you wouldn't believe.
Nobody's even *thinking* football—cartwheels, that's all they want.
Crowd goes bananas. Super Bowl fever, they're all screaming for
more cartwheels . . . Curt Gowdy's shouting the play-by-play . . .
TV cameras zoom in on me—instant replay, slow mo, the works.
I'm famous! Fans swarm onto the field and . . . And that's when it
finally *happens*. Cheerleading, the main event. No sidelines
crap—it's me they want—they came to see *me*. Just a billion
beautiful cartwheels. They love me. They really do, just love-love-
love. Who cares about football? War's over. Just *love*. It's all completely reversed. At half time the two teams trot out for a cute little twenty-minute scrimmage and then—bang—back to the
action—me and my cartwheels."

There was a moment of quiet, then she nudged me and lifted
up her sweater.

"My breasts," she said, "they're nice, aren't they?"

"Fabulous," I said.

"For a Cowgirl, though. Not huge or anything, but they're—you know—they're nice. I don't need a bra."

"I see that. Cover up now."

"I'm not too old?"

"Just right," I said.

Sarah frowned and examined herself.

"And my legs. I'd probably have to start shaving again, but they seem—"

"Very pretty legs."

"You think so? Be honest."

"Perfect," I said. I helped her up. She wobbled a bit, laughing, then straightened up and took my face in her hands and kissed me hard. I could feel the structure of her jaw. When she pulled back, there were tears in her eyes.

"The dream," she said softly. "You see the point?"

I didn't but I nodded.

"Love," she said.

She didn't cry.

She smiled and said, "Love, that's all. I want it. God, I do want it."

The rest seems to slide away.

I remember her black eyes, flecks of orange and silver, how she kept smiling at me. "Love," she said.

And then what?

Hindsight, foresight. But which is it? I can see her jerking up in bed that night, or perhaps another night, still trembling, hooking a leg around me, and maybe it's then when she says, "I'm *dead.* I'm all *alone.*"

Is it possible? Can we read the future?

Do our bodies know?

I remember holding her.

"No," I tell her, "just a dream."

Which is how it was and still seems.

A curious year, fast and slow. I can see Sarah practicing cartwheels in the backyard. She winks at me and yells something—I don't know what—then she goes up into a handstand, ankles locked, toes at the sky, and she holds it like that forever.

Or I see her squinting into a mirror. She winces, shakes her head, and begins applying a coat of Blistex to her swollen lip. After a second our eyes meet in the mirror. Sarah cocks an eyebrow. She nods and says, "All right, tiger, Congress is in session. But no fancy lip action."

Naturally there were realignments in our relationship, certain taboos and touchy subjects, but over those months we more or less patched things up.

It was an exercise in tact; the questions were always implicit.

One evening she found me paging through a world atlas. I was studying topography, tracking the Rhine toward Bonn. Sarah came up behind me. I didn't see her, or hear her, and it was a surprise when she placed her fingertips against my throat.

"Wrong continent," she whispered, "wrong woman," then she left the room.

In the morning the atlas was open to South America. Rio was circled in red. Europe was missing. At breakfast, as we were finishing our coffee, Sarah sniffed and said, "Love and war. If necessary, I'll wipe out the world."

For the most part, though, the days simply vanished.

I remember watching the war on television.

The same old reruns. There was a malaise, I remember, a weariness that imitated despair.

Ned Rafferty came down with the flu—a vicious case, fever and diarrhea. I remember dipping a washcloth into a basin of cold water, wiping his face, thinking what a nice guy he was. Even sick he looked strong. I can see his gray eyes aimed at the attic, how his beard framed a smile when he turned toward me and said, "Get *out*, man. Go. You're crazy if you don't."

A slow recovery, but he made it.

And then chronology.

On Valentine's Day, Ollie and Tina announced their engagement. They were married a month later—Nevada, I believe. The telegram mentioned a honeymoon in Mexico.

On March 29, 1971, Lieutenant William Calley was convicted of premeditated murder.

My father died on the twenty-first of April.

"Sit down," Sarah said.

Then she told me. I forget the sequence—network sources in Montana—a hot line—and then she told me. All I remember is when she said, "Sit down."

Forty or fifty hours seemed to drop away.

Daylight, then dark, then airplanes and a rented car and telephone poles and mountains and patches of snow. I suffered tunnel vision. Objects popped out at me: the A&W off Main Street, my father's Buick parked in front of the house.

"You understand the problem?" Sarah said. "About the funeral. We can't . . . I mean, it's a problem."

We spent the night in a motel up in the foothills. Rafferty was there, and Sarah, and the hours kept falling away. I remember sitting under cold water in the shower. Then daylight again, and Sarah cut my hair, and I was wearing a suit and a blue tie and black shoes.

A car ride, I remember that.

Then climbing.

"I'm sorry," Sarah said. "You understand, though?"

I watched through binoculars.

Ned held me by the arm. Sarah stood off to the side. We were on a hill overlooking the cemetery and I could see the entire valley below, the highway running east-west through town, the golf course and the water tower and the slim white cross over the First Methodist Church. The sky was a smooth, dusty blue. There were birds, too, and cattle grazing along the hillside, and a brisk wind that pressed Sarah's skirt flat against her hip. Farther down, the sunlight made sharp elongated shadows where it struck headstones and human figures.

I tried to focus on physical things. A good man, I thought. There was nothing worth dying for, but he always died with such dignity.

The binoculars gave it perspective—close up but also distancing. I studied the lead-colored coffin. That square jaw of his. He never ran or wept. A brave, good man. The wind was high and chilly, but there was bright sunshine as I brought the binoculars to bear on a mat of artificial grass at graveside. My father would've laughed. "Plastic grass," he would've said. He would've looked at me and rolled his eyes and muttered, *"Plastic."* I felt myself smiling. I could see him dying under floodlights at the county fairgrounds. He always died so beautifully. "Well," he'd say, "let's get this show on the road." He'd wink. He'd tell me to look smart. "What the hell," he'd say, "at least you got yourself a haircut."

But it wasn't worth dying for.

Nothing was, and I would've told him that.

Sarah touched my arm.

"All right?" she said.

I nodded and gave her the binoculars. After a moment she handed them back.

"If you want," she said, "there's some brandy. He wouldn't mind, would he? Your dad?"

"I guess he wouldn't," I said.

"Just a drop, then. To beat this wind."

"One drop," said Rafferty.

We moved to a cluster of granite boulders and passed the flask. Rafferty slipped an arm across my back. It was a brilliant day, but the wind made my eyes ache.

I fixed on dignity.

Down below, things seemed much too small. I recognized Doc Crenshaw and Sarah's father. It was all in miniature, the coffin and the hearse and the flowers and my mother. Even with the binoculars, she looked curiously shrunken. Worn down, I thought, and much too old. She wore gloves and a brown coat and a small dark hat, but no veil, and she stood slightly apart from the others, facing my father's coffin. She seemed nervous. When someone offered a chair, she made a quick motion with her hand, as if startled, then shook her head and remained standing. Surprise, I thought. We know it can happen but when it happens there is always surprise. I felt it myself. Grief, too, but the surprise was profound.

"Your mother," Sarah said, "she seems okay."

They were praying now.

To the north and east the mountains were bright purple. While they prayed, I thought about chemistry sets and lead pencils and graphite. Odd thing, but I finally saw the humor in it. I was an adult now; it didn't matter. I would've told him that. "Graphite," I would've said, "what a moron." I thought about how things happen exactly as they have to happen, but how even so you can't help feeling some bewilderment.

When the prayer was finished, the minister moved to the head of the grave, the wind ruffling the pages of his Bible. There were no voices, of course, but it was easy to imagine.

The binoculars helped.

I brought the hole into focus. I saw my father kneeling in front of a Christmas tree—colored lights and ornaments—and he was smiling at me, holding out a package wrapped in silver paper. He wanted to say something, I know, but he couldn't move or speak . . . I saw him mowing grass in deep summer. He had his shirt off, the hair wet against his chest, the smell of gasoline and cuttings, but he was locked behind a lawn mower that wouldn't move . . . I remembered a game we used to play. The Pull Down Game, we called it. He'd lie on his back and I'd hold him by the arms and he'd struggle and try to get up, but I'd keep pressing down—I was a child, six or seven, I didn't know my own strength or his—and after a while he'd give up and say, "You win, you win." I had him pinned. He couldn't move, like now. I saw him lying flat and looking up at me without moving . . . I saw him that way . . . At night sometimes, when he drove off to sell real estate, he'd flash the taillights at me—it was a special sign between us—but one night he forgot to flash them, and I was furious, I couldn't sleep, and when he came home I wanted to grab him and hit him and ask why he forgot to flash the goddamn taillights. I wanted to yell, "Why?" And there were other questions, too. A million questions I didn't dare ask and never would. What about Custer Days? The fairgrounds—why did he die? What was the point? Honor? Irony? What? I wanted to know. "I was just a kid," I would've told him, "I *hated* it, every fucking summer you always *died*." I would've pinned him down. I would've demanded answers. The

Ping-Pong table—better than nothing, wasn't it? Why the jokes? Why bring up graphite? What about the bombs? Real or not? Who was right? Who was wrong? Who's crazy? Who's *dead?* I would've climbed all over him. "You son of a bitch!" I would've screamed. I would've yelled, "Why?" Why so gallant? Those bright blue brave eyes—the world could end—he didn't flinch—no one did—why? The *world,* for Christ sake. Why didn't he cry? Why not dig? Why not do something? Dig or cry or something? Right now, it could happen, couldn't it? Yes or no? Why such dignity? Why not anger? Why did he have to go and *die?* "Bastard!" I would've yelled. Through the binoculars I could see him squirming. I *had* him, though—he couldn't move—so I'd fire the questions at him. The war, for instance. The whole question of courage and cowardice. Draft-dodging: Was he embarrassed for me? What did he tell people? Make excuses? Change the subject? Secretly, in his heart, would he prefer a son with medals and battle ribbons and bloody hands? I would've kept after him. I would've hugged him and held him down and asked all the questions that had to be asked. I would've told him what a great father he was. Such a good man, I would've said. I would've said all the things I wanted to say but could never say.

You brave son of a bitch, I would've said. I love you.

I tried to say it but I couldn't.

It was all grief now. I looked away, at the mountains, and later Sarah laced her fingers through mine and said, "I think it's finished."

Below, people were mingling and shaking hands, sliding off toward their cars. Doc Crenshaw had my mother by the elbow. For a long time I kept the binoculars up, but finally there was just that relentless wind.

"William," Sarah said.

I nodded.

"Another minute," I told her. "Go on ahead, don't worry. Just one minute."

I smiled to show I was in control.

When they were gone, I watched the sky and tried to find

some words. A bright, sunny day, but the wind made it hard. I wanted to talk about my life. Apologize, maybe. Tell him I'd be making some important changes. How it was time to stop running, and how I'd need help, but how, when the moment came, I'd pretend he was right there beside me under the yellow spotlights.

I had a last look through the binoculars.

The coffin was still there, unburied. I studied it for a while and then said goodbye and followed Sarah and Rafferty down the hill.

The hours fell away.

We had dinner that night at a restaurant near the motel. Around midnight Sarah went to bed and Rafferty and I stayed up late making plans. When I mentioned the guns, he looked at me and said, "You're sure?" and I said I was, and he smiled and said, "Positive thinking."

I slept hard for the rest of the night.

In the morning I took a wrinkled scrap of paper from my wallet, went to a pay phone, dropped in some quarters, and placed the call.

"What you have to do," Chuck Adamson said, "is make it quick and clean. Cold turkey. Move, that's all I can say."

"I'll need time," I said.

"Time. That can be arranged."

"A place to go."

"That, too," he said. "Time and place, I'll handle it. From there on you'll have to draw your own map."

Behind him, the capitol dome had lost some of its shine. Otherwise not much had changed.

Adamson slouched in his chair, taking notes.

He was older, of course, and balding, but he still had those sad copper-colored eyes. Still jittery and preoccupied. I felt at home. I could almost hear him groaning—"You think *you've* got problems"—but instead he opened a desk drawer and took out a photograph and examined it for a moment and then handed it across to me. Surprise, but I was smiling. A handsome child: blond hair and a cowboy shirt and a big smile.

Adamson reached out and touched the photograph.

"Square one," he said, "tell it to me."

It took nearly a week. I started with the binoculars; I told him that I'd come to appreciate his fascination with telescopes. "That's what it *feels* like," I said. "My life, it feels like it's happening inside a telescope."

Over that first afternoon I laid out the chronology, or what I could remember of it. Peverson State and my poster and Ollie and Tina, and then Sarah, and the war, and Ebenezer Keezer and Nethro and life on the run, and then Bobbi—it was hard to get the order straight—but then Bobbi—and a missile rising over the Little Bighorn, and guns in the attic, and uranium dreams, and my father, and a sleek black submarine, and how in retrospect it all had the shape and logic of a chain reaction, cause becoming effect and then cause again.

When I finished it was dark.

"Well," Adamson said. Then he rubbed his eyes and took me home with him.

It wasn't what I expected: a huge old house on the outskirts of Helena, white clapboard with black shutters and a wraparound porch, and a cocker spaniel and a pretty wife and four terrific kids, the youngest just a baby. He put me up in a spare bedroom. At dinner that night, it felt as if I'd rejoined the world. Lots of laughter. Adamson clowning with the kids, a parakeet diving through the dining room, his wife shaking her head and smiling at me—a madhouse, she meant.

After dinner we played Careers. And then late at night, when we were alone, Adamson dished up ice cream and we ate it standing up at the kitchen counter.

I laughed.

"Well," I said, "this explains it." I made a gesture that encompassed the entire house. "I mean, listen. Now I know why you're so miserable."

Adamson licked his spoon.

"Right," he said. "We'll talk about it in the morning."

But we never did. For the next five or six days I led him through the chronology again, slowly. It wasn't therapy; it was purely practical. When I told him about Sarah, he asked the essential question: Why didn't I go with her? There was no answer for it. Trust, I said. Or no trust. Did I love her? I did. Did she love me? She no doubt did. Then why? I shrugged: there was no answer for it. It wasn't our universe. I didn't know. Not our universe, that was all I could say, except no trust, or not enough, or the inability to see how it could end happily. But I didn't know.

If you can't imagine it, I said, it can't happen.

I told him about Bobbi.

That much I could imagine. Why? he said. I didn't know. It seemed possible.

I told him about Ned Rafferty. A person is defined by the quality of obsession, I said, and Ned Rafferty was a quality person. Ollie Winkler was not quality. Nor was Tina Roebuck, nor Ebenezer Keezer. Sarah was high quality.

"And you?" Adamson asked.

I thought about it. Up in the air, I told him. My obsessions were sometimes quality and sometimes not. Nothing lasts: that was not a quality obsession. But there was also Bobbi, and peace, and that was quality.

For many hours we went over these things, shifting back and forth, but the purpose was never therapeutic, it was always practical.

A serious problem, Adamson said. There were legal issues. There was the question of surrender. How exactly to go about it, and when and where, and all the attendant logistics. There were consequences to consider. Prosecution, maybe. Maybe jail. And beyond that, he said, there was the whole matter of deciding on a future for myself. "Not just any future," he said, "we're talking *quality*," and then he asked the simple, practical questions. Did I want a house to live in? I said, Yes, I did, very much. Did I want children? I did. What about a career? Geology, I said. What about love and happiness and peace of mind?

"The point," he said quietly, "is that you have to try to picture the exact circumstances. The shapes and routines, the things you want. A blueprint. Then go out and make it happen."

"I understand," I said.

"Do you?"

"Yes, I think so. Take charge, you mean."

Adamson shook his head,

"What I mean," he said, and paused. "I mean you're not a child anymore. Nowhere to hide. It's a grown-up bitch of a world."

On the last day we spent a few hours in his office and then he drove me over to the bus station.

It ended where it began.

"Cold turkey," he said. "Time and place, I'll set it up. From then on it's your life."

There was a final trip to Key West. When I explained my decision to Sarah, she nodded and said she'd been expecting it. "No hard feelings," she said.

It took a full day to pack up my things.

That evening we sat in the backyard, just holding hands, letting the sun go down.

In bed, she said, "I have to ask this. Did you ever love me?"

"Right now," I said.

The next day she took an early-morning flight for Miami. She was gone when I came down to breakfast.

"It's you and me," Ned Rafferty said.

We ate pepper omelets and drank Bloody Marys. In the afternoon we switched to gin, and then later, after dark, we rinsed our glasses and drank vermouth.

"Among the spirits," Rafferty said, "we are presently well spiritualized, I would say."

"I would say so."

"To the spirits, then. To spirituality in all its diverse guises. To firewater."

"And firesticks," I said.

"Of course. Firesticks, too. But that comes later, does it not?"

"Later, I apologize."

"Think nothing of it." He bowed and smiled. "Firewater

now, firesticks later. One must approach it with orderly spirit, must one not?"

"One must," I said.

We drank vermouth on ice until the ice ran out. There was a winding-down feel to the occasion, a happy sort of sadness, and for a while we permitted ourselves the quiet to let it happen.

Later I felt myself smiling.

"You want the gist?" I said.

"Definitely. Couldn't do without it."

"The gist," I said, "is I'm pretty damned fond of you."

"That's the gist?"

"That's it."

He looked at me. "I accept with pleasure. Finest gist ever spoken. I recommend we spiritualize it."

"We shall," I said.

There was no ice but I stood and made a speech about how we had become like brothers over the years, many scrapes, many untold thicknesses and thinnesses, and then Rafferty made his own speech, which was eloquent, and then we paused to remember our absent colleagues, which required solemnity and the last of the vermouth.

"To dear Tina," Rafferty said, "and to Ollie, our honeymooning brethren. May they find joy in the overripened flesh."

"Poignant," I said.

"I thank you, sir. And to Nethro. And—let me think—and let us praise Ebenezer Keezer. May he stew in stir. May his darkest dreams come true."

"And Sarah," I said.

"Certainly. And God bless Sarah Strouch."

I looked at my watch.

"So now?" I said. "I believe firesticks might be in order."

"I believe so. Shit-faced, I believe."

"The attic, then."

"Most definitely," said Rafferty. "The spirit most definitely beckons."

It was a two-hour job. Earlier that morning, after Bloody

Marys, we'd rented a van and tacked up curtains along the rear windows. The Gunmobile, Rafferty called it. We worked as a team, hauling the plywood crates down to the kitchen, then pausing for spiritual sustenance, then loading up the van.

I drove, Rafferty rode shotgun.

"Advance to the front," he said loudly, "we must commence without compunction. Destiny, all that. Compunctionless. No more compunctions."

I was intoxicated but not stupid. I took it slow up Roosevelt Boulevard, past a glitzy strip of neon along the Gulf side, both hands on the wheel, one eye closed, hitting the turn signal when I swung north onto Highway 1.

The road went dark after a mile or two. Rafferty switched on the radio and sang with The Doors.

After a time he put his head back.

"I am overindulged," he said. "I am not well. I am the victim of impacted spirits."

"Pull over?"

"No. Commence. Impacted upon."

Then he chuckled and sang with the music. I measured the road with one eye. The hour was late and the universe was not entirely stable. To our left, I calculated, was the Gulf, the Atlantic to our right, but otherwise we were navigating a course between topographical unknowns. The Doors sang and Rafferty harmonized— *We're gonna set the night on firrrre.* I concentrated on the center line.

The darkness was not altogether comforting, nor the unknowns, and I was down to one eye.

"How far?" I said.

"Firrre!" Rafferty sang, then shrugged. "I have no compunctions. Two miles, I would gauge. The running of guns is not—how shall we say it?—not yet an exact science."

"An art," I said.

"Quite so. Art. Artsy craft, even crafty craft. Could be a song in it."

"There could."

"Shall I sing?"

I took a bead on the center line.

"Firrre!" he sang.

There was no traffic. The road was flat and seamless, very narrow, and the sound of the engine mixed nicely with his baritone. The darkness amazed me. I thought about Sarah for a while, with something like passion, but then I decided it would be better to stop thinking. Then I thought about Ebenezer. This would not please him, I thought, nor Tina, nor Chekhov, so why then think about it?

Ahead was the smudge of Lower Sugar Loaf Key.

Deceleration, I thought, and I let it glide. I pulled off onto the shoulder, backed into a rest area at the Atlantic side, cramped the wheel, set the emergency brake, switched off the systems. Each operation demanded diligence.

For a few minutes we sat listening.

The blackout was total. Rafferty sat up straight beside me, holding his head.

"I detect no light," he said soberly, "at the end of this particular tunnel."

"Ready?"

"Of course. No light, no compunctions."

Outside, there was a strange sort of silence, flying insects and tidal splashings along the roadbed. Commando vibrations: comportment was paramount. Dignity, I decided, and I felt brave and competent as we established a beachhead.

When the guns were unloaded, we took off our clothes and waded in with the first crate.

It rode low and heavy. Awkward but it floated. Close in, the water was warm and marshy-smelling, barely up to the knees, then cooling as we waded out. I had both eyes open. I could see birds and fireflies off in the mangrove. Vaguely, I wondered where the stars had come from; there were flashings, too, and reflections, but for once I felt powerful.

We steered the crate straight out.

When the water came thigh-high, we pried open the lid. The

guns lay muzzle-to-stock, oiled and fleshy, overlapping, like tinned sardines.

"Such beauties," Rafferty said. "You'll have to grant the obvious, They are true, ball-breaking beauties."

He touched a tooled barrel.

"Works of art," he whispered.

Then he said, "Oh, well."

We tipped the crate sideways and pushed it under and waited for final sinkage. There were soft bubbling noises. Presently a sheet of oil rose up and gathered in flecks of orphan light.

"In a way, you know," Rafferty said, "it amounts to tragedy. Just in a certain way."

"It's a token," I said.

"That's what I mean. Tragedy. Fucking token."

He ducked underwater. While he was gone I watched the oil spreading out, smooth and shiny. Even in the dark it had some color.

Rafferty came up smiling.

"Token," he said, "I guess that's something. Something positive, isn't it?"

"I think it is," I said.

"No compunctions?"

"None."

There were fourteen crates altogether, then the ammunition. It was sobering labor. The footing was slippery with turtle grass and coral; in the mangrove to the east there was the nighttime babble of birds and reptiles and creatures I didn't know. Mostly, we sank the crates whole. Once, though, we took turns disposing of the weapons individually, which was gratifying, standing naked in salt water and grasping a cool black barrel in both hands and using the shoulders as a pivot and spinning with the arms, then a howl and a snap of the wrists, then listening for the splash, and then saying, "Well done," or saying, "Positive dynamics," and then laughing.

Otherwise it was mechanical, just sinking guns. We inclined toward silence. We pressed the crates under and watched the bubbles. At one point, as we waited for a car to pass by, I found myself telling him about Chuck Adamson. Cold turkey, I said. Had to be a clean break. Too bad about Sarah—I did love her, I said—it just wasn't our universe. Did he understand this? I shook my head and said I didn't understand it myself, but did he understand? She was *in* the world. I was *out* of it. Did he understand this? She wanted engagement, I did not—was this understandable? Different universes, I said. Rafferty lay back in the shallows, floating face-up, and after a moment he said he understood, but he reckoned he would have to stick with her anyway, because he only knew about one universe, and here it was, and that was his way of looking at it. But he understood. Then he asked what my plans were and I told him I was trusting Adamson to work things out. "Just go," I said, "anywhere but crazy." Rafferty laughed and said crazy was a wonderful place not to go.

Then we hauled out the last crate and pried it open and committed it to the bottom.

In the van, heading for town, I thanked him for his partnership. More than a token, I said. Something positive. For my father, partly, but mostly for myself.

He sat with his eyes closed.

"Men of virtue, are we?"

"No," I said. "Just positive."

At the house I showered and put on a coat and tie and inspected myself in a full-length mirror. I looked presentable. The smile was straight and full, almost happy. The skin was copper brown, the hair was just a shade short of blond, and the eyes had a bright blue clarity which gave me pleasure.

I have a theory. As you get older, as the years pile up, time takes on a curious Doppler effect, an alteration in the relative velocity of human events and human consciousness. The frequencies tighten up. The wavelengths shorten—sound and light and history—it's all compressed. At the age of twelve, when you crouch under a Ping-Pong table, a single hour seems to unwind toward infinity, dense and slow; at twenty-five, or thirty-five or forty, approaching half-life, the divisions of remaining time are fractionally reduced, like Zeno's arrow, and the world comes rushing at you, and away from you, faster and faster. It confounds computation. You lose your life as you live it, accelerating. Which is my theory, and which is how the next eight or nine years went by.

Chuck Adamson's word was gold. Time and place, he'd promised, and he set me up in a small cottage in the foothills outside Fort Derry—no frills, but comfortable—eight miles from home, close to the old sources but far enough away. Always, to his credit, he was practical. He covered the rent, helped to furnish the place, bought me a pair of hiking boots and a beat-up Volvo and a Geiger counter. "Time and place," he said, "so draw your map." He never pressed me; he let me surface in my own way. On weekends, sometimes, he'd come to visit, but for the most part the time was my own. I became a householder. I learned how to regulate a wood-burning stove and how to spend the hours of night without terror. Just the simple things. Doing dishes became an important piece of business; it seemed civilized and honorable, a matter of consequence. Once a week there was garbage to dispose of. There was a floor to sweep, a woodpile that required vigilance and wise husbanding. Eventually, I knew, I would have to begin squaring the legal circles, but for that first year it was enough to let the days accumulate. I camped out and collected rocks and devoted many hours to my Geiger counter. It was all acceleration. Alone, listening through headphones, I followed the trace elements along a stream that led where it had to lead, as I knew it would, and at the source there was just the steady click of a geological certainty. It was my secret, though. I lived with it. Naturally there were times when the solitude pressed in hard, and I'd think about Sarah and the others, but then I'd think about the mountains and tell myself, No, that's finished. Here it is, I'd think. Right here. Lying in bed at night, or sitting at the stove, I'd take satisfaction in the shadings of sound and temperature, the most minute increments in the density of silence. I noticed how even cobwebs cast shadows. I noticed how geopolitics made no perceptible difference in the movement of dust against a lighted lamp. For me, at least, the war was over.

The rest was a silhouette.

June 1971. I drove into town, parked on Main Street, and walked home. My mother did not seem much surprised. When I came in the back door, she said, "I *knew* it."

There were changes. Her hands, when she touched me, were raw and bony, smaller now, and her hair, when we kissed, was thin and gray against my cheek. Her eyes were milky. Her voice was like straw when she said, "I did. I *knew* it."

But the silhouette was my mother's.

That night, and the next night, I slept at home. And my mother slept with me, in the same bed. It was just closeness, but we did sleep together. I explained that it wasn't quite over yet. Not everything, I said. I told her I'd made the break. I held her when she cried—she was my mother—and I told her about the cottage and how Adamson had arranged it and how I was close by now and how I needed to be alone to sort things out. "But I'm here," I said, "I'm home," and we talked quietly and then slept together, but it was nothing except what it was.

Christmas Eve 1971. I remember a fine long-needled spruce and a pitcher of eggnog and my mother getting tipsy and a card from Sarah which said: *Love me?*

November 7, 1972, an electoral landslide, but it didn't mean a thing.

Then Christmas again, and Nixon bombed Hanoi. Eleven days. Forty thousand tons of high explosives. But I reached out and found quietus: It was someone else's war. Just a silhouette, form without content.

Then early spring 1973, a Sunday, and Chuck Adamson and my mother came to dinner. There were blizzard warnings. A hard wind, I remember, and sleet turning to snow. The cottage windows frosted over, but things were snug inside, and we ate turkey and drank wine and played Password.

"Pencils," my mother said, and I said, "Graphite," and Adamson was amazed.

Acceleration.

That half decade of rapid-fire history. Like a wind tunnel, wasn't it?

On August 9, 1974, Richard Nixon said goodbye. He received his pardon on September 8.

In January 1975, the North Vietnamese Army began its final push. Ban Me Thuot was overrun on March 11. On March 20, Hue. On March 30, Da Nang. And then Quang Ngai and Chu Lai and Pleiku and Qui Nhon and Nha Trang and Kontum.

That fast. There then gone.

On April 17, Phnom Penh fell to the Khmer Rouge. The city was empty within four days.

A wind tunnel—am I wrong?

Silhouettes. Four days, an empty city. Form without content. And in Vietnam it was full retreat now. Children dangled from helicopters, and NVA troops were playing pinball at Cam Rahn Bay, and on April 30, 1975—that fast—the decades collapsed into a twenty-second dash up the steps of the presidential palace in Saigon, and then it was finished.

Take a breath and it's 1976.

There were fireworks and tall ships. Amnesia was epidemic. Gerald Ford: My life was like his presidency; it happened, I'm almost certain.

In late summer of that year, 1976, there was another card from Sarah. It was a Kodachrome photograph of Rio at twilight, a little slick, but pretty, pinkish-blue reflections on water. I felt a kind of smiling sadness, though not really sadness, because in that water I saw what our world might have been, and in a way, I suppose, now was. I saw what she meant by commitment and passion, and it was present in that other universe, as love was also present, and as it would be present always. I thought about her a great deal; I'm sure she thought about me.

On my thirtieth birthday, October 1, Chuck Adamson suggested that now was the time. And I agreed.

There were lawyers, of course. It was not easy but it was not hard either. Like visiting the dentist: You squirm and tighten up, and maybe there's an ache, but then it's over and you touch your jaw and shrug and walk away. There was no jail. There was no *trial*. There were formalities and papers to sign, even pleasantries, and in the end it was almost a letdown, not enough hurt.

On January 21, 1977, President Jimmy Carter issued a blanket pardon—ten thousand draft-dodgers shot full of Novocain.

I began my graduate studies in February. Geology, it was a natural, and for the next two years I went underground in an entirely new way. I was an adult. I learned about the world we live in, all of us, which was finally a world of real things, sandstone and gold and graphite and plywood and art and books and bombs and the particles which make these things, and how each thing is vulnerable, even Bobbi, who was no longer a fantasy, but real. My dreams were glass. There were no flashes, not even a glow. I was hard and sane.

I completed my master's in June 1979.

A time of miniaturization, it seemed. Our cars were shrinking; our daily affairs were printed on microchips. Across America, the streets were quiet. Richard Daley was dead and Gene McCarthy was in seclusion and I spent the last summer of that decade in the Sweetheart Mountains, deciding. Before me was the rest of my life. What I wanted above all was to join the world, which was to live and to go on living with the knowledge that nothing endures, but to endure. It was a matter of choice. I didn't give a damn about missiles or scruples, all I wanted now was my life, the things of the world, a house and whatever hours there were and the ordinary pleasures of biology. I was hard and sane and practical. I wanted Bobbi, who was real.

And I knew where to start.

If you're sane, I realized, you take the world as you find it.

Science dictated: The uranium had to be there, and it was.

All summer, and through the fall, I followed the trail up into the high ground, homing in, and by mid-October there was no doubt.

On New Year's Day 1980, Sarah and the others came to visit. In a sense, I suppose, I was expecting them. Except for the years, nothing much had changed. There was some gray in Ned Rafferty's beard, a few extra pounds at Tina Roebuck's beltline, the usual wear and tear. It was good to see them. Ollie Winkler was a Christian now, and before dinner he led us in prayer, then we ate lamb chops and talked nostalgia. For the first time I felt at ease in their presence. Like family, I thought, and I was one of them— hard and sane and practical to the end.

Around midnight, after the others had turned in, Sarah and I sat on blankets in front of the wood stove.

"Son of a bitch," she said. "Almost nine years. Not a word."

She meditated for a while, then put her head in my lap.

"Kiss?" she said.

Later we held each other. Her skin felt cool and foreign. She laughed when I told her about the uranium.

"Well," she said, "it's a crime, isn't it?"

I said, "No."

Then I laid out my plans. It wasn't crime. It wasn't selling out. I was an adult, I said. I was able to take the world as I found it, and to use it, and to make what I could of it. When she asked about morality, I shrugged. When she asked about the flashes, I smiled and quoted Yeats: *We had fed the heart on fantasies, the heart's grown brutal from the fare.*

Sarah thought about it.

"Oh, well," she said, "at least we're rich."

CRITICAL——— ————MASS

12

The Nuclear Age

WE HIT PAY DIRT on the twelfth day out. By the twentieth day we knew exactly what we had. I'd been confident all along, and the data were there to back me up, but that didn't prevent celebration when Ollie ran the clicker over that pile of hot rock. On February 4, 1980, we bought the mountain. Rancher Roe reckoned we were setting up a commune, or maybe a new close-to-the-clouds religious establishment, but even so he couldn't wait to unload. At the registry of deeds he kept saying how, if he had it to do over, he'd most surely lead the hippie life himself. I never saw a man so willing to please. When it was done, we rented an electric typewriter and group-composed the letter. I handled the technical stuff, Rafferty the prose, Sarah the legal ins and outs. Then I sat down at the IBM Electric and cranked out seven copies, one for each Sister. We mailed the letters and waited. That was the hard part: two months before the first tentative reply, another month before Gulf brought in its exploratory team, two more months before we got any sort of bidding war going, then forty days more before Texaco doubled BP and we finally signed the papers. A straight cash deal—it had to be that way. No options, no pie-cutting, no deferred payments. The check was for twenty-five million dollars. Of course, there wasn't a banker in town who'd touch it, so we ended up in Ned's van, the whole gang, heading for First National in Helena. Along the way we stopped. There, on the banks of a shallow creek, we conducted a ceremony. It was silly, but the ladies insisted, so we each tossed a chunk of precious ore into the water, and I uttered a few solemn words, and we left two clickers behind as a gift for the next generation.

In the van, halfway home, Sarah cuddled up against me and asked how I'd be using my cut. It wasn't something I wanted to talk about. Buy a town somewhere, I said, or maybe a sinecure at Harvard.

"Geology?" Sarah asked. "No other dreams?"

"Well," I said, but of course she was right. "I guess I'll go to Bonn."

"In reference to what, exactly? As if I didn't know."

"A girl," I admitted. "A woman—I'm in love with her."

We rode along for a while. Sarah said she'd never seen Bonn. Not even a postcard. Could she come along?

We made Helena at midnight. It was Saturday's midnight, which meant another idle day, so we selected a motel advertising a heated pool and sauna. I suppose it was a combination of things— the van, the way Ned had let his hair go, Tina's behind-the-times peasant costume—but, whatever, the night clerk insisted on cash up front. He was just a kid. "We're good," I said, and I showed him the check: "*Texaco's* good." The clerk shrugged and claimed it was one of those computer foul-ups—extra zeros—and we ended up depositing our last hundred or so. The kid was smug about it. When he asked how many rooms we'd be wanting, I held up a finger and said, "One," and before he could smile I moved the finger to his nose. "Day after tomorrow," I said. "Watch out."

"No kidding?"

"Day after tomorrow. You're out of work."

The kid smiled and handed me a room key.

"Yes, sir," he said. "And don't forget, shower before you use the pool. New house rule."

We spent Sunday in the water. It was our last full day together, the Committee, and there was lots of talk about where everyone was headed. After all the nonsense, it boiled down to the predictable. Tina and Ollie were returning to Key West, where they would soon be very well-heeled revolutionaries. Ned Rafferty talked about buying himself a piece of property somewhere, maybe horses, maybe cattle, he couldn't decide. He glanced at Sarah, who kept quiet. At times sadness intervened, but we fought it off—much splashing and dunking. It was a heated outdoor pool, big and comfortable, and we made the most of it, floating side by side, holding hands, turning sentimental in the way smart people do, hipping it, finally coming straight out and saying how much we loved one another and how it wasn't the money that made it good, it was something else, the time together, all the ups and downs, and how we felt older and sadder, and how we hadn't done much to change the world but how the world had changed us, and how the whole thing was like camp. We hated ending it. Ollie said he'd heard tell of rich lodes up in British Columbia. Ned said he'd heard the same stories. We'll do it again, we said, but bashfully, with the sophistication of senior citizens who know better. Tina cried. Everybody hugged and kissed. "Maybe we should pray?" Ollie said. Nobody wanted to pray, but we knew what he meant.

In the morning, after some delays, we opened up substantial bank accounts at First National.

"We're even now," I told Sarah.

She nodded soberly.

"Even," I said. "No debts either way."

Ned Rafferty drove us out to the airport.

"British Columbia," somebody said, and we all said, "Can't wait, same time next year," but not one of us was feeling wealthy.

In the terminal there was more hugging.

Ollie went first. He shouldered his duffel—a waddling, funny-looking guy in his cowboy hat and fancy boots. After a moment, Tina pecked my cheek and tagged along after him.

They boarded a Frontier Airlines flight for Denver.

Ned and Sarah and I waved at the windows, then Rafferty said, "Where to? Portland? Samoa?"

I said I was headed the opposite way. So did Sarah. Rafferty gave us a lift back into town, but this time there was little emotion.

"My problem," Rafferty said, "is I can't cry."

We shook hands and then it was down to Sarah and me.

"There's risk in this," I told her.

"Accepted."

"Thing is, I do love her."

"You did," Sarah said. "Perhaps."

"So."

"So let's find out," she said. "The uranium, that was a gamble, too."

Wrong, but I nodded. The uranium had to be there. That was science, this was something else.

"Ready?"

We were on the corner of Elm and Moore. Across the street was a parked tractor, and beyond that was the capitol dome, and far off were those mountains we'd plundered.

"Ready?"

"Ready," I said.

Sarah slipped her hand into my back pocket, took out my wallet, and put it in her purse for safekeeping.

"Let's at least keep the risks to a minimum," she said. "How do we get to Bonn?"

First, though, I bought myself a motel. The night clerk took it pretty well. So well, in fact, he almost ruined the pleasure; it was a relief when he got a bit testy near the end.

A night later we were over the Atlantic.

"So let's have the data," Sarah said.

"Bobbi Haymore. Married a guy named Scholheimer. Bobbi Scholheimer."

"Bobbi?"

"She can't help it."

"I suppose not." Sarah levered back her seat.

"She *can't.*"

"I know that. Unfortunate, though. I'm sure she's a doll."

"You want to hear it?"

"Everything."

We were alone in first class. Two of the flight attendants were already sleeping, and the third had gone back to help in coach. The jet seemed to fly itself.

"Well," I said, "it was like getting shot by a stun gun. Just happened. The smile, maybe, I don't know. Something clicked— the passion thing. There it was. When I saw her the first time, it was like I'd known her all my life, or before I was born. One look, you know? I'm sorry." Sarah listened with her eyes closed. I could see movement beneath the lids, darting motions; I knew it was hurting but I had to get it said. I described the night flight and the bad dreams and the martinis and poems and hand-holding. "Couldn't forget her," I said. "All in my head, I guess. I'd keep seeing her face, hearing that voice, and sometimes—I *am* sorry— but sometimes I'd make up these stories about how we'd run away together. Pictures. Little glimpses."

Sarah laughed. "And me?"

"You were there, too."

"Steady Sarah. Go on, you're breaking my heart."

The jet made a slight adjustment to starboard.

I told her about the airport stakeouts—just a game at first, but then a desperate game, something to live for and hope for—an obsession, I admitted—and then I talked about the chain of events, how the trail led to Manhattan, then the phone calls and the navigator and finally Scholheimer.

"Hot pursuit," Sarah murmured.

"I guess so."

"And then?"

I shrugged. "And then nothing. Called her up. Told her—you know—told her I loved her. Big confession. Big hopes. All those stories and pretty pictures . . . Anyway, she was nice about it. A couple of times I thought, God, it'll *work*, I could hear this—I don't know—this *willingness* in her voice. So after a while I asked if we could have dinner or something, or run off to Hudson Bay, and then she laughed, but it was a nice laugh, like wistful, and she told me, No, she couldn't, because she was going to Bonn, and there was this married guy she was going with. 'The guy's married to me,' she said. Just like that. But sort of sad, too. 'The guy's married to *me.*' That's all I remember. Except I wanted to ask about that grass she gave me. Grass—what's the grass mean? This time I'm asking."

"She sounds swell," Sarah said.

"Yes, but I love her."

Sarah was quiet. She covered herself with a blanket and watched the flashing green light at the edge of a wing.

"Grass," she finally said, and sighed. "If I'd only known it was so easy. Grass galore. Poems, too. Would've pinned them to your ears. 'What is love? 'tis not hereafter; Present mirth hath present laughter.' That turn you on, William?"

"Let's just wait. See what transpires."

"I'll eat her alive," said Sarah.

In Paris, the choice was either a train that afternoon or a plane the next morning, so we took the train. Sarah said it was best to keep up the momentum. She didn't want things fizzling out in some quaint hotel room. For the first hour or so we sat up watching the suburbs and grapes go by, then Sarah began making up the berth.

"It isn't just that I love you," she said. "I mean, we've committed *crime* together. Doesn't that count for anything? Aren't we thick as thieves, you and I?" She pulled the shades and undressed and got into bed. There was a red bow in her hair, a cigarette in her mouth. She looked lean and unladylike and smart. "William," she said slowly, "the girl won't even recognize you. Things have changed. You've changed. The uranium, for God's sake. What's she to make of it? One look, she'll see you've lost that crazy edge of yours. Mr. Normal. Ban the bomb to boom the bomb. Denim to sharkskin, plowshares to swords. How does dear Bobbi-cakes cope with all that?"

"I'll explain."

Sarah sniffed and kissed her kneecaps. "Rancher Roe?" she said. "You'll explain how we conned that poor old fairy? Take a *look* at yourself. Not a moral fiber to be found."

"I'm sweet, though."

"Nixon was sweet. Oppenheimer was sweeter. Einstein—

sweetest old geezer who ever lived."

"Yes, but Einstein warned us."

"That's how sweet he was! Invents the end of the world, then sounds the alarm. Isn't that how relativity works? Szilard was a sweetie, Fermi was a pussycat. Just like you and me, William. We're all such charmers."

"If you're feeling guilty—"

"Guilt?" she said. "Forget it, man. Guilt went out with culottes. It's a new world."

Sarah crushed out her cigarette and winced and stroked a thick red blister at her lip. It was a blemish that had been recurring for years now, but here, in the flickering light, it seemed to have its own organic mandate. I wanted to reach out and brush it away.

"Face it," she said, "we're *established.* Donated our scruples to the highest bidder. Buckled, snapped, sold out. Sweet Bobbi will see the change."

"Enough," I said.

"Am I a nag?"

"A little." I watched her massage the blister. It was the color of her nipples, almost exactly, and it did the same thing for me. I locked the door and took off my clothes and squeezed in beside her.

"You love her, William? Really?"

"Pretty much."

"Maybe we should take separate compartments."

"If you say so."

"But maybe not," she said. "In a case like this, proximity's important."

"Fine," I said.

We made Bonn late the next morning. Sarah wanted to get right down to business—no last-minute waffling, she said—but I needed a day for reconnaissance and planning. No mistakes. Ten years and more I'd been dreaming about this, how one day I'd pack my bags and take off after her, chase her to the ends of the earth, do it right this time, show her what a brave and sane and exciting man I am, make her beg for me, buy her furs and jewels, the things of the world-as-it-is, real things, show her how life is meant to be lived, show her what she'd missed. I was done with half-assed fantasies. I was a pragmatist. Let the world stew in its own bloody juices, it didn't mean a damn next to Bobbi.

"You want it too bad," Sarah said. "You can't win."

I told her to wait and see.

We found a room near the government district, unpacked, then went out for lunch and a walk. It was the burning end of August. There were giant shade trees along the Rhine, and bridges and boulevards; there was a sidewalk café where we ate sausages on brown bread and drank beer. We were beginning to feel rich. We rode the riverboats, bought cameras, bought clothes, dined elegantly at a high rooftop restaurant. Sarah looked great. She looked tan and aristocratic, silver earrings and a Cyd Charisse dress that was made to dance in, so we danced slow to jazzy music, then we rented a hansom that took us clomping through the wee-hour streets.

"A question," I said. "Put yourself in Bobbi's shoes. A night like this—will it win her over?"

Sarah snuggled close. She had a shawl around her shoulders. Her shoes were off.

"Depends on the vibes," she said.

"How are they?"

"Ho-hum, sort of. This is Europe, man, you have to wear your wealth more freely. Take it more for granted."

"What about the basics?"

"Passion," she said. She showed me a brown leg. "Otherwise it gets soupy and she starts thinking of you as something sweet. Like Fermi and Einstein. Take some chances. Get violent."

"Like so?"

"Harder. We're talking *violence*."

The hansom circled through a park. I practiced violence for a time, then got sleepy, and Sarah ended up paying the driver and seeing me to the room.

In bed, she cried.

"This lip of mine," she said. "I'm not hideous, am I? I mean, I'm still kissable?"

"Absolutely."

We kissed cautiously. Afterward, with the lights out, Sarah slipped a pillowcase over her head and came in close for warmth.

"Idiot," she said, "I love you."

In the morning I began making calls. There wasn't much to go on—a few vague possibilities. All I remembered, really, was that her husband had taken a position as a visiting lecturer in prosody at Bonn University; Bobbi had planned to teach English to the children of embassy officials.

But all that was nearly a decade in the past.

"A cold trail," Sarah told me.

She lay in bed as I made the calls; after each strikeout she kissed me and said it wasn't meant to be. I tried the university, the American Embassy, and the central APO mailroom in Bad Godesberg. No one knew anything. In part, it was a problem in detection, teasing out clues, but there were also the complications of language and uncertainty and Sarah.

"It's an omen," she said. She was at the foot of the bed, legs wrapped around a phone book. "Tell you what. Let's get married."

"Not that simple."

"It *is* simple. Get hitched in Istanbul. Honeymoon in Venice and then settle down in some nifty castle on the river Rhone."

"Nice thought," I said, and frowned at her. "Maybe I should try American Express."

Sarah put her head in my lap while I dialed.

"Man and wife," she said lightly, not quite teasing. "We'll do it right. Have portraits done. Those rich, dark oil jobbies that age so nicely. Hang them in your hunting den. You'll call me Lady, I'll call you Sir William. Dine each evening at eight sharp. Very proper, you know. I'll run charity balls and you can chase foxes with your friends. Late at night we'll talk pornography. We can *do* it."

American Express had never heard of Bobbi Scholheimer.

"William, for God's sake, don't you *love* me?"

We had breakfast in bed, then I tried several hotels and pensions, then the German-American Club, then each of the banks. I was getting desperate. Somehow, for all the wasted years, I'd always thought that when the time came it would be easy. Ring her up and plead my case and start making children. I'd run through the image a million times.

"Hey, look here," Sarah said. She went up into a handstand at the foot of the bed. "Command performance. How does Bobbi match up?"

"Stop it."

"I'll bet she can barely stand on her *feet.*"

"Sarah—"

"Balance, man."

She curled her toes toward the ceiling, the muscles at her hips correcting for the wobble in the bedsprings.

"Is she cuter? Perkier? No shit, I can be perky, too." Sarah came down to the kneeling position. "Coy and shy and mysterious. Demure as all get-out. Sublime. You want sublime?" She crossed her arms on her chest, bowed her head, and smiled. "Gee golly, sir, I don't commit Congress on the first date. Am I blushing?"

I looked away.

"Listen," I said gently, "we can't accomplish anything this way."

"Accomplish *me*, William."

"Let's just—"

"I'm sublime! I am, I'm brilliant. You can wear my Phi Beta Kappa key around your neck, we'll go steady. My doctor says I've got this gorgeous womb—ovaries like hand grenades—I'm built for motherhood—I can cook and rob banks and manage money. I can sew. I know how to make pickles. Just name it."

"Get dressed."

Sarah sighed. "I hope she's dead."

"Then there'll be ghosts."

"Who cares? Hope she got hit by a *tank*—nothing left but tread marks and maggots. We'll build a memorial to her somewhere in southern Illinois."

We spent two days making the rounds of every school in the city. Sarah complained that it was too much like FBI work, like tracking down Most Wanteds, but still she insisted on tagging along. It was rough on both of us. We interrogated teachers and headmasters, paged through old yearbooks, wasted hours at the embassy, placed ads in the three daily newspapers. Nothing. At night, while Sarah slept, I'd sit up and study *Martian Travel.* It was all I really had of her. And a few threadbare images: the way she moved, the blondness and blue eyes, the voice that never seemed to alight on nouns or verbs. I remembered the phone call—her light laugh when I declared myself. Flattered, she'd said. She understood. Dreams were wonderful, but we had to be practical, we had to be adults, and then she'd gotten around to the business about being married.

Well fine, I thought. If it was practicality she wanted, acceptance of the world-as-it-was, I was ready now to take her on a uranium ride to the ends of the earth. I'd be dead-hard practical; I'd toe the line; I'd take her as my wife and build a house and lay in supplies to last a lifetime—whatever she wanted, whatever practicality could buy—and then, when the lights went out, when the established planet went hot like a cinder, then we'd uncork that last bottle of Beaujolais and turn to the civil defense channels and congratulate each other on how splendidly adult we were. It didn't bother me a bit. All I wanted was to end the world with Bobbi close by.

And there was Sarah, too.

As we went into the second week of the search, she began moping. She slept in a closet. She drove the bellhops crazy with elaborate late-night orders and penny-pinching tips. At lunch one day she gave me a memento of our times together, a lavender envelope containing the scented shavings of pubic hair. "It isn't grass," she told me, "but it'll grow on you."

She was relieved, then depressed, with each new dead end.

"A proposition," she said one evening. "What we'll do is, we'll set up a basic-training business for all the up-and-coming provocateurs. Like at Sagua la Grande, only franchise it, spread the risks around, establish branches in all the major capitals. Terror's the fashionable thing. A wide-open field—Beirut, Jerusalem—the market's there. Say the word."

"I'll sleep on it," I told her.

She smiled. "You do that. Dream the good dreams. The closet's all yours."

Next morning we turned up our first hard lead. The Dean of Faculty at Bonn University remembered Scholheimer and Bobbi. "Lovebirds," the man said, and shook his head. "They go *kaputt*." He was a portly old gentleman with red cheeks and an ivory cane. Leaning forward, wheezing, he pulled out a soiled old photograph and carefully presented it to me. It was Bobbi in pigtails. *"Liebchen,"* he said. "Make many men cry. *Auf Wiedersehen*, Scholheimer."

"In other words," said Sarah, "a bad-ass bimbo."

The old man nodded.

"Bobbi, she squeeze the juice out of rock, *freilich*. Break the husband heart."

"Right," Sarah said. "Yours, too, I'll bet."

"Bitte?"

"Keep talking."

The language barrier was formidable but Sarah managed it. Apparently the marriage had not been a long one—Bobbi had walked out after two months; Scholheimer had returned to the States with a chastened perspective and a pocketful of poems. "Bimbo," the old man said sadly. He fingered the hem on Sarah's skirt and went on to explain that Bobbi had taken a job teaching sixth-graders at the American Air Force base in Wiesbaden, 130 kilometers southwest of Bonn.

The man's eyes dampened. He patted Sarah's knee.

"All many years ago," he said. *"Herzen und Schmerzen.* You find my Bobbi, you say I still love. *Alles vergessen."*

Sarah put the snapshot in her purse.

"Count on it," she said grimly, "I'll deliver the message."

That afternoon we rented a car and drove for almost an hour along the Rhine, through Königswinter and Remagen, then a straight shot to Wiesbaden.

An adjutant recognized Bobbi's photograph.

"Angel," he said. "Sweetest thing on earth. She your sister?"

"Yes," I said.

"Some sister."

"I know that. The whole family knows."

"An angel," he said flatly. "Wings. All of it. How'd she hook up with that bastard hubby of hers? Schlum, Schultz?"

"Scholheimer."

The adjutant bit down on a pipe. He was a trim, polite man of forty-five or so, whiskey lines along the nose and cheekbones, but still healthy-looking, the ruddy tightness of a long-distance runner. "Scholheimer," he muttered. "Shit on a shingle. Bobbi deserved better."

"Angels do," said Sarah. She crossed her legs and looked at him with understanding. "You knew her pretty well?"

"Ma'am?"

"I mean, you *knew* her. That way. I can tell."

The man wanted to smile. He filled his pipe from a leather pouch, tamped it down, and struck a match against his desk. There was a hesitation before he shrugged. "Yes, ma'am, I guess you could say that. She was my daughter's teacher—damn fine teacher, too. Kids loved her. So the marriage goes bad, hubby's out of the picture. I took up some slack." He turned toward me. "But, sir, I'll tell you something, it was real romance. Your sister, she was no troop groupie. I hope that's understood."

I nodded.

"Romance," he said, "the genuine article. She used to slip poems under my pillow."

"God," said Sarah, "she must've been a darling."

"Roger that. Even my daughter said so."

The adjutant pulled a piece of ruled paper from his desk drawer. He smoothed the edges and passed it across to me.

"Martian Travel," he said. "Go ahead, read it."

"I already have."

"Your sister's got talent. One day I woke up, she was gone, and maybe a week later I found that poem in my Class A's. Made me feel like a million bucks. She had this way with words."

"Sure," Sarah said. "Like a Xerox machine."

"Ma'am?"

"Nothing. She writes like Shakespeare."

"Affirmative," said the adjutant. "Maybe better."

It was easy after that. At last report, he said, Bobbi had returned to grad school, this time the University of Minnesota. She was a Golden Gopher. Early the next morning we boarded a Lufthansa flight for New York.

"The thing that gets me," Sarah said at forty thousand feet, "is the way you've written off our whole relationship. You don't talk about it, you don't think about it. All Bobbi. No Sarah. What the hell *happened?*"

Her eyes showed fatigue. She was quiet for a moment, then searched for my hand.

"William, I'm quitting."

"No."

"I am. I've had it. The end. Give it up, otherwise I'm bailing out."

"One more week?"

"Impossible."

"Sarah, I need time."

Eyes closed, she glided over the clouds. "Sorry," she said, "I'm done."

"All right, then."

"Sure. All right."

But over New York she said she loved me; at Kennedy International she said she'd give it a while longer.

We took a nonstop to Minneapolis, spent the night in separate beds, then walked across town to the U of M. It was bright September. Freshman season, kickoff, the rush, and the campus was clean with Swedes and maroon and gold and Big Ten fever. We'd won the peace for them. Hair was out, health food was in. And it was our labor of a decade ago that made all this possible—straight-legged jeans, Jantzen shirts, ears wired for sound, the serenity of higher education. "Memories moribundus," Sarah murmured. In the administration building, she hummed a tune that had been fashionable during occupations of such places, or in jail, or in torchlit parades for amity on earth. Her voice was husky.

Boys in letter jackets stopped to ogle. She wore high heels that went snap-click in the waxed hallways. Her nylons gleamed. She had the posture of a model, a moneyed alumna, classy and chic, stunning; she could still stop traffic. She hummed and ignored the jocks while I bribed the assistant registrar. "Inflation," the man said crisply, "is the evil of our era," for his price was high; then he slipped me the records.

Bobbi had enrolled in 1978—a master's candidate in fine arts. She'd completed the program in ten months, record time, and the transcript was monotonous with A's and B's. A professor named Rudolph was responsible for the A's. We found him in the faculty lounge, a tall and very bitter man. "She *deserved* A's," he snapped. "Johnson gave her B's—Johnson's the one she ran off with. Should've *flunked* her ass!" Then the anger came. Last he'd heard, she was working as a tour guide at the United Nations. "The princess of Dag Hammarskjöld Plaza," he said. "What a waste. All those goddamn A's."

"This Johnson?" I said.

"B's! Claimed she needed incentive."

"And now?"

Rudolph cackled. "The scrap heap. B's didn't cut it. Hope he's peddling candied apples, that's what I *hope*. Hope she dumped him hard."

In Manhattan, we took two rooms. Sarah insisted. That evening we talked tactics, went out to dinner, then spent the night together. There wasn't a word spoken. I kissed her on the lips, a healing kiss, tracing that red blister with my tongue, memorizing its shape and texture, knowing it would eventually be all I remembered, or almost all. In the morning she was back in her own room. I spent an hour in a barbershop. At noon, by arrangement, I met Sarah outside the hotel. We went arm in arm toward the East River.

Twice we circled the UN, then Sarah led me inside.

She spotted Bobbi outside the Security Council.

"There's the jackpot," Sarah said. "I'll retire to Rio. Good luck."

"You're a neat lady."

"She looks adorable. Really, she does. I'm crazy about her uniform."

"Well."

"You're sorry, I know."

"More than that. If it doesn't work out, I'll—you know—I'll arrange another search party. You know?"

"Rio," Sarah said. She was backing away, still holding my hand. "I'll leave a trail of bread crumbs. You be Hansel, I'll be Snow White."

"I am sorry."

Sarah's eyes were colorless.

"I'll grant you this, she's one in a million. You'll get your money's worth. Everything you deserve." Sarah walked out the revolving door. Then she came in again and slugged me on the shoulder.

"Bye," I said.

"You're an asshole."

"Rio."

We bought a limo and drove to Helena and took over the top floor of my motel.

I stayed away from nostalgia. Sarah had warned me about that. "You've led a nasty life," I said, and I ticked off the betrayals—me and the navigator and TWA and Scholheimer and NYU and the Air Force and Rudolph and Johnson and the United Nations. It was a hard speech. Here and there I shouted. "You can't *stick*. You don't know what commitment is. You can't want a thing and get it and still want it. You quit. You're unfaithful. Iron deficiency. Anemia of the will. No magnetic glue. You drop off men like leaves off trees, by the season. You're selfish. You're fickle. You don't attach to things. You don't believe in causes *or* people, and what else is there? Essence, existence—you can't cope with either. You flit like a fucking fruit fly. You can't hold on. You can't endure. You're shallow and cowardly and vain and disgusting— you're probably mad—that's what madness *is*—can't stick, always sliding—you're an ice rider, a melter, gutless and hopeless, and I love you with all my heart, and I swear to God—I swear it—I'll never let you go. Never. That means *never*."

We soaked in the motel's big green pool. At night we watched television, anything but the news, and then we got married.

We honeymooned in the Sweetheart Mountains.

Each morning was a miracle: I'd wake up and take a breath and reach out to make sure.

I'd hold her tight, squeezing.

And in 1983 we had a daughter this way, Melinda, whose presence brought happiness and new responsibility. As a father, as a man of the times, I was more determined than ever to hold the line against dissolution. When the newspapers warned of calamity, I simply stopped reading; I was a family man. The motel turned a modest profit. I attended monthly meetings of the Chamber of Commerce. We coped. We had our disputes and found solutions, we vacationed at Yosemite, we raised our daughter with discipline and love. At the back of my mind, of course, I feared that someday I might wake to find a poem in my pocket, but Bobbi was always there. Through her poetry, which she would sometimes read aloud, she permitted access to her secret life. She was devoted. She made soft love. She was a wise mother, a patient wife.

The balance held.

It was not a fantasy.

We prospered in a prosperous world. We took our showers as a team, the three of us, and there was peace and durability, a kind of art. On Halloween we bobbed for apples. We designed our own Christmas cards, hand-stenciling Bobbi's poems on fine white parchment. We shared things—our lives, our histories. Once, on a whim, I took Bobbi up to have a look at the uranium strike. The season was pre-winter, twiggy and bare, a desolate wind, and I held her arm and pointed out the scars left by man and machine. I showed her where the mountain had once been. With my hands, I shaped it for her, explaining how we'd followed the clicking trail toward riches, and how, at a spot roughly between Orion and the Little Dipper, in the age of flower children gone sour, we had come across the source, the red-hot dynamics. It was science, I told her. Morality was not a factor. Bobbi said she understood. Yet, for me, there was something sad about the disappearance of that mountain, because it was now a pasture, flat like Kansas, with pasture weeds and mesquite bent east with the wind. We found a pickax and a burnt-out bulldozer and a No Trespassing sign with the Texaco star preserved by heat and cold, bright red, friendly-looking as symbols go.

"Somewhere," I said, as I stashed the sign as a souvenir, "the mountain is still there, it's tucked away in silos across the Great Midwest. It isn't gone, you just can't see it."

Bobbi asked if this scared me.

It didn't, not then. But back at the motel, two or three years later, it did.

A Sunday afternoon. I was sleeping. It was August, and I was out by the pool, a calm summer Sunday, the gentlest Sunday of all time, a day of rest, and even in my sleep I could hear the lap of water and tourists splashing—business was booming, Montana was the Energy State—and there was the feel of Sundays forever, a lawn mower buzzing, a child laughing, a steady hum beneath all things. And the sun. And a breeze that wasn't really a breeze and made no earthly sound as it swept the Sunday like a Hoover. This was sleep. This was the day of perfect union, when Christians barbecued. A day for picnics and lazing. I basked like a lizard. I wasn't dreaming, just drifting. The sun—that full *sun*—the sun was part of it. It was a Sunday like no other Sunday. It was a day without spite or malice, not an evil thought abroad, not a word of blasphemy, not a sickly deed; a day when, by some incredible chance, one shot in ten billion, the human race quieted as if in church. Disembodied, dusty, I felt like fragrance, I could've made chlorophyll.

Afterward, I told Bobbi how it happened: "Just this drone at first. Maybe a mosquito, like that. Except the sound was way up. *Way* up. Nobody else noticed. Everybody in the pool kept splashing, having a great time, they didn't *notice*, and the drone kept getting louder and louder, like this screechy whine, like—like I don't know what—like from outer space. A whistle sound, sort of, but it wasn't a whistle, it was something else. Like this, like *wheeet*. You know? Just *wheeet wheeet*. So I sat up. I saw these weird ripples in the pool. Then this vortex, swish, a whirlpooly thing, like when water goes down the toilet, and then—maybe it was the heat or something—but then I looked up and there was this huge zipper across the sky, a big silver zipper. And it was unzipping itself. That's what I saw. That's how it happens. A zipper opens up."

Bobbi was gentle. She kept close to me that night, and for many nights afterward. If I wanted, she said, we could make some changes. Would I like to travel? Go back to school, maybe? Pursue a career? I thought about it, then shook my head. All I wanted was for her to stay with me. Always. *Fidelis ad extremum.* I looked straight at her. "Fidelity," I said. "It's absolute. I won't let you leave me."

Her smile was opaque. Not much later she composed a poem called *Leaves.* Lush imagery, but I didn't quite understand it.

> *What do the leaves mean?*
> *Autumn comes to fire*
> *on hillside flesh,*
> *but you ask:*
> *What do the leaves mean?*
> *The oak, the maple, and the grass.*
> *Winter comes and leaves*
> *and each night you touch me*
> *to test the season.*
> *Here, I say, and you ask:*
> *What do the leaves mean?*

A year later we sold the motel for a handsome profit. We toured Europe, and the Orient, then returned to build a house in the Sweetheart Mountains. It was a large, expensive house, with decks and fine woods, not a neighbor for miles. To be safe, though, I bought up the surrounding land and spent a summer fencing it in. I installed a burglar alarm and dead-bolt locks on all doors. It was a lovely sort of life, Bobbi said, horses and hiking, our daughter, but even so I could sometimes feel an ominous density in the world. The stars seemed too tightly packed. The mornings were too short; the nights collided. Beirut was a madhouse. The graveyards were full. In Amarillo, they were manufacturing MIRVs, and in the Urals there were Soviet answerings in kind, a multiplication.

And me—I stewed. At night I would often wake up and squeeze Bobbi for all she was worth, which was everything. The flashes were killing me.

Density, I thought. Implosion, not explosion, would surely end the world.

It wasn't mental illness. By and large I was happy. The world spun on one axis, we spun on our own. Bobbi worked on a translation of *Erlkönig*, I putzed around the house, Melinda grew smart and beautiful.

We were homebodies.

On November 8, 1988, Chuck Adamson was elected mayor of Helena. When the polls closed, I remember, there was a gathering at his house, which by midnight became a victory party, and we were all there, his wife and kids and cocker spaniel, and Bobbi, and my mother, and many people I didn't know. I remember dancing with my mother—hard stuff, no waltzes—her hair bluish now, the way she snapped her fingers and rocked without modesty. I remember delivering an oration. It had to do with the governorship, how Chuck was a shoo-in if he kept his nose clean and his eyes on the shining dome. It was stirring rhetoric. We were all very drunk and very happy. Later, I found Adamson off by himself, sitting in a stairwell with a drink and a glum expression in his eyes. The dog was curled up in his lap. "Mr. Mayor," I said, "what's the sadness for?" and Adamson fixed a stare on me, a long one. He wasn't acting when he said, "The usual." I knew what he meant. Nothing more was said. I sat beside him, and we listened to the party, and after a while we went back in.

My mother died on January 10, 1993.

And that summer Bobbi disappeared. She was gone two weeks; her diaphragm went with her.

That was the worst time. I loved her, she loved me. I was almost sure of it. So why? I'd go to the medicine cabinet and open it and just stand there. It was like watching a hole. The diaphragm, I came to realize, was one of those objects whose absence reveals so much more than its presence.

In mid-June, Bobbi returned as abruptly as she left.

She put her bag down and kissed Melinda. She gave me a look that meant: Don't ask.

But I did. I wanted specifics. Where exactly, and who, and what was said and done. I wanted to know these things, but I didn't want to know, but I did, I wanted to know and not know, and what I most wanted to know and not know was why. Bobbi was forthcoming in her own way. She did love me, she said. But then *why?* Why couldn't it be absolute and perfect and final and lasting? Her smile was uncontrite. When I asked about the diaphragm, she said it was only a precaution—I believed in precaution, didn't I?—and when I asked where, she said it didn't matter—she was here, with me, now—and when I asked who, the navigator or Scholheimer or the adjutant or Johnson or someone new, Bobbi shrugged and went off to wash her hair.

I followed her into the bathroom. I kept asking why. It was more than asking, because I opened the medicine cabinet and showed her the hole and yelled, *"Why?"*

Bobbi worked up a lather with her fingertips. The shampoo, I remember, was lime-smelling. She looked at me in the mirror. She was back, she said. Couldn't we let it go at that? I remember sitting on the edge of the tub, smelling limes and picturing the diaphragm. It was round and rubbery and discolored to a white-brown. Two weeks, I was thinking. Why? I pictured the tube of spermicide. Bobbi in bed: blond and long-legged, those narrow hips, how she made love with her eyes open, not moving much until near the end, when she would reach behind her head with both hands and grasp the vertical grillwork on our brass bed and make a sound like a bassoon. But the diaphragm was there between us. It was there even when it wasn't, or especially when it wasn't, and it was there now when I asked, *"Why?"*

She dried her hair with a red towel.

She closed the bathroom door and sat beside me on the tub. She did not smile. Because, she said quietly, she was a breathing human being. Because she was not a dream. Real, she said, and it was time to accept it.

Then she quoted Yeats.

Brutal, she said.

For several months afterward, through the summer and fall, I expected to find a last poem nailed to my heart. I couldn't sleep. In bed, I watched her eyelids. I plotted tactics. Ropes and locks and dynamite. I felt sane and brutal. *Dig,* a voice whispered, but that came later.

There were stresses and uncertainties, an in-between time, and then one day near Christmas Sarah and Ned Rafferty drove up in a jeep. They needed a hideout.

"Just for a month or so," Sarah said, kissing me, then Bobbi. "Till things quiet down."

She was wearing mink. Piled high in the back of the jeep were Christmas presents, boxes of Swiss chocolate, a frozen turkey, and an armed nuclear warhead.

"So far," Sarah said, "the Air Force doesn't even know it's gone. Ignorance breeds calm."

Rafferty hugged me.

That evening Bobbi cooked the turkey and I put a record on and Sarah chatted about the terrorist life. She was not a terrorist, of course, or not exactly, but she enjoyed the wordplay. "You wouldn't believe how tough it is," she said. "Not all glamour and fun. I mean, shit, nobody gets terrified anymore." She looked at Melinda. "Excuse the shit."

After midnight, when Bobbi and Melinda and Ned had gone to bed, Sarah curled beside me on the couch.

"Home, sweet home," she said softly. "Your daughter, an absolute honeybun. How old? Nine? Ten?"

"Ten."

Sarah sighed. "Ten biggies. The magic number." She put her head in my lap. "Naïve Sarah. All that time I kept thinking, Hang in there, baby—he'll be back. Wanted to be wanted. Not a peep." She tapped my wedding ring. "Anyway, it's still politics as usual. Key West, the old Committee. Not quite the same, I'm afraid— mostly just dreams. Super Bowl, remember? Never made it. Cowgirls won't have me. Look at this skin, William, like cowhide, that's what the tropics do. I'll be tan till I die."

"It's perfect skin," I said.

"Old."

"And perfect."

She laughed and kissed my nose.

"So here's the program," she said brightly. "We kill Bobbicakes. Sell your daughter. Blow this house up then hightail it for Rio. Two days, we're home free."

"Not funny," I said.

"Add your own wrinkles."

"There's Ned, too. You're lucky."

"Yes," she sighed, "that I am. Magnificent guy. Loves me dearly, you know. Not a string, just loves me and loves me."

"Well, he should."

"He does. Love, love, love."

I waited a moment.

"So look," I said, "what about that warhead?"

Sarah coughed and rubbed her eyes. She'd lost some weight—too much, I thought—and without the mink she seemed skinny and poor-looking. Unhealthy, too. The blister at her lip was hard to ignore.

"The warhead," she said, and shrugged. "Actually, I guess, we could've built our own—Ollie had the blueprints. Who doesn't? But that wouldn't make the same waves. Had to swipe it. These days, it takes real drama."

She stared at the ceiling.

"God, William, I do miss you. But anyhow. The bomb. Ebenezer—it was his brainstorm. Proliferation, you know. Dramatize the problem. Show what could happen. One last shot, so we got

organized and pulled it off like you wouldn't believe. Like with
the guns, that easy."

"And now?"

"Yes, now's the problem." Sarah pulled off my wedding ring
and popped it in her mouth and swallowed. "They wanted to *use*
the damned thing."

"Use it? You mean—"

"Blackmail. A demonstration project or some such shit. Set it
off in the desert, wake up the rattlesnakes. I don't know. Headlines. Ollie was crazy about the idea—Tina, too—she wouldn't
stop quoting Chekhov. Some terrorists. *Threats*, that's what scares
people. A difference of opinion, you could say. So Ned and I, we
had to reswipe the warhead. Packed it up one night and took off.
And now we're badly wanted."

"I see."

"By our own comrades. That old gang of ours. They want the
bomb back."

We were quiet for a time. It occurred to me that life has a
way of tidying up after itself. I remembered my Ping-Pong days,
but then I remembered the grief.

"Sarah," I said, "I want that ring back."

"In due time," she said.

Later we put on our coats and went outside.

It was snowing hard. Sarah lay down and made angels on the
lawn, then she led me to the jeep and pulled back a tarp and
showed me the warhead.

"There's your mountain," she said.

She brushed snow from the nose cone. It was the size of a
large cantaloupe, smoothly polished.

"Seventy-two pounds," she said, "but think what it would do
to Las Vegas. New model—Mark 24 or something, I forget." She
slipped her arm through mine. Her voice seemed faraway. "Graceful lines, don't you think? Like me. Bombshell. If you want, we can
run away together, you and me and Mark. Tuck us in at night, tell
us bedtime stories. Great sex, I bet."

"Enough," I said.

"Touch it, William."

"Not necessary. No."

"Your big chance. Cop a quickie. *Feel* it."

"No."

"Touch."

She took me by the hand and pressed it down. The metal was cold. No surprise, I thought. Just cold and real. I felt a slight adhesion to the fingers when I pulled away. I nodded and said, "Get rid of it."

"Of course."

"I mean it, Sarah."

"Yes. You always do." She tapped the warhead. "For now, though, we need storage space. Three weeks. A month, max. Look at it as a good deed. For me."

"Temporary?" I said.

"Oh, sure," said Sarah. "Just temporary. Like everything."

We lugged the bomb into the tool shed, covered it with rugs, and locked the door.

Outside, Sarah hugged me hard.

"I love you," she whispered, "and that's final."

We celebrated the holidays like a family. Rafferty and I chopped down a tree, Bobbi and Sarah made pudding and pies, there was mistletoe everywhere. On Christmas Eve we set up an electric train for Melinda. We opened gifts and sang carols and drank rum toddies. On Christmas morning, before breakfast, Sarah returned my wedding ring.

The days afterward were lazy. I remember snowshoeing and quiet reminiscence. Beneath the surface, however, there was renewed velocity: that Doppler feeling.

Late one night I heard crying. It was Sarah—she was crying hard—and it went on for a long time, all night it seemed. But in the morning, when I asked about it, she shook her head and laughed and said, "No way, man. Not crying. I don't indulge." It was that kind of velocity. The kind that moves beneath things, as blood moves beneath skin. There were no flashes. No sirens or pigeons, nothing so vivid. I'd sometimes find myself gazing at the tool shed. Normal, I'd think. Things in their place; the absolute normality of the abnormal.

There was some apprehension, yes, but the bomb didn't disturb me nearly as much as Sarah's lip.

It was badly inflamed. Bruised-looking and scary—movement beneath the surface.

Dangerous, I thought, and one morning I told her so.

Sarah smiled and touched my wedding ring. "A love disease," she said. "It'll clear up once we get married."

"Seriously."

"Ugly, am I?"

"It should be looked at," I said. "By a doctor."

Sarah laughed.

Not funny, however. At the end of January, she complained of fatigue. A dark, thimble-sized scab formed at the corner of her mouth. Tiny black veins snaked across the surface of the blister. Her speech faltered. She had trouble coordinating past with present.

In February there were periods of dizziness; at night there was crying.

"Mommy!" she'd scream.

She'd press a pillow to her face and curl up at the foot of the bed and scream, "I'm dead!"

For a week or two it got better. Then it got much worse.

"Dead!" she'd yell.

One evening she used a needle to drain the lip. There was infection and severe swelling. In the morning, when I brought breakfast to her room, she pulled a pillowcase over her head.

She was cogent, though.

"Well," she said cheerfully, "this smart-ass mouth of mine."

Rafferty sat in a rocking chair near the bed. His eyes were dull. He looked at her for a while, then left us alone.

Gently, I tried to lift off the pillowcase, but Sarah stopped me.

"No, please," she said. "Leave it be. Just for now."

The room smelled of medicines, Campho-Phenique and Xylocaine. For several minutes I sat in the rocking chair and tried for silence.

"A doctor," I finally said. "You know that?"

"Not quite yet."

"Sarah, I won't let—"

"Not yet," she said. "No hospitals. I can't be alone like that."

"You're not alone."

"I *can't* be."

She turned away from me. It was a bright winter morning, and the curtains were open, and the sunlight made little trails along the flesh at her arms and ankles.

Lying back, she seemed to doze off.

Then she said, "William, you know what I wish? I wish— don't get upset or anything—but I wish we'd had some things together. The two of us. Just certain things. I wish I was pregnant. It's corny, I know, but I really wish that."

"It's not so corny," I said.

"I guess not. Sounds that way, but . . . You know what else? I wish there was more time. A billion years. I wish I was floating on this raft in the ocean somewhere, like somewhere romantic, and there's this island with palm trees and waterfalls and stuff, but it's not exactly a desert island because we've got all these kids running around barefoot, and I'm pregnant again and it's a real hot day and I'm just floating on this raft—no sharks or anything—so whenever I want I just sort of slip into the water and go down to the bottom and get cool, and there's this baby inside me, this thing we *have* together, and then when I'm cool I come up to the raft again and lie there and get hot. Pretty corny, I told you. But that's what I wish. I wish we could just float. I wish you'd make love to me. You can't, I know, but I still wish it."

"I'd like that," I told her.

"But you can't?"

"No. But it's not corny."

Sarah took off the pillowcase and sat up. She wasn't quite smiling, or crying, but it was a little of both. Even with the lip, I thought, she was a very striking woman. There was still a great deal between us.

"If you kissed me," she said, "could you live with it?"

"I think I could."

"Might be contagious."

"There's the risk."

She came to the rocking chair. "Go on, then," she said, and almost laughed. "Just keep that tongue in your mouth. It'll be wonderful, I promise."

It was not cancer.

A form of encephalitis, they told us. A viral migration along the pathways between lip and brain.

She was operated on in Helena, she came home to recuperate, there were convulsions, she died in March.

Which is how it happens, that fast.

We know we will live forever until that instant when we know we will not.

"God," she screamed, "something's haywire!"

"There, now," I said.

"William?"

"I'm right here."

"Where? I can't *think*."

"Don't, then," I said. "Just don't think."

In the last week there were hallucinations. The cortex liquefied. The viruses consumed her thoughts. The left eye roamed in its socket, her face darkened, there was puffiness along the jaw, she had trouble swallowing, her arms and fingers twitched, her breathing became fast and shallow.

"Am I dead?" she asked.

Another time she jerked up and said, "I *want* something! I forget what—I *want* it."

We took turns sitting with her. She was never alone. When she died, Ned Rafferty was there. He came into the kitchen, where I was shelling peas, and he looked at me and said, "I loved her best."

The funeral was quick and somber.

When it was over, I asked Rafferty what he'd be doing with himself. He thought it over, then said he'd probably stick with the gang, they were family. He didn't cry much until later, but later he cried a lot.

After all, she was dead.

"I'm dead!" she keeps yelling.

Not long afterward, the others showed up. Ollie and Tina and Nethro and Ebenezer, they were all shaken by the news, their grief was genuine, and for more than a week we catered to a morose household.

When they left, in early April, they took the warhead with them.

And later that summer they died by gunfire in the tropics. There was tear gas, I remember. Bullhorns and sharpshooters and a burning safe house and a bomb in the attic—all the networks were there, a TV spectacular.

In the autumn I suffered a minor breakdown.

And in the winter, when Bobbi said she needed space, when she suggested a trial separation, I was comforted by the final passage of a poem in progress: The balance of power, our own, the world's, grows ever fragile.

13

Quantum Jumps

HE HOLE SNORTS and says, *Do it.*

It's a smug, self-satisfied voice. Constant chatter all night long—*Star light, star bright! Shut me up with dynamite!*

Below, in their hammocks, Bobbi and Melinda sleep beautifully, and the backyard shimmers with the lights of Christmas, and here, at last, I've come up against the edge of an imposing question: What now? Three hours till daylight. Soon, I realize, it will be time for absolutes.

Chasm! Spasm!

The hole releases a steamy, insinuating laugh, then coughs and belches. I can smell its breath.

I lie back and watch the lights.

Certain truths appear. I love my wife. I loved her before I knew her, and I love her now, and I will not let her go. I'm committed. I believe in fidelity. I will not be separated. One thing in my life will last and keep lasting and last forever. Love is absolute.

What I need now is silence, but the hole has a mind of its own: *Here's a good one . . . Jack be nimble! Jack be slick! Jack me off with a dynamite stick!*

I shake my head: "I'm not interested."

The hole snickers.

Oh, yeah, you're interested. I'm the mouthpiece, you're the brains. Now and never. Do it.

I'm wired. I'm hot. But I know the difference between life

and death. When the hole hoots and says, *Home, sweet hole,* I don't respond, not even a shrug. I get to my feet and do some exercises. A clear, calm night, but there's a dynamic moving through the dark. I'm at wits' end; I can't think beyond black and white. In a time of relativity, I wonder, how does one achieve absolutes? Separate, Bobbi said. She was gracious about it. She smiled and said she loved me. But then she said separate—she needed space—what does space mean?—and later there was a poem called *Space Walk*—walk on air, walk away—but I can't be relative about it. I won't let it happen. Trouble is, what now? I want to nail our hearts together. I want no space between us. I want wholeness, without separation. I want it all, now and forever.

The question is simple. In this age, at this late hour, how do I make a happy ending?

The odds, I know, are poison.

It's a real world and it's dangerous. Science takes no prisoners; the atom forecloses; there are no epilogues. Here, at the rim of the hole, I can see what I'm up against. I can see Sarah dying. A burning safe house, oceans boiling, cities in ash. I can *see* it. A Titan II missile: ten feet in diameter, 103 feet tall, 330,000 pounds of launch weight, a flight range exceeding 6,000 miles, two engines, five megatons of no-bullshit firepower. It's out there. It's deep in the Kansas soil—you can touch it, man to metal—you can walk the underground corridors and press your fingers against the cool, damp technology. There it is. Just look: the whirring exhaust fans, bright lights, no shadows, the chrome launch console, the red box with its two silver keys, the coffee pot, the photographs of loved ones, the clocks and computers and holstered pistols, the crew-cut missileers in their spit-shined boots and SAC-blue uniforms and daredevil scarves. It is in fact there. And here's how it happens. Topside, it's a hot Kansas day. A record-buster—roasting heat. It's witch weather. A freaky black atmosphere and high winds and high voltage. Just look and say the words: Nuclear war. Kansas is the creeps. Tornado country, ghost country. Say it: Nuclear war. Look at it: black-eyed Susans and sunflowers staring at you from roadside ditches, vast fields of wheat, the sun and soil. And it happens. There's lightning now, huge neon Z's, a violet virga, and then the sky divides itself into two perfect halves—one hemisphere bruised and ugly, the other bright like summer—and the crease opens up like a smile over that Titan silo. This is it. A sudden wind comes up. It's hard to stand, but you lean against the wind. You ponder the hemispheres. You see a small plot of land enclosed by barbed wire; you see a cow grazing; you see a farmer on his tractor; you see a little boy circling under a pop fly; you see a parked Air Force truck and a tiny white outbuilding and a stenciled sign that reads: "Deadly Force Authorized." You consider running. You hear thunder. You watch a 700-ton concrete lid blow itself sideways; you say, "Oh!"; you see a woman run for the telephone; you see the Titan rising through orange and yellow gases—there's still that wind and that Kansas sun and that grazing cow—and you gawk and rub your eyes—not disbelief, not now, it's belief—and you stand there and listen to the thunder and track the missile as it climbs into that strange smiling crease in the sky, and then, briefly, you ask yourself the simple question: Where on earth is the happy ending?

Kansas is burning. All things are finite.

"Love," I say feebly.

The hole finds this amusing.

I am all there is, it says. *Keyhole, rathole, asshole, eyehole, hellhole, loophole, knothole, manhole, peephole, foxhole, armhole, sinkhole, cubbyhole, pothole, wormhole, buttonhole, water hole, bullet hole, air hole, black hole, hidey-hole . . . I am that I am. I am that which nearly was but never will be, and that which never was but always will be. I am the unwritten masterpiece. I am the square root of infinity. I am one hand clapping. I am what happened to the dinosaurs. I am the ovens at Auschwitz, the Bermuda Triangle, the Lost Tribes, the Flying Dutchman, the Missing Link. I am Lee Harvey Oswald's secret contact in Moscow. I am the anonymous tipster. I am Captain Kidd's treasure. I am the uncaused cause, the unnamed source, the unindicted co-conspirator, the unknown soldier, the untold misery, the unmarked grave. I am, in modesty, Neverness. I am the be-all and end-all. I am you, of course. I am your inside-out—your Ace in the Hole.*

There's a sharp grinding sound. Rock slides against rock, a perilous shifting.

Go on, do it. Dynamite.

"No," I say.

Light the fuse! What's to lose? Like a time capsule, except we dispense with time. It's absolute! Nothing dies, everything rhymes. Every syllable. The cat's meow and the dog's yip-yip—a perfect rhyme. Never rhymes with always, rich rhymes with poor, madness rhymes with gladness and sadness and badness . . . I could go on forever. I do, in fact.

"Lunatic," I say.

Can't have sorrow without tomorrow.

"Crazy!"

The hole laughs and sings: *Oh, I got plenty o' nuttin', an' nuttin's plenty fo' me.*

I shut it out. I squat down and fold my hands and wait. For what, I don't know. A miracle, I suppose, or some saving grace.

I'm not myself.

It's a feathery hither-and-thither sensation, like riding music, slipping up and down the scales of my own life. A balmy night in May—May 1958—and I grab my pillow and run for the basement and crawl under the Ping-Pong table and lie there faceup. I hear my father calling out my name. I smell the dank, sweet-sour odor of mildew, the concrete walls and basement moisture. "Easy, now," my father says. He takes me in his arms and says, "Just a dream, cowboy, just a bad, bad dream." But he's wrong. It's beyond dreaming. It's right here and it's real.

Balls to the wall! the hole yells. *Off your ass, yo-yo!*

The Christmas lights sparkle all around me.

There's no other way.

Reluctantly, I move to the tool shed. I bend down and lift a crate and hoist it to my shoulder. There's a queer sense of standing a few steps outside myself, a nonparticipant.

I carry the explosives across the yard.

Just the mechanics.

I use a pickax to chisel out three notches along the rim of the hole. I study the angles. I lay in the charges, crimp the caps, wire it up, test the firing device. I'm careful. I concentrate on each task as it comes.

When the surface work is done, I set in the ladder and climb down and prepare three more charges against the base of the north wall.

Dark down here—I stumble. I drop a blasting cap and jump back, then I spend five minutes searching for it on my hands and knees. *Pitiful,* the hole says, or maybe I say it, or both of us together: *All thumbs, no nerve. Fire and ice—poetic justice!*

I find the blasting cap.

An omen, I think. Then I wonder: Do we find the omens or do the omens find us?

Riddles!

I won't be rushed. I work slowly, at my own pace.

The hole seems to press in closer, and there's a foul, clammy smell that makes me wheeze as I wedge in the last stick of dynamite and lean down to hook up the firing device. I feel queasy. It's partly the stench, partly my own misgivings. No hurry, I tell myself, just follow the sequence—attach the copper wires, turn the screws, make sure it's a solid connection.

Done.

And what now?

I kneel at Melinda's hammock. She sleeps with a thumb at the edge of her mouth, her tongue taut against the lower front teeth, her expression frank and serious. I stroke her hair. I want to cry but I can't; I want to rescue her but I don't know how. There are no survivors. When it happens, as with Sarah, the proteins dissolve and the codes are lost and there is only the endless rhyme. I feel some remorse, and even grief, but the emotions are like ice, I can't get a grip on them.

What's wrong with me? Why am I alone? Why is there no panic? Why aren't governments being toppled? Why aren't we in the streets? Why do we tolerate our own extinction? Why do our politicians put warnings on cigarette packs and not on their own foreheads? Why don't we scream it? Nuclear war!

I love my daughter, I love my wife. It's permanent. Gently,

with love, I smooth the blankets around Melinda's neck and shoulders, kissing her, surrendering to a moment of intimacy, then I
turn and go to Bobbi and stoop down and put my arms around her
and say, "I love you." I rock the hammock. I'm frightened but I
keep the vigil, just waiting, cradling the firing device, watching for
the first frail light of dawn.

Once, I drift off.

There's a fluttering in the darkness, like wings, and I snap
awake and jerk my finger from the yellow button.

I lock my hands together.

So much can go wrong. Madness or malfunction, simple evil,
an instant of overwhelming curiosity. Like a child with a chemistry set, and the instructions say, "Never mix X with Y," but the kid
starts wondering, *What if?* He's human. He has to know. Curiosity, that's all. A noble instinct. A craving for secrets. And so one
day the kid creeps to his room and opens up his chemistry set and
cautiously sprinkles out a little X and a little Y, just to *know*, and
it's the discovery of a lifetime. There are no more hypotheses.
Knowledge becomes perfect and absolute. And again there's that
simple question: A happy ending?

If you can imagine it, I remind myself, it can happen.

But imagine this: Nuclear war.

A dark movie theater and you're eating buttered popcorn and
someone shouts, "Nuclear war!"

You laugh.

But this: "Fire!"

Drop the popcorn and run. It's a stampede.

And then again this: "Nuclear war!"

Shrug? Shake your head? A joke, you think?

Imagine the surprise.

In the dark I hear someone chuckling, which startles me, but
it's just the hole. *T minus nine,* it says softly. *Like falling off a log.
We'll all dream the same sweet dream—pure metaphor, that's all it
is. Push the button.* Its voice is smooth and mellow. It recites nurs-
ery rhymes. It tells stories from the Bible, as if reminiscing, adding
and subtracting here and there. *Amen,* it says. *T minus eight, the
century's late.*

I try not to listen.

I watch the night reorganize itself, the movements of stars and shadows. The patterns tend toward stasis.

God knows, I don't want it this way.

Folded in forever like the fossils. I don't want it but I can see it, as always, the imprints in rock, the wall shadows at Hiroshima, leaves and grass and the Statue of Liberty and Bobbi's diaphragm. Here, she can't leave me. The fossils don't move. Crack open a rock and she'll be curled around me. Her smile will be gold and granite. Immutable, metamorphic, welded forever by the stresses of our age. We will become the planet. We will become the world-as-it-should-be. We will be faithful. We will lace through the mountains like seams of ore, married like the elements . . .

Jackass! the hole says. *Very pretty, very stupid! Push the fucking button!*

It scares me. I'm tempted.

I put down the firing device and stand and try to shake out the brain waves. I'm capable of atrocity. Lucid, entirely practical, I feel both powerful and powerless, like the stars. I make myself move. I circle the floor of the hole, feeling my way, but also not feeling—which is what scares me—then I sit down and check the safety on the firing device and stare at the walls and look for signs in the darkness. I see myself crawling under barbed wire at Sagua la Grande. Flares and tracers. The terrible things man will do to man. I see the wreck of the *Thresher.* I see my father dying under yellow spotlights. He won't stop, he's a professional, he keeps dying. I hear sonar. I hear Melinda yelling, "Daddy!" I hear Bobbi's warm blond voice, scanning itself, free verse on the brink of blank. She needs space, she tells me. She pins *Space Walk* to my pillow. There's a transworld look in her eyes when she sees my rage, when I take a scissors to her diaphragm, when I burn the poem, when I tell her no one's leaving. I see her sleeping. It's after midnight, and I kiss my wife's cheek and quietly slide out of bed. No lights, no alarm. Blue jeans and a flannel shirt, then out to the backyard, where I pick a spot near the tool shed and begin digging. I won't permit separation. It's final. Am I crazy? Maybe, maybe not, but I see black flashes against a chrome sky, scalps in a punch bowl, mass going to energy. And there's more. Because I also see a white stucco house in the tropics. The roof is burning. It's live television, all the networks are there, and cops and SWAT teams and smoke and sirens, and Ollie Winkler is shot through the mouth. The front door burns slowly, like charcoal. The dining-room drapes are burning. Ollie moves along the floor, toward Tina, but he's shot again, in the hip and head. Tina hides in a closet. But the closet burns, and the bedrooms and attic. I can smell the heat and tear gas and burning plaster. Ned Rafferty coughs and smiles. His face is wax. He keeps touching himself, but his face sticks to his hands, he can't fix the melting. "The gist of the gist," he says. He raises a hand, as if to point out a lesson, but the hand curls into a claw, and Ned Rafferty burns. The gunfire seems distant and trivial. Holes open up in the walls, and there's a shower of sparks from the ceiling, and the doorbell rings, and Tina Roebuck cries out from her burning closet. It all seems phony and impossible, except it *is* possible, it's real, people truly burn, the skin goes black to gray, the bowels open, the fingernails peel back and the bones glow and there are snappings and splinterings, burning sugars and phosphates, burning enzymes, the body burns. Nethro is shot dead. Ebenezer Keezer topples sideways and burns. The safe house burns. In the attic, a warhead no doubt burns. Everything is combustible. Faith burns. Trust burns. Everything burns to nothing and even nothing burns. There are no foot-prints—the footprints burn. There are no messages in bottles, be-cause the bottles burn, and there is no posterity, because posterity burns. Cement and steel, it all burns. The state of Kansas, the for-ests, the Great Lakes, the certificates of birth and death, every written word, every sonnet, every love letter. Graphite burns. Churches burn. Memory burns, and with it the past, all that ever was. The reasons for burning burn. Flags burn. Liberty and sover-eignty and the Bill of Rights and the American way. It just burns. And when there is nothing, there is nothing worth dying for, and when there is nothing worth dying for, there is only nothing.

The hole makes a sound of assent.

Nothing.

The night seems to stretch out like elastic. Melinda turns in her sleep and looks at me with half-opened eyes. "Hey, there," I whisper, and she nods, then tucks her chin down and sleeps.

If I could, I would save her life.

I let myself sway with the night. Bobbi's breathing. The influences of the moon.

And later Sarah appears. She does a cartwheel on the wall. Then she giggles and says, "I'm *dead!* You know what dead is? You get this malaise. You forget to wash your hair. You're bored stiff. *I'm* dead." How much, I wonder, is real? Like those phone calls back in high school, I can still dial and break the connection and hear that husky voice of hers. It's not unreal. Right now, as she goes up into a handstand, it's neither real nor unreal, it's just dazzling. "Love you," I say, and Sarah smiles and says, "Oh, well— better late than never. Except I'm dead. Too bad about Rio, though. Would've been a gas." She sighs. She pecks my cheek and sits cross-legged on the wall. "But don't apologize. No problem, I'm dead. What's new with you?" So I tell her about the hole and the dynamite and the implausibility of happy endings. The bombs, I say, are real, and Bobbi wants to leave me. Sarah listens carefully. When I feel sorrow, she comes off the wall and goes inside me for a time, then hovers near Bobbi, frowning. "Well," she says, "if I weren't so dead I'd say hit the switch. We'll run away together. That island I told you about." She kisses Bobbi's lips. "So then. The fantasies didn't pan out?"

Then she takes the firing device from my lap.

"Hold me," she says.

Along the rim of the hole, the Christmas lights are soft and mysterious, and Sarah takes her place in my arms. I don't know what to tell her, except it wasn't our universe.

She seems to stiffen.

"Such bullshit," she snarls. "I'm *in* the other universe. Nothing *here!* Washout—colossal fucking drag. You should've loved me. You know that, don't you? We could've been happy. All those places we could've seen, Paris and East Berlin. That honeymoon I never had. Oh Christ, we could've had it. Diapers and rattles and all those nights together. Is that too sentimental? I don't mean to sound morbid, but I'm dead, and there's only one universe that counts. You should've loved me. That's all I mean, we should've made promises to each other and kept them, like vows, and we should've unzipped each other and crawled inside and been honest and true and loving, just loving, all the time, and we should've done everything we didn't do. We should've taught each other things. We should've had Christmas together—is that silly? Eat lobster and open the presents and make love and go to church and believe in God and make love again and light candles on the tree and listen to records and have oyster stew at midnight and go to bed and smell the pine needles and sleep and wake up and still be together. It's a little sad, isn't it? It's sad that we could've been so happy."

Later, in the dark, she says, "Why did I die?"

I don't have the answer.

Sarah nods and says, "I thought so."

And later she reads my thoughts: "Doesn't seem real, does it? I don't *feel* dead. Maybe I'm not. Maybe it's something we dream up to make our stories better. Maybe so?"

Then comes a long silence.

"Sarah?" I say, but she doesn't speak.

She's dead.

Like my father, like all of them, she died and dies and keeps on dying, again and again, as if repetition might disclose a new combination of possibilities.

"Oh, Lord," I say, but I don't know what to ask for.

I smell daylight coming.

The hole says, *Now and never.*

I lift the firing device. It's light in my hands, or seems light, box-shaped, an aluminum casing with a small plastic safety catch and a yellow button. The copper wires wind off toward the north wall. All it takes is a touch. Not even courage, bare volition. It occurs to me that I'm not immune to curiosity—so easy. I think about Ned and Ollie and Tina, my father, my mother, and it's the simple desire to discover if the dead are ever truly dead.

In the absence of hope, what can we hope for?

Does love last forever?

Are there any absolutes?

I want to know what the hole knows. The hole is where faith should be. The hole is what we have when imagination fails.

"Hey," Melinda says.

Something moves inside me.

"Hey—"

She makes a languid, woozy motion with her arm. After a moment she sits up in the hammock, rubs her nose, turns her head slightly to one side, and looks at me without recognition.

I feel unsteady.

There's a sudden compression when she says, "Daddy?" Enormous pressure, it's too much for me. I place the firing device at my feet and get down on my hands and knees and practice deep breathing. The hole, it seems, is in my heart.

"Daddy?" Melinda says.

"Here, angel."

"Where? How'd I get down in this . . . God, it's dark. Where's Mommy?"

"Mommy's fine."

"Yeah, but—" She stops and touches her flannel nightgown. Her eyes wander. She looks at the granite walls, then up at the Christmas lights, then down at me, then at the firing device. There isn't enough light to make out her expression, but I can easily imagine it. "Man oh man," she says, "what's going *on?*"

It isn't a question, though. She knows.

Her eyes, if I could see them, would be blue and full of wisdom. Drawing conclusions, perhaps. Maybe a little frightened.

I'm still on my hands and knees. The squeeze is on.

No dignity in it, but I don't trust myself to stand.

Melinda stares at me.

"Daddy," she says, "what's happening?"

I keep smiling. I want to go to her but I can't manage it; I make a queer crabbing motion, knees and knuckles. It's a balance problem. I'm embarrassed when I feel myself slipping—I can't get traction.

The hole cackles.

Dynamite!

Melinda seems startled. I'm smiling at her—it's all love—but she recoils and hugs herself and says, "What?"

"Nothing, baby."

"I *heard* you."

"Nothing."

"That *word*," she says, "I *heard* it. You *said* it, I *heard* you! I can't *believe* this."

She's wide awake now.

Quickly, she gets out of the hammock and takes a step toward me and stops and glances at Bobbi and then steps backward. All I can do is smile. She takes another step backward.

There's silence while she makes the connections.

"Get up," she says sternly.

"In a second."

"Daddy."

"One second, princess."

She puts a thumb against the edge of her mouth.

"No," she says, "I don't *want* a second. I want *out*. This hole, God, it smells like . . . Let me out!"

"Melinda—"

"Out!" she shouts.

I can see her eyes now. She glares at me, then spins around and moves to a wall and hits it with her fist. "Now," she screams, "I want *out!*" The Christmas lights give her face a splotchy blue and red tint. She kicks the wall. "Now!" she screams. Her eyes keep roving—quick, jerky movements of the head, up and down.

When she spots the dynamite, I pretend it's not what it is. It's not evil, I think. Not murder, not sorrow.

"Oh, wow," she grunts.

With her left hand, gingerly, she reaches out and nudges one of the copper blasting caps.

Reality impinges.

"Baby, don't," I say.

It's a discovery for both of us. Melinda wipes her hand and turns and looks at me. I can't explain it. Just the sadness of discovery, the dynamite and the wiring and the blasting caps, and when she looks at me—not accusing, only knowing—there is nothing that can be said or done. She bites down on her lip. She wants to cry, I know. Her tongue makes a light clicking noise against her teeth.

I'm helpless. I'm aware of the night's pure harmonics, but I can't make myself move.

I watch her trace the wires back to the firing device. Stooping, she inspects the plastic safety catch; she clutches her nightgown at the throat. Not murder, I remind myself. There is no evil in it, no rancor or shame, and we are all innocent and unsullied and sane. Even so, I suck in my breath when she finds the yellow button.

"God," she says.

And she knows.

Now, at this instant, we share the knowledge that there is no mercy between fathers and daughters. We will kill for our children. Our children will kill for us. We will kill for families. And above all we will kill for love, as men have always killed. Crimes of passion. As terrorists kill. As soldiers kill for love of honor and love of country. Just love. And when there is no love, there is nothing worth dying for, only nothing, and Melinda knows this.

She picks up the firing device.

"I don't care what," she says, "I'm not afraid of you. I'm just not."

"I know that."

"I'm *not*."

"Fine, then," I tell her. "But be careful, okay? Be extra careful."

"Don't move, Daddy."

"I won't."

"Stay right there," she says. "You better not even move, because . . . You better not."

"Careful, baby. Extra super careful."

"I mean it. You better *not*."

She carries the firing device to the far side of the hole, near Bobbi's hammock. I do the calculations. Five or six paces between us, maybe four seconds. Hard to be sure. Would my legs work? What about the shock? All the imponderables.

"Sweetheart," I say, very softly, "I wish you'd—"

"Don't move."

"No, I'm not moving."

"If you do, though, I might—you know—I *might*. Just stay there. Just be nice, don't scare me."

A gallant little girl. And smart. She keeps her eyes on me. We both know. She reaches out and shakes Bobbi's arm.

"What's wrong?" she says. "How come Mommy won't wake up?"

Again, I smile. "Just can't, I guess. Maybe—I don't know— maybe Mommy forgot how."

"Forgot?" Melinda says. She makes a motion with her shoulders. "That's stupid. Not even funny. It's almost . . . How'd I get down here in the first place? Just dumped me in, I suppose."

"I carried you, baby. Both of you."

"You could've dropped me, though."

"I didn't."

"Yeah, but I mean—" Suddenly, almost falling, she sits down and clamps her arms around the firing device. "I don't *mean* that!" she yells. But she doesn't cry; she doesn't dare. She measures the distance between us. One hand flutters up to her ear, as if to brush away an irritation, then she flicks her thumb against the safety catch. "I mean *this* thing. I mean, *why?* I always thought you sort of loved me."

"I do," I say. "I do love you."

"Okay, but I mean, how come you almost tried to blow me up? You did, didn't you?"

"Never."

"You *did!*"

"No way. Never. Careful, now."

For a moment she's on the verge of crying. She puts a finger near the button.

"Scared?" she asks.

"You bet I am."

"Don't move, then. Better be real scared."

"I am," I say. "I'm scared."

She runs a hand across her forehead. I know what she's going through, I've been there myself.

"Don't think I'm chicken," Melinda says, "because I'm not. And if something bad happened, I bet you'd be so goddamn sorry you couldn't believe it."

She makes a small, incongruous fist and holds it over the firing device and screams, "Goddamn!"

There is nothing I can do.

"Goddamn!" she cries, and the hole laughs and says, *No survivors!* and Melinda yells, "Stop it!"

We sit facing each other from opposite sides of the hole. She's crying now; I can see her shoulders shaking. "Daddy, please!" she says. "Let's get *out* of here!" And if I could, I would do it. I would take her in my arms and be calm and gentle and find safety by saving. God, yes, I would. "A joke," I'd say, "just a big silly joke," then I'd carry her up the ladder, and Bobbi, too, both of them, one in each arm, and I'd laugh and say, "What a joke." I'd be a hero. I'd do magic. I'd lead them into the house and brew up some hot chocolate and talk about the different kinds of spin you can put on a Ping-Pong ball. And the world would be stable. The balance of power would hold. A believer, a man of whole cloth, I would believe what cannot be believed. The power of love, the continuing creation—it cannot be believed—and I would therefore believe. If you're sane, the world cannot end, the dead do not die, the bombs are not real.

Am I crazy?

I am not.

To live is to lose everything, which is crazy, but I choose it anyway, which is sane. It's the force of passion. It's what we have.

When I get to my feet, Melinda whimpers and says, "Stay *away* from me." But I'm willing to risk it. I'm a believer. The first step is absolute. "Daddy," she says, "you better not!" But I have to. I cross the hole and kneel down and lift the firing device from her lap and hold her tight while she cries. I touch her skin. It's only love, I know, but it's a kind of miracle.

In the dark, Sarah's smile seems hopeful.

"Another universe," she says. "A nice little miracle, that's all I want. You, William. I'll never stop wanting."

But it isn't real.

Not Sarah, not the Bomb. Nuclear war: just a fault line in the imagination. If you're sane, you accept this. It's easy. Sarah winks at me, still flirting, and I nod and embrace my daughter.

At daylight we climb the ladder.

And that, too, is easy.

I hustle Melinda into the house, turn on the shower, test the temperature, and tell her to hop in.

She looks at me through the steam.

She nearly smiles, but doesn't.

"I'm a grown-up *girl*," she says. "You can't just stand there and *watch*."

"No, I guess I can't."

"God. What a father."

"Right," I say.

I close the bathroom door, listen for a moment, then return to the hole. It's a fine summer morning. I take Bobbi from the hammock, holding her as if we're dancing, and when she opens her eyes, the hole seems to laugh and whisper, *One more clown in the screwy cavalcade. Hickory dickory hope.*

It doesn't matter.

I'm a realist. Nothing's real.

Bobbi goes first, up the ladder, I follow behind with the firing device. I turn off the Christmas lights. The sky at this hour is purple going to blue. The mountains are firm and silent. There are morning birds in the trees, and the grass is a pale dusty green, and I love my wife. She leans against me. For some time we stand together in the backyard, and later I lead her into the house and make coffee and sit with her at the kitchen table. There is little to say. I ask how much space she needs; I ask if we could stay together a while longer. Bobbi touches my hand. Her eyes, I notice, don't quite focus. Her voice, when she says anything's possible, comes from elsewhere. She's thinking of other worlds. But she does smile. She lets me love. In her heart, I suppose, there's a lyric forming, but even that doesn't matter.

I have a last piece of business.

Outside, I pick up the firing device and take shelter behind the tool shed. Nuclear war, it's a hoax. A belly laugh in the epic comedy. I flip up the safety catch, crouch low, look at the sky, and put my finger against the yellow button.

I know the ending.

One day it will happen.

One day we will see flashes, all of us.

One day my daughter will die. One day, I know, my wife will leave me. It will be autumn, perhaps, and the trees will be in color, and she will kiss me in my sleep and tuck a poem in my pocket, and the world will surely end.

I know this, but I believe otherwise.

Because there is also this day, which will be hot and bright. We will spend the afternoon in bed. I'll install the air-conditioner and we'll undress and lie on the cotton sheets and talk quietly and feel the coolness. The day will pass. And when night comes I will sleep the dense narcotic sleep of my species. I will dream the dreams that suppose awakening. I will trust the seasons. I will keep Bobbi in my arms for as long as she will stay. I will obey my vows. I will stop smoking. I will have hobbies. I will firm up my golf game and invest wisely and adhere to the conventions of decency and good grace. I will find forgetfulness. Happily, without hesitation, I will take my place in the procession from church to grave, believing what cannot be believed, that all things are renewable, that the human spirit is undefeated and infinite, always. I will be a patient husband. I will endure. I will live my life in the conviction that when it finally happens—when we hear that midnight whine, when Kansas burns, when what is done is undone, when fail-safe fails, when deterrence no longer deters, when the jig is at last up—yes, even then I will hold to a steadfast orthodoxy, confident to the end that E will somehow not quite equal mc^2, that it's a cunning metaphor, that the terminal equation will somehow not quite balance.